It rumbled the hill burrows and shook a family of foxes from their

hole. Critters scattered through the night. Crows swooped, gathering

in an ominous, squawking cloud, their congress interrupted. They

hovered over the cliffs, waiting—they knew this sound, this rumble

that meant a wall of iron was about to come barreling across the gap.

Sometimes, it would leave behind an unlucky something for breakfast.

PRAISE FOR THE WORKS OF KIN S. LAW

"Adventure is what I expected going into this book, and adventure is what I got. The atmosphere was entrancing, the airships were captivating, the action was spot on. I can't wait to see what the author has in store for us next!"

- Mystery Author, M. W. Griffith

"A different take on the steampunk genre. Most stories tend to explore the contraptions invented had the Industrial Revolution taken a different path, and the world remained stuck in the Victorian Era. Using Mark Twain as a pivotal character will likely bring about a chuckle or two."

- M. P. Ceja, InD'Tale Magazine

"It's a fun story about a diverse group who comes together to save the world, something we've seen many times, but what sets this story apart is the quality of the writing- great dialogue, cool world building and wonderful characters, especially the women. Rosa and Vanessa are prickly, strong, smart, and capable, and couldn't be more different from one another. No damsels in distress in this Pirate story, I loved those ladies."

- GoodReads Reviewer

"The characterization of the four main characters is exceptionally well done. The plot is a weave of two quests. The first is to find out who is stealing famous landmarks like Big Ben and the Eiffel Tower, and of course to fight them and thus return the landmarks. The second is to find Albion's mentor, Captain Sam Clemens, and resolve the issues that caused their separation. The fantasy elements were quite interesting and the author has been very creative."

- ARC Reviewer

SPECTRE

of WAR

KIN S. LAW

SPECTRE OF WAR
Lands Beyond: Book Two

CITY OWL PRESS
www.cityowlpress.com

Cover Design by Fodor Miklós, and Tina Moss. All stock photos licensed appropriately.

Edited by Heather McCorkle.

For information on subsidiary rights, please contact the publisher at info@cityowlpress.com.

Print Edition ISBN: 978-1-944728-53-3
Digital Edition ISBN: 978-1-944728-54-0

Printed in the United States of America

To my love, with whom the last eight years

have been better than all the spices of the East.

PRELUDE
A PICTURE HOUSE SCENE

A black murder rose from the wound of a cliff, a bloodstain against the royal purple of the lavender meadow. Moments later their alarm was justified by a whistle howling through the valley, long and low.

It rumbled the hill burrows and shook a family of foxes from their hole. Critters scattered through the night. Crows swooped, gathering in an ominous, squawking cloud, their congress interrupted. They hovered over the cliffs, waiting—they knew this sound, this rumble that meant a wall of iron was about to come barreling across the gap. Sometimes, it would leave behind an unlucky something for breakfast.

And then the train was upon them, a hellish clatter, a tempest of wind-scored iron. For a moment the skin of the night was given a necklace of shimmering fire, the valley lit by a glittering arc from one sheer cliff side to the other as the train crossed the trellis bridge. The wind tore ahead of it and in its passing the old steel shook with uncommon speed. The foxes fled in terror. The murder, buffeted by the wind, tumbled headlong through the air.

In the train's wake an inky patch followed, flowing across the flowers, a soundless shadow upon the ground.

Past the valley, the train screamed through a countryside far too open to feel safe. She was fleeing something, her engine pumping away at her gilded baroque flanks. Her engines sighed and groaned through three big pairs of boxy vents in her sides. Her cars rattled and tipped as she raced. Pistons blurred. Still the shadow followed, eating up the tracks, flowing over the caboose with its oblivious diners inside. One man shuddered over his Lobster Thermidor, feeling a chill.

The shadow nibbled on the coach, and as if making up its mind, surged forward as a black patch against the gilt and glimmering passenger cars. It ignored the third, the second, and even the first class passengers, aiming for the car just behind the sleek black of the hopper car, studded with glowing coppertop fuel pods.

The meager light made the black seem to grow deeper, the shadow larger, until all of a sudden it wasn't a shadow anymore but claws of night reaching from a vast storm cloud hovering over the train. There came a pop and a hiss. Two smaller shadows detached from the cloud and came spinning down, leaves on the wind. The car below took their landing harshly—they had barely been introduced. It shook from side to side, its protest rattling its way down the train. But the train's visitors paid it no mind, digging their stormy claws deep into their prey. Shudders rocked the cars as their teeth bit deep, exposing the innards to the wind.

There came a flash of light, and the shadows glowed for a millionth of a second. One of the passengers had leaned out to use a photogrammer, hoping to catch a shot of the thing shaking the cars. In the next second, the hand-held bauble was gone, snatched away by the roaring wind, but not before it illuminated a lumbering and grasping thing as tall as a house: shapes of yellow and black, glistening brass tubes, exposed, rotating gears.

Eldritch fingers dipped into the ragged roof of the train car. Secondary flares shot into the night, tiny suns lighting spots on the train car. Silhouettes, shadow-puppets suddenly lit in gun flashes too small to see anything by. A horrible shape, like a mangled starfish, tumbled headlong to the tracks as a shot rang out: a man tumbling from the roof. Heavy shudders shook the train, sparks of metal clashing with metal. The train's vents erupted with fire. A great red hand hung in the air, its fingers opening, descending.

And as suddenly as they had come, the shadows were gone. The gunfire stopped. The engine rumbled on, perhaps half as anxiously as before, its whistle still sounding through the night, its proud flanks scarred and pocked by the grasp of alien hands.

1

THE CHAMBERMAID OF SCOTLAND YARD

Inspector Vanessa Hargreaves sighed, fidgeting at her Norwegian pine desk. Her straight-backed chair made an easy scapegoat for her discomfort. Eventually she picked up a lighter from one of the bundles of notes and photograms spread over the otherwise-neat workspace. It was one of the old flint wheel ones with a wick, none of the newfangled liquid apertures, and it caught every time. With her other hand, she held the letter out and watched as the open flame lapped up the sparse words.

Sorry, Vanessa, you're beautiful and a wicked good time, but I can't wait for you forever. I'll remember our night in Dover, how beautiful you looked silhouetted against the sunset, the smoke of the rail and the surf on our toes.

Affectionately, Martin.

Her stomach gurgled, painfully. Bad beef? Not likely.

She'd absconded from seeing Martin four times—twice for work, once for her ward, and the last because she couldn't bear to tell him the experience was par for the course. He ought to write a book about it: *Seeing Vanessa Hargreaves, a Fruitless, Lonely Endeavor.* Martin was a good-looking one, too, just an inch shorter, so she was always looking into his mussed night-clerk hair. A good shag.

Worse still, he had been *nice*.

She simply hadn't the time. Two days without sleep left her arms slack in their white cotton sleeves and her stomach prone to upset. Her office was small, and shelves of intelligence and constables' reports crowded in on either elbow. By the light of her wall lamp, her flaxen strands glimmered where they escaped her neat bun. Her corset's cheap stays dug into her back, even though she'd made it a point of fashion and progressivism to wear it on the outside, loose enough so she could avoid a stabbing if she saw one coming. Work was a weight that wrung the blood from her brow, but not one she could easily place aside.

The ghosts of profanity constantly haunted her lips. But she just let the flames lick closer and closer until the bite touched her copper rings. Then she opened her hand and let the wisp be sucked out the window.

The only consolation was the view. Victoria Embankment was a bustle of steaming hansoms, their lights rivaled by the boats on the Thames and the zeppelins drifting by overhead. Sometimes Hargreaves liked to sit on the benches and watch ladies and good-looking gentlemen come drifting by, cycling in the brisk evening. But not tonight. Tonight's entertainment consisted of overdue reports and a plethora of cases. She picked at them halfheartedly. As true night came to the streets below rattling traps and horse-drawn carriages replaced the cycling folk. The steam engine and clocked equine were the preferred mode of travel; they were symbols of wealth and power clopping past on steel hooves, their flanks liveried to match their owners' elegant greatcoats and modish bustles. Night blurred all the handsome lines of the vessels now, and every conveyance glittered, a constellation of gliding stars.

After five minutes, she cast aside the report with a sigh of frustration. She didn't care what people called them, automata, gears, or steam golems, to her they still looked like Mordemere's terrible kobolds, with their scissor claws.

Hargreaves' thoughts drifted back to her adventure on the *Huckleberry*, together with the reckless Albion Clemens. Apart from a chance sighting in the paper, she hadn't seen any of them since. Just as well—their airship had flown under no banner, which made all of them pirates. If they hadn't also saved all of Europe, the crew would have been liable to be hanged, despite their status as cult heroes in the back rooms of pubs, picture houses, and penny dreadfuls. They had stopped a madman from... what exactly? Hargreaves wasn't sure. Destroying the world? From the reports scattered before her, the world had not changed an iota. Far from being saved, it seemed the world was having a grand old time destroying itself.

It had only been two years. It was two years since steamcraft mogul Valima Mordemere opened the door to a Copernican revolution. Though Mordemere's magical machine, the *Nidhogg*, had been lost over Eastern Europe, the alchemic madman had already sold a number of weapons to the militaristic Ottoman Empire. Much reduced by the advent of airships choking their trade, the former crossroads empire was mustering to retake its former glory. The Knights of the Round were Pax Britannia's only edge. Still, Her Majesty would have to prepare for things to go pear-shaped.

The blueprints of Mordemere's clanker armor, his kobolds, and various other strange inventions were on file in his old atelier in Leyland, and her boys were making a killing from the shadow of the Ottomans looming over the horizon. In the *London Times* at her elbow, Vanessa Hargreaves could just make out the adverts for Doctor Adams' Miraculous Fuel Additive and Professor Dahl's Spectacular Coal-Saving Spirits. She threw the paper aside, only for it to land with Elric Blair's latest novella glaring at her from an ad. The air pirates were up to their old tricks, it seemed.

In a word, the world was changing. People were finally selling their horses and filling their stables with clean-puffing sedans and mild-mannered steel steeds. London's air was cleaner than it ever had been, but it was not without a cost. The coming of the automata reminded everyone the wonders at hand were wartime steamcraft. Those iron giants, two stories tall and fearsomely strong, were essential to the rebuilding of Westminster and the other parts of Europe devastated by Mordemere. With them lumbering about even in civilian capitals, it was believed the Ottomans dared not infringe on the West.

The automata were also a double-edged sword. Clever criminals could overpower the Metropolitan Police Service simply by possessing one of these large, powerful machines. Despite the Ministry of the Interior's adamant insistence on strict controls, one Leyland automata had already been involved in a sensational robbery. Highgate Bank's steel vault had been emptied a month ago, the culprit making off with more than a hundred thousand pounds of notes and coin. The Highgate bank job had been done with punctures of the vault's hinges, then ripped away with incredible force. It was an unprecedented and hence unprepared-for event. Constables arriving on scene reported the managers simply stood there, staring in a befuddled manner at their impenetrable steel door lying on the bank's marble floor like a crumpled toffee wrapper.

Hargreaves drank deeply of her cold tea. It helped, but not by much. The night was muggy, the beautiful metropolitan cityscape in a Turkish bath. Sweat dripped down her graceful neck and pooled unladylike in her bosom, steaming up the new badge at her shirt pocket—the badge that read Scotland Yard, Metropolitan Division Six.

"Your Majesty, Your Majesty, Your bloody Majesty," Hargreaves blasphemed casually, a daughter bemoaning a mother popular at the pub.

The fact of the matter was, Her Majesty Queen Alexandrina Edwardia Victoria III was directly responsible for the mountain of work all about Hargreaves. The queen had commissioned MD6 after the Calamity Over Europe to address steamcraft crime. What it meant, in practice, was Hargreaves had become the chambermaid of Scotland Yard. Whatever refuse the other units could connect with a newfangled steam engine or automata misuse was directed to her for disposal. Every cuckoo clock that sprung into someone's eye was shoved at MD6. It was all she could do to document the cases, and dole out what enforcement she could under the sorely lacking framework of British law. If she could just hang one perpetrator, she would feel a bit better about her job.

A pile of documents shifted on her desk, and Hargreaves pounced on the stack of criminal case files to keep them from toppling. When they were straightened again, a fresh *London Times* article lay revealed, earmarked that very morning. She cursed—this should have been brought to her attention right away.

The story read: *Witnesses at Paddington reported the arrival of the ten-thirty Montmartre Express, a fifteen-car passenger train from Paris, sans one car. When the Gallic engine glided through the glass-and-iron wall of the station, only the platform and wheels remained of a missing car, leaving a gap where Scotland Yard's vigilance ought have been.*

"My word, what a lashing," Hargreaves sighed. It represented an odious amount of monetary damages, and bore all the marks of a golem crime. The French insurance companies had been quick to pay, but not without a smirk tangible in their telegraphed paperwork. France did not as yet possess automata craftsmen, although their engines were excellent for the purpose. The spite was thicker than Vacherin Mont D'or.

Unfortunately the case would have to wait—it was too late to call on Temple Mills, where the victimized engine had been sent. Suddenly aware of the dwindling embers, the inspector yearned for a comfortable fire. Perhaps a good book to take her mind off the case. Thankfully, there was something almost as good nearby, so she grabbed her riding coat and goggles to go to it.

Stepping into the smoothly tiled, utilitarian corridors of the Yard, she took the back stair and descended into the bowels of the building. The smoothly plastered walls became raw iron pilings and mortared brick. Damp dripped from every crack in the wall. This close to the Thames, it could not be helped. The training rooms were down here. With guilt, she remembered she hadn't been keeping up with her judo instructor's sparring sessions.

Past the padded practice rooms and locker areas, she finally reached her destination. Hargreaves breathed deeply. The scent of lift compound took her back to the refreshing showers aboard the *Huckleberry*. Camouflaged behind an old archive door, Scotland Yard had secretly hollowed out two levels of concrete and pipe. Some cheeky monkey had scribbled "You Must Be" on the office's temporary window plaque, over the mysterious anagram:

M.A.D.

The inspector turned the tumblers to the clockworked lock, and opened the door to the cellar rooms.

"Oy, don't you be standin' there, lass!"

Hargreaves had to duck and roll in perfect, Yard-trained form, over her shoulder so her corset didn't break her back. Just in time— something enormous buried itself into the wall behind her. . For one madcap moment she wondered who had let a freight train into her department. But that notion dissipated as a cloud of mortar and dust blossomed, glinting here and there with the touch of chrome.

"Cid!" Hargreaves shouted, but the grizzled figure stuffed in a set of work overalls was already bumbling over to the disheveled inspector.

"I was just patching her fanny and she up and waltzed away from me, Inspector. Blasted heap of junk," the gruff old mechanic said, one thick hand massaging away a stitch in his side. He looked through a dense, salty beard and tinted goggles to behold a foot-long wrench in his other hand, as if he had forgotten to put it down. "These tinkers think they've the measure of Mordemere, and stuck all sorts of rubbish in this big fella. The madman's forgotten more than they ever knew!"

"Peace, Tanner, peace," the inspector soothed. She gently nudged the aged mechanic away from the twitching piece of machinery embedded in the cinder wall. Two stories of whistling, hissing steamworks continued to scrape green paint and sparks from itself until, quite suddenly, a billowing cloud of steam vented into the lofty chamber. The titan ground itself to a halt, one steel claw coming to rest against the wall.

"From the case on Friday?" the inspector asked. "I thought we were scrapping it for parts."

"We were, Maman, only Hallow saw ze big one had a tougher chassis."

The explanation came from behind Hargreaves, in the form of a raven-haired youth in dirty work clothes. Her grubby linen skirt ended at the knees, where slender copper sculpture took over for the girl's shins. In places, Hargreaves could see completely through the tubing and fluted metal. Even after two years, she sometimes caught herself staring at the slender French girl, thinking about the day she pulled Cezette Louissaint from the belly of an abomination.

Cezette had been reborn covered in ichor and maimed from the knees down. She had been small, seeming at first to be no more than nine or ten, but after two years of decent food and clean baths, the girl had blossomed into a young woman, and now looked closer to fifteen or sixteen. If asked, the girl couldn't tell for sure. She had spent too long locked away before her transformation to know.

Cezette did not seem to mind her predicament. If anything, she was fond of showing off her clockwork legs with elaborate ballet extensions and pirouettes, albeit only to the crew down in this garage. There was a necessity to sequester Cezette underneath Scotland Yard and off the London streets, lest she be kidnapped for her beautiful new limbs. Steamcrafts were worth a lot in money and innovation these days. Cezette had taken this isolation in stride, but sometimes Hargreaves felt she was stifling the young lady. Besides the regular tutoring Hargreaves provided, Cezette expressed a distinct interest in automata. In that spirit the inspector had arranged a place for her in M.A.D. working with the best mechanic Hargreaves had ever known. The girl had taken to the machinery like a duck to water.

"I did try to stop the child and madman," said a reedy male voice joining the discussion. "But I think I set them off instead." The pasty complexion of Jean Hallow appeared like a ghost out of the cavernous dark. Born of an Englishman and some species of white bread, he seemed indigenous to the caves, part of it.

Hargreaves had found Jean in a dusty records room. She had been investigating a larceny case at the start of her new appointment. Jean Hallow had, uncannily, produced a trio of unsolved robbery cases off the top of his head. From those files they had deduced the locked room cases had been accomplished through the strategic deployment of street urchins, not some elaborate engine or apparatus. They fit much better through the chimneys, were cheaper to acquire, and were easily replaced when they died of groin growths.

Hargreaves had requisitioned Jean Hallow's service at her earliest convenience. With one of the Yard's difference engines at his disposal, the archivist was invaluable at staying on top of the endless stream of rubbish from the other offices. Invaluable, if a bit private. Hargreaves did not care to pry into the man's affairs. He had plenty to teach Cezette and that was all that mattered.

Hargreaves constantly found herself grinning at the motley crew. Cezette Louissaint, Cid Tanner, Jean Hallow. Here was the Yard's newest section, the Mobile Automata Division, tasked with maintaining and deploying heavy steam support to MD6. Despite the overwhelming necessity for automata in all sections, the top brass had deemed the entire department Hargreaves' jurisdiction, deferring to Her Majesty's judgment.

"What have I said about firing up the gears when I'm not around? You lot are lucky it's one in the morning, or I'd have the Commissioner down here cracking some heads. Bloody great shock, you'd think it were Mordemere back from the dead!" shouted Hargreaves. She breathed deeply, trying to slow her heart. Her aitches were showing. Her stomach twitched, unsettled.

"Sorry, Maman," Cezette said sheepishly. "But there's so little to do 'ere! Jean brings me all ze books I want, but it is *très difficile* to be not two blocks from *la bibliothèque*. If I were allowed to stroll Hyde Park I might not feel so... *existential!*"

"Good word," said Hallow, but quickly turned away when Hargreaves shot daggers out of her eyes.

Cezette's tutor was right to feel proud, but Hargreaves didn't need his cheek. Besides, she felt guilty about not being able to allow the youth to wander just anywhere due to her valuable legs. Cezette had been under the thrall of the alchemic madman Mordemere. Who knew what secrets still lay beneath her skin, behind her eyes? M.A.D. seemed as good a place as any for the precocious child. At any rate the automata kept her stimulated... It was a costly diversion, Hargreaves saw now, but she didn't have a better answer for her ward yet.

"Just... don't do it again," said Hargreaves, a bit limply.

"*Mon Dieu! Je m'ennuve!*" Cezette cried, and stomped off in a metallic huff.

"And you, Jean, you should have known better," Hargreaves finished, conveniently turning her ire on the pale figure still lurking about the gear bay.

"I did know better," Jean managed, "but I am afraid our little Cezette is still afraid of the deeper tunnels, where the automata would do no harm."

"*C'est* where you keep your logic engines." Cezette whirled, mounting a protest. "Who knows when it will be logical to murder me in some dark corner?"

"M.A.D. is already taking heavy flak for our huge independent budget. Sanctioned by the queen or no, I don't want to pay for knocking down Scotland Yard," Hargreaves continued, walking past Cid, Cezette, and Hallow. Her diversion from the office was certainly working. "I'll be just an hour or two. Please keep this place shipshape while I'm gone.""Yes, ma'am!" came a chorus of voices. The inspector sighed.

Hargreaves' heels clicked neatly on the utilitarian concrete, echoing down the tunnel. She left the main headquarters under Scotland Yard, passing through where Hallow had just entered. Her hearty crew had given her more reason to vent.

When Hargreaves commissioned this MD6 headquarters, she didn't have much choice in the location. With the airways taken up by the Royal Navy, and the various crooked streets of London unsuitable even for some horse-and-fours, there was only one way of deploying her forces into the city swiftly—the underground tunnels. Some twenty kilometers of unused, often undocumented, sunken rail passages made the perfect conduit for their operations. Moving a couple of tons of steaming steel from Victoria Embankment to Dartford took only twenty minutes. Not to mention, there were other fringe benefits.

"Alphonse tonight, Maman?" Cezette asked as Hargreaves approached the hangars sunken into the tunnel sides. The little mechanical ballerina had not made a sound, but Hargreaves was becoming accustomed to the prosthetic legs working a little too well. She would rather the girl walk silently than not walk at all. Sneaking up behind her was just Cezette being precocious.

"It's the Gaelic-Seven," Hargreaves said, "not Alphonse."

"Shh! He'll hear!"

"Hell's bells! Yes, Cezette, I'll have Alphonse tonight. Take your things," Hargreaves said. "I'll give you a ride home."

"Maman, I will take ze velocipede," Cezette said. "Tolstoy needs fixing."

"You'll come along in an hour, or you'll not get any dinner," said Hargreaves. She much preferred discipline to talks about school. She hadn't much experience as a mother, but she remembered her own youth. Structure and order, that was the trick. That had gotten her through Maple Cross, that and the Yard's strict programme of training.

Now, though, the inspector tried to hide her disappointment as Cezette turned on her heel and trotted back the way she had come. The townhouse tended to get lonely with just the landlady for company.

She rounded the corner at bay number seven. A heavy switch allowed arc floodlamps to reveal the chrome metal of Alphonse standing at attention, waiting for her patiently in a cradle of wrought iron. The cockpit was set in the chest cavity, behind a thick chest plate enameled with St. George's cross. She could see from the hollow of the neck, under the chevron plate of Alphonse's helm. A stechhelm, or frog's head, squatted over the huge shoulders.

"Right," the inspector said. She climbed the short flight of stairs in the hangar and jumped into her familiar seat aboard the Gaelic-Seven. After she trod on the starter of the ten-foot-high automata, the pressurized furnace caught with a pop.

Satisfied no prying eyes were about, Hargreaves gave the control surfaces a loving stroke. The machine made her feel comfortable, protected, in control. Thick hoses connected to the Yard's boiler rooms infused the automata with piping-hot water. The pulse of the metal made it seem almost alive. With the Tesla lamps glinting off the unicorns and lions emblazoned on his pauldrons, Gaelic-Seven always seemed to resemble a large ogre dressed as a knight. Tonight, however, Alphonse was not on a mission of battle, but of escort—he was Hargreaves' dance partner for the evening.

"Allons-y, Alphonse!" Hargreaves sang along to the hum of the gear's movements. She was trying out something from a recent picture-house feature, quite a silly piece—something to do with time travel. Tommyrot, of course, but she quite fancied the hero. She was halfway out the door before the realization hit her.

"Bollocks, now that imp's got me calling you Alphonse," she cursed into the wind. She would have to correct herself on her way to the crime scene tomorrow.

2

ASSAULT AT TEMPLE MILLS

Morning sunshine basted the machinery cathedral of Temple Mills Rail Depot. Every coal mote lit up in the beams. Vanessa Hargreaves stood slack-jawed.

The inspector was not a fanatic of dirigibles like Rosa Marija nor an admirer of road engines like Albion Clemens, but she was a British woman, born and bred. Her love of trains had been put into her by rattling tracks, clean steam, and station teashops. Those sensations always meant a trip to Brighton Beach, or a visit into London. Decades of post-war propaganda infused Britain's superiority in every rivet, and the romance of travel was lacquered into smoothly appointed rail cars. Initiation into the Metropolitan Police Service had further strengthened her love of locomotives. The railroads were the pride of Queen and Country, and thus, the secret pride of Vanessa Hargreaves.

Temple Mills dwarfed anything Hargreaves had ever seen. The old water mill, she had been told, originally housed eight train-roads, but these had been long since expanded. Pipes were laid, track set, the wrought iron sculpted into trefoils, escutcheons, Neo-Victorian shapes. On either side of the entrance stood a brace of statues, one of a young, battle-ready Athena, clutching a spear and a round aegis painted with the Union Flag. The other was Hermes in flight, god of travelers. The Knights Templar who originally owned the mill would have balked at the grandeur, or taken it for granted—they were imperialists, after all.

Inside, tracks threaded in from the expanse of yard, feeding up, down, and through the five stories of sturdy masonry. Locomotives were everywhere Vanessa cared to look, triple-deep and parked on vertical rotaries, like gun chambers loaded with comfort and fine dining. Chained to enormous pistons, the rotaries shunted each car, track and all, through three levels of the building. Their idling boilers filled the enormous space with a stifling wet heat, and a pervasive smell of soot.

Outside, Alphonse sat gleaming, an Olympian cousin to these steel titans. Parked immediately before him, just inside the entrance, was a shining Pullman sleeper car, a true George Pullman, no doubt shipped at great cost from America. The dull red paint made for running the great desert expanses of the American southwest had begun to discolor in the English damp, peeling in great swatches as the stuff shrank and pulled away from the metal. On the same rotary, a little to the right and above the car was a second sleeper, an English Barclay in comforting green. Directly below that was a squat caboose, shorter by half and sharing the rotary slot with a diner car.

"If you look to the front of that rotary, you'll see the *Fenchurch Flyer* herself," came a voice from behind Vanessa Hargreaves.

She turned to behold a greasy mechanic as different from M.A.D.'s Cid Tanner as could be. Hargreaves had first met the pirate shipwright aboard Albion's Huckleberry. Naturally, she thought all engineers were old, crotchety, or some combination thereof. Far from stopping her poaching him, those qualities had been a comfort when Tanner decided to accompany Cezette to London.

This mechanic was shaggy, young, and tanned despite the English sunshine. Best of all, he seemed unfazed that Hargreaves was out and about without a chaperone. England was being pushed away from such restrictive customs by the young, charismatic queen, but the old vestiges remained in places.

"Pardon me, I must have startled you," this man now said in a perfect, nondescript accent. Hargreaves recognized it as a distinct sound, as regular as the broadwaves' or picture house announcers'. Of course, a naturalized Moor, she decided, having not settled on his specific origin. It did not seem polite to ask upon first meeting—some traditions were worth keeping over others.

"No pardons necessary. I was clearly admiring the *Flyer,* and appreciate the introduction," Hargreaves said.

"I'm the foreman, Thomas El-Nevazar. We are about to line up the formation now, if you would like to watch." The foreman, apparent because of the whistle he now blew, signaled the operation to begin. Hargreaves became transfixed.

Before her eyes, the rotary began to spin laterally, with great ratcheting sounds that reminded her of Alphonse's lumbering bulk. Whole sections of track rotated before her, carrying their seemingly monumental loads of cars. As each car was lined up and hitched behind the golden chrome of the *Fenchurch Flyer,* a block of tackle and chain as large as her waist drew the engine forward, slowly building the train as easily as a child might connect a model railroad. The mechanism allowed any car to be separated from the series for service, without the cumbersome rail switching she normally associated with these operations. The *Flyer* slid smoothly forward, through the cathedral formed by a trellis of steel columns.

"Oh, bravo!" Vanessa cried. The *Fenchurch Flyer* sat gently puffing on the rails, like some great, golden, benevolent serpent.

"Thank you, Miss...."

"Inspector," Hargreaves automatically corrected, but toned down the edge she normally used for the uniformed constables. "Vanessa Hargreaves."

"Here about the *Montmartre Express,*" El-Nevazar said, "we've had a flock of constables survey the bloody thing already. One more pretty one wouldn't hurt. The baggage car's parked in the back."

Separated from the train proper, the damaged baggage car was not on a rotary, but had been moved to a quiet corner of the depot. The little platform stripped of walls and roof looked naked and sad to Hargreaves' eyes. According to the report, what baggage remained had been sent to its owners, and now only shredded fragments of sheet metal and strangely intact wheels were left of the once-handsome car.

Hargreaves touched the jagged, saw-toothed edge of the destruction and was reminded of the Highgate bank job. The steel had been crumpled like tissue paper.

"Definitely automata," she whispered. She cursed the constables who were more concerned with relaying baggage than they were with the case. In doing so, they had removed valuable evidence, leaving Hargreaves in the dark. Not a clue remained to her eye.

Yet, that was why she had called Arturo C. Adler, wasn't it?

"A bat could see it was the work of a steel golem, my dear Inspector," came the piercing, high-flown voice. On cue. Most irritating. Hargreaves pinpointed the source of the annoyance below her, and spotted the young detective wriggling out from a maintenance ditch underneath the baggage car. Startled, she nevertheless suppressed the urge to squeal. Instead, she merely stepped back so he could not see the color of her knickers.

"How can you see anything from that hole?" she shot back gamely.

Arturo straightened up before replying. It was a dubious process that involved brushing down layers of scalloped linen sleeves threatening to drown his loud purple vest. Impressively, not a drop of grease clung to the cumbersome garment, but he did spend an inordinate amount of time brushing a bluish dust from one sleeve. A lens, disguised as a monocle, hung from his breast pocket, and a bong hung on his belt loop. None of it was as flashy as Arturo's hair, a shock of platinum that veered back in a series of hard spikes. The color was a recent affectation he would grow out of in a week or two. Hargreaves spotted his green greatcoat slung on a nearby rail, itself a shimmering double-breasted horror, and threw it over to him.

"My regrets that you are late, Inspector," Arturo said nonchalantly as he drew the sleeves over his shirt. Now, he looked merely eccentric, like a Roman candle caught in a bottle. He drew an intricately cast pocket-watch from the folds of sleeve vomiting from the coat. "Your telegram did say nine in the morning, but it cannot be helped. Scotland Yard is quite a ways from Newham."

"How did you...." Vanessa began, instantly regretting it. Her jaunt on Alphonse had not cleared her mind of the *Montemarte* case, and she had ended up collapsed atop a newsprint headline, "Temple Mills," triple-underlined, in her office.

"That you slept last night in your office? Your corset laces are drawn four millimeters too tight, a desperate attempt both to straighten your skirt and to hide the deplorable condition of your blouse. Your boots, though tasteful, are practical, flat, and scuffed, with secure buckles in lieu of laces, all signs they are part of your professional wear. Tweed coat still has some crumbs on it, Mr. Sanders' Pork Pie from his cart on the embankment if I'm not mistaken. I have written a monograph on the types of street food detritus commonly found in London, you know...."

Hargreaves touched her hat impatiently, which only let Arturo continue his deduction. It didn't escape her that Arturo had left the hat alone in his verbal skewering—it was a felt top hat that accented her hair perfectly.

"Most damning, your hair is dry and your skin dark under the eyes, a trait shared by those cursed to sleep on the planks they call cots in the Yard's vernacular. Please do not test me, Vanessa Hargreaves," Arturo quipped smugly. "If you'd like a demonstration, I can shed some light on this ruin of a train car that seems to have stumped you so royally. That is why you called?"

Hargreaves simply harrumphed. As Arturo turned his self-satisfied mug to the train's twisted carnage she attempted to smooth down the wrinkled blouse and skirt. Her original intention was to highlight her bust to draw attention away from her clothing, creating the illusion that her ample front was overflowing from her neckline. What lay under her thigh-highs was usually enough to accomplish seduction, while maintaining the tweed look so useful for a London copper.

Arturo C. Adler was a completely different type of man than the dashing pirate Albion Clemens in that he seemed to care nothing for Hargreaves' charms. Still, she never liked his taking the piss out of her efforts.

"The constables had the baggage car stripped. There's nothing of value," Hargreaves said, if only to prompt Arturo's snide put-down. He fell for it hook, line and sinker, though not much prompting or taunting had ever been needed. The two had been drawn together time and again for the very purpose of crime scene investigation. Arturo came running from his Camden Town house sometimes before the inspector sent for him.

"As I observed on the Blackfriar Bludgeoner case," Arturo said with a distinct cadence, beginning to flow into his rhythm of crime scene analysis. "Inspector Hargreaves sees all that I see, yet understands nothing. The very method of destruction speaks volumes. Look here, where the metal is rent from its bolts. The even, smooth punctures along the edge! The striation pattern and stress marks! The roof!" He slipped his monocle out now, and instead of placing it on his eye, hovered it between himself and the car. Squeezing the rim, the lens flexed: now concave, now convex. Arturo was plucking clues from empty air with his fingertips.

"There is no bloody roof, you imbecile." Hargreaves feigned a barb. Had Adler been looking, the amateur detective would have remarked upon the sardonic hint of a smirk on her face.

"Precisely! The fact there was an automata involved is obvious— no, there *were* automata! One to drive in some sharp, pointed instrument." He gestured to the puncture marks, now brutally obvious to Hargreaves. Most solutions are, after someone points them out. "Let us call it Driver. A second golem must have been present to clip and pry open the breach. Let us call it Priser. The very lack of a roof indicates that either Driver or Priser, or perhaps even a third automata, entered the breach with the precise plan to destroy the roof. That indicates the loot was probably cumbersome, perhaps too large or heavy to extract swiftly."

"An airship!" Vanessa now cried, and Arturo gaped slightly at her momentary burst of genius. He tried not to let it show, and Hargreaves had to be quick to catch the minute widening of Arturo's eyes.

"Precisely," Arturo said, recovering. "An airship provides both the ability to move the item and the heavy golems," he said, hopping onto the baggage car. A peculiarly ragged hole lay at his feet. "And here, this is where the ship anchored itself, with an anchor launched by steam, with great force. Note the salts left by the evaporation. Now the question is: what was stolen?"

"I called you because I needed your forensic abilities. I'll track down the loot and the perpetrators," Hargreaves said, feeling the familiar caution she always felt about Arturo. If the stolen item in question were valuable, she didn't put it past Arturo to retrieve it himself and sell it to the highest bidder. He was quite good enough to do it without Hargreaves ever suspecting a thing, a fact she bit her thumb at savagely.

"Do not be silly, my dear Vanessa, I must know what the motive was if I am to track these ingenious malefactors."

"'Inspector Hargreaves' to you." She took a quick inspection of her surroundings; one engineer and a foreman, not quite a coop, but enough to start a fair clucking in the *Times*.

"With all we've been through? Why, do you or do you not remember that moonlit eve under the shade of the iconic, raven-graced Tower, standing over the conquered Crown Jewel thief Argento de Maupaussant, under the eyes of none but God, when you professed your undying—"

"Oy, get off of there!" A cry came from above, interrupting the prattling detective mid-boast. She felt the air shudder before she heard the workman scream, cutting through their banter like a knife through butter.

"Arturo!" Vanessa redirected the cry, and she was not a moment too soon. Lithe and observant, yes, but if not for the warning, the spry detective could not have avoided the tons of sleeper car silently falling on their crime scene from the rotary above.

The gleaming chrome and black iron wheels came groaning and shuddering down just behind Arturo's heels as he leaped off the baggage car, which promptly exploded in a nova of wooden splinters and lost bolts. The tinkling of pieces shot out of their mountings had not ceased when Hargreaves helped the detective up.

"Almost went tits up, I did. What the bloody fuck?" Arturo was spitting dust, but Vanessa was not looking at him. Rather, she was scanning the lofty ceiling of the train depot, where the rotary that dropped the sleeper car on them still quivered.

"Things haven't quite gone pear-shaped yet. There!" she cried, spotting the whisper of a jacket darting behind a boiler on the upper level. Her boots squealed with her leap towards the maintenance stairs, the .22 already sitting warm in her hand. As she passed a railing, she tossed her hat to spin neatly on top of it, for safekeeping.

"Tosser tried to crush me!" Arturo was hot on her heels.

Out of the corner of her eye she saw him wielding a tiny weapon with a pistol grip. The barrel had a funny shape, almost like a silver iced cream.

"Cut him off!" she said, indicating a clear access route that led to the northern exit of the depot. The gaping maw was still admitting steaming, huffing engines, looking to her and any criminal like the liberating gates of St. Peter. Vanessa lunged down a narrow alley formed by train cars crowding the upper level of the depot. Each step came down on grating suspended over two stories of steel trains, their stoked furnaces an inferno of gnashing gears. Ducking swiftly between the rotaries, Hargreaves tried to assess the number of assailants. It had been a surprise attack, and the enemy hadn't stayed to finish the job. They had fled, so they did not outnumber her and Arturo. That meant one person, and if Vanessa Hargreaves were trying to escape after a surprise attack, she would be hiding—

"There!" she said under her breath, and whirled round a handhold with the .22 up and ready. Nobody was in the cabin, save cold ashes and one lonely shovel leaned up against the wall.

Instead, the expected attack came from above. In a tangle of shadowed limbs tipped with leather-wrapped steel, hard vice grips closed on Vanessa Hargreaves' gun arm, followed by the weight of a small, fast opponent—the kind of sparring partner she hated, like a bloody Amazon monkey.

Some kind of mask covered the assailant's face, but when she struck one of the arms, it was wiry and covered in muscle, like punching rocks wrapped in butcher paper. She felt a stab vest under the tight jacket even as she threw the assailant's weight off her. The .22 Tranter skidded to a halt, hanging over the lip of the walkway.

Her weapon lost, Vanessa sidestepped into the opponent's space even as he spread-eagled against the cars on both sides, arresting his fall. She knew for a fact it was a mistake to sacrifice her superior range. Little blokes had all the fast jabs and dodges normally kept at bay by her long legs. Cramped in by cars on both sides, her limbs wouldn't get the leverage she needed for a punishing blow.

Time to get close and untidy.

Hargreaves tried a right feint, following up with a devastating stomp that made use of tight quarters, but her foe *jumped*, splaying his feet against the sides of the cars like a great spider. So that was how he ambushed her! Before she could react, he planted a short jab to her right cheekbone, high enough to make her see stars. She fell backwards while lifting her knee, so when the assailant's feet hit the ground his gentleman's sausage would be gelatin. With a shock, she felt her kneecap connect with nothing, perhaps something soft.

"Hargreaves, down!" Arturo's voice barely made it through the pugilistic haze, but in her periphery she saw the spiky-haired detective behind their enemy, leveling his strange weapon. Hargreaves pressed herself flat to the ground.

There came a taste of pennies on her tongue, and suddenly her ears filled with a riotous din. Blue arcs crashed between the steel walls all round her, like Tesla lighting freed of their glass bulbs. Tongues of sparkling, crackling light danced along the tracks. A mad scientist's experiment had been uncaged, bubbling the paint and scoring black marks where they touched.

"Mother of God!" she blasphemed. Thankfully, Arturo's aim was true and their mystery assailant took the brunt of it in the back, tumbling through the gap between two train cars.

"Ach!" Arturo said as Vanessa got up. Something smoked and fizzed in his hand, throwing off sparks, and with another curse he lost his hold on the weapon. With a final crackle, a piece of it popped off and buried itself in the wood of the walkway, two inches in front of Hargreaves' nose.

"You could have killed me!" Hargreaves shouted. "What is that, a prototype death ray?"

"Never you mind; the quarry is getting away!" Arturo said, and he was right. A smoking trail clinging to the air was all that was left of their mystery man.

"Adler...." Hargreaves fumed. She scooped up her .22 and the death ray in hand, leaving Arturo gaping. Darting left and right, she followed the faint trace of a burned tyre smell hanging in the air, all the while thanking the fashion gods shin-high pencil skirts were not a la mode this year. Yet corsets and bustles were. Curses.

"Went that way, ma'am!" hollered one of the workers overhead, before ducking back into the safety of a cabin. El-Nevazar!

"Your country thanks you!" Vanessa shouted, and took the route indicated, only to emerge from the cathedral of rotaries and soot-smeared track into a moving labyrinth of chugging locomotives. The glaring white English sky seemed to taunt her with its sudden brightness, revealing every detail of the yard—except for her mark.

Persistent to the last, Hargreaves dashed into the mess, her coattails flying tweed wings. She vaulted through baggage cars and over linkages like the jumps at Kent. After ten minutes of fruitless search, she skidded to a halt in the clinker.

"Blast it all!" Vanessa cursed. The slippery saboteur could be anywhere, on any number of trains or cars. There was no way she could track the smell in all this coal smoke. She braced her elbow against a gleaming red mail train, trying to slow her heart. As she plodded back to the exploded crime scene, she passed the stoic Alphonse, sitting there like a lump of shiny Christmas pudding.

"Fat lot of good you were," she mentioned in passing, a barb the machine took without complaint.

Back at the baggage car, she met the kneeling Arturo, who seemed to be canvassing the scattered pieces of the crushed crime scene. He seemed completely unfazed by the near-death experience, and was instead absorbed in his search.

"What a fine mess this is," Vanessa said, "I've just gone and lost our one real lead, my crime scene is smashed to bits, and what the hell are you doing with those nuts?"

"Not this particular lug-nut," Arturo was mumbling. "It was stuck in the board about there, so with the force of the explosion... eureka!" He straightened up, all five-foot-six of bottle-green detective, clutching a gold hexagon between two fingers.

"I'm a size six, firstly, and secondly you forgot the champagne," Vanessa said, wiggling her fingers.

"This is no ordinary lug-nut," Arturo said, completely ignoring her desiccated tone. "It is a twelve-gauge gold alloy timing nut, with the presence of point-zero-zero-five percent gold and twenty-five percent carbon slivers commonly known as adamant."

"I'm glad you've taken a shine to someone else's nuts," Hargreaves said, channeling a certain helmswoman in her annoyance. Curse those pirates and their uncouth influence!

Arturo removed a flask from his inner pocket, and the strong herb scent that effused between his lips told Hargreaves it was his favorite laudanum, a strong port laced with plenty of opiates and absinthe. His victory drink.

"Adamant is a hideously expensive material that has a significant reaction to fuel additives, and one that has become favored by my arch-nemesis, Professor Halley Blackwater, alias Doctor Shock."

"Oh, Lord, not this again." Vanessa rubbed her temples, a gesture she reserved just for Adler. "Arturo, you have no nemesis. Professor Blackwater is an expert in economics, not bloody metallurgy. Besides, he's been on a book tour in America since July, and won't be back until Guy Fawkes Day."

"Are you his press agent? No, a spy! How are you so aware of his movements?"

"You knucklehead, because I've had to protect you from the Yard. The Professor's filed seven different complaints against you since you two met!"

"He's no academic lily-white, he's a criminal mastermind, I tell you! He wouldn't dirty his hands with this ground-level fluff. This is part of some bigger plot."

Hargreaves heaved an enormous sigh. Arturo was a great help, unfailing in his attention to detail and clues, but perpetually inept at seeing the bigger picture. Nobody could mastermind hundreds of crimes in nearly every Steam Age country, as Arturo was fond of accusing Professor Blackwater. Hell, even Clemens hadn't gotten to Venezuela yet.

"In any case, the nut couldn't have come from the sleeper car. Give it here." Fast as lightning, the lump of metal was in the inspector's hand.

"The distributor is either Sturluson Metallurgy or Logan

Alchemics, their London offices being 42 Patch Street and 744 Wilde Street respectively. But I doubt you will find much there, for the nut is cast in American customary, not metric or Imperial standard," Arturo said to Vanessa's back. He brushed an imaginary piece of lint off his jacket, which was immaculate compared to Hargreaves' begrimed duster. "It's Shock's, I say."

"Bah."

"And can I have my gun back, please?" Arturo continued.

"Confiscated," Vanessa said coldly even as she turned the clue over and over in her hand. She examined the serial number, and the odd grooves. "And you'll tell me who supplied it to you so I can arrange a raid."

"Trade you for the real addresses?"

"No deal," she said. The amateur detective knew how to bluff, but it was not in his interest to feed her false information. He enjoyed the mystery too much. "And one of these days Proscribed Substances is going to have your dealer in cuffs."

"Fellow by the name of Tony Macmillan, in Whitechapel. He assured me it would shoot straight."

"Thanks, Art," Vanessa said. "I'll let you know what this turns up."

"No, you won't," Arturo said mildly. "But I'll find out anyway. I always do." He walked away, whistling a merry jingle.

***

It took her all of ten minutes to slip Alphonse into one of her underground entrances, a municipal pump house. Once inside, a ramp led down into the catacombs beneath the city where Hargreaves guided Alphonse by Tesla lamps down the branching tunnels, using a copy of a pre-Elizabethan map Hallow had procured from a private archive. She avoided her office where constables were waiting with more idiotic cases, and headed straight down to her lair in the M.A.D. machine shop.

"Reckon ye mate be right about this being American. Yanks make a fine grade of steel, so long as it's for shooting or stabbing," Cid Tanner supplied when Hargreaves showed him the little nut.

"This can't be a dead end. I can't just hop a zeppelin to America on one lead," Hargreaves complained.

"No. Sturluson or Logan will know who made the thing even if they don't know the way themselves," Tanner said. He paused, taking in Hargreaves disheveled, and chuckled. "Looks more like you need a cold shower."

"Cid...." Hargreaves cautioned. She had had just about enough cheek today. Unfortunately, Hargreaves in the part of detective had no idea whodunit, save the tenuous connection to the Highgate bank robbery, or, God forbid, Arturo's Doctor Shock. Besides, the Highgate case had been open and shut. It had been a polite young gent called Michael O'Toole, in deep with bookies who gave him an ultimatum: rob a bank, or lose your fingers. O'Toole was the perfect rube—no ties to the mob, single, no children, just a nobody clerk from a nobody brokerage firm.

O'Toole had been caught spending his ill-gotten gains trying to catch a ship to Melbourne, and he had no idea how his metal partner had arrived to his door or where it had gone after the deed. The industry was too young to have any sort of standardization, so it could not be traced.

Back in the hall outside her office, Vanessa Hargreaves sighed at the sight of the *Gwain* floating outside the window, on regular patrol of metropolitan airspace.

If only I could spot the buggers from the deck of the Gwain, Hargreaves thought wistfully. The confidence-inspiring bulk hung suspended in mid-air like a fairy mountain, her foothills still scorched black from recent battles. Her maiden-and-shield figurehead still flew proudly.

Hargreaves also found Cezette Louissaint waiting there with the office's modest tea service ready. The girl turned. She had just been setting out some biscuits, the pistachio ones Hargreaves liked. Her legs clicked softly, hidden by a voluminous skirt. Hargreaves' own, actually.

"Oh, you little—!" Hargreaves said. "How many times have I told you not to sneak up here?"

"They're like to think me some gentleman's daughter, in this couture," said Cezette nonchalantly. It was true—the dress was blue French linen, cut with a mild gothic fishtail, just the style to hide the girl's legs. The disguise was good enough for a building full of detectives.

To drive home the point, Cezette set her feet primly and lowered herself into a chair with a barely perceptible whirring. Hargreaves harrumphed, setting aside her coat. She held no such vanities as to compare herself to her ward, but she had to admit Cezette had at most a year or two before suitors would begin to materialize like slugs.

"Well. I suppose you shall be mother?"

"Yes, Maman," said Cezette obediently. She poured a cup with the milk in first, setting the cup before Hargreaves. It was strong Ceylon and just how she liked it. "I am beginning to like the English habit quite well."

"And your manners are beginning to match," added Hargreaves. "Hallow is teaching you admirably."

In accordance with an unspoken compact, neither of them spoke about Hargreaves' work. Instead, the afternoon was spent talking of things large and small, such as Cezette's favorite automata, her progress on their shared book of the week, or which austere persons Hargreaves had glimpsed that day. The inspector was unfazed by these ministers and society belles, but Cezette was fascinated by them, so Hargreaves kept notes of them in her notebook filled with sketches. Cezette was working on another of Hargreaves' dresses to fit her slighter frame, really one of her undercover costumes Hargreaves was all too glad to be rid of. By the by, the hour for tea was gone, and Hargreaves poked her head outside so Cezette could make a stealthy exit.

"It's clear. Go, go!"

"Maman!" Cezette protested as Hargreaves nudged her out. "This is no dirigible raid! I will look *au naturel* walking at a measured pace."

"Oh. Yes, you're perfectly right, of course." Silly, Hargreaves. How many times had she gone undercover herself as some countess or other? Before Hargreaves could do anything more, the girl leaned up on her iron trotters and threw her arms around her. Her lips landed soft on the inspector's cheek.

"Right." Back in her office, Hargreaves breathed milk and honey from her tea, trying to control her flush. She had never thought she was the maternal type, yet this girl brought something out in her that she couldn't deny.

The day's pleasantries over too quickly, Hargreaves braced herself for the work ahead by talking aloud. "Step one: alert the hospitals and constables to look for burn victims, five-foot-four, trim and fit." Hargreaves sent out the alert over the Metropolitan Police Service tube net, a system of telegraph lines and Morse lantern codes between dirigibles. Within the Yard building itself, the act amounted to a hurried scribble stuffed into a latching ball, sent via vacuum tubes throughout the building's walls. She doubted the overworked constables on the ground would bother, but it was worth a shot.

"Step two: put in a tip to the powder sniffers on the sixth floor, look for a Tony Macmillan in Whitechapel, store of illegal sparkers." She scribbled this note as well, rolling it tight and setting her wax seal on the tin ball before putting it in the bolt-action slot in her wall.

She had taken the piss out of Arturo, but truth be told Scotland Yard's problem with the weapons based off of Mordemere's designs was an ongoing one. Firearms Division desperately needed the tip-off, as Arturo well knew. One out of nine ladies of the evening in Whitechapel could cremate an unruly client where he stood. Likely as not, the guns smoked their owners as well, leaving a blackened corset like the fossilized skeleton of a raptor.

"I'd like to see Ruddy Jack put up against this lot," Hargreaves jested grimly at the thought. Proper police business done with, this left her with one last task.

"Step Three: Investigate Logan Alchemics and Sturlusson Metallurgy."

True to form, Hargreaves trusted Arturo to do one thing, and nothing else: carry laudanum. She took the five-minute trek to Hallow's office, deep in the M.A.D. catacombs. The place was as spooky as Cezette always said, full of clicking machines, strange smells and unspooling ticker-tapes like wraiths in the dark. A disused hand-cart was parked at the terminal line, full of machine parts and rolls of paper.

Jean Hallow himself sat like a monolith, near a niche he had outfitted as an office. The telegraph lines converged here, eaten up by a large Turing machine. Like Arturo, Hallow was another man immune to her charms, but she tried anyway, tipping her ample bosom close as she looked over his shoulder.

"Excuse me," Hallow said, and reached past her for the punched card with her data on it. Hargreaves sighed.

The information Arturo gave was the truth, and would have earned brownie points if Hargreaves was in the business of handing them out. Instead, she chose to commandeer a squad cab. Sometimes, one needed the extra finesse of arriving in a squad Fjord, over the imposing, outlandish Alphonse.

Sturlusson's was a townhouse parked between two equally gravelly tombstones of the type. A short stair led up to the parlor meeting room, with a mahogany mantelpiece holding up a glass case containing a harpoon. Obvious signs of Nordic heritage were strategically placed all-round the dominating, four-seat Queen Anne meeting table. Hargreaves picked up a deceptively heavy cube of some layered mineral, which seemed out of place there.

"That would be durandite, not something just any garage tinker can make," came a voice from her right. "Franklin Feerick, I represent Mr. Sturlusson's interests in Her Majesty's Britain."

Hargreaves gave the man her investigator's once-over. Short, hair nearly transparent with age and trimmed round the pate of his head, the bespectacled Feerick looked the very picture of gentility—the perfect salesman. Eton, Hargreaves guessed, but could not be sure. The accent felt off, somehow, as if he hadn't completely acquired a taste for it.

"Inspector Vanessa Hargreaves. Your man relayed to you my business with your firm?"

"Yes, and I am very pleased to be able to help a member of Scotland Yard, particularly an inspector of such high standing. Please, sit. Would you like refreshments?" The two took seats at a corner of the Queen Anne.

"Your investigation into the horrible calamity was well covered in the Times, even dramatized at the local picture house in a five-part series. I recognized your name straight away," the elderly gentleman said as his butler appeared with English Breakfast. Hargreaves had not seen any bell pull. The butler was a large man, but seemed ill at ease, and the bone teacups were a subtle mismatch to the eggshell saucers.

"Most Londoners remember only the name Albion Clemens," Hargreaves said. "The anonymity suits me well, but I appreciate a man who reads the entirety of his queen's testimony."

"Journalism is a dying art," Feerick sighed. "A man may interpret anything he likes when he has the sepia-toned photogram in hand. People will believe his story. It takes a certain clarity to stitch together the gestalt. But I digress. May I see the sample?"

Hargreaves was beginning to like the prompt, business-driven attention. She produced the nut in question, while Feerick produced a glittering loupe with a showman's flourish. Almost sleight-of-hand.

"Yes, this is indeed adamant, of a gauge very specialized for automata. Your source was remarkably well informed."

"Are they used for quite powerful automata?"

"Difficult to tell. Luckily, unlike its mythic counterpart, real adamant is not indestructible. Its weakness is the fantastic cost of its making. The trace components are very dear."

"A person would need large amounts of capital to produce it," Hargreaves prompted, thinking of the Highgate robbery.

"And the right metallurgist. We at Sturlursson's consist of eight percent of the global adamant market, and this is not one of ours. In fact, the gauge appears to be American."

Hargreaves read the frown on Feerick's face.

"Is there a problem?"

"Unfortunately… if the gauge is American, the problem is yours. The liberated colonies have significant internal trade between their states, and are especially guarded in military applications. Isolationist, you see. It may well prove their domestic market in adamant outstrips the whole of Europe's."

"I suppose I will find those heavily taxed products at Logan's?" Hargreaves sighed. This clue was proving more elusive by the second.

"Indeed. They are a major source of American gauge parts here in Britain."

Hargreaves bid Feerick goodbye, and headed some blocks to Wilde Street, a short, narrow cobble alley blocked off by stanchions to prevent hansoms from getting stuck in its winding corridor. Logan Alchemics was a far cry from Sturlusson's, comprising of merely one crooked two-story plaster structure advertising offices in New York, Sheffield and Detroit. It wasn't Whitechapel, but there were a couple of townhouses that looked to be upper-crust brothels or private opium dens. That is, nothing illegal, but enough to throw shade.

Hargreaves rang the braided bell-rope and was shown into a cozy study as different from Sturlusson's professional office as Bag End was from Rivendell. Cubbyholes and bins full of documents protruded from every corner, while a merrily tumbledown hearth blazed in one wall.

"You'll have to excuse the state of the office, we normally take orders by post or telegraph," the whip-thin servant said to Hargreaves, and it took a second for her to register the man's familiarity with the office to mean he was the proprietor, not the help. He seemed not to mind her standing in his foyer, and did not offer her so much as a seat, let alone the kingly reception she had gotten earlier.

"I am not here to place an order," Hargreaves snapped. She showed him the odd little nut of adamant, dodging it left and right as his attention flitted from one thing to another.

"That's a Mendenhall if I've ever seen one. The serial is in Courier," the man said briskly, slurring his 'that' so it sounded like 'fat.' Was it his normal accent, or was he simply overworked? Difficult to say.

"And you are?" Hargreaves said, a little annoyed.

"Thomas T. Thatcher, Managing Director, and if you'll excuse me I'm very busy." The hawkish man with the unfortunate combination of name and affliction leaped from perch to perch, plucking a scroll of paper here, retrieving a fountain pen there, and always consulting a heavy ledger open on his desk. Hargreaves decided to cut the crap and showed him her badge.

"Inspector?" Thatcher said now, noticeably slowing down.

"Yes, and I'm investigating a theft involving automata that used this part."

"Won't have much luck," he answered. "Mendenhall went under. Was a shop fire, I hear, and the shareholders lost faith. Official in today's wire."

"What kind of firm was it?" Hargreaves pounced.

"Strictly priva'e, very hush-hush. Listen, Inspector, automata parts is a very young industry. Cannibalizes from other steam-works as much as it can. A firm like Mendenhall decides to experiment but does not understand the engine's danger, it has an accident. Happens all the 'ime."

"All the time," Hargreaves mused, which seemed to put Thatcher back to speed. "I need to know the latest order for them that came through this office," she pressed.

"Less than a month ago," the director answered after an industrious flip through his ledger. When it came to business, his voice was steady, and his t's enunciated. "Here is a copy of the order invoice, several 'iming nuts, pressure cylinders, engine bolts... odd...."

"What is it?" Hargreaves asked, and for the first time Thatcher stood motionless, looking at the invoice.

"This seems like a large order. Type Four Piling Driver attachments were adapted from construction engines, cranes and shovels, and are supposed to last years."

"Piling Driver?" Hargreaves felt like she just struck gold. "Tell me, Mr. Thatcher, who made the order?"

"A... Feerick. Franklin Feerick. 42 Patch Street, London."

***

When Hargreaves burst through the front door of the handsome townhouse in Patch Street, Feerick was gone. The office door hung ajar, as if to drive in the point that nothing of value had been left.

The rooms besides the ones she had seen were unkempt and dusty. She crept through the dwelling with her .22 Tranter out, but found the only people in the house locked in the attic. They were all dead. The men showed signs of having been trapped there for some time. There was a woman in the room who wore a maid's frock.

"Damn!" she cursed. "I was too bloody late. Damn and blast!"

Hargreaves covered her mouth from the smell of urine. This was murder by neglect. But she was accustomed to horrors worse than this by now. Hargreaves descended the stairs and found a police box nearby. The blue box was roomy enough to hold an inebriate. More importantly, the locker in its front held a telegraph apparatus. The machine accepted her inspector's key, unfolding like Oriental papercrafts, and she hastily tapped out a message to Scotland Yard on its typewriter controls.

Clockworked porcelain tabs spun her message out through the ether, and in a moment, spun again to tell her help was coming. The contraption's serenely ticking logic gates were an immense comfort. When she had been a constable, she had had to memorize every one of Leibnitz's blasted telegraph codes, tapping them out in binary on a knackered rubber knob. One of the anachronisms of the age: When at sea, use Morse. Leibnitz, though, to summon horse.

Hargreaves hunkered down to wait. "I expect the real representative for Sturlusson's is in here somewhere," Hargreaves told the detective inspector on call who arrived to help with the case. Hargreaves was pleased to see a fellow woman inspector in the Yard's service, even if the woman brought a cadre of sleepy constables and a flashy ambulatory engine in her wake. They drew far too many people for her liking. To the other inspector's left, a couple of clocked horses stood serenely chewing the stray clinker in the road. Children reached up to pet them, gingerly, avoiding the flaming grates in their chests.

In the back rooms, Hargreaves found a raided kitchen and pantry that looked as if no maid had touched it in months. A study adjacent to the front room had been hastily stripped of recent maps or plans, pins dotting wallpaper still flagged with little triangles of yellowing parchment. The dusty room was where Arturo C. Adler found the inspector, knee-deep in records.

"Damn! Blast everything!" Hargreaves said.

She tossed a nearby ship in a bottle out of an open window. A couple of cats shrieked their protest as the bottle shattered below. Hargreaves continued to harangue Arturo for a few minutes, comfortably, as if he were an old shoe she might wear to dance her frustrations out on. Arturo looked on mildly until her fit had subsided, before she resumed civil speech.

"I've just been comparing the constables' account of the Sturlusson warehouse to the records kept here. There is already a discrepancy, mainly minor components, but a large space was recently cleared, large enough for two automata and a steam lorry to carry them. I've contacted the port guards, station masters, and Captain Leeds of the *Gwain*, to be on alert for any train, ship, or dirigible carrying our fugitives."

"You saw nothing out of the ordinary, and the man was helpful and cooperative," Arturo said. "It may comfort you to know this Feerick or his contemporary abused the maid frequently during their incarceration. We'll put him away without delay. There's no moral ambiguity here—not like Maple Cross."

Was that a smirk on his face? Impossible to tell. But Hargreaves knew the psychology. He was trying to guilt her out of her rote by-the-book response to see the case in a different light. Maple Cross was before they'd met, but Hargreaves had been livid the first time he brought it up. He had gone out of his way to find out everything about Hargreaves. Maple Cross was not something one spoke of simply to be crass.

Arturo traced a finger delicately between the pins on the wall, imaginary lines sketching the form of shadowed plots. Hargreaves found it remarkable he could read her, a distinguished graduate of the Academy trained in criminology. How old was he? Twenty-two? Eighteen?

"Those people were locked right upstairs. I passed beneath where they were bound," Hargreaves said matter-of-factly. "I'm a homicide investigator, Arturo. I can read murderous intent from across the deck of an airship. This subterfuge, following the money across countries, it's not in my comfort zone."

"You're giving up?"

"I just don't understand why the queen gave me the job," she said, the first sign of fatigue creeping across her brow.

"If she could, she probably would have given me the honor," Arturo answered wryly. His gaze now traveled the writing desk, and the bluish sand embedded in the surface cracks.

"Like as not give you the excuse to raid Professor Blackwater's laboratory."

"Please, a criminal mastermind would hardly hide the maleficent fruits of his labors in a laboratory. Some secret room or such is in order. Haven't you ever read a penny dreadful or seen a picture at the Odeon?"

"If it were you, how would you proceed?" the inspector asked, momentarily startling Adler. "I have no motive, a suspect that could be halfway to Devon by now, and a crime that is rapidly growing more public despite the Yard's and the queen's expectation of me."

"I for one would question that expectation," Arturo tossed back at her. "It seems like the queen was expecting something to happen. Why else would she assign a trusted homicide inspector, one of her best agents, and a personal friend nonetheless, to a position like yours? You have complete authority over any case involving unusual steamwork apparatus. You command a squadron of metal soldiers and genius-level subordinates. Best of all, you can operate with total impunity, because nobody wants your job."

"What are you saying, Arturo?"

"I'm saying we should ask the queen why you are really the head of MD6. This bluish dust, here?" Arturo scattered some in the air, brushing it off the table in a fine blizzard. "I found it filtered through the boards underneath the *Montmartre Express* baggage car as well. It's a very fine tracking agent, with an oxidation marker that changes very gradually—the color indicates the amount of time since it was applied. Anyone who touched the booty would have brought it with them, unnoticed. The thing is, only one agency in all of Europe uses it: MI6."

"By Queen and Country. British Intelligence," Hargreaves said with a mixture of awe and religious terror.

"Now do you think my Shock conspiracy is delusional?"

"This is very different from your boogeyman Shock. How long?"

"The color indicates the tracker was applied when the *Montmartre* stopped in Paris—I believe that is when possession of the cargo was given over to Intelligence. The Ottoman threat is looming just over the east, Inspector. What could British Intelligence be transporting that warranted such secrecy?"

"Whatever it is, they don't have it anymore. Catching the thieves is out of the question—one lorry in a city stuffed with them, the proverbial needle in a haystack."

"Based on the unique nature of the parts we found, we may assume some connection to American nationals. Let us ignore their motives for the nonce, and examine their possible strategy." Arturo's chin rested on his breast, his slender gloved digits pick-picking at the pinned cardstock on the wall as if it were a captured chess piece. "Transporting it back to America is out of the question, thanks to your preemptive measures. Not to mention the attacker we put in his place at Temple Mills. That is, if transporting it is their aim. They will most likely play their next move quite safe."

"Barring any covert involvement, the mooring ports, Paddington, and the docks are all alerted to the presence of the missing item," Hargreaves said, a thought even now occurring to her. "I expect Intelligence already has people covering those exits, ever since the train arrived."

"A single pawn may creep amongst the knights and bishops, becoming a queen just in time for checkmate."

"Hide, eh?" Hargreaves meant to berate him, but suddenly the word struck a chord. "Right. That is exactly what I would do, if I were an American national. We don't tell our constables and customs officers to look for the automata Driver and Priser, but for the transportation of the large cargo. We are perfectly aware their owners can abandon the heavy steel golems. Why can't this cargo be abandoned as well? What if it is some advanced steamwork, or even a prototype weapon? These are no petty thieves; they are capable men with some intelligence, who may know what they are stealing even if we do not. They do not need the cargo itself; they merely need to know how to *build it*."

"By Horatio, you are absolutely right!" Arturo cried with a smirk, as if he hadn't thought of it first. "They must be hiding, squirreled away somewhere in London with some alchemist or engineer trying to pry open the box of secrets as we speak! That must be why they chose Sturlusson in the first place. The firm supplies every alchemist and engineer in the city."

"And when they have those plans, they will leave their conspicuous equipment behind, spiriting the weapon away. How long will that take? If it is a blueprint, we will have no way of knowing who is carrying it, by train, ship, or air."

"At all costs," Arturo C. Adler said to Vanessa Hargreaves, his face flushed with the scent of the chase. "We must convince Her Majesty to tell us what was in that box."

3

THE GOOD PHYSICIAN

"Do you know the story of John Snow and the Broad Street pump handle?" the Queen of England asked Vanessa Hargreaves.

"Yes, ma'am. Doctor Snow stopped a fatal outbreak of cholera, saving thousands of potential London victims," Hargreaves answered from her perch atop a wrought-iron chair. Its Neo-Baroque curves dug into her lower back despite the lavishly printed cushions and swooping rests. Sprung and clocked fixtures within it were supposed to form perfectly to her back. A beautiful chair, undoubtedly, but it may as well have been an iron maiden.

Rather than Buckingham Palace or even Westminster, the heir to Hanover took her afternoon tea on a Soho rooftop, spears of sunshine blasting through facets of crystal glass the size of front doors. Waving fronds tinted the light green in places where the gifts of foreign dignitaries had been planted, including a majestic stand of bamboo, a small vanilla tree and Her Majesty's ancestral favorite, a towering mangosteen in a blue china pot. Hargreaves glanced nervously at the door she had come through, where a brace of sharply suited gentlemen in tailcoats and wigs had been fuming with impatience. She wondered how long they had been waiting, and was quite sure the elder had been the Minister of the Interior.

A servant poured rich, amber Darjeeling from an enamel pot.

Everything was the color of lapis lazuli, from the teapot to the checkered tile floor, even Her Majesty dressed in a tasteful spring riding suit. High, soft boots and trousers, Egyptian cotton, practical and understated. A turquoise brooch in the shape of roses set off the shades of blue. Every piece of Her Majesty's wardrobe spoke late-twenties independent woman, of the dynamic type found in every level of England's most affluent firms. A wide-brimmed, violently cerulean confection shielded the royal brow from the sunlight, and a faux bustle spilled from the royal derriere most fetchingly.

"Most of the residents felt Snow was doing them a disservice, that his germ theories were nothing but the ravings of a discredited physician," Her Majesty continued, sipping and looking out onto the coal-stained London cityscape. "Without his groundbreaking research, we might not have the vaccinations or antigen ampoules Albion General uses every day. In many ways, the warnings I and members of Parliament are espousing daily are being treated like Doctor Snow's earliest efforts: noble, correct, but unless we do something drastic, ultimately useless."

"Your Majesty is referring to the Ottomans," Vanessa said dutifully, pushing down urgent business in favor of Her Majesty's good graces. Her stomach complained, twitching. "If the size of the force we discovered under Leyland is any indication, the emperor has poured the last of the empire's coffers into Mordemere's army of horrors. Parliament is unwise not to listen."

"There is no need to humor me," the queen said, "speak your mind."

"Ma'am," Hargreaves said, and chose her words carefully. "I think your efforts are admirable, but perhaps encouraging military action is unwise so soon after our brush with destruction."

"I am only a figurehead, Hargreaves. I am not a commander," the queen said, the first wrinkle of a smile playing across her generous Hanover brow. She was nothing of the kind. Hargreaves knew Her Majesty had loyal agents posted at every level of government, moving the country with a gentle smile and a veiled dirk. As one of those weapons herself, Hargreaves knew Her Majesty as both the holy virgin and the wise witch.

As Her Majesty spoke, she toyed with the dark burgundy fruit at her place, held by a gilt china bowl much like an eggcup. The queen teased out the juicy white pips with a demitasse silver fork, taking her time in savoring the subtle tropic taste.

"Tactical action is beyond my sphere of influence. My contemporaries and I only wish to have some contingencies in place should Parliament decide to make fools of themselves. Should the Ottomans make some incursion west, a possibility that Lord Gerard refuses to see as dangerously real, Parliament shall move for an alliance with the other western powers. Prime Minister Falstaff sees it as an inevitability, and has prematurely christened it the New Western Alliance."

"It will detract from funding the recovery," Vanessa said. "At a time when the nation's investments are being overbid and undercut by American venture capitalists."

"We still have Britain's steamcraft industry, those ghastly automata makers swelling the royal coffers," the queen said, flirting with less than royal etiquette in her echo of Hargreaves' words. "The Americans claim to possess their equal, but I have yet to see one tin finger."

Hargreaves squirmed uncomfortably, sensing the topic of conversation being swept aside like the last of the Queen's unfinished mangosteen. In a flurry of gloved service, her fruit was replaced with the fluffiest cassis scones Vanessa had ever seen.

"Your Majesty, there is an urgent matter regarding your assignment to me," Hargreaves said, choosing a moment when the queen's royal mouth was busy on a veiled bite of pastry, cream and jam. "You are familiar with the *Montmartre Express* incident?"

"Not for nothing are we called a police state by our detractors. I have the finest aerial Navy and the most disciplined law-keeping force in Europe to handle these matters, not to mention the best Scotland Yard has to offer." Her eyes rested pointedly on Vanessa's blond head.

Victoria III might have enchanted the entire Parliament into radical recovery measures, or charmed rooms full of diplomats into welcoming a tidal wave of goods into their homes labeled 'Made in

Britain,' but Vanessa Hargreaves wasn't fooled. She had been one of the queen's secret confidants, and as close to a friend as someone in Her Majesty's position could have, even before the Mordemere incident. After a full minute of polite staring, the Queen of England relented.

"Oh, all right. It's not a bomb, if that's what you're thinking," Her Majesty quipped, as if speculating on the color of a new frock. Vanessa's stomach churned uncomfortably.

The queen's words were chilling, but it was this quality that had brought Hargreaves to her attention. Her Majesty was remarkably old-fashioned, and her Victorian fascination with murder had brought her servants to Hargreaves' door all those years ago. The difference between ordering a scone and ordering an execution was only a matter of pitch for the queen.

"What have they taken, Your Majesty?"

"You understand I did not wish for any word of it to escape. I have every confidence in you and Intelligence, Hargreaves, but I do understand the difference between a dagger and a sledgehammer."

"Then why put me on the case?" Hargreaves said, all etiquette forgotten.

"I tire of Parliament," the queen sighed. "You've no idea how much fiddling about goes on behind the tapestries. Before my subjects decide their queen has done quite enough meddling, I intend to force the issue. Sometimes your most delicate instrument is the one that will break down walls."

Hargreaves had to snicker at her queen's appraisal.

"Hargreaves, look here," the queen said now, her hands briskly grabbing the teapot to the shocked look of her serving staff. One sugar, two, three went in and was macerated in a flash. Then, even more scandalously, she proceeded to do the same for Hargreaves. If anything, it showed every servant in the room was a trusted agent of the crown. Nothing would leave this room, not even gossip.

"The economy will take care of itself," the queen went on. "If there's one thing we Britons are known for, it's our management of money. War, restoration, lending to other afflicted countries, I trust my subjects to muddle through somehow. If we become embroiled in a conflict, Parliament will have to pay more than sovereigns."

"Is it so bad, ma'am?"

"War is nigh unavoidable. The Ottomans have been in a state of stagnation ever since dirigibles made their trade routes obsolete. You've seen what Mordemere's creations can do, and you were the one who made the incursion into Leyland and saw the Ottoman Balaenopteron. In my back garden! The gall!"

The queen attacked an innocent biscuit that had been sitting on her saucer, devouring the sovereign-sized morsel in a scandalous four bites. Then, more calmly, she followed it up with a sip of tea.

"The army has had the devil's time stocking automata in preparation for those monsters, and the Royal Navy lost one of the Knights in the last debacle. We're spread thin as it is, and I'm in the middle of negotiations with the Nipponese so we can pull back our Pacific legions. If there's any advantage to be had, I want Great Britain to have him."

"Him, Your Majesty?" Hargreaves' eyebrows shot through the glass roof.

The queen was not caught off-guard. Rather, she smiled a grim line that chilled Vanessa to the bone. Victoria III leaned back in her seat, eyes enrobed in shadow even in the scintillating sunroom.

"Three agents, Hargreaves. MI6 has never lost so many, not since its inception, not on one case. It's the newfangled automata, my dear, so powerful, and used so deviously... it's King George and the American minutemen all over again, shooting our officers in the rough."

"Ma'am, what was stolen?"

"I imagine there is a mole in Intelligence, which makes your involvement all the more necessary. I regard you as a capable inspector, Hargreaves; you've earned that right. But don't presume to overstep your bounds."

"Your Majesty, I... I would never," Vanessa stammered quickly.

The queen took another cup of tea, and as Hargreaves received hers, the serving man slipped her a thick sheaf of papers.

"The box was a coffin, Hargreaves. It contains the body of a colonial officer, the last remaining of many from Bombay. A Sergeant

Victor Cook, who was beset by a disease twice as contagious as consumption and even more gruesome. He showed symptoms on the twenty-ninth of March this year, and died on the first of April. A cruel joke, that. Here is the file."

Hargreaves picked up the beige folder and looked through it. The photograms were horrendous, even in sepia. She choked back her rising gorge.

"Sergeant Cook was a good soldier, and his was the only body we saved from the Indian heat. We sealed the body in a hermetic coffin and had it routed through civilian channels to avoid suspicion, through a firm based out of Venice. Bonham's agents were ambushed on the Parisian terminal, and I would be lying if I said it were not good fun watching the Frenchmen sweat. We worked with the *Direction Intérieur* putting his box on the train, barely able to contain the automata violence."

"What good would it do even if I do find it? You mean to use this… this corpse-maker… against the Ottomans! For God's sake, we have to find his remains. If the thieves open the container…!"

"Obviously that was not the situation we planned. Lord Howser has Intelligence in his back pocket, and God knows what those cloaks and daggers had in mind." The Queen sighed, as if the whole mess could have been avoided by the simple expediency of tact. "Fortunately, within the military there are still forces loyal to their Queen, chief of whom are the Knights of the Round. My intention is for the naval forces to retain control of Sergeant Cook. At the least, I can insure this weapon is delivered into the midst of my enemies, instead of used in some grab for power. I will not stand idle while a trump card lies in my grasp, Hargreaves."

The queen's face was set in stone now. It was the face of a matriarch resigned to her choices. Deep down Hargreaves realized she might have made the same decision in her place, and thanked her stars the choice was not hers.

"This is wrong," Hargreaves managed. "Christ, half their forces might be unmanned steamworks. Do you really think this will turn the tide in a war that might never come?"

"War is no phantom!" The queen nearly hissed the last word.

"The spectre of war is very real, but the angel of fortune favors the prepared. Retrieve this ghastly package for me, Inspector, and do it quietly. You know as well as I what may happen if you do not. Will you be our Doctor Snow, or will you be the ignoble constable who stands in his way?"

Seeing the troubled look on Vanessa's face, the queen extended one delicate hand to grasp hers. Hargreaves looked up, shocked by Her Majesty's gentle, undecorated fingers.

"*You* are my trump card, Hargreaves. You were assigned MD6 because I have every faith in your abilities, in how you play by the book, but also by your knowledge of when to throw the book out of the window. You can do this."

"Yes, ma'am," Vanessa Hargreaves said and got up without another word. She left the Queen there in her sunroom, surrounded by her tropical foliage like some Amazon princess. Hargreaves had a nasty feeling that she was not any trump card, but a wild card in a game where she did not know the rules.

***

"I want every machine shop, forge, and chisel-chucking monkey in London searched, I want every physician and physiologic alchemist raided, and I want it done immediately!" Hargreaves said back in the police cab below the Queen's luxurious Soho loft.

"And I want a boiled sweet every time a Whitechapel tart nips my gentleman's sausage," Arturo C. Adler answered her. "But we can't always get what we want, now can we?"

"Suddenly the voice of reason? Bugger off, Adler," Vanessa huffed heavily into the cramped cabin, her breath competing with the boiler steaming outside the windows. She and Adler were the only people in the utilitarian vehicle, a Fjord signed out of the Yard pool. Grinning bars reinforced the front grille, and the roll cage inside featured handy lock-points to cuff a perpetrator's hands. Right now, Vanessa felt she might need to lock herself in before she did anything stupid.

"You found out what it was," Arturo said blandly, his eyes never leaving the beige folder Hargreaves set between them.

"Yes. You had better take a look while I get on some reckless driving."

Taking the wheel, Vanessa hurled the heavy Fjord into London traffic, letting the white and black of the cab's police markings clear the way for her lead foot. While she marked London's streets in smoking India rubber, Arturo's brows knit gradually closer together until the wry cynicism made them a single furry worm across his face. He closed the file with a snap.

"If the queen goes through with this, she could be tried for war crimes," Arturo said.

"She knows. Her Majesty doesn't want to make that call unless she must," Hargreaves answered him. "I know it sounds extreme, but I've come head-to-head with the monsters the Ottomans bought from a madman. It's not an inconceivable tactic, though one of last resort. At any rate, we have to live with that mistake now, and I just want to focus on finding our perpetrators."

"Before they open the box."

"Precisely," she said, and parked the Fjord in a long skid. A line of East End warehousing stood opposite, conveniently off a canal. Merrily playing in the still pool of a lock, a pair of ducks ignored Hargreaves and Adler as they stepped out of the car. The Sturlusson mark was stenciled on one of the warehouses.

"Do you think they took the canal?" Hargreaves said, examining the ramp that led off into the waterway. There were recent signs of movement, but that could have been from the regular steamboat shipments to other warehouses.

"It's possible. The locks will admit boats that can take automata weight. I doubt it though. Feerick made a fast getaway."

Hargreaves looked at the drop of the lock, a ten-foot enclosure made by hinged doors, operated by nothing more than a clever manipulation of the water. An outlet to the Thames lay at the mouth of the canal, but it was too far to get to before the Yard's dirigible scouts were called to canvas the area. They would have needed to move the two automata one boat at a time, raising and lowering the lock each time.

"From Sturlusson to this warehouse, Feerick must have made a similar drive to the one we just did," Hargreaves supposed. "That accounts for my trip to Logan's, leaving about twenty minutes for the interval of my conversation and notifying the constables."

"In twenty minutes, where could they have gone?" Arturo mused along with her.

"It is likely Feerick will want to either study the coffin or extract the contents for stealthy departure. Hermetically sealed coffins look like any other hardware or steamwork container. They will not know what is inside or have an easy job of opening it," Hargreaves said, the photograms from the file in hand. She didn't want to touch them with more than a thumb and a forefinger, as if the record itself was contagious.

"*D'accord.* If they're working for someone higher up, however, they will want to transport the entire package. Let us assume they moved their entire operation to a backup location, *oui?*"

"I hate when you speak French, Arturo," Hargreaves complained. She pushed open the heavy sliding door to the warehouse, and was greeted by the silence of a thousand packing crates and boxes. The slight breeze stirred up the dust and smell of mildew, unavoidable this close to water. Vanessa observed a row of skylights, and gas lighting.

"We are probably looking for a space like this one," Arturo said, looking round. "Adequate lighting for their automata maintenance, good open spaces to test movement, access to multiple avenues of escape, and within twenty minutes of this location."

"That narrows it down, but the constables have already scoured the area downstream of the canal and within twenty minutes range. It's as if they disappeared into a cave."

"Has anybody looked upstream?" Arturo asked.

"Why? It's impossible to go upstream. The canal narrows."

"Impossible for a boat, perhaps," Arturo said. "Look here: the tracks for the large lorry are not imprinted too deeply in the gravel."

"You're suggesting they took off on automata?"

"Stepping right up the shallow canal? Why not? An empty lorry driven away by an accomplice would have blended right into traffic."

Hargreaves spared no more words, but backtracked to the canal. Most of the embankment was built of square gray masonry or ancient stones dating back to Roman times, but further along the algae shifted to green grass, still bright for autumn. Soon the verdant path yielded to softer, less packed loam, where Vanessa found what she was looking for.

"Footprints," she said victoriously, observing the tracks while stepping carefully around them. The track was enormous, a square divot in the earth as if a line of filing cabinets had been dropped into the path.

"One of them was in the river. The dirt is a little disturbed here where it climbed up for some yards," Arturo observed keenly as only he could. Not to be outdone, Hargreaves squinted at the tracks.

"The other followed the path, and it was carrying our box, perhaps a little clumsily," she said. "The tracks are sunken in more, and there are signs of dragging where the coffin slipped." Hargreaves felt the bite of fear again, as she considered how one unfortunate rock would have loosed a Biblical plague on London.

The two investigators made their way along the tracks, to passersby a well-matched couple on a romantic waterway stroll. Hargreaves' long legs kept up a good pace through the oddment of gardens, storage lots and public parks the canal wound itself through on its meander of the East End. Arturo's tightly wrapped trotters were surprisingly deft in their Oxford shoes, dodging the occasional cyclist with little effort.

They were in a residential neighborhood. The bridges over the canal were only iron walkways between cloistered clusters of biscuit-cutter homes. The trail marched up a wide dirt ramp and onto some gravel that held tracks nearly as well as the mud bank. In the near distance, a tall pastel government housing development reared over the crooked chimneys. Hargreaves thought, with some resentment, of the importance of repairs in this corner of the city, compared to the restoration of Westminster. Rotting holes full of sooty rainwater stood gaping like gangrenous wounds between the neat, square brick dwellings of Londoners. These knots of squalor had never been repaired since the War. There were hundreds of cloistered nooks for criminals to hide in.

"Here, Adler," she whispered, foregoing his first name's audible consonants in favor of the surname. She used hand signs to point out a large building, connected to a Gregorian-style church, with the wide doors and stalls of a stable. All of the shutters and doors were closed. The tracks disappeared in the general area, but there was no sizable building other than the stable.

"Jackpot," she said, using a word the pirate Rosa Marija used to say when she won their games of mahjong.

In the back of the stables, a metal bucket held the remains of a mask and dark jacket discarded in haste. The edges looked raw and brown where they had fused to the man's back, and were cut with a sharp knife.

"Please tell me you don't have a sparker again," was too much to sign quietly, so she opted for waving her .22 and glaring at Arturo. He responded by producing a much more sensible 9mm magazine pistol, likely a German variety. They flanked around the stable, confirming the exits, and Hargreaves barred the rear door with a handy beam of wood. Around the front, a covered walkway connected the stable to the church proper. Hargreaves attempted to restrain Arturo.

"No dice," he whispered. "I have your back."

"Fine. But there will likely be little cover in there, and they will see us as soon as we go in."

"All the more reason," Arturo insisted. Even his platinum spikes seemed to shiver. Hargreaves shrugged, reconciling herself to what help she had. She didn't have time to call in reinforcements—these thugs might have left already.

With a finely placed boot, Hargreaves stormed the place.

"Metropolitan Police Service!" she cried. "Hands where I can see them!"

"The pigs!" someone shouted, and suddenly the air rang with gunfire. She wouldn't have expected it in the middle of Britain. A parked phaeton made the nearest cover, even as a lantern exploded in most vulgar fashion behind her.

In a moment, she had the measure of the place; two of them, one in the rear stall near the back door, and a second behind a wheelbarrow three slots from the back. Now, Hargreaves thought, they will try the door and I can get the jump on them.

What she hadn't counted on were the automata, still warm from

Feerick's escape.

"In the gears!" she heard a gruff, American voice say, the one who had said 'pigs' instead of 'rozzers.'

"Bollocks!" Hargreaves cursed, and a second later rolled out from under the phaeton to see a yellow shape smash through the rear door with a box the size of a morgue drawer.

"Now what, Hargreaves?" Arturo yelled, suddenly beside her. The two of them were pinned by a sudden flurry of shots. A split second later, thundering steps told her the second golem had followed its friend.

"Get the car, and when you pass a police box call for backup! Ask for Tanner or Hallow in Mobile Automata Division, and tell them to bring Alphonse!"

"I'm not good enough to back you up, but this Alphonse fellow is?" Adler protested, but to empty air.

Vanessa Hargreaves didn't stop to see if her orders were obeyed, trusting instead to Arturo's sense of urgency and hound-like knack of finding prey. She dashed past stomping, neighing horses and through the splintered hole of the stable. Then, she did a double-take.

Two minutes later found Inspector Hargreaves riding bareback on a chestnut mare, galloping across the green meadows of Mile End Park. She rode gripping the mare's flanks with her thighs and swatting at the buttocks with an appropriated crop. Her bright blond hair flapped freely, like the banners of a charging knight. She certainly didn't feel particularly gallant—rather, she felt she'd probably cocked everything up.

"Faster," she urged the delighted horse, her eyes fixed on the lumbering yellow forms in the distance. Construction yellow, she blithely observed with her inspector's sense for details. Construction automata had been appropriated for the crime, large and bumbling. Alphonse moved with much more grace, but he was smaller by a head.

Flat out across the green, Hargreaves vaulted the fences of a low cricket pitch with barely a glance, the mare huffing and bulling her way through the field with wild abandon. The crazed gallop cut across a rolling hillock and put her within audible range of the villains.

"Stop!" Hargreaves yelled, and fired off a warning shot to

emphasize the point. The mare had an even temper, and did not buck. "You have no idea what you're carrying!"

The two lumbering titans did not miss a step, not even when Hargreaves rode around and cut them off. She could even see the pilots' heads, Feerick in one and a bald head peeping from the other's chest cockpit. This one carried the coffin, a matte, riveted truncheon for all the swinging the golem was putting it through. In reply, the golem simply swung the heavy weight in a circle around its waist joint, a roundhouse blow that nearly took Hargreaves' head off.

"Christ on a platter!" Vanessa blasphemed, pulling the panicked mare back. She let them flank her, moving around the slowing mare. She shied away from the thundering feet, falling back inexorably despite Hargreaves' best efforts.

Suddenly, like a bolt from the blue, the countryside rang with the sound of a constable's whistle, followed by the rumble of something heavy off to her right.

"Alphonse!" she called in delight, recognizing the silver glint. Two more automata came into view, all of them loping quickly to her. One of them was the Yard's other auto, a shuddering horror little removed from Mordemere's kobolds. The other was the domestic recovery, hastily done up with the unicorn-and-lion livery of M.A.D.

"Maman!" the familiar voice of Cezette called from Alphonse, sidling up to her. She yelped when the inspector leaped the short yard from the horse's back and onto the automata's arm. From there, Hargreaves made her way to the pilot's seat.

"Cezette? What are you doing in there? Budge up!" she said, undoing the girl's loose harness and forcing her out of the seat. She took the controls herself, and, feeling for the familiar lever, activated Alphonse's rolling mode. There was a clunk.

"Mon Dieu!" Cezette yelped, and the machine surged forward.

Beneath their feet, Hargreaves felt the boilers and gears in Alphonse's abdomen pulse pleasurably, pushing the automata forward on hooves of India rubber. Alphonse's ankles contained piston-powered wheels padded to handle hard London roads. The grass might as well have been smooth pavement as it whizzed past, until Hargreaves found herself suddenly on top of her prey.

"You git! Get down from there," she cried, feeling herself channel the pirate spirit of Clemens. She accelerated the heel of Alphonse's foot into proximity with the closest golem. There came a grinding crash as both machines rolled atop the carpet of turf, rending the soil aloft in a shower of loam.

When Hargreaves righted Alphonse, she found herself face-to-face with Feerick, whose machine had developed a rather large dent. She also found herself alone. Cezette had tumbled out, landing neatly on two spring-heeled feet. Long stockings hid their true nature, but human legs would never have taken the fall. She was now sprinting ably away from the fray. Hargreaves felt the pang of maternal guilt. She hadn't thought of her charge, and though no harm was done, she knew she'd let the chase get the better of her.

"Feerick!" Hargreaves yelled. "The game is up! Give up and disembark from the golem!" The other two M.A.D. automata, Jean Hallow and Cid in the pilot seats, were cautiously flanking their own prey. Hargreaves had Feerick all to herself.

A hoarse yell came from the yellow machine. Striped black and yellow, the construction automata had been built to sustain heavy loads, practically bulging with purpose in its square shoulders and mesh-lined joints. The arms ended in heavy three-fingered pincers, ridged and deadly-looking.

"Priser," Hargreaves confirmed to herself, even as her opponent swung round a straight right. The blow jarred the teeth in her skull, even though she had thrown up Alphonse's arm in a block—Priser was heavy.

Never before M.A.D. had a royal peacekeeping authority engaged in automata-to-automata battle. Pistols were useless here; the shivering machines quickly becoming impossible to aim from. One might hit it as surely as a barn, but unless a bullet whizzed magically into the cockpit, the person inside was as good as bulletproof. Hargreaves found herself recalling Yard training, the psychology of a criminal, and the writings of Freud and Schopenhauer. An automata was an elegant solution to the hedgehog's dilemma. Covered in steel plate, one might wall oneself away from the world, absolutely protected from being hurt by the quills of other people. She saw how it might appeal to someone like Feerick, brilliant at deception but physically feeble.

What became apparent, as she fought, was the need for pugilistic instincts. When Priser's heavy pincers rammed forward, they jostled Alphonse hard enough to make steam hiss from the joins. Priser was heavier and taller than Alphonse, but Alphonse had more ratchets, making him more agile and more dexterous. As if to make the point, Hargreaves found a hole and landed two jabs, right-left like comets, pushing back Priser's chest until the mesh sprang out of it.

"Bloody Nora!" Vanessa cursed as she weathered the next barrage of punches. Each blow vibrated through her body more than the bass of a picture-house, and each jostle was a roller-coaster dip with no rails. Priser continued to move, and Feerick was not encumbered at all by the damaged chest.

Vanessa Hargreaves was not out of the fight. She found her rhythm slowly, her hands working the various levers and foot-pedals to make Alphonse jump and dodge out of the way. The more she became accustomed to Priser's movements, the more Feerick seemed to be punching in a blind panic. Priser was limited not only by the range of the construction golem but by Feerick's own dwindling hope of escape. He wasn't even trying to use those monstrous pincers. If it were one of Mordemere's kobolds, Alphonse's front would be a mess of shreds by now.

Well, if he wasn't, then Hargreaves would. She used Alphonse's fingers to grapple for Priser's outstretched pincer, pulling it forward. She rode the momentum, and pushed back, at the same time positioning Alphonse's foot. Like a toppled mountain, Priser fell backward over the tripping limb, in a perfect, police-trained judo trip.

"Down the rabbit hole," said Hargreaves in a fugue of battle calm. The earth shook as Priser bit deep into the loam, digging a deep furrow in Her Majesty's front lawn. When they cracked the hatch, Feerick would be knocked quite unconscious by the blow, crumpled against the metal.

"So what now?" Arturo asked in the shadow of the crumpled, defeated form of Driver.

The remaining Yard automata had flanked the construction golem, avoiding the whistling pile driver that punched canned-ham holes in the turf. At first, the massive, wild machine had the upper hand over the Yard automata, but the oversize construction equipment proved more of a hindrance than a threat. After a bit Cid's domestic began to jerk. It threw its heavy limbs round and round uncontrollably as it had in M.A.D. headquarters. The flailing blows pitched into Driver, and both toppled against Mile End's beautiful foliage. The fearsome driver pin stuck in a tree, its hydraulics choked by branches, allowing Hallow's automata to pierce the boiler with a truncheon the size of a lamppost. Steam billowed out in a painful whistling cloud that cooked the leaves on their branches.

"Now we move the Cook box back to Yard for quarantine." Hargreaves nodded Alphonse's head towards the matte black drawer sitting in its own crater, where it had been dropped. She couldn't bring herself to call it what it was: a coffin. Luckily, the seam had been riveted and welded; the containment procedure for the body had been absolute. Whatever lethal bug was trapped inside, it was staying there. Constables moved the moment the thrashing was over and the box seemed safe to handle.

"By the book, Inspector?" Arturo called up to Hargreaves. His eyes showed nothing, but the set of his jaw indicated to Hargreaves that the swarm of constables would become a problem. Hargreaves had to agree, but how would any of them open the Cook box? There was no window to see in. For the moment Her Majesty's dirty secret was safe.

Hargreaves disembarked from Alphonse, marveling at the amount of superficial damage he had absorbed. Dents and paint scuffs dotted the gear's armor. She went to Adler and the two of them stood on the grass a little apart from the constables trying to pry open the cockpit of Driver. Unlike Priser, this automata had been sealed with a heavy plate hatch, with the operator holed up within. Cid shouted hasty directions from his automata, while Hallow on the ground was shoulder-deep within the machine's exposed workings.

"The conundrum is on my mind as well, Adler," Vanessa answered him in a low voice as they watched. She knew very well once Intelligence heard of M.A.D.'s successful mission, they would waste no time in securing Sergeant Cook's body for their own study.

The thought of Great Britain using such monstrous tactics in any situation made Hargreaves sick to her stomach, but she couldn't think of any ready remedy. If she did anything but hand over the box to the shadows lurking under the Union flag, she would be branded a traitor. Yet, was there no other choice? There was but one hope, if she dared; getting the box out of the hole would require automata assistance. That meant MD6 had to be involved, and that presented some opportunities.

Hargreaves liked to think she did know her queen well enough. The woman was no figurehead, but a powerhouse of connections and intrigues. Even when Her Majesty hosted Parliament at her summer home in the Isle of Wight, her agents in Whitehall and the Diogenes Club maintained a covert network of chambermaids and butlers loyal to the crown. How could Hargreaves evade that kind of power? No, what had to be done had to be done now, while she was in possession of the box. She didn't know enough about the plague to risk its destruction. What if she threw the box into the river and poisoned all of London? What if burning it simply set the demon loose?

"Damn!" A shout came up, and Vanessa snapped out of her torpor to see the hatch on Driver pop loose, dumping the spidery Hallow onto the turf below. He seemed unharmed, perhaps surprised to be suddenly in sunshine and greenery. Several constables were on hand with revolvers and truncheons, but that proved unnecessary.

"Bollocks," Hargreaves muttered under her breath, a profanity that stung her English Protestant lips as much as the acrid smoke rising from the cockpit. The pilot was dead, choked on the leak that had built up behind the hatch. Most likely an exhaust line had ruptured in the struggle, filling the cramped cabin with coal smoke. Speaking of butlers, it was the butler from Sturlusson's who had served with the mismatched tea cups. Vanessa hoped he had been knocked out. She was not prepared to entertain the possibility of groping in the hot, choking darkness for a latch or lock, fast running out of air even as one roasted to death.

Cid walked his automata over, using the hands to provide a platform for the rescuers to remove the body. Its face was horribly contorted and blackened, Hargreaves saw as the automata rolled the corpse gently onto a tarpaulin. She knew at once it had not been he who attacked her in the train yards. The arms were too short and the muscles too dense. This was a man closer to Feerick's age, whose physiology had been adapted to heavy labor, not acrobatics.

A terrible certainty struck Hargreaves. There had to be a third accomplice.

4

Hargreaves Hatches A Plot

Vanessa Hargreaves' Fjord tore into Scotland Yard, and hot on their heels were Yard engines bearing their quarry—one long truck for the automata and a shorter, covered cab for the box. She had reluctantly given Cezette control of Alphonse again, after a stern talking-to about leaving M.A.D. without Hargreaves' say-so. The convoy made straight for the access ramp, a guarded back entrance that would serve to keep the papers at bay. Soon the journalists would crowd the narrow streets with their photogrammers and portable gramophones, cranking their arms off for a recorded quote. A sound-bite. Remarkably apt, given how cutting words without context could be.

But for now, Hargreaves was alone in the vehicle with Arturo, and they both knew it was now a race against time. British Intelligence would be converging on them now that the Cook box had resurfaced.

"There has to be a third accomplice." She tugged at her shirt with a grimace, which was soaked through. Alphonse tended to produce that effect.

"It would seem he was recovering in those stables," Arturo answered her.

In lieu of a partner, Vanessa Hargreaves found herself bouncing ideas off Adler instead. He seemed to arrive at a conclusion preternaturally, but for every time Hargreaves slapped herself for missing an obvious clue, she had to hold on to any shred of sense in Arturo's bewildering train of thought. It didn't help that he was right nearly all the time. Often she was tempted to purchase a supply of coca at the nearest snuff shop to catch up to his ranting. The only thing stopping her was the smug look of satisfaction Arturo would undoubtedly wear.

"Your stocking is torn," Arturo pointed out when her accelerator foot came into view. Vanessa observed the run, a line of fraying thread like a mauling. Then again, she thought, brilliance comes with a price.

A blessing of cool cellar air and calm darkness met her as she climbed from the Fjord, but Hargreaves knew she had precious little time to enjoy it. She gestured wildly for the automata to be moved to the back, funneled into the bay just outside the catacombs, and the short cab into a Yard garage.

Even though the other constables had brought Feerick in just before her, Intelligence had probably already sent their agents ahead. She took the stairs two at a time, arriving on the heels of her constables before the interrogation room. Straight away, she instructed them to leave her alone with Feerick, hoping Sergeant Cook would stay below the Yard in the interim.

"Right," Hargreaves said, attempting to keep her cool despite the four flights of stairs she had just run. "Fancy meeting you again."

Franklin Feerick's neat composure had decomposed like a week-old corpse, and now he sat slumped on the interrogation room's hard bench as if he were grateful for the seat. Strings of his sparse hair hung over his face, and he looked defeated. Good, Hargreaves thought. This will make it quicker.

"I want answers," Hargreaves said, preferring brass tacks and clichés over the lengthy process of breaking down a witness.

"So would I," Feerick managed.

"What do you mean?"

"We're a band of petty thieves, Inspector. We operate in the shadows, we weren't prepared for three Yard golems running a merry chase through Mile End Park. What was in the box that was so valuable?" He sounded about to break down, actually.

"Someone hired you to steal it," the inspector pieced together.

"Yes, of course."

"All three of you?" Hargreaves asked.

"Yes. You figured it out after you pried poor Gregor's body out of our golem. There were three of us, Gregor the Strongman, me, Faustus the Clown, and the contortionist Orb Weaver. We were part of a circus troupe that broke up a year ago."

"Orb Weaver attacked me at Temple Mills. To cover your tracks," Hargreaves prompted. She thought of the way the contortionist had scrabbled over the engines, exactly like a spider.

"Yes."

"Who hired you, then?" Vanessa started to ask again, but the opening door cut her off.

"Inspector?" A young constable stood in the doorway, a recent Academy graduate by the smooth jaw. Hargreaves bit her lip—she didn't know this one. "The Commissioner wants to commend the inspector responsible for M.A.D.'s successful mission. Your presence is requested in the press room."

"Can't you see I'm in the middle of an interrogation?"

"Yes, but he was adamant about making a good impression, ma'am. You know how he gets."

Vanessa cursed, knowing full well the feeling of being given the runaround. Then again, the room had only one door, and no windows save a small one over the aperture. Easy to lock Feerick in.

"I'll be back," she said to Feerick, and locked the door. If Hargreaves had turned back at the last second, she might have seen the look of horror on his face. Of course, when Hargreaves rounded the three flights of stairs and down the hall to the press room, there was nobody there.

She barely had time to spit out an expletive before dashing pell-mell back up the stairs, shocking several clerks and young constables on the way. Even before she reached the interrogation room, she could see the glitter of glass in the hallway, and the broken window over the door where the Orb Weaver had squeezed himself in.

A shard of glass lay bloodied on the table next to Feerick's open throat.

Hargreaves took the shortest way to her office, not stopping for anyone. She had no pretensions of catching up to a murderer who could slip unnoticed within the Yard and noiselessly murder a witness. Yet, she had one hope. Orb Weaver had come with two aims: Feerick, and the Cook box.

Turning a corner, she spotted the Commissioner fending off a gaggle of paper-men. Doing an about-face, she darted up the rear stairwells and through the holding cells to a chorus of wolf-calls, finally making it to her office.

In a flash, her coat flew across the room, followed by the damp shirt. Hargreaves was anything but unprepared. In her closet hung a backup outfit, a utilitarian waist jacket cropped at the waist to facilitate the quick draw on her .22 Tranter. Slipped between the laces of a deep purple underbust bodice was a line of hidden slugs and a bit of cash, accentuated by a darted hip line. She also grabbed a fresh linen blouse that reminded her of Arturo C. Adler for some demented reason. Her torn stockings were rubbish, so she replaced everything with riding trousers, made of a good elastic weave that clung to her hips.

If she was to face the treacherous Orb Weaver, her next stop would have to be the armory. She'd danced this waltz before, and did not intend to go unprepared. A pair of constables guarded the secured room, who made a record of every weapon and officer who left with it. No dice, Vanessa concluded. Instead, she pulled her duster back on and clicked her buckled boots over to Firearms Division. There a friendly inspector thanked her for her assistance in their raid of Tony Macmillan's Whitechapel basement, which had been stuffed to the rafters with a stash of five hundred illegal sparkers.

"Inspector, would you be so kind as to show me the confiscated weapons? I'd like to compare them with the one we liberated at the Temple Mills train yard," Vanessa asked with just a dash of a golden smile. Alfred Davies, thirty-four and happily married, was not immune to Vanessa Hargreaves' statuesque physique, particularly in her current getup. Anglo-Saxon ancestry was strong in her family, with a dash of Swedish grandmother and a Scottish great-aunt somewhere. It gave her strawberry-and-honey locks and a fabulous bust perched on a tall frame that Artemis would approve of—she had a hunter's body, an archer's stance. Her legs went on forever under the duster. Soon enough Hargreaves found herself in Firearms Division's evidence room, a fifteen-yard space jammed with gun lockers and racks of bagged weapons.

"Like Christmas Eve at Em and Ess." Hargreaves smiled. She strode past the racks of strange prototype sparkers glittering with toggles and dongles, heading straight for the matte black racks in the back. Tucked between all the muzzles and magazines was a fashionable bandolier belt. To accessorize, Hargreaves chose the following:

1. One 9mm Browning, of a collection of illegally brokered American arms, magazine loaded. Assorted ammunition.

2. Four potato mashers, souvenirs from a successful terrorist intercession. The bombs fit snugly in her duster, hanging on loops of fabric.

3. One 14-inch 'Bowie' knife, lifted off an Australian stowaway. Satisfied with her armament, Hargreaves turned when something caught her eye.

4. A palm-sized sparker in a fetching chocolate brown. "It worked on Orb Weaver once; at the very least it will scare the living daylights out of someone."

5. Lastly, almost as she was leaving, she picked up an object that resembled nothing more than a spindle of wire, a fishing hook, and a canister of Chantilly crème. Almost a child's toy, really, that had been lifted from an inebriate in the tank who died from drink. The man had been far too gone to explain what it was, but the sharp-eyed inspector thought it might come in handy if she ever wanted to cross from one airship to another in a hurry.

Just outside her office, she nearly ran down the man in the bow tie standing there with a bouquet.

"What the deuce—! Martin?" said Hargreaves, her mouth agape.

Martin, her ex-beau as of two days ago, took a step back. He took in Hargreaves, standing there loaded for bear. He opened his mouth, which flapped a bit. Then he quit it and just held up the flowers.

"Oh... oh dear, these are lovely," said Hargreaves. She took them in hand, smiled, and jammed them back into his. "But you really have terrible timing." She spun on her tall bootheels and marched off. "Toodles!"

For some reason, that felt more real than anything she'd felt in a long time.

When she turned the corner, Vanessa Hargreaves stopped again, barely restraining herself from using her bevy of armaments on what she found there. She cursed a blue streak of blasphemies.

"Going somewhere?" Arturo C. Adler said from his casual perch in the hallway of Scotland Yard. He waved away the attractive clerk he had been speaking to, her arms filled with pressed copies.

"I suppose you deduced my plan as easily as you saw through our perpetrators' intentions," Hargreaves said, beginning to stride down the corridor and away from Adler. Not surprisingly, he began to follow, struggling to match her long steps. "Feerick's dead."

"Bollocks."

"Slippery wanker got in through the window."

"You are aware that, by taking Sergeant Cook's body yourself, you're exposing yourself to fire from above?" Arturo reminded her. Luckily, there was nobody else in the corridor. Arturo's demure date had darted into a side office in a dizzy of disappointment. "Intelligence won't take kindly to you running off with their ace in the hole, and the Yard won't understand at all."

"You are aware the hair products in those maddening spikes will catch fire if you walk too close to the lamps?" Vanessa shot back. Seeing the earnest look of concern on Arturo's face, she reeled it back. "The box isn't safe in Scotland Yard either. Look how easily you got around in here. The three of them were circus performers together and highly skilled thieves after, but Orb Weaver had no problem killing Feerick."

"Feerick is dead?" said Arturo.

"That's the acrobat done it, a right jellied eel. But right now, I don't want either him or the military getting hold of Cook." Hargreaves reached the stairs, and took them at a gallop.

"Whatever agents employed Feerick and his two cohorts, they know the box is in the Yard, and it won't be here long. What they don't know is who will be moving it, which will be me," Hargreaves declared. "I've already sent word ahead by telegram. All the arrangements are made." She had done no such thing, but if it was enough to steam-roll over Arturo, it seemed like a good thing to say. Vanessa did have a plan in mind; she just hoped the box would still be there. She felt distinctly less dagger and profoundly more hammer.

"How are you going to move it?" Arturo said, but their destination soon put a plug in his mouth. Vanessa slipped through the dungeons of the Yard like a sylph, headed not for the covered short carriage but for M.A.D. headquarters.

"Drat," she cursed as soon as she stepped through. It was a milling sea of people eager to see the Yard's shining metal knights. Not only were there Yard engineers following Cid and crew's instructions in the automata repairs, there were higher-ups, including the Commissioner, milling around congratulating everyone. Where had those engineers been for four months? She cursed the Yard's avarice for good publicity. On the bright side, there were too many press and personnel here now for anyone to pay her any mind.

The shop was further crowded by the presence of both Priser and Driver, slung up with chains in the middle like trophies. Hargreaves caught scattered announcements by Commissioner Clarkson, informing everyone they were going to repurpose the illicit automata for M.A.D.'s use.

Taking advantage of the hubbub, Hargreaves and Arturo wove through the parked lorries, homing in on the sugarplum fairy floating at the periphery. Cezette Louissaint had put on some long overalls to hide her shins, and stuffed her hair under a cap to approximate a mechanic's young apprentice. But her features were still finely sculpted and distinctive. Hargreaves would have to give her a lesson in disguise later. If there was a later....

"Where is Alphonse?" Hargreaves asked Cezette, taking care to keep some machinery between herself and the crowd. This would be the third time the big automata had aided her in this investigation. She was beginning to think of Alphonse as a guardian angel.

"In the parts room to the left. Clarkson and his cronies still think the box is an engine. Not an alchemist's bone in their bodies," the little French girl said with no small amount of satisfaction.

"Is Alphonse ready to go?"

"As ready as he'll ever be. I filled him up with coal and water, *et un petit* amount of blue," Cezette answered. She peered at the inspector through a pair of baffled riding glasses, likely part of the disguise. It also made her big eyes even more waifish and forlorn. Perhaps she knew what was about to come.

Vanessa held the girl close, trying to communicate her deep gratitude. It did not seem fair to abandon this girl she had scooped out of the innards of Mordemere's abomination. When a new head of M.A.D. was appointed, she doubted Cezette would be considered an asset. Hargreaves hated what she was about to do, but Cid and Jean would have to take care of the girl.

"You'll need a diversion," Arturo said. She felt him touching her bottom, and slapped him roundly.

"Oh," she said when he resurfaced with one of the potato mashers and a red flower on his face. "That seems a bit extreme. These are the good guys."

"I'm just going to destroy Priser. The automata's armor should contain the explosion," Arturo said, still wincing and rubbing his face. "You should be my assistant sometimes. I need a strong right hook with me when I go detecting."

Vanessa Hargreaves nodded, then, wincing, said, "I definitely owe you a favor for this, Adler."

"I like it when you call me Arturo," he said, smiling. "You only say Adler when you're angry."

Leaving the two by the lorry, Hargreaves snuck past them and through a lowered shutter on the left side of the room. She ducked to avoid the sharp edge. Inside, she found herself in an isolated room much like Firearms Division's evidence locker. Instead of weapons, the racks were full of machine parts: boiler piping, long wrenches, and oiled copper artifices sharing space with more common parts like nuts, bolts, and gaffer tape. In the very back, half-veiled by a tarpaulin, sat Alphonse, his boilers slowly popping and simmering with fresh embers.

Knowing she didn't have much time, Hargreaves ripped the tarpaulin off and began to climb the automata. When she got to the cockpit, she observed a harness of steel cable had been looped over Alphonse's back, supporting the matte black of Sergeant Cook's box. She shuddered, imagining the pox-ridden body inside.

A simmer of voices coming from beyond the shutter told her Arturo had made his move. There were curious voices, reassuring ones too, people thinking he was just another engineer. Seconds later, a snap-bang shook the cavern. Screams sounded. The shutter stopped most of the noise, whipping about like a living thing, but the air shook with the force of the explosion. Wasting no time, she put Alphonse into rolling mode and dropped an anvil on his accelerator.

With a shearing, screaming tear of metal, the big automata smashed through the shutter and into a thick curtain of smoke, similar to the one that had killed Driver's pilot. Dimly she beheld a pile of yellow parts on the floor, but not the platinum flare of Arturo nor the dim blue of Cezette. Arturo had tossed a bomb inside of one of the thieves' automata, containing the explosion.

Sparing no second glance, she accelerated Alphonse round the shop and up through the ramp on the other side, coughing and spitting as she went.

"Thank you," she whispered, unsure of anyone's fate in that basement, least of all her own.

INTERLUDE I
UNDER THE VERDUROUS SARGASSO SEA

In the cities on the shores of the Atlantic Ocean, a parasite was taking hold.

Like all parasites, this one camouflaged itself against the surrounding foliage. It took the colors of its prey, breeding, spreading. But nowhere was it more prevalent than with the market barge *Verdurous,* which made a slow circuit of the Sargasso Sea every three years. Winding gyres took in the currents from the north and the south, those whirling eddies that pulled in the flotsam of trade and stranded seafarers in the age before airship travel. Now those abandoned waters were home to another sort of flotsam: the human kind.

The parasite stalked the sun-bleached market tents and crawled through the dark passages belowdecks, taking root in the dim alleys between eateries, sleeping quarters, and workshops. Hunched piles of shivering rags were the evidence of its passage, and stilled, sprawled bodies in the blackest bilges were its strange fruit.

But such things were still unknown to the intrepid Inspector Vanessa Hargreaves, who had taken up with the airship *Schwartzhaus* out of London, bound for New York. She had purposefully found her old friend and captain, Zampano Ivanov, who would hide her if they were stopped by the Royal Navy. Alphonse and the dreaded Cook box were stowed safely below decks, but Hargreaves had bit her lip until the crane lifted away and a tight tarpaulin was drawn over her mechanical friend. She didn't feel safe until the bloated, heavily armored airship drifted away from the Murkwood moorage towers and lurched across the Thames, headed over Reading, Bath, and the Bristol Channel to find the open sky of the Atlantic beyond.

Only when they had got that far did Hargreaves bother to inquire on their itinerary, which Zampano revealed to be a little circuitous. They were avoiding heavily trafficked channels, which suited Hargreaves just fine. But they were also making a few trade stops, which was a little out of the way. Still, the air outside the pea soup of London was crisp, and she had her own small cabin to retire to and plenty of good Russian poets to read in Zampano's library, which had been the first thing he had refurbished when he purchased the *Schwartzhaus* from a German trader. The strong tea aboard was sweetened with beet sugar, a welcome novelty. It was enough to hold her until the *Schwartzhaus* stopped to trade on the *Verdurous'* northerly loop, before heading the rest of the way to New York.

As she stepped off of Zampano's airship and onto the plate steel of the *Verdurous'* market deck, she breathed deeply an ocean air layered with ship's oil, fried food, and subtly rotting vegetable matter from all the detritus floating in the Sargasso. Zampano raised an eyebrow and Vera, Zampano's right hand, visibly held her nose. Hargreaves took in the experience. The bouquet was simply nonexistent high on the decks of an airship, and it was a useful thing to a detective inspector. For instance, she could tell the social strata at a whiff: profitable traders at the top, with their perfume of gardenias and musk. A middle layer of hucksters, vagabonds, and jacks of all trades with their richly spiced potpourri of lies and dirty deeds. There was a relatively small amount of old piss hidden under everything, which meant the place was booming with business—or they simply made the vagrants walk the plank.

Zampano had docked amongst a veritable storm of airships, their balloons and pressed gas hulls rubbing against each other in a profusion of colorful clouds. Though Hargreaves was anxious to be on her way and keep the Cook box far from prying eyes, she also knew there was little chance of someone finding them on a mobile market barge like the *Verdurous*. Zampano had put it like this: "When I held pirates and murderers in Siberia, they speak of ports like this, like the *Straight Hook*. Is place to go when you don't care for the Tsar to catch you at play, *da?*"

Through this colorful banter, Hargreaves gathered moving ports were popular with pirates for their dislike of authority and multitude of services. Security through transience; if your place of dirty dealing was moving, it was harder to hit. The barge had once been a ship-shipping ship, one of the few steam-powered hulks that were capable of hauling seafarers within its capacious innards, or salvaging entire airships when they were downed at sea. A thousand feet across and five thousand feet long, the *Verdurous* had been designed as a horseshoe, with the bow and stern of the barge open to allow easier salvage, and sealed bows on the arms of the horseshoe. Each arm held a deep stack of decks, well-tunneled with passages to allow crews access to various levels of the ship being hauled. Steaming lifts carried cargo from one level to another. At both sides of the stern, huge gears rose from the depths of the barge, pistoning sets of cams up and down like great oil wells. They drove the paddle wheels that moved the ship from below.

When the *Verdurous* was decommissioned, its captain had gone rogue, citing unpaid wages and horrible dental benefits. He had taken the barge out to the tempestuous gyre of the Sargasso Sea, where the fickle aeon storms made for treacherous sailing. As if that weren't enough, when the Sargasso was calm the aeon fog was known to make sailors go mad. Men saw horrible apparitions. Somehow, the crew of the *Verdurous* were able to circumvent those effects, and it was legend itself as to how. Over the years they had raised the loading keel to become their market deck, and built dozens of bridges, envelopes, and towers, until the *Verdurous* was the Atlantic icon it was today.

Hargreaves expected a grubby collection of rogues, scalawags, and oily underhanded scoundrels. Instead, the *Verdurous* turned out to be bright and colorful, and reminded her of Brighton Beach. She peered towards the distant edge of the barge, but she couldn't see where the deck ended and the ocean began. There was only a profusion of tents, an ocean of fabrics, bright stripes and spots under huge wooden billboards. Most of the boards moved, ratcheting back and forth distractingly and laced with the bulbs of arclights that would surely be a sea of stars in the night. The air smelt like sea salt, with a prevailing musk of grilled clams, fried fish, ginger beer, and potted shrimp. There were other smells too, but those were unfamiliar, a collection of whimsies from every shore in the world. She winced, as the criers' and barkers' voices reached her ears.

"Vigils! Colossus Vigors and Vigils, only a dollar apiece! Impress the missus! Stay awake longer; be more productive!"

"Hot off the press! *Columbia—Peerless Amongst Her Rivals!* Learn how America became the greatest nation on God's green earth!"

"If it took a second shot, you're not buying Hamish Arms! Good guys trust Hamish for fast, smooth action. Money-back guarantee!"

It was difficult to walk, actually, with the bear-like Zampano at her back and the tight press of criers on every side. She nearly fell over into a stall full of spices, cones of yellow turmeric, rich brown cinnamon, and blood-red mace. The proprietor opened his mouth and Hargreaves cringed, expecting rebuke. Instead, she got a smooth, practiced catalogue of the spices she had nearly gone face-first into.

"What is it you Brits say; sod off, wanker," said Zampano, waving an enormous hand into the proprietor's face. "Is not good to get close. Is like zoo, or prison, *da*? The tigers will take an arm if you let them."

"Hang the tigers," said Hargreaves. She reached behind her, coming up with a very small arm clutching a purse; Hargreaves' petty cash. An urchin had nearly pickpocketed her whilst she was dangling over the bloody cardamom. "It's the mice you have to watch for."

Hargreaves tucked the purse into her bosom, smacked the child's buttocks, and shouldered her harness a little tighter under her duster. As she turned back to Zampano, there came a rustle in the crowd somewhere behind her. Hargreaves looked back at Zampano's ship docked between the roast chicken stall and the saltwater taffy, where a small crowd began to gather. Impossibly, a swirl of even brighter color appeared between all the variously attractive tents. A ribbon of cloth soared high overhead, followed by a sizzle of bells that cut through the crowd with its promise of jingling hips.

"Ah. That would be Vera Jasper. Is good show, we go, da?" said Ivanov gruffly. In addition to running a crane, fixing steamcraft, and being a champion at chess, Vera had mentioned offhandedly she could also belly dance. The small dusky girl hadn't agreed to show them, citing the tightness of the *Schwartzhaus'* decks, but when the *Verdurous* was proposed as a trade stop, Vera had wanted to "make a little extra coin at the bazaar." Apparently the way to gain so many skills was to take every opportunity that presented itself—Hargreaves knew the feeling.

Zampano seemed embarrassed, even though his affection for Vera was plain to see. Vera had not paid Ivanov for passage; she was exchanging services, and the captain had not wanted the crew to think those services were untoward.

"Go on then," said Hargreaves. "Go watch Vera dance." Ivanov blushed beet-red, every part of his pale Russian skin lighting up.

"It is nothing! I simply wish to... that is, I am only curious... you will be fine on your own?"

"Yes, yes, Ivanov. I doubt my pursuers will have followed us this far. Now go," said Hargreaves, laughing. "Besides, I have something I want to look into."

As Zampano made a massive wake in the crowd, Hargreaves let out a deep breath. She was torn. On the one hand, she enjoyed the jovial banter with her old friend. Zampano had been invaluable during their fight with Mordemere, giving the *Huckleberry* her valuable hideaway just before Moscow and tracking the Russian airship traffic. On the other hand, Zampano stood out like an ugly couch. No, what Hargreaves needed to do, she needed to do with a set jaw and a stealthy step. There were characters of ill repute here on this barge, and she needed to grill them about the American automata used to rob a moving train in the French countryside.

Besides, Zampano was concerned about nothing. Inside her carpet bag was a veritable armory taken from Scotland Yard, along with baubles shed won off the ship's poker table. Trinkets, really, ranging from a stash of smoking weed to a Remington rifle with a custom scope. Hargreaves had brought the cream of the crop. She grinned and stepped into one of the many open stairways into the bowels of the market barge. As she arrived onto the landing, somebody rushed past her and disappeared into the passages. A second person appeared, sallow and ill-shaven, clearly chasing the first. Beads of sweat covered his face, and a hungry look darkened his eyes. Hargreaves cared not why the second person looked so furtive, but when he shoved past her quite rudely, she turned her shoulder and put out her foot. When the sallow man hit the floor with a clang, she was already around the corner.

Oh, yes, Vanessa Hargreaves could take care of herself.

***

Far below the top deck of the *Verdurous*, nefarious doings were happening that Vanessa Hargreaves knew nothing about.

For instance, the person who ran past Hargreaves and disappeared into the passages was one Hopping Hare Lewis. She ran past Hargreaves without making note of the inspector and plunged headlong into the passages, taking the first turns she could see in the unfamiliar deck. Clothing stores, clockworks markets, and shamanic healers appeared and disappeared in a flash as she dashed past them in her strong calfskin riding boots. Her linen skirt swished around them, brushing walls on both sides as she squeezed through a gap in pile of old junk leaned against the ships' cargo containers.

For good measure, she dashed down another stair and found herself in a red light district, where the men whistled and catcalled to her. She was about to take umbrage when she realized her plain bodice had come loose, and she looked a lot like the women working the halls of this level. Good; at least she would blend in. The lanterns on this level glowered at her in various shades of crimson, arc and gas lights crammed into the ribs of the bulkheads. Colorful silks veiled the passages, making it hard to tell where she was going. Lewis slowed to a stop, trying to calm her heart by leaning against the outside of a quiet enclosure that had been cobbled together with tenting and tin sheets.

As she caught her breath by the curtained windows, she started, but it was only her reflection in the glossy dark glass. Lewis had never thought of herself as pretty, but she did not kid herself either. Her strong jaw and aquiline nose might be considered masculine, but Lewis knew her rich brown skin and strong equestrian's hips were very desirable. But as the blood returned painfully to her brain, she didn't think pleasure was her pursuer's intent. He had been too drawn, his look too hungry, and she didn't think the *Verdurous* was bad enough to simply put up with that sort of behavior. Trade didn't happen unless there was some stability, Lewis knew it from traveling all over the West... and farther.

Somebody had scrawled "Explicit Endeavors Undertaken Economically" over the door of the enclosure. It was a saloon of some kind, or a pub, and a burlesque dancer stared at her curiously from within. Lewis smiled awkwardly and moved on at a brisk trot. Her frontier frock, obvious heritage, and the eagle feather behind her ear made her stand out further from the mostly European and African passengers. She didn't want to leave an impression, in case her attacker knew the barge better than she did.

Was it her imagination, or did a few people here have the same hungry look? The attack had come from shadows just like these. With every step it seemed like the alleys just grew deeper, the looks transformed to low plotting. Eyes glinted in the dark, their whites nearly pushed out by their dilated pupils. Strange how all of them had the same look—like they were staring out at a far-off land.

Lewis was going into bad territory, she could tell. The red lanterns were gone, and the materials in the walls were closer to junked than upcycled. Desperately, she turned corner after corner, trying to find her way out, but only when she tripped over a pile of rags that turned out to be a gaunt, reeking woman, did she realize she had only run deeper into the slums of this barge. But by then, it was too late. The darkness was full of glinting black eyes, and they surrounded her now.

"Stay back!" said Lewis, and she took up the nearest thing that might serve as a weapon: a broken, rusty pipe. Despite her youth running free with the horses of her tribe, she was winded. There was not enough room to exercise on the airships, and she had been traveling for a long time. She had told her father she wanted to see the world, and she had, but that had meant taking up the white man's airships and the white man's clothes. There were white men here, certainly, but there were freemen too with their inky skin, though it was hard to tell them apart. Everybody was covered in a layer of grime, and they clutched strange devices in their hands. Each of them had one, and as they crept around her, surrounding her, the contraptions made odd clicking noises. Like the ticking of a clock....

The first of them took her unawares, and Lewis felt the blow drive across her back—the attacker had been too short to get her head. She cried out, painfully, but felt her lungs catch. She had run too hard, and now she was winded by a second blow, somebody punching her in the dark. The third hit hamstrung her, and it felt like there was something sharp in the attacker's hand. Not a knife—a point, like a needle. Hopping Hare Lewis fell, and as she did she felt the needle drive deep into her shoulder. Then another, in her thigh, and another at her arm, in the crook of her elbow. People held her down now, and she tried to flail, but only felt the needles tearing at her inside her arms. Lewis took a deep, ragged breath, and with the fullness of a voice that could carry over the prairie, gave a piercing scream that was swallowed up by the bodies piling over her.

***

"This woman... I have seen her before," said Hargreaves as she watched what passed for the barge's constables inspect the crime scene. She sipped her tea, trying to remember where she had seen the striking face lying on the floor of the open-air cargo lift. The woman's skirt billowed around her, stained a bright red, and her rich brown skin was gray. It looked like she had bled to death.

Hargreaves had spoken with a few shady characters in the decks of the market barge. As it turned out, the *Verdurous* dwellers were more concerned about African and European trade than American. When she asked about American steamcraft, the local fauna simply laughed. There was no steamcraft trading from America, they said.

"They might as well have installed a blockade," said one man, a merchant on one of the machine shop levels. "We hear a lot of propaganda but nobody buys American anymore. Plenty of Ubique universal parts for tractors or cranes, just nothing for new automata.

Their steel was really hot on the market just after the war, though."

There didn't seem much point in investigation until she reached America, so Hargreaves had decided to rejoin Vera and Zampano, only for this unpleasantness to begin unfolding beneath her. The inspector sat at a high platform jutting out from what had once been the barge's auxiliary bridges. One of the levels had been claimed by a respectable teashop that made actual cucumber sandwiches. The observation deck had been made into an outdoor garden full of small bonsai. It would have been pleasant if it hadn't overlooked the cargo lift, which had been called to service from the depths of the barge in the middle of high tea and inspired several workmen to cry out as the body rose to the top deck.

"I have it," said Vanessa Hargreaves. "This woman rushed past me as I ventured into the barge's lower levels."

"Are you sure?" said Vera Jasper, who seemed very comfortable at the tea table, out of sight of the view below.

"Yes. For an inspector of Scotland Yard, recalling small details is an occupational boon. Clearly she did not run fast enough...."

"If you are wondering why she is dead," said Zampano as his enormous sausage fingers closed around a delicate cup, "it is no mystery. She was—" And he said a word that sounded like 'napitok.'

"Pardon?"

"Drank. Drained. Ah, in the English... like the *vampir*, *da*?" continued Zampano. "But there are no monsters in the dark. It is called 'Chasing the Rabbit.' But I have never seen so many marks. Usually the rabbit lives."

"I know of this," said Vera Jasper. "You mean to say the murderer was Going to Wonderland."

Vanessa Hargreaves looked back and forth at the pair, until Zampano relented and explained.

"It is an opiate. A drug," said Zampano. "I am not sure how it works. But you can always tell who is a user. They have a far-off look in their eyes, like they are living another life elsewhere."

"If they are coming after you, they will have it in hand. The drug comes in an ampoule," said Vera. "Like a doorknob. Round, with a glass portion, and a needle that pops out of the thin end."

"You should not know such things," said Zampano. He seemed paternal, and for an instant Vera seemed annoyed. She was older than she looked, thought Hargreaves.

"The user needs to get a small amount of blood," said Vera, hardly pausing. "It is mixed with the drug inside the ampoule. Then it can be injected into a vein or slowly infused through a gravitator."

"You are very knowledgeable," said Hargreaves, with a touch of the unsavory.

"I have worked with Wonderland fiends before," said Vera, and fell silent.

"Not just anybody's blood will do," said Zampano. He seemed eager to ease Vera's discomfort. "Some say travelers are best. That is why you will hardly find it in Whitechapel or Dover, where trade is mostly local, or London, where travelers are under your queen's protection. But it is common in Istanbul or Glasgow, under the large airship routes, and a cancer in wandering waystations like the *Verdurous*. Perhaps the chasers are seeing what the travelers see. That is the rumor, *da?*"

"Da, Ivanov," said Hargreaves. She thought about the places she had already been, and the sights she had seen. Experiences that she had paid for in pain, and the people she had connected with because she had chosen to go with them, parley with them, fight with them. Suddenly the opiate called Wonderland disgusted her.

"You are thinking of something, Inspector," said Zampano Ivanov. "You want to catch the person who did this horrible thing. Do not. You will only draw attention, and you will draw your pursuers to us."

"Investigations are best done unseen anyway," said Hargreaves. Judging from the various strongmen and gunmen putting the woman's body into a covered stretcher with stoic indifference, the *Verdurous* did not have a single detective to serve them. Blast it, even if she had become a traitor to Queen and Country, she was still a police inspector. Overhead, a dull gray cloud cover slowly blanketed the barge with a light mist. Perfect—overcast, wet, and dreary. Just like home.

"I'll see you later," said Hargreaves, darting up from her seat. She dashed past the grasping hand of the airship captain, which, full of scones, was quite ineffective at detaining her.

"We leave at fourteen hundred hours!" called Zampano, a little helplessly. Vera sipped at her tea.

***

"Our Steam Age," said the man with the hookah pipe, as the smooth, Hellenic shapes of a dancer's legs pirouetted in the vicinity of his turbaned head, "is fairly decadent, isn't it?"

They were seated in front of a stage at one of the many pleasure palaces in the warrens of the *Verdurous*. Hargreaves had stuck out her chest a little at a couple of bars and storefronts, and within minutes gathered that someone who wanted to chase the rabbit need only find a Kamala Singh in the Dusky Forest club. It was reputable, a bare-ankle spot and not a bare-everything spot, which everybody seemed eager to mention to a beautiful woman like Hargreaves. Was it for her protection or some moral standard? Either way the mildly accented quips felt insulting. Hargreaves did not fear dark alleys or the rogues. Rogues usually had reason to fear her.

She certainly had no moral guff with exotic dancers either—they were not so far removed from her own undercover work. She was happy to see a young girl working in a place where inappropriate behavior made large bouncers appear, their muscles rippling under fashionable silk vests.

A redheaded lass was working the dance floor and a lowly moor was enjoying the show. For a moment Hargreaves wanted to protest that the moor ought to be serving, not the girl. The imperial racism instilled in Vanessa Hargreaves by decades of propaganda reared its ugly head, daring to suggest the superiority of whites over the whole world. It was inevitable, the product of being trained by Tory sergeants and a private English education. "This is an English world. We allow you to live in it." It was a phrase slowly being picked to pieces by progressivism, but its ghosts were persistent.

Hargreaves shrugged it off. Besides, she wanted Singh for something legitimately bad: dealing in this so-called Wonderland, and indirectly causing a woman to die. He was her lead, but therein lay a problem. She had no doubt the strong bouncer men would come if anyone threatened Kamala Singh.

It was likely her golden beauty that made Kamala Singh wave her to the seat beside his. Singh himself was a man of indeterminate age, anywhere from thirty to fifty, but he behaved like a lecherous old man. His gray beard came to a point, and gold rings shimmered at one eyebrow—a sure sign of an untouchable fixture of the *Verdurous*, that Singh could wear valuables where anybody might yank them from his face.

"Decadence comes in many forms," said Hargreaves, as the tinkling of bells masked their conversation. "Mr. Singh... I hear if one wanted to purchase a little decadence, you are the man to come to."

"I carry many things," said Singh. "At a very reasonable rate."

"Even if one were, ah, to want to chase the rabbit?"

"Then decadence carries a high price," said Singh, without pausing. He was suddenly all business, accustomed to this. His voice felt oily, disgusting. "Eighty for a trip down the rabbit hole. Rental is free on the first trip. Four hundred English sterling for your own gear."

Hargreaves held down her gorge and shifted in her seat. She had taken the precaution of taking off her duster and undoing two buttons on her blouse. She'd worn a lighter corset beneath, in beige, just high enough to hold her front up. Her .22 Tranter was stowed in her boot, and her belt became a loose hoop accenting the swell of her hips. Between the just-visible edge of her underthings and the tightly fitted sable tights, she wanted Singh not to know which part of her to look at. It would blind him to the deceit in her eyes.

"And pray, what manner of coin does a man of means and measure like yourself prefer?" Hargreaves said quietly. She uncrossed and re crossed her legs, letting the heels drift in the air. The dancer jingled furiously, giving her a dirty look—*not on my turf, you tart.*

"Ahhh," said Singh. His mustaches quivered. "Perhaps we can conduct business in private? The proprietor lets me use his office." There was only one lush at the nearby bar, and he was so deep in a bottle he had come out the other side.

"Do let's," said Hargreaves. Singh took the lead, then Hargreaves got up with leisurely slowness, letting the tension build. Singh gestured towards a curtain of beads. Hargreaves walked through into a dim hallway, more of an alley created by the meeting of two shipping containers. The top was open to the bulkhead of the *Verdurous*. The ends were blocked off with planks, and crudely soundproofed with layers of rugs. She could feel the eyes crawling up and down her backside as she crossed to the other container door.

Singh didn't wait until she got there before he slammed her to the wall. His hands crept over her blouse like questing fish. One shot inside, popping a button. Hargreaves felt the difference in their height as a tickle of mustaches at her back and a bump just over her knee. She heard a fumble of fabrics. Disgusting.

"You're a tall drink of water... you'll have to kneel so I can choke you properly," said Singh. His hand shot to her throat, but couldn't get much purchase. "Not to worry; you'll only pass out at the end... because you like it so much."

"Haven't you been doing this trade awhile?" said Hargreaves, letting the hands roam. She put her arms on the shipping container wall and slid them up, out of the way, as if Singh's passions were hard to curtail. She shifted slightly to her side. "You always pass... to the left!"

In a flash, Hargreaves stuck out her rear and twisted back, letting her arm lead her body. Momentarily, she saw Singh's expression; eyes wide, open in pleasure as her curves brushed across his hips. Then her elbow found his larynx, not a hard blow but a stunning one, and he gasped, voiceless. Seizing the moment and his arm, Hargreaves flipped him around and put her heel to his knee, forcing Singh to the ground. Singh squeaked, harshly, in pain. The whole thing had taken two seconds, but it left Hargreaves standing over a panting, wheezing man completely in private.

"Now then," said Hargreaves as she pivoted away from Singh's flailing arm. She hiked the other one up, and elicited a painful squeal. She tried not to enjoy it too much—this man had been instrumental in the death of a woman not an hour ago. He had sold something that made people attack travelers. Hargreaves gave a heroic effort to resist, but in the end she gave in to temptation and yanked Singh's arm to a point just before it would break. Singh eventually gave up and planted his free hand on the painted steel of the floor, where she fought the urge to stomp on it. Submission was good, and she needed to reward that.

"Mr. Singh, you'll get your voice back in a moment," said Hargreaves. "I need for you not to scream when you do, or else I shall break your arm, and I daresay it will be a low point in your day. I don't have much fondness for hurting people, but then again you seem to be a man of little conscience and this disgusting hand was just stroking my fine French underthings. So if I were you, I would answer my questions succinctly, briefly, and with all speed."

Singh didn't say anything, so Hargreaves did take the chance to stomp her heel on his hand.

"Yes!" croaked Singh. "Yes, bloody bitch, I'll talk! Mother promise, Father promish, Brahma bloody promish!"

Hargreaves had no idea what that meant, but he was slurring and had dropped the subtle Indian accent for aitches. She took that to mean her coercion was working.

"Oh, I see you're a cockney underneath? What happened to the exotic opiate dealer nonsense?"

"Just ask your blasted questions!" hissed Singh.

"I want to know about the girl," said Hargreaves.

"What girl?"

"The girl who got killed today."

"I had nothing to do with it," said Singh. Hargreaves gave him the old Yard enticement, pushing his arm down lower until it creaked.

"Arghhh—Okay! Okay!" said Singh. "You know the dancer inside? She's the donor for Wonderland. You buy from me and you buy from her. She gives a great high, lady, I ought to tell you—Arghh!"

"So it's different from person to person," said Hargreaves.

"Right, would you let go of me arm?" cried Singh. He seemed much younger, probably in his twenties. The mustaches were peeling off his face with the sweat dripping from his chin. "Meredith's been everywhere; she's my go-to. The stuff takes you wherever she's been, yea? I tell all my customers, you go off-script, it's your own head you're mucking about."

"Off-script," repeated Hargreaves. "You mean…."

"Yea. Anybody who's been through the veil."

The Gray Veil. The gateway to the Lands Beyond. Hargreaves knew it was real, but sometimes the place sounded like a myth. Rumor had it there were many worlds behind the veil, gardens of Earthly delight and palaces of perennial pain. This was something she didn't know enough about. Did Wonderland truly take someone beyond the veil without moving from an opium den couch? If so she was beginning to understand why some would go to such lengths as bleeding a girl dry.

"You're saying you have people here who buy from you and attack travelers?" said Hargreaves. "Who? Tell me!"

"Bad for business and such, yea? It would do me good if whoever did such a thing should disappear," said Singh. He was beginning to recover, just a bit, becoming accustomed to his new lot in life. "Hey, from here your legs look jolly good. *Arghh*, all right, all right, come off it!"

"You think I am here to sell you a contract?" said Hargreaves.

"You're no rozzer," said Singh. "You're a killer. Stone cold."

Hargreaves was now honestly taken aback, and she nearly released Singh. She had killed, before, but only once in the line of duty and to save an innocent. She certainly didn't believe herself to be a simple cutthroat.

"I am not going to kill anyone," said Hargreaves. "But someone needs to find out what happened to the girl and—"

"We know what happened to the girl," said Singh, almost pleadingly. His arm looked like a wet brown noodle. "A few of my misguided clients took to her with too much gusto. Does it matter who? The barge captain will hire cutlasses to clear out the bottom levels, regardless of whether those vagrants did it. I don't give a damn about them. Vagrants don't buy much."

"I just want to know why," said Hargreaves, a little guarded. Her bottom was tensing in a way that meant she didn't really have a leg to stand on. She felt a little foolish, even though she was the one in control.

"Why?" said Singh, nearly in tears. "Why do we do anything? For pleasure, of course. For need."

That made her let the man go. Singh immediately toppled to the floor, scrabbling and holding his arm. He lay there for a moment, obviously in pain, staring hatefully at Hargreaves. He reached into his robes, but the inspector caught the motion and stepped on his elbow before Singh could finish pulling out a weapon. Hargreaves reached into her boot for her .22, leveling it at Singh.

"Slowly. Use the bad hand," said Hargreaves.

When Singh's shivering hand emerged, it held a small glass globe with filigree all over it, and a small screw on one side. Hargreaves plucked it from his fingers, like a date, and nearly pricked the man with the needle that shot out of the screw. When she turned the screw, the needle came in and out. The globe looked empty, but a second later she realized there was a thick, bluish liquid inside. If she squinted, she could make out the words spelled out by the filigree: "Drink Me."

"For the pain," said Singh, but he had already seen her disquiet, so Hargreaves let him go. He disappeared through a hidden panel in the passageway, back to the warrens of the market barge. No use for a dealer when the violence was happening *en masse*. How many other dealers worked in the shadows? Singh was probably only the most visible one. Who would she bring Singh to anyway?

Hargreaves made her exit brazenly, through the front, with her hair still mussed by her encounter. Let the guards and the dancer think what they would. She had what she wanted. Or did she? Now Vanessa Hargreaves wasn't sure, and as she left she felt the cold weight of the knob of Wonderland in her hand. It felt bigger than it was, like a doorknob, and not something the size of a cherry.

Hargreaves hadn't thought this through, really. She had come looking for a case to solve, to feel like the inspector she used to be. In a well-ordered society, the inspectors would track down whodunit and arrest them. The culprit would be locked up, preferably forever, and society would be a little safer for it. Cut and dried... but here on the *Verdurous*, she doubted the barge would have space or spare victuals to house a murderer indefinitely. Half the visitors had probably killed out of survival. She knew Zampano had. She knew the crew of the pirate airship *Huckleberry* had, and Hargreaves would trust Clemens and the crew with her life. But sadly, she wasn't there now, and she missed her ragtag pirate crew dearly.

If anybody stepped out of line on the *Verdurous,* they would probably be thrown off the top deck and into the calm depths of the Sargasso. The gyre of aeon water was already full of the refuse of a dozen countries, pulled into the whorl by unseen currents. What were a few more pieces of rubbish?

Now Hargreaves knew what to look for, she saw the dancer Meredith had henna markings all down one arm, suggestions of peacocks and flowers up and down the smooth brown limb. When she moved just the right way, she saw the little circle of henna that marked the crook of her elbow. It was the perfect place to stick a needle. Hargreaves shuddered, but she flicked the girl a coin that Meredith caught appreciatively. Hargreaves held a finger to her mouth in a gesture of silence before she stepped the rest of the way out of the Dusky Forest. As she did, she thought she heard Meredith's voice drift to her ears with the jingle of bells.

"It's no use going back to yesterday. You were a different person then."

But when she looked back, there was no sign that the dancer had ever opened her lips.

For unfathomable reasons, Hargreaves clung to Singh's hateful bauble as she made her way deeper into the decks. Vagrants were not hard to find. They lived in the bad places, the slums and the bilges of the world. Hargreaves couldn't hope to bring anybody to justice, let alone the number that all those needle pinpricks suggested. It put her in mind of Caesar.

So what was she doing heading deeper into the dark decks of the *Verdurous'* bowels? There was something she was looking for, she knew that much, but if asked Vanessa Hargreaves had no ready answer. This wasn't something that could be fixed with a cuppa or a good pint; this was something she wanted to sort out before she left with the *Schwartzhaus* and Zampano.

Past the nightlife portions of the barge, the *Verdurous* was laid out like any other settlement. Vast levels devoted to manufactories and workshops, sprinkled clusters of dwellings like anthills dug out of the firmament. A glittering set of rooms housed a meat-cutting floor, with enormous, slick black Atlantic tuna strung up like hanged men. There was a whole deck full of steam, with people covered head-to-toe in boiler suits and goggles in it. It smelled strongly of sea salt. Hargreaves checked the plaque on a lift—the engine room and water distillery, where the Sargasso was drawn to fuel the great boilers and condensed for drinking water. Next to it, a room for sorting all the junk in the water kept many people busy sorting and tossing. There were bicycles, and old medicine bottles, and wind-up tin toys, amongst stranger things.

She first noticed the people following her when she passed a pawn shop on the lower levels. Hargreaves was not unused to the behavior exhibited by the glinting pairs of eyes in the darkness: lurking, scrabbling, and oozing through the passages, trying not to let her catch them staring. It was a lot like the fans of her picture house series back in London Town. Sometimes they would pop out of blind alleys and ask for Hargreaves' autograph. Here, Hargreaves feared the eyes would not come out unless *en masse*, and with other glinting things to hand.

Instead of clutching her duster close to her body and exhibiting the body language of a victim, Hargreaves walked straight and with purpose, keeping her coat open and her back straighter than a railroad tie. She kept her blouse titillating and her hand on her Tranter, ready at a moment to pull it out on some foolish soul who jumped the gun.

As she went along she counted her blessings. Thank you, Scotland Yard, for all those acting lessons. Hargreaves tried to embody herself with the qualities of somebody who frequented the slums of a mobile pirate market every day. A loan shark, perhaps, or a high-stakes bookie. She imagined stepping into a space between packing crates and haranguing the women there for protection money. It was a game she played that allowed her not to feel afraid in a terrifying place. It let her keep her head as she turned a corner and looked for the nearest way back up into the light. But every blessing had a razor-sharp lining. She was counting on her undercover acting because she had left her carpetbag full of weapons with Ivanov. Stupid, stupid.

Instead of upwards, Hargreaves rounded a bulkhead to find a narrow channel into the very bottom of the barge. The hull sloped down and away into a fogged gloom, where the bilge sloshed. If she turned around she would be showing herself as a lost lamb, ripe for the pickings. So the inspector forged ahead.

At the bottom of the barge, there was a slick of incredibly salty water sloshing slowly back and forth. It was strong enough to leave the air brackish and harsh. The rafters were hung here and there with sickly green lights, almost as if Hargreaves had accidentally discovered a sort of rotting underworld below the confectioner's glitz of the market deck. Her watertight boots were a centimeter deep in the wash, and it left a green film on her raised heel.

Hargreaves stood on a landing that branched off into eight or so platform walkways, assembled out of the sort of flotsam that was dredged out of the Sargasso Sea. Tin and tarpaulin, cable and old meat cans. After taking a moment, Hargreaves stepped confidently out onto one, even though she had no idea where it went. Immediately she could feel it rock and give under her, but she kept going. The feeling of multiple eyes following her from every nook and cranny had only grown stronger, though they were hidden in the dark.

The walkway led through the enormous bilge that ran under the entire barge. Out over the sloshing bilge, it was possible to see a little farther, but nothing there pleased the eye. This had once been where the *Verdurous* took on water as it hauled heavy ships back and forth across the world. Their displacement left high water marks on the deck above and on the bulkheads. Half the supports were rusted, replaced with thick beams and columns that looked like they were harvested from wrecks. Vanessa Hargreaves felt like she was in an enclosed marsh dotted with the carcasses of trees, and not inside a vessel.

Hargreaves started running when she counted six people following her. She could see the walkways jostling, their submerged surfaces sending out wakes across the bilge. Worst of all there were two ahead of her, at the end of the walkway. So at one of the thick supports she took a sudden turn and sprinted off down a thin plank, her boots raising a spray of drops.

As she predicted, Hargreaves managed to score a few seconds lead on her pursuers before the bilge began to roil with the ripples of many footsteps. Basic *Art of War* tosh, really; she who acts first shall win the day. Her training was comforting as it came rushing to mind. Afternoons in sun-dappled window seats spent reading old war texts from the Orient, accounts by Arthur Wellesley of Waterloo, and practical urban tactics from the likes of Dupin.

But really, there was no salve for the terror of running from fiends in the dark. And they were fiends, of that she had no doubt. When the bilge rocked particularly strongly, she caught a glimpse of them through the fog: emaciated bodies wreathed by filthy rags, moving like shades across the drowned planks. One of them had a knife, a happy dirk that shone in the green light.

Hargreaves put her training to good use as she ran past a thick pile of forged iron supports, a strong remnant of the original ship's bones. The edifice of riveted beams climbed high to the ceiling, and it had also acquired a sort of islet of detritus piled high over the water line. Everything was filthy and green, but it was dry and the surface firm to step on.

Even from high ground, she was only able to shoot the one with the dirk as he came barreling past. Not an instant passed after that before another man was atop her back. Where the blazes had he come from?

She threw her weight just so, tipping the assailant forward in a practiced judo throw. The pile of reeking cloth, skin, and bone tumbled through the legs of yet another fiend. The two of them tumbled over the edge of the islet, and there were the burbling screams of the tangled drowned.

Then they were all over her, and Hargreaves felt the stab of a needle drive into her collarbone, missing her vein by an inch. Something hard battered her cheek and she felt surprise in addition to pain. It had been a naked fist, nothing but skin and fragile bones that crackled as they struck her relatively wholesome, well-kept body. But the fiend's broken hand did not stop him, and Hargreaves twisted as best as she could to avoid the swarm of kicks and stabs raining on her. The dastards were filling up the knobs in their hands. She could see the globes filling with droplets of her life, turning the glass to onyx in the green light.

Through the pinpricks of pain and her focused attempts to sock a few of them with fisticuffs, Hargreaves found herself strangely empathetic. How many of these needles did it take to kill the woman on the deck? It was a million paper cuts, death from a slow bloodletting. And if there weren't only three of them, Hargreaves might have stood no chance of surviving.

She felt three of the needles sink in before she pulled the .22 Tranter out and shot another one of them through the skull. In the dim light, the blood from the back of his head looked black, like an unnatural liquid that filled the air with a rank coppery smell. Was it a woman? Or a man? The body that fell to the water was too thin and ragged to tell.

The others shrank back, torn between a desire to live and a desire to live *somewhere else*. Hargreaves could read it in eyes now visible through layers of rags; a glazed, distant look, as if they were only visiting on this plane and their real lives were going on elsewhere. Just stepped out for a tea break; be back in two shakes of a lamb's tail. The glass knobs in their hands were the doors to another world. Hargreaves looked around at the destitution of the bilge, and now she could see the slum hovels that had sprung up at every dry spot available. There were at least a dozen pairs of eyes in the distance, shades who were not quite so brave as the ones right before her. Maybe the life these fiends were headed back to was one more worth living than this one.

Instead of shooting another one, Hargreaves drew the Bowie knife she had the good sense of keeping on her person and instead of in the carpet bag. Her clothes were already spotted with dark drops, so when she drew a shallow cut across her arm it wasn't anything inconvenient, merely painful. She was already too highly strung to feel it very much. Hargreaves let the drip go into a nearby vessel, a sort of trencher that might have once been a sink or a plaster fountain. It elicited a gasp from the denizens. The blood was fresh, the scent almost flowery compared to the sick fluids that ran in their own veins.

"There. There's your trough of blood," said Hargreaves. She

thought of Maple Cross as the drip slowly lined the bottom of the trough. "Though I warn you, what you find there may make you want to come back to this Tartarus. My life is... not for the faint of heart."

The nearby shades fell upon it with a fury as soon as Hargreaves stepped away. As she bound up her cut with a scrap of her blouse, they came from every corner of the bilge hold, flowing past her in a rippling wave. Ignoring her, they dove for the sacrifice of blood, pushing and jostling each other as they dipped the needles in the fluid. The first of them fell to the ground, the glass knobs pulsing at the crooks of their arms. Their faces were vacant, blissful, and then as the stuff took a dark turn they simply weren't.

Suddenly half the rabbit-chasers lay incoherently writhing on the floor, and others stared in horror at the empty globes they had just put inside their veins. Hargreaves wondered if they were seeing the pictures of Sergeant Cook's mangled, plague-ridden body. She wondered if they were experiencing the engine room of the *Nidhogg*, that terrible place with the mangled lives holding up a city in the sky. She wondered if they were seeing Maple Cross, but she couldn't be bothered to ask. She was too busy running.

It wasn't until Hargreaves was out of danger, back to the front of the Dusky Forest did she grow faint. When she looked down she noticed her forearm was drenched in red, but the arm felt distant, not quite a part of her. Had she cut too deep? The thought drifted through, looking for an alarm bell to ring.

Hargreaves clutched at the ramshackle tin of the club for support. When the arms came round to hold her she nearly shot the dancer called Meredith, who had come out to see what was climbing the walls.

"Come inside. You're scaring away the customers," said Meredith. She had a musical voice, the same voice Hargreaves heard leaving the club the first time.

"The dealer... Singh...."

"He's not here," said the dancer. "I am pretty sure you scared him away for a few weeks at least."

"Good...." said Hargreaves.

Meredith led Hargreaves into the club, and back into the alley where Singh had been subdued. They ducked into the second storage container, where there was a storage room for liquors and a simple curtain partitioning a performer's ready room. The dancer sat the inspector down on a dressing stool and put some water on to boil, with a kettle on a nearby coal brazier. When the water was boiling, the dancer put long strips of linen in and wrung them out to clean Hargreaves' cuts.

"Why are you helping me?" said Hargreaves as the dancer bound the longest cut tight with a cooling liniment.

"You were kind," said Meredith. The blood was stark against the dancer's pale skin and henna marks. "Though the coin you gave to me will not replace Singh's custom."

"Apologies," said Hargreaves.

"Do not concern yourself over it," said Meredith. "I have wanted to see someone plant Singh one for a long time."

"Then why give him your life's blood?" said Hargreaves. "Why, when his poison merely makes all those wretches living under your feet?"

"You have seen the bilges," said Meredith. Hargreaves slowly recounted what happened after she left the Dusky Forest. At the end of it, Meredith sighed. "It is not supposed to be like this."

"How else can it be?" Hargreaves was beginning to recover a little strength. Meredith set a cup of broth before her that had been in a small pot, and the stuff helped a little more. There was a silence as Hargreaves hesitated before sipping at the broth gingerly.

"You gave them blood yourself," said Meredith. "Why did you do it?"

Hargreaves had no ready answer for that. Without concern for modesty, Meredith began to strip off her dancer's bells and veils. The body beneath was lithe, but well-cared-for, and she had fine proportions. The clothes she drew from a small locker and on over herself were tough, but showed as much skin as her costume. This woman needed no training to appear confident and not to be mucked with.

"I suppose," said Hargreaves slowly. "I suppose those people must feel as if they are traveling on airships when they take the... the substance. This Wonderland."

"Headlong down a rabbit hole. Yes," said Meredith. "That's how they describe it for me."

"You are used to caring for wounds. You have done this many times... but you have not tried it?"

"I'm not going to be here for long. I go from place to place; I don't need an escape," said Meredith. She sounded almost merry, but it could be because Hargreaves was fading in and out. The voice drifted out at times. "I've lived the things those rabbit-chasers want to experience. I can always sell a little blood to get by. Some of them get a little too addicted to it, okay. Not my problem. Someone else will come along with another knob for them soon enough. But you've lived it too. And it's not enough."

"I wanted to share it. Spread the misery around," admitted Hargreaves. "This stuff has aeon in it... I can feel it. And aeons react to emotions. I think it helped me to see other people reacting to what I've gone through... it makes me feel stronger." She had to stop to take a breath and steady the spinning room. How much blood had she lost? "I have an objective measure of how well I've handled things. I know I'm not crazy."

"It doesn't always show them what you've seen," said Meredith. "That's just an easy way of telling someone about it. Sometimes... sometimes it shows them things too true to see. Too blinding."

"You have tried it," said Hargreaves now.

"Just the once. And maybe you should too," finished the redheaded girl. She was finished dressing now, but she pulled her skirt up to reveal a spot on her thigh marked out with henna whorls. "Give me the one you have. The knob you got from Singh."

Hargreaves, in a state of almost dull compliance, took the Wonderland knob out of her pocket and handed it to the other beautiful woman. Instead of taking it, Meredith clasped Hargreaves' hand to her skin, pressing the needle tip into her thigh. The woman's flesh was warm and ruddy, pulsing gently with the same sort of good feeling that animated her dance. Meredith's head leaned back, and the expression was a blend of lip-biting pleasure and a frown of pain.

Then the dancer was gone, her dull colored hairpiece and

traveler's roll surely hiding her amongst the crowd. If she bade Hargreaves any words of farewell Hargreaves did not remember. She was busy staring at the glass knob in her hand. With a drop of Meredith's blood in it, in the light of the coals and the warm yellow lamps, the Wonderland inside the globe was the rich crimson of a ripe pomegranate.

***

Hargreaves got back to the *Schwartzhaus* with plenty of time to spare, but her dirty, bloodied clothes caused Captain Ivanov to go into quite a state. He immediately called for all the ramps to be withdrawn and the ship to lift off, and with a good number of harsh Russian expletives. Hargreaves expected huge Cyrillic letters to float burning across the docks as the huge captain pointed and hollered to his men. His concern was frankly quite endearing.

It took a few minutes for Zampano to settle Hargreaves back in her cabin, but by then preparations were almost ready for the ship to leave. Twilight purpled the sky, and it was a bad time to leave, really, for any airship. Storm clouds dusted the horizon, and the sea was ominously dark. Hargreaves uttered some apology for interrupting Zampano's trade, to assurances that Russians were incredibly efficient and also cared little what others thought of them. Zampano stood in the doorway, a little awkwardly for a moment, before adding a final word.

"I am sorry you did not get your man," said Zampano Ivanov. "You must be very disappointed."

"Just gutted," said Hargreaves. "Can't be helped. Good night, Ivanov. I am very tired."

"Good night, Inspector," said Zampano. "I will order my men not to disturb you."

"Thank you."

Hargreaves closed the door of her cabin and slumped into the stiff cot. The porthole outside was blurry, streaked with a sudden rain. Hargreaves watched the *Verdurous* slowly get pulled into the storm brewing beneath its keel. She felt glad to be on her way, and glad she was aboard an airship high above that dreadful bilge. The cot felt good and hard, a lot like the ones in the Yard barracks.

Five minutes later the *Schwartzhaus'* deck tipped as it veered north, away from the *Verdurous* and on towards New York. An empty glass globe rolled across the floor of Vanessa Hargreaves' cabin and came to rest against her clothing locker, which was well-stowed and placed under the washstand, which faced the cot. For that brief respite before the storm, her face rested against the thin pillow. Hargreaves was dead to the world, and she could not be happier for it.

Later, when she went to the mess for dinner and Zampano's men came in to batten down the porthole, one of them remarked on the odd stain against the side of the inspector's washstand. Under bandages stained brown by old blood, the metal of the sink was the crimson of pomegranates.

5

NEW YORK,
THE LUMINESCENT CABARET

Stan Burgess' Luminescent Cabaret sat like a glittering jewel in the coal-heap of the Bowery. Vanessa Hargreaves hadn't arrived in New York more than three days earlier, but she felt such places drew her like a moth to the flame.

The neighborhood in New York smacked of Whitechapel for its cheap sleaze, doorjamb dealers, and closeted charlatans. It held a touch of Camden Town, full of starving artisans, craftsmen, and academics. Only, instead of knackered booths under thin tarpaulins and the lapping sounds of canals under vandalized steel bridges, Hargreaves found the shady characters of the Bowery nestled on sunken stoops of tenement buildings, amidst a constant clatter underfoot of what the Yanks called a 'subway.' Unlike the proper underground, and the Camden Town she found a ready analogue for, everything had the peripheral glint of gang markings she did not know, boundaries she never felt in the crossing. The dirigible flutter of passing peacekeepers overhead offered no reassurance.

Flickering lamps made the nightclub feel almost like an oasis. Hargreaves' long, ebony limousine steamed up to it, giving her a good long look. A red-robed sidewalk offered a long queue of finely dressed bourgeoisie waiting to see Lumina Von Venus, in the act that had gripped the ton in a fever of burlesque passion. The building had been a theater, hosting everything from magic acts to the first picture-screens, but the rain-streaked marquee held only four words now, three rows high. Stan Burgess had spared no expense.

Hargreaves marveled at the irony of Gotham. Two blocks away from the mink-swathed ladies in their pearl collars and the bearded top-hats reeking with ambergris were men who sold coca, who would sooner shank a customer than give him his change. Coca was illegal in the free state of New York, and in thirty other states, a fact that stymied some Brits from even crossing the pond—they were used to their afternoon pickup. A bit of digestive, or a headache remedy.

"Burgess is expecting me," she said to the large wall of meat blocking the underwhelming front door. The bouncer molested her with his eyes before letting her pass through the ornamental glass and thick curtains. Inside the spacious lobby, Hargreaves made out the posters of the acts on display: Rocket Rand in the *Object of Self*, Cammie Alberta in *The Whimsical Mr. Murderer*, Jeanne Pauletta in the *Sweetish Sickness* and other toffish, avant-garde titles. Everything was tastefully lit, with crystal lamps on walls patterned with orange blossoms, above varnished oak wainscoting.

A magnificent candle chandelier dripped slowly into its own wax pans high above. It cast its light through a hexagonal contraption of tinted glass onto vague Judaica moldings, likely a remnant of Gotham's construction magnates. In quite post-modern fashion, and in keeping with the avant-garde subject material, there were carved marble teats at the bar, dispensing drinks. A grand stair framed the lobby along the walls, and directly between them was the oil poster for the main attraction: Lumina Von Venus, in *Beethoven's Fifth*. She stood clad in bowler hat and white coattails, the very picture of demure seduction. Vanessa shifted uncomfortably. Where had she seen those bedroom eyes before?

Shaking the déjà vu from her eyes, Hargreaves focused herself. She hadn't allowed the boys at the precinct to dress her up in this slinky Parisian couture to impress the society Gothamites, and she certainly wasn't about to stand still and let the bored diplomats and dirigible barons get an eyeful. *It hasn't even got a bustle!* Vanessa found herself thinking, swishing her hands in the general area. Her backside had never been more exposed, even though she was accustomed to trousers.

Sure enough, when the coat-check girl took her knee-length pea coat, more than a few coiffed heads turned to get a gander. A Rhône-red, ankle-length burst of ruffles bloomed above her sweetheart bust, barely veiled by a modish gear-print shawl and matching, elbow-length sable gloves. Her hairpiece was a raven feather, a flower of iridescent ebony round a glittering garnet that showered a cluster of lesser gems in a netted veil over her left eye. Her hair was a torrent of gold over her bare back.

Paying no attention to the gaping apes, Vanessa Hargreaves marched her coal-black Flamme Regale heels across the lush carpeting, up the flight of stairs with the gilded railing, and onto the mezzanine, refusing all offers of assistance. The prim, slender fingers trailed the railing on the right and her small rose-red pocketbook in the left, with her lipstick, powder, and .22 Tranter inside. The suits attempting to show her to the box were visibly stunned by her appearance, a fact Hargreaves counted on; she wanted maximum impact for Burgess, a man famed for his feminine indulgences.

"Mister Burgess will be along when the show begins," the usher told her once her derriere touched down pertly on the plush box seating. The luxuriously Old Victorian box with the bucket of French champagne startled her for its existence in the middle of New York. When the uniformed servant left the box, she relaxed her tense shoulders and allowed herself the luxury of reminiscing.

***

Vanessa Hargreaves had taken the one route she could, to Mirkwood-on-Thames, where the sky was dark with the clouds of airships amidst the forest mooring towers. She took Alphonse with her, and Sergeant Cook's plague-ridden corpse on his back. Ships of all makes and often dubious origins berthed at the Mirkwood, everything from bloated German touring zeppelins to the exotic dragons of Chinese junks, the wings of their sails veined with battens. She was quite sure one would take her to America. Or if not, another pirate port where she could find a way there.

Since the train thieves had been caught and her act of sabotage had not yet danced the telegraph tightrope, it was a simple matter to barter passage with an old friend; Zampano Ivanov, Russian airship commander turned Siberian prison warden, turned dirigible merchantman after the Mordemere cataclysm. The old Russian bear had a perverted sense for profit, and with the Ottomans ready to swarm, he had jumped on the bandwagon.

"Hargreaves! Velcome!" Ivanov had embraced Hargreaves with a grizzly hug in front of dozens of dock passers-by. "Have to claim territory, see, or other aeronauts will not leave you alone. Some have not seen a woman in months. Da?"

"Da, Ivanov, da," Hargreaves laughed with the gruff, bearded giant. Ivanov had shed his furs in the relatively warm English climate, but his beard and bursting businessman's vest set him apart as much as a wolf's pelt would have.

"Who is she, Ivanov?" came a voice from Ivanov's shadow. Out stepped a short, limber woman in a rainbow-embroidered kaftan. Tumbling gypsy locks reminded Vanessa of Rosa's, only these were so black they gleamed blue, framing a creamy brown face. Ribbons and intricate braided cloth decorated her from veiled head to bare feet. Cinching at the ankles finished a billowing garment not quite trousers, yet not quite a skirt.

"Inspe… Vanessa Hargreaves. Knew her through yellow dog," Ivanov said.

"She won't be in our way?" the woman named Vera said suspiciously, glancing at the golden hair, the too-pale skin of the London native. Her eyes were like flat onyx.

"Not in the least, Miss Vera," Hargreaves said, extending the olive branch.

"Miss Vera?" the little lady repeated, as if the polite title had been inconceivable a moment ago. She cannot be more than twenty-four, Hargreaves thought at the time, and a petite one at that. Just looking at the girl's hips made her trousers feel tight. Something bothered her about Vera, but she could not place a finger on it.

"Vera Jasper. Make with the friendly," Ivanov had said, and

shooed the two of them aboard. As it happened, Zampano Ivanov's new ship, a refurbished German zeppelin called the *Schwartzhaus*, was bound for New York. She carried a load of British tea, Egyptian linens, and a caravan of Romani, which explained the origin of Vera.

New York was a fine destination, a hub of all things illicit. Hargreaves would simultaneously be in exile and able to investigate Feerick's employer. Hopefully it would be enough. She had had plenty of time to think about the sticky treacle that was now her life. Hargreaves knew she was acting against orders, but she also thought Her Majesty would not operate without some secret agenda. It was entirely possible Her Majesty had engineered all of this, like some benevolent watchmaker. Or some diabolical chess master....

The Ottomans were just reaching northward into German and Russian papers. Small skirmishes in the guise of pirate raids, the incidents were nonetheless harbingers of a concerted effort to push for strategic bases in a future war. Sergeant Cook's resting place was now a wild card, leverage the Queen could use all the better for its being in one of her agents' hands.

In the meantime, Hargreaves was forced to while away the time spent traveling the Atlantic. True to form, Ivanov employed a crew of skilled men, mainly his former Siberians. Ivanov employed Vera Jasper in the roles of navigator, ship's hand, cook, and all manner of odd jobs.

The journey proved smooth, and the springtime Atlantic was as peaceful and calm as could be asked for. The only memorable incident came near the beginning of the journey, towards twilight one evening when Hargreaves stood at the railing watching Mamadu shoot gulls. He wielded a bowgun in the same way Hargreaves would a rifle, seeking and taking down the circling birds so they fell onto the deck. Later, they would be roasted in the ship's galley, their fishy flavor not unpalatable to Hargreaves' tastes.

Tracking one of these animals, Hargreaves suddenly marked a speck of twinkling, sapphire light in the distance, too low to be the North Star and in the wrong direction. It threw out mirages of strange lights, in all different colors, and though Hargreaves pretty much knew what it was, she felt the need to voice her doubts. Somehow, having someone else confirm it made the illusion solidify in her mind.

"What is that?" she asked aloud, and was startled when the high voice of Vera Jasper answered.

"That is the Laputian Leviathan shimmering in the sky," Vera said directly to Hargreaves' right, causing her to whirl about. "They call it the Sargasso Siren here in the Atlantic, or the Sargasso Scourge, for the illusions it casts on all the ships passing under it."

"A scourge?" Hargreaves had said, thinking of her own role in creating it. It must have drifted there, borne on the aeons' own unfathomable currents.

"Yes. It is only a misnomer. It is more curiosity than scourge, and only those willfully entering the Sargasso Seas succumb to it. The effect is pleasant to watch."

Hargreaves thought she could see the shadow of the Union Jack in the shimmering light, and perhaps a softer shadow of a pirate zeppelin somewhere underneath. She shook the image out of her head.

The crossing took about three weeks, with a good tailwind, and during that time Hargreaves formulated a plan of sorts. It was only because of the intricate cubbyholes that riddled the *Schwartzhaus* that Hargreaves was able to hide both the Cook box and Alphonse. Once the customs agents in their crisp uniforms were gone, Hargreaves could look out the portholes and see a magnificent Ferris Wheel spinning gently over a cloud of fanciful lights and fairy floss. Bright Tesla arclights worked into words proclaimed it the 'Wonder Wheel.'

Alphonse and Sergeant Cook safely hidden, she took the King's County train line to the British embassy in Manhattan. With the right confidence, name-dropping, and a reliance on the nature of Britons to be Britons, she managed to convince the diplomats she was British Intelligence, and they put her in contact with inspectors in the New York Police Department. Oddly, the inspectors were only called 'detectives,' which put Hargreaves unpleasantly in mind of Arturo C. Adler.

Detectives Sancho Ortega and Frank Ferrera were the equivalent of Firearms Division back at the old Metropolitan. The two men were carbon copies of each other in brown and ruddy, with identical mustaches and identical paunches. They spent a lot of time with their eyes on her bodice and legs, an involuntary response she nevertheless took vanity in, and advantage of. Certainly they were sharp. No amount of cleavage would make them miss the .22 in her shoulder holster.

Apparently, the partners were something of a black sheep in the department. Most of the officer material had names like Kelly or Connor, not Ortega or Ferrera. Hargreaves took all of two minutes to figure out she had been foisted onto the pair as some kind of routine abuse, and that they were taking it in stride. As gratitude, she was a little more liberal with her assets than normal, but it didn't take much strutting and posing to make them show her to one of the major suppliers of illicit automata parts in the country. Black as the night were Stanley Burgess' dealings, and Hargreaves felt a distinctly feminine intuition she would find some kind of clue about the Cook box at his Luminescent Cabaret.

"That is Burgess' own pleasure palace," Ortega said from the anonymity of a squad cruiser. Desertion of the native fauna and the quieted Tesla lighting made the daytime facade of the Cabaret seem camouflaged against the Bowery, a sleeping predator with its colors hidden in a restless crouch. The three lawmen studied the place from the cab of a powerful Feint Stallion. Occasionally a grubby-looking informant would come by and deliver a report on the neighborhood. Once, a beat uniform appeared and immediately turned away. He'd recognized the car, and didn't respect the pair even as much as the vagrant had.

"Most of the automata deals are far out of our jurisdiction. Our colleagues on the take turn a blind eye to the petty crimes," Ferrera said after one such exchange. He didn't so much as drop a 'fuggedaboutit' but there was a definite confidence exuding from him, a New York bravado Hargreaves found pleasantly soothing. Were he a stone lighter, and some years younger, her honor would have been sorely tested.

"He's snug as a bug with the top brass," Ferrera said. "Burgess is well connected with Ubic, the American arm of Ubique. Obviously they can't declare the alliance openly, but it's rumored old Stan owns a good portion of the company through dummy firms. Ubique also sponsors the precinct's basketball team."

"Everything from our uniforms to our calculating engines comes from Ubique." Detective Ortega, by contrast, was soft-spoken and gentlemanly in his Latin accent, somehow disarming in how welcoming he appeared. The inspector knew the type, a friendly uncle who spoke cleanly and smoked much.

Rumors of the criminal strata in the Big Apple were notorious. From derelict to dirigible, scoundrels of all kinds found a home amidst the sunburst ziggurats of the city. Chinese triad syndicates made backroom deals with Italian mafia. Bowery minnows hawked cheap whores to Wall Street sharks. In a city as fraught with corruption and deceit as New York, Hargreaves guessed the strange duo had been put together, and assigned to her, a foreigner, because they were not good old boys. They likely were as honest as could be found.

"But?" she prompted.

"But we all know what the deals are. Prostitution, obviously, though he lets the girls run the cabaret. Very high-class, too, so I hear," Ortega said.

"Smokescreen. Pimp is a pimp," Ferrera disagreed.

"Illicit substances," Ortega continued as if his partner weren't there. "Coca and poppy, mainly. Most of the muscle on the lower east side is his. He also supplies smaller gangs with equipment, sometimes...."

"Automata weapons," Hargreaves answered, glimpsing the black portion of her plan. "Right, boys. How do you think I can get in to see him?"

The two detectives looked her over, and Hargreaves blushed; she regularly used her charms for her own gain, but this was something different.

Ferrera summed up succinctly. "Dame like you? Don't have to ask."

***

Sitting in the lush box, sipping the notorious gunrunner's champagne, Hargreaves felt somehow transformed. All her hard edges served her no use here. She needed to be soft and alluring. A barmaid, a farmhand, and a waitress, she had gone undercover in positions where she could be a fly on the wall. She had not often posed as a society peacock, in the spotlight at all times. It made her feel conspicuous, objectified, and bulbous. Even more disconcerting, the character she played was supposed to be looking for a fat tomcat to restore a depleted family fortune. A cougar, on the hunt.

Hargreaves had told Burgess as much in her letter, banking on both his taste for women and the potential connections 'Duchess Valerie Von Hammerson' would have in the Old World. Von Hammerson would be the legitimate society face of Burgess in Europe, something he should be very interested in possessing.

Her box looked on a luxurious theater arrangement, but staring at a blank curtain wore on her patience. Keeping a duchess waiting was criminal even for Stan Burgess. Just as she was contemplating leaving in a huff and rescheduling the interview, the lamplight was extinguished in the theater.

"Blimey." Vanessa couldn't help herself, as gentle riffs rolled through the room, a uniquely American torrent of notes she recognized as 'soft jazz.'

Somewhere in the orchestra pit was a glinting organic shape of the instrument, someone playing along to a device a lot like a calliope. On stage, an equally lulling play of light began to grow into a soft, steady glow Hargreaves recognized as filtered, softened arc lighting. Fancy stuff for a cabaret.

A woman stalked, feline, on stage through darkness like jungle. Hargreaves saw the slim lines and small breasts and recognized her as Cammie Alberta from the poster outside. Cammie got up from all fours, and the lighting playing across her nude form showed up like leopard spots.

Flash! A hissing beast, caged.

Flash! Needle-sharp points of fingernails.

Flash! Wildly tossing hair, the feral look of seduction a tonic, an ounce-shot of life zipping through the crowd, infectious, insatiable.

Hargreaves felt the chill of the performer's art shoot up her spine, the beauty and attraction, even though she had seldom felt arousal for her own gender before. Undercover work was in essence performance art. Hargreaves watched, rapt, as another woman came into the cage and the two writhed around each other. Legs opened and closed, always tastefully hiding each woman's gentler parts, matched with a genius orchestra that rose and fell in mounting notes.

Finally, Cammie closed her lipstick-red mouth on the other woman's neck, whose ample curves rose and fell in a pantomime of a small death. A cheery, humorous number replaced Cammie onstage, with women in ragged wigs and severely damaged dresses.

In between the first and second acts, Hargreaves felt rather than saw the lean form of a man seat himself beside her in the box. Rapt as she was by the country music and the beautiful women on stage, she nevertheless noted the severe cut of chin, and the scent of a man in the prime of life. She pretended not to notice, keeping her eyes on the show. It was a wonderful show, and the illusion was not difficult to create.

The third act was a shadow show, created in different colors by Tesla lights. The women stripped off gloves, garters, and other intimates, showcasing their wonderful physiques in silhouette more beautifully than full frontal nudity ever could. Xylophone and harp tickled the air as each woman teased the straps off perfect landscapes of Venus. In Vanessa's periphery, the man who seated himself held his head in his palm. Though he did not look at her, Vanessa was self-conscious of her own curves.

There was an intermission after the third act, and once the lamplights flickered into life, the man beside Hargreaves spoke at last.

"Many people think cabaret is a sleazy strip show or some kind of bordello advertisement." It was a refined voice, a metropolitan voice, a Manhattan voice. It also sounded rehearsed, a set piece that ended in suggestively veiled bedroom props. Hargreaves knew when she was being seduced—or at least a fairly good attempt at it.

"Do they?" she asked, allowing Burgess his theater. Burgess seemed to adore drama. Though he was educated, and his clothes were extravagant luxury, the very tip of his finger tapped always a rhythm against the arm of his chair. It betrayed a certain boredom, impatience. With a minimal gesture he called a man to replace the empty champagne. With another, an usher below dragged a man bodily out of the theater, a man whom Hargreaves recalled had been catcalling in a very ludicrous manner.

"People regard burlesque as theater, as art, as drama. Is it prostitution? By its very nature art is prostitution; an artist sells more than his body for his art. A painter blinds himself studying landscape, a musician deafens his ears searching for soul-lifting melody, and a dancer opens herself to the sound of applause."

Hargreaves imagined he had repeated this little speech many times. Burgess took deep succor with the rarefied air of the enclosed box, as if the smell of champagne, decades of cigars, and the bouquet of Chesterfield sofas could sustain the minuscule bellows of his lungs.

"Cabaret is like any other art. It is sacrifice."

Despite the theatrical quality, Hargreaves listened with rapt attention. They fell not in her ears but across her back, chilling her to the bone. This was a very dangerous man, Vanessa suddenly realized, with all the certainty of experience and Yard training. The rich words and silken delivery were nothing but a mask. He was more dangerous than the thief or murderer. Vanessa Hargreaves had been trained to handle those. This man was a monster of a different color.

A psychopath.

"Mr. Burgess," Vanessa began, but was shushed by a rapid finger movement, as if Stan Burgess' name was anathema to his own ears.

"The show begins," he merely said, and Vanessa turned to behold the stage once again.

This time, the darkness of the cabaret filled with light, a vital, sudden flare amplified by the sudden hiss of sodium bulbs. It was as white as could be, betraying only the slightest tinge of yellow from igniting wire. The stage was flooded with brilliance, all ghosts fled.

An impossibly high heel stepped through the curtain. One piano note, high C. Tiptoe, tip. The leg retracted. Then again; piano, here, there, dance, tease. Fishnets seemed to rear high like an animal scenting, then scoot back into its lair behind the curtains. Slowly, timed perfectly to a rising introduction of piano, the animal probed with a pure white sleeve, pawing at the air with black tips. The cufflinks were orange blossoms.

Bit by bit, the leg was joined by the right hand, and the left, cradling a cane. Black bowler hats seemed to dance a jig quite otherworldly. Almost imperceptibly, the lights dimmed, and the audience reared forward to catch the curves emerging from the curtain. There! A coat-tail! A bit of firm derriere!

The music stopped.

Four notes dropped like a bomb, one-two-three-four all at once, the last invading and taking over the fifth space, the true space, *Beethoven's* space. Lovely music, such as Hargreaves could not deny. The music of the ages! White coattails joined firm, lush flesh. With the bomb of the fifth, the dancer struck out! A kick! A flourish! A pirouette!

Suddenly the curtains rose and the stage was full of golden dancers, topless, with exaggerated eyelashes and wide collars toothed like gears, all queer, all otherworldly, all seductive. Like pips in an orange, Hargreaves thought, as the procession drew into a circle round the ecstatic mocha-skinned woman moaning her passion into the bowler hat.

Vanessa Hargreaves sucked back her gasp into a gulp of shock.

Her old friend the airship pirate Rosa Marija stood poised up there, starkly naked under her tailcoat.

6

OF BURGLARIES AND BURLESQUE

"Quite a… beautiful… show," Hargreaves complimented the cabaret later, in Stan Burgess' private parlor.

"From a woman as radiant as the sun, that is quite the compliment. Cabaret is, if nothing else, a celebration of women by women," Burgess answered, tipping his top hat. He chilled her. The words were like a carefully chosen blinds, his eyes flat and dull like a shark's. His audience crowded around, held not so much by the content but by the feel of the words, the velvety way he said them. A psychopath is the ultimate extrovert.

"Splendid as always!"

"Bravo!"

"And will we see such a performance at market? Hmm?"

"Leave Old Burgy alone. But honestly, what do you think of steel? Bullish or bearish?"

Bourgeoisie crowded in on either elbow with brandies and cigars, a dense miasma of ownership. Hargreaves was choking on it. In the far corner, Rosa Marija stood with the other dancers, swathed in handsome silk robes. Her eyelashes and makeup were outlandish in the close quarters. No doubt she remained as naked as the day she was born underneath. Hargreaves resolved to work her way over as soon as the fluttering admirers scattered.

The parlor was cozy, set in a converted, smaller theater of the old picture-house, and lit with comforting gas instead of Tesla. Velvet cordons roped off the entry to an old projection booth. In the smoky glow, Hargreaves observed Burgess wore a silk-backed pinstripe vest and pointed Italian shoes. She nearly missed her cue to blush.

"Thank you," she said to Burgess, just in time to be introduced. She looked nervously into his eyes, but it seemed as if she had said the right thing in present company.

"What business might a countess have with a common cabaret owner like Stan Burgess?" Burgess said. The self-deprecation came out perfectly natural, not a hint of ego. It was frightening.

"The duchess," she intoned as dulcetly as possible, "Valerie Von Hammerson simply desires a social evening with New York's finest members of gentry… but of course you have no royal family." The accent was easy to fabricate, but the dance was unfamiliar. She had come prepared to sort the gentry by station, occupation, and personal wealth, but nobody seemed to have any of those Victorian preoccupations. This was a pleasure palace, not the social rat race of parlors in London. What mattered seemed to be instant gratifications: momentary trysts, trips to the powder room. Fruit from the tree. A group of gentlemen snorted from a mirrored plate. Others were gambling in a back room, occasionally raising an uproar.

"You've certainly made swift work of New York society," a chalk-faced woman with doe-brown eyes quipped at Hargreaves. She looked in her twenties, but clung to a graybeard glittering with gold and full in the paunch. "The Luminescent Cabaret is a Gotham tradition, and Burgie here doesn't invite just anyone into his parlor."

"Like a great big spider he is, choosing all the juiciest morsels for himself," said another woman of similar ilk. Blond locks framed an ermine collar, dusted with flakes of ash despite her long cigarette holder.

"Now, now, Burgess," interrupted her distinguished-looking husband, a man with a multi-lens monocle permanently jammed into his head. An air pirate affectation? Perhaps the colonials hadn't forgotten they came from pirate stock. "You mustn't keep the rest of us guessing. How did you find the means to invite a duchess, when none of us were even aware royalty would be gracing our shores?"

"It was a spur-of-the-moment fancy. My dear Aunt Marilyn owns a manor outside of Boston, and Stan was good enough to offer me entertainment during my brief layover," Hargreaves lied through her teeth. Was the first name too much? To Burgess, she gave a knowing look, hoping she played the part of the sheltered nubile well enough. Thankfully, the sharp proprietor evidenced a detached affirmative.

"Is that Marilyn Ann Roth? Why I had heard she had no family..." whispered one guest. A chill dropped across Hargreaves' bared back.

"My Luminescent Cabaret has a distinct reputation for distinguished guests." Burgess now took over the conversation. It was difficult to read his face. There was a simmer of names, Princes of Far Arabia, Nipponese Captains of Industry, and Very Important Bankers. His skillful manipulation of the crowd hadn't escaped her, though.

Society banter grew wearisome, slowly grinding down Vanessa enough that she began disengaging herself from the crowd. It was an incredibly homogeneous one—everybody in dinner jackets, the women like herds of beribboned, sculpted cattle. On Ivanov's ship she'd seen women veiled for their gods, gentleman scholars, even one Icelandic hunter, a vast, muscled veteran who had found her fortune and was seeing the world. It made for a bubbling cauldron of company.

To her lasting relief, Rosa Marija saw fit to glide through the crowd and materialize next to the plate of smoked salmon. "Fancy seeing you here, gorgeous," Rosa Marija breathed in her ear. Hargreaves nearly jumped out of her slinky gown, blushing red enough to match it.

"Fancied seeing your fanny, Rosa Marija," she said in return, and a Cheshire grin spread like butter across the beautiful air pirate's face. Glitter and makeup masked her lush dark features, but Rosa Marija seemed to exude glamour. Likely she looked fabulous in just about everything. Or nothing.

"There was spirit gum over the good bits," Rosa Marija remarked, disguising their conversation by gesturing towards the various plates and drinks on the table. Between delicate tidbits, Rosa moved the conversation to a corner, pretending to entertain Hargreaves. Just a bored, wealthy duchess condescending herself to a thespian thrill. Hargreaves snacked daintily at the hors d'oeuvres, though she wished the guests weren't there so she could really get stuck in. Airships made Midwestern beef and Maine lobster available in Britain, but they were still dear and not happy regulars in a detective inspector's household.

Rosa Marija's hair was done up in a complicated nest of clips, but the glittering sumptuousness of a few stray locks flowed over her neckline like liquid caramel. Hargreaves felt the stares of the surrounding gentry at the two beautiful women conversing together, one blood and gold, the other mauve and mocha. She almost didn't catch Rosa's familiar brand of pirate guff: "Sort of like gaffer tape, only it doesn't hurt when you don't have hair there."

"Right; I get the gist." Hargreaves halted Rosa before she got too riled up. Her grin was exploding out of either side of her face. "What does Albion have to say about this?"

"He suggested it, actually, but I think his original plan was to come here in drag. It was supposed to be a one-time recon, but the loot has been hard to extract and the work is surprisingly satisfying. I'm sure you saw it."

"Oh, I saw everything, thank you." Hargreaves hid her face behind a bit of sliced flank steak on a party pick. "Your show is a smashing success."

"Of course! Who do you think I am, someone less gorgeous? Mustn't jabber; Cammie is right over there. Anyway, I bet we're both here for the same reason. This is a bad place to talk."

Rendezvous delayed for the time being, Hargreaves allowed Rosa Marija's coltish legs to stride away into a clot of pipe smoke and testosterone, her hands fluttering and fending away the drooling patrons. Amazing. How was it done?

When Hargreaves turned to spot Burgess, however, she found the host missing in action. Perhaps he had been diverted by a society dame. After another half-hour of verbal backgammon with the trophy wives and dirigible barons, Vanessa Hargreaves finally extracted herself from the mass of patrons. It seemed these New Yorkers were used to bandying about the town at all hours, but a real duchess would find a prudent excuse to end the evening at a decent time.

Ortega and Ferrera met her a few blocks away in their crotchety Feint.

"Inspector?" Ferrera inquired through their rolled-down windows. "Was Burgess as much of a cad as we thought?"

"On the surface? A perfect gentleman. Now if you can just turn your heads toward the street, I believe I shall shimmy out of this dress."

Hargreaves was as fed up with the tight gown as she was the night's unsuccessful raid. How does a lady hide a decently sized gun without even a bustle? While the sheepish detectives kept a polite distance, she shrugged on a more practical blouse over warm leggings and a thigh-high wool skirt. She sighed as her tortured feet found familiar places in her good boots. Her coat went over all, including a sturdy gun belt holding her new best friend, the Browning from her stash. Her Tranter lay safe in one boot.

"I shall endeavor to investigate the cabaret," Hargreaves informed the two detectives, who looked a bit overwhelmed by her gear, and her bare limbs rising and falling in the back seat.

"You will need help, *señorita*," Ortega offered, but the inspector shook her head.

"I do not wish to implicate the city," she said. Privately, she did not want an incident to turn up the fact she was not actually British Intelligence. Some things were just too complicated to explain, and for everything green and good, she did not want the Americans to get their hands on Cook. "It would be better for you to stay. They will have a hard time noticing one woman."

Even if the two detectives wanted to protest, she did not let them. Instead, she gave them a winning smile before running back to the Cabaret. The bouncers, remembering her scintillating entry, did not balk at letting her back in. She didn't even have to pretend she'd forgotten something; her coat just reminded them of the goodies underneath. Back at the party, she slipped quietly along the stairs, and then up into the cordoned-off projection door. As she expected, the door also let off onto a corridor so well-padded there could be no doubt of the place's less than savory reputation. She could almost feel the night market pulsing on the other side of the walls.

"Now, we will see about your records, Burgess. If you are every bit the scoundrel you are the gentleman, you ought to be keeping tabs on just about every automata criminal in the city," Hargreaves reassured herself. It wasn't a bad assessment. New York was the capital of the New World. Still, Hargreaves felt as if she was reaching too far. She had come because of a tiny machine part in the wreckage of a crime scene, and there was no guarantee an American had done the deed. She couldn't go back to Britain without something to show for it, but the automata nut was the only lead she had.

Inside, Rosa met her not far down the corridor. She had changed into a satin number with a sable coat, but her strappy stiletto heels still looked untouchably gorgeous. Hargreaves knew better. There was likely twice her stone in blades and sharps inside the sumptuous coat.

Rosa looked expectantly impatient, standing next to two glasses of Vanessa's favorite rotgut gin. Rosa's was already empty. "Really? I was so easy to read?" the inspector said, glumly downing the shot. Its fires chased the autumn chill from her spry form.

"We raided a rum runner's stash together in Barcelona. I'm used to how you look when you scope out a joint. Sort of screwing your face together, like you bit into a lemon. Don't worry; Burgess was more interested in your bust than your eyes," said Rosa Marija.

"I will monitor my tells more in the future," Hargreaves said through gritted teeth. "Say, what were you looking for?"

"Burgess doesn't simply deal in girls and automata," Rosa mentioned offhandedly. "Half these rooms are filled with clothes and jewels for dressing up his ladies. Likewise, half his cellar is filled with illicit parts, rare art nobody else can fence, and loot he can afford to keep until the pigs forget about it. Custom jobs are sort of his kink."

"And you've been pinching them left and right...." Hargreaves deduced.

"Bingo. Everything too hot to move eventually gets to Burgess. He's the only one on the eastern seaboard knowledgeable enough to take apart and file down the endless strings of serial numbers without blowing himself up. Guns, of course, but clockwork for gears, too."

Rosa's explanation did not sit properly with the inspector. For one thing, it seemed too difficult to steal and resell the items after Burgess put in the laundering. For another, long milking operations didn't seem like Clemens' style.

"Come now, what are you really after?" Hargreaves was tempted to say. Instead, she opted to keep quiet. This was American jurisdiction, after all, and besides, the inspector had developed a burlesque dancer's worth of flexibility in her morals during the last few months. Stealing from a crime kingpin was just dandy in her book.

"Not to sound suspicious, gorgeous, but why are you here? What business does the Queen of England have with Stanley Burgess?" Rosa asked now.

"None of yours," Hargreaves evaded. "But if you can show me to his records rooms, I can compensate you for the aid."

"I can compensate. Not 'the Crown,'" Rosa remarked. "I could call for a guard. They know who I am."

A moment passed between the two, and Hargreaves' lips tightened almost imperceptibly. Rosa's sardonic grin never faded.

"Come on, we're past all that," said Rosa. Without another word, she marched off along the corridor. Hargreaves breathed a sigh. It was good to have friends.

Hargreaves could only follow, admiring the complete discretion of the place. Behind the scenes, Burgess' pleasure palace bore none of the frippery and frosting of the burlesque. Each of the doors they passed looked as if they were storerooms, windowless and whitewashed, without even numbers adorning them. Still, there were hints of fragrances and small moans drifting out from behind the thin tenement doors. Hargreaves blushed, and hid it in her collar.

At the end of the corridor, another door led into a dark chamber. It took a moment for Hargreaves to realize they were high above the boxes of the main amphitheater, lights extinguished after its stars quit the stage. A catwalk led round the perimeter, strung with complex, bulky apparatus. Candles and chalk to produce the magic of burlesque.

Rosa led the way, round the catwalk towards a door set atop three steps. It was an awkward, cramped arrangement. The walls were tumbledown and rotting, leaking insulation here and there. When

Rosa opened the door, more steps led down again, this time to a makeshift walkway laid across some bare girders. Chip wrappers, damp boxes, and tobacco ends crammed every nook and cranny so badly it took Hargreaves a moment to realize they were traversing the beautiful avant-garde ceiling of the amphitheater. To think, the bourgeoisie of New York gathered each evening to sit under a metric ton of rubbish.

"Here. It used to be a projection booth, but now it's used as a storeroom for the arclight engineers. Some of the old picture-house reels are still there, but the rest has been converted into Burgess' records office. Nobody comes up here but Burgess, and then only rarely," Rosa all but whispered. She opened a second, thicker door, and stepped inside the booth. "We can talk normally here. The booth is insulated against sounds."

"You thoroughly scouted the place," Hargreaves remarked as soon as the door closed behind her. Inside, the booth wasn't large, maybe twice the length of a woman lying down and very narrow. It was, however, quite tall, featuring a ladder stretching up to a roof access trap. Wedged into a corner sat a small desk, cleaned off and ready for use.

Against the opposite wall crouched a privy with no door, and a large tangle of boxy machinery mostly obstructing their view of it. This was the old picture projector, with its prominent cannon-like lens and intricate film spools. Much of the bulk belonged to a rectangular metal box in the body of the apparatus, which revealed a triple shelf of bound black notebooks when opened.

"There you are," Rosa indicated in a humored kind of way. "Now can I be party to the workings inside that gold-plated noggin of yours, Hargreaves?"

Something in her voice suggested to the inspector their meeting so fortuitously was not due to chance. Perhaps fate had thrown in Vanessa Hargreaves' lot together with this pirate crew again—or perhaps, they were the very villains Hargreaves was after. Was Clemens capable of pilfering a weapon of such horrifying implications? No, absolutely not, Hargreaves decided. But if he had no knowledge of the contents of the box... Yes, it was a definite possibility. He might only think it was very valuable. In such a case, the pirates had every reason to waylay or exploit her.

Hargreaves kept her thoughts to herself. She reached for the closest notebook and began to leaf through. Rosa Marija hadn't steered her wrong; these were in fact Burgess' gunrunning records, written in neat blocky print and meticulously organized. Debits were marked in red, and everything was written in guarded shorthand, but it was all there. She recognized prominent airship pirates, international gang leaders, and high officials in Ubique. A veritable stock exchange of death.

Rosa Marija looked around with a seemingly bored expression on her face, but Hargreaves knew her better than she let on. The inspector looked for the fingers: still and even like a stalking spider. Rosa was paying rapt attention. Hargreaves was supposed to find something here, was she?

The notebook she held was the most recent. From the date headings, Hargreaves counted back a full month, and selected the appropriate volume. This detailed some sales Burgess had bartered or mediated, mostly dealing with percentages he had a cut in. In a minute, she noticed something odd.

"Rosa, were you casing the place as far back as a month ago?"

"No," Rosa replied. "We started at the beginning of the month. It was lucky. Burgess hadn't been hiring any new girls for a long time. When we stepped in, it was like he had a sudden windfall, three girls at once."

"It makes sense. His illicit revenue stream, according to the abbreviations here, dropped off the map after three months of non-stop gain. See, these months are all red." She slapped at the entry with the backs of her fingers. Businesses were all the same, black or white. "But a large deal came in at the beginning of the month."

"You Brits have a golden touch with accounting," said Rosa. She ignored Hargreaves' narrowed eyes. "I snuck Alby in here when we started. He saw the same thing, but he couldn't figure out why."

"Mordemere's fall must have rippled through the underworld. This is bad, very bad," Hargreaves thought aloud.

"How bad, exactly?" asked Rosa, maybe a little too anxiously.

"If we assume these sales are guns and automata parts, there's only one large, legitimate buyer," Hargreaves continued. "The Ottomans. They've been stockpiling since before Mordemere and the *Nidhogg*. If they're stopping, it could be a prelude to an intrusion into Europe."

A chance to mull over the matter never presented itself. Rosa Marija had been correct in assessing the insulating nature of the room—it had been as quiet as the grave, besides their own voices. Only one aperture marred the hermetic seal: a window cut to allow the projector egress, corresponding to a hole overlooking the amphitheater. Hargreaves almost missed the wisp of movement there, visible for a brief moment in the gap. Someone was coming!

"We must go. Is there another exit?" said Hargreaves calmly. Rosa Marija pointed at the ladder reaching from floor to ceiling. Quite a bit of debris stood in the way, old film reels and dusty boxes of equipment likely writ with the history of the old building inside them. They clambered over these shaky footholds one at a time, reaching a spot just out of sight as the door rattled with the sound of an unexpected visitor. Burgess?

Hargreaves motioned silently for Rosa to stop, about to open the heavy trap above them. Noise would have drawn the visitor's gaze up, but they were fortunate. The room was narrow enough to push one's gaze down towards the equipment, to avoid the feeling of being in a well. So long as they stayed quiet, they would be safe.

The ladies' hardy patience won out. The intruder was not Burgess, but one of Burgess' men, carrying a dim gas patrol lantern. Hargreaves held her breath when the stocky youth made right for the ladder. The youth rummaged through the pile of debris purposefully, lifting a few specific boxes until he had the right one. Inside, she spied a yellow stack of papers. The tough did not bother to pause, pulling the lone stool in the room close to him.

In the dark, the tough began to masturbate, one hand leafing through the girlie mags at a leisurely pace, the other working business-like in his trousers.

Hanging over the projection booth with one hand, Hargreaves covered her mouth. Inspector Vanessa Hargreaves had seen some of the goriest cases ever to come across Scotland Yard's Homicide desks.

The moniker their black-striped ambulances had in the streets of London said it all: Meat Wagons. She had seen men with their heads caved in, men stabbed so many times their guts spilled into the street, and men flayed by syndicate professionals into steaming, naked piles. She had been in the Core of the *Nidhogg*. But she had never seen a man in private, flogging the monkey for everything he was worth.

She had gone on the pull, of course, but encounters were fleeting, awkward and brief. Naked passions made her want to bury her eyes in her hands, but she couldn't tear her eyes from the scene below. Meanwhile, Rosa Marija was having a ball, quietly laughing hard enough to jiggle her rounded buttocks over Hargreaves' face.

"Keep doing it. They'll fall off, you see if they don't," Hargreaves replied, when the tough was finished and all sign of him had disappeared from the catwalks. Only an abandoned handkerchief remained, sticky and stinking in the booth with its sweaty detritus.

"Oh, God, the look on your face was too good," Rosa guffawed. "Come on, we don't want to run into our stallion downstairs. Up, up. Come on!"

"That's what he said," said Hargreaves, and they chortled merrily as they made their way out through the roof access.

INTERLUDE II
B.O.E ON THE GHOST TRAIN

Winnie Lee-Smith watched the men put the small freeman boy into the hopper with the rest of the dead ones. The clacking arms of the client's collection apparatus (for that was what she chose to call them, as opposed to gigantic spiders made of metal and the stuff of night terrors) always made her nervous as they dropped the cargo inside. But for the whiteness of teeth and the palms of hands, the deep umbers and cocoa browns in the twilight might have been coal or coffee beans half-filling the hopper.

Winnie sighed. Not for pity, or her rising gorge—both stopped a long time ago—but out of a detached sense of professional pride. The client had expected a full delivery of thirty barrels. When the company was unable to deliver last month the client had sent these rattling, chittering collection apparatuses to help speed business along.

With the previous day's haul the load would add up to twenty-two barrels, stretched to twenty-seven if they put in an extra cycle of processing. The client would not be happy, but the sub-par barrels would be mixed in with the single-press barrels and overall she thought she just might get away with it.

"Winnifred? Looking for a Winnifred here," cried a delivery man. He rolled a hand truck through the loading dock, clipboard in one hand.

"Here. It's me. And it's Winnie," she said in a piercing voice. That was routine—it was the only way to get these big construction men to notice her.

"You don't look like a 'Fred,'" said the delivery man as he rolled to a stop. He held the clipboard just out of reach.

"I get that a lot," said Winnie, and flashed her badge. The delivery man reluctantly handed over the clipboard and she signed for the items. There was always the off-chance he could be a government inspector in disguise, but judging by his leering at her professionally cut pencil skirt and mini-bustle, he was only a delivery man.

And it was her gosh-danged birthday.

Winnie's parents were Southeast Asians from the Canton region, and they didn't understand the difference between a man's name and a woman's name in the West. They also did not understand which names were first and which were last. Her brother was named Lincoln Lee, which was convenient in the northern states. He went by Link in the South, where he ran telegraph shipping junctions for Ubique. But Winnie, with her sublimely archaic given name, was constantly mired in a swamp of androgyny, so much that she had cut her hair to a knife-sharp bob in an attempt to own her looks.

Winnie adjusted her spectacles, making sure the horn rims sat perfectly placed so she wouldn't have to see anyone's faces. She double-checked her figures against her own much more impressive clipboard, making notations in the appropriate notches so the marks weren't just in pencil, but depressed into the hard cardstock. The Ubique marquee graced the top of the clipboard's brazen housing. It was the latest model, absolutely quiet, fresh from the Clockworks Department. Tiny gears whirred in a corner beneath clear glass, surrounded by bezels buffed and brushed to a high shine. When she flicked a tab at the top, the spring-loaded spreadsheet widget automatically did the calculations with a slider that traveled the width of the paper.

In a moment the armature finished rolling over her marks with its rounded pins, and a tiny nib scratched out a figure at the bottom of the spreadsheet. The result: twenty-eight barrels, better than Winnie guessed. But that also made it more likely the client would be unhappy with the sub-par barrels. She would just have to take the gamble. Brooklyn was not yielding any more to fill the hopper, and it wasn't anything Winnie could help, no matter how she fudged the numbers.

They'd had to cut a few subcontractors from the payroll. Her superiors couldn't understand why the numbers were so shoddy even with the client's equipment. The truth was the winter hadn't been as hard in the last few years, and her normal contractor had expended far too many assets subduing—no, harvesting—the material. Had to keep the terminology right in her head, or there was no coming back from that slippery slope. Her bosses would probably ask her what she had done that quarter to increase vagrancy and keep up their bottom line. She shuddered to think what would happen if they missed the target again, even as an innocuous freight car rattled in the nearby rail yard.

The Ghost Train was coming very soon.

Winnie headed back up from the loading dock to her office, situated in the second story of the building. The Ubique facility sat hunched over a strip of rail that joined the main line a little ways away, but the building itself was in a fashionable neighborhood. Coffee houses and fashion houses sat in the high industrial ceilings of the old ateliers, while nightclubs received their employees at anonymous ground level doors

Winnie stopped at the one in her building, fussing with the barista. She had a special rapport here. As a diminutive Oriental woman high in the company, she had a certain power and mystique that went all the way to the coffee house. Her usual barista, Joshua, never failed to make just what she wanted or put on her favorite B.O.E album. Sometimes he brought the order up to her office. It helped that the one time Joshua made a mistake Winnie had let him make it up after hours in a back room. Winnie was not above downplaying her age either. These Westerners seemed to have no idea how to judge hers. Her string of coffee boys had left knee dents in the filing cabinets over the years.

As for the coffee itself, Winnie was a recent vegan, a practice that was common in the Lands Beyond. News of healthy foods, exercises, and the latest fashions flowed down the grapevine to Winnie's ears, each bit of information extracted at the source from trader ships that came through the veil. Like most other executives, Winnie followed the trends of the Beyond religiously. As of last March, Joshua knew she took almond or frontier flax milk only. Being able to follow airship follies at a moment's notice helped denote one's social rank and ability to expend frivolously, which meant better access to the upper management. Winnie looked forward to sipping soy lattes as far from the steaming grinders as she could get. Shipster Crap was what entertained the owners, after all. As Link sometimes said, shit rolled downhill.

Back in her office, Winnie filed the document from the clipboard. She first fed it through a copy press, which took a similar slider read of the page and produced thin newsprint copies. One she kept in her desk, and two she sent off to Accounting for filing and matching toward subcontractor payouts. That was official terminology. "Payouts." Not "Wages," which would implicate Ubique as the employer, not as the client to the contractor. Not "Fee," because that would cut out the contractor's piece of the pie. Never "Bounty," oh God.

The papers went in vacuum tubes that sucked the letters off through the building. The last she put into an envelope with a strongly worded letter, and sent it to the Mail Room for sending out to their contractor. A deficit of this magnitude will not be tolerated, your rate will drop accordingly, yada yada yada. Her inbox had the usual mix of interdepartmental memos, but someone had failed to screen her mail properly and there were three hate letters mixed in with the rest. Winnie sighed when she peeled the first open: an angry tirade from a subcontractor on the lack of contracts being dished out, and claims of legal violation. That was why they had made it to her desk, the legal ramifications. Even though Winnie knew these were likely futile claims, she still had to file the letters with Legal, and that meant a mountain of paperwork. She decided to put on B.O.E's latest album, *Ramona*, and got out her angriest pen. The experimental industrial sound was different, but that was what Winnie loved about B.O.E. Always on the outside, looking in to the mainstream.

Toward afternoon, Winnie checked in with the Telegraph Room. The client had checked in not two hours ago and would arrive in the morning, bang on time. There was a sense of nervousness that lived in the office but did not affect the dock loaders. The loaders and machinists who knew how the sausage was made treated it no differently from another job.

But everything about the client scared them, and management didn't go into the work floor unless absolutely necessary. In the hall, Winnie ran into the foreman, Semyon Gorvinsky, who was the sort of stuff they made drill sergeants, sous chefs, and copilots out of. He seemed hectic, but confident they would meet the schedule. They were starting the barrels on the preliminary processing now. As Winnie bid Semyon a good day, she noted the brown hand sticking out of a grinder apparatus in one of the work rooms. That would not do—Semyon needed to fix those latch covers.

The Telegraph Room was near the first-floor coffee shop. Winnie decided to stop by for her afternoon brew. Inside, the sunset was a dusky fog against the plate glass and redbrick. Whitewashed walls soared up to the industrial ceiling, the same one that hung over Ubique's work floor and the loading platforms. Rising high into the space were the large bean gravitators, filters, and cold-brew coils for the custom espresso machine. High ceilings helped to disperse the jets of steam that vented out over the wooden bench seats of the café. Plumbing parts held most of the furniture together, and the baristas were impeccable in vests and manicured beards.

The café was the height of Shipster Crap trendiness. Really, it wasn't so much a place to have coffee as an appropriate place for Winnie to be seen. Even the name of the coffee house was textbook aesthetic: Sixty-Four Roasters. The number suggested an allusion to a time or an address that only meant something to the proprietor, and "roasters" separated it from the commonplace cafes where coffee came out of a tin. The implied exclusivity of fresh beans roasted on site and ground to order lent it an air of authenticity. In truth the owner of this café was in part Ubique, and there was nothing personal about the place. The plumbing fixtures came by the foot, an exact replica of the coffee shop at their tower offices in San Francisco. There were carefully engineered differences, of course; the wood had been reclaimed from an old, derelict coach building manufactory, for example. Different Yonder artifacts lived here, anchors and other trinkets on the walls. But that veneer covered up the drip-perfect consistent coffee, the souvenir carry cups, and the tea sandwiches made in manufactories a lot like the Ubique hopper room. Needless to say, Winnie stayed away from the sandwiches, but even the coffee came in pre-roasted bags that attached to the measurement fixtures in the grinders. Ubique did not trust the baristas to spoon out a measure of coffee. Even the clientele looked the same, all in slick pencil skirts, Shipster fashion top hats and faux dirigible breeches. In the coffee house, there were two things worth having besides the coffee: people Winnie needed to know, and people who had something to trade. People came to a corporate coffee house to figure out which of the others were prey and which were predator. She hadn't become senior executive of Human Resources (distinct from the senior executive of Staffing, who handled employees) by chance. She had traded in favors, clandestine contacts, and, yes, sexual arrangements to get this far. That was the nature of the game, and Winnie was very good at playing. So Link could have his café racer haunts, but Winnie had Sixty-Four Roasters, which kept food on the table and Winnie in baristas in the back room.

Her cappuccino was ready.

Winnie let the barista come over and put it on her tiny reclaimed-wood table. The foam filled the warmed cup from brim to soup-bowl-sized brim. Perfection. The barista had drawn picture-perfect cam and cog latte art into the top. As the barista left, Winnie remarked on the taut, perfect buttocks on him. Not John, but someone named Logan, who was new. Winnie took a seat where she could see the whole café. She had outgrown the customers who frequented Sixty-Four, but that was why she came to watch them. The view from the top was... in a word, exquisite.

Really, that was the only reason why she stood a chance when the terrorists burst through the front door.

***

Winnie was sitting with her back to the wall, and in a corner, when the bullets came through the front of the café. They perforated the pair of power women who had immediately grabbed the seat in the front when they came in, so the floor-to-ceiling windows lit them in the best possible afternoon light. Now the gunshots lit them up in shades of bright crimson, the dots splashing across the tops of their lattes and ruining the cute kittens laboriously dripped into the foam.

For a moment Winnie froze, stock-still, as the bodies lay on the broken glass and blood began to pool. The world felt as it had been taken from her and violently shaken, then returned. In shock she turned at a small sound, to find there had been somebody walking through the hall opposite the window and had been wounded in the crossfire. It was the same place Winnie herself had come from: one of two entrances to the café. It led back to her offices at one end and the rail yard on the other. Slumped to the floor, the hurt man twitched for a few seconds, then was perfectly still.

"Nobody move!" said someone gruff who clambered in through the smashed window. He was enormous, just big enough to scrape both sides of the window as he came in, and he had a Collier eight-shot pistol in one hand and a sawed-off shotgun in the other.

"Or these women get it? You dolt," said the second figure, who appeared to be a woman. For a moment Winnie was confused by the lack of pencil skirt and heels that didn't prop her two inches higher. But then the utilitarian leather and riding chaps resolved into the shape of a well-squared woman with a rifle held in both hands and thick, shaded goggles obscuring the top half of her face.

A third man came in through the front door and stood off to a corner. With his tall hat, the coat sweeping his heels, and the enormous crossbow, he looked a little bit like a witch hunter from Protestant New England. This man had a pretty yellow handkerchief tied round his face, but that did nothing to soften the terror of his deep voice as he spoke loudly and clearly into the room.

"Women and children on the floor. We just want Winnifred Lee-Smith!" said the Crossbow Man. When nobody moved, he raised his crossbow and laid a stream of quarrels into the custom gravitator, sending glass and coffee raining down on everyone. *"Now!"*

So they did—what else could they do? The women slid off the perilously rickety café chairs and the men stood on shaking legs, remained standing, or pissed themselves. But Winnie, as she pressed her face to the perfectly clean, meticulously chosen, hexagon tiles of the café floor, counted on two things that might possibly, just possibly, get her through this.

One: she hadn't seen anybody who knew her from work. Everybody here was on Ubique's second shift or from the other company that leased offices in the building.

Two: these terrorists thought Winnifred was a man's name.

The terrorists spread out to three corners of the café, kicking over tables and poking people with their weapons. Shotgun reached the spot closest to Winnifred and began aiming his guns at the various café customers. His shoes smelled terrible. Like breakfast and old blood, which was probably exactly what it was. She sensed from their movements that they were accustomed to combat.

Think, Winnie, think! She told herself. Who had military training and bore a grudge with her? Of course; the laid-off subcontractors!

Meanwhile, Rifle and Crossbow had respectively taken up positions behind tables near the door and window, evidently prepared to deal with the next eventuality—the police officers who arrived, their klaxons screaming in their steaming chaser engines. Red and blue lights lit up the immaculate whitewashed walls.

"Come out with your hands up!" cried one of them. "Police!"

"No!" cried Rifle, who set up a shot using a reclaimed naval pump condiments table as a steady tripod. She squeezed, and people screamed when the shot rang like a bell through the cafe.

"What do you want?" cried the same officer, unseen outside the café. Evidently Rifle had hit a soft spot. For good measure, Crossbow stepped up and unloaded an entire drum of quarrels through the window, a hail of barbs plunked like piano keys against the chasers and the street outside. The weapon hissed as its steam canister vented gas. Crossbow reloaded casually from a bandolier under his coat.

"He's got a point," said Rifle, not moving from her spot. "How do we know we have Winnifred Lee-Smith here? We don't know what he looks like."

"Doggonit, you told just about everyone here we don't!" said Shotgun. He picked up a half-empty latte, drained it, made a face, and smashed the cup inches from Winnifred's nose.

"We will know soon enough. Our contact said he always takes his coffee here at four in the afternoon, just before a delivery," said Crossbow. "Let's give our man some time to show himself."

The rat bastard! Was it John the barista? Any of her baristas. Or her superior? Was it Melinda from Accounting? Oooo, Winnie had just known Melinda was after her job! Really the sniping wasn't anything bitter or conniving. Mostly Winnie was trying to distract herself from the skirt-soiling terror that threatened to shake her to pieces. But after a minute passed, then five, then ten minutes of nobody doing much of anything except rounding up the men near the window as human shields and waving some guns about, Winnie relaxed as much as she was going to. They wouldn't figure out who she was any time soon. Winnie could wait them out until the authorities decided to storm the place.

It was Shotgun who grew impatient with proceedings and barked hoarsely into the tense atmosphere.

"This waiting is hard on my bad knee. Do we really need this Winnifred?"

"That's the signature on the checks. And on the forms that laid us off, numbskull," said Rifle. She had left the gun propped on the condiment table and found a mostly-untouched free trade macchiato to sip while she watched the street outside.

"We get him," said Crossbow as he paced smoothly around the café, "and we get to Ubique. We hold their top man hostage and we demand the payment of our proper wages."

These simpletons! thought Winnie. Ubique wouldn't give two damns about one of their mid-tier managers set up in Red Hook She didn't think those Cali suits knew where that was in Brooklyn. Winnie had been setting herself up for a headquarters position in San Francisco when she took the special client's job.

"If it makes you feel better," said Rifle, "hold each man by gunpoint and ask them if they're Winnifred. We're only dragging this out so Ubique can get a negotiator down here."

"That sounds like a hoot," said Shotgun. Without further ado he fired, making one of the hostage's knees into hamburger. "Whoa Nelly. I forgot to ask."

"You splendid, murderous bastard," said Crossbow as a scream cut through the air. "That's rock salt. That's why the darkies down Colorado way are so scared of you."

The man writhed on the floor, clutching at his ruined knee. His mouth gaped in a silent scream. Winnie covered her mouth as the blood crept by her. Oh Goddess of Mercy, she thought, and clutched at the jade pendant at her neck. If Shotgun found out Winnie was Chinese, what would he do? Some small part of her was quivering in shame, too. That man had gotten hurt because of her.

No. Because of the Shotgun man. Slippery Slope.

"Stings," commiserated Rifle, though it sounded like professional detachment. Winnie knew it when she heard it.

"Let that be a lesson to you all. If you are Winnifred, best speak up now, or my associate here will do much the same to you," said Crossbow. "We've time to burn and ammo in the plenty, but when the negotiator arrives we want our bargaining chip."

Winnie felt her blood run cold as the various menfolk began to plead or whine, insisting they weren't Winnifred Lee-Smith. Some of them showed identification cards, and those that had photograms of themselves were shooed to the floor with the women. Eventually only Joshua and Logan, the baristas, were left along with two other men. Evidently Sixty-Four Roasters did not issue photogram identification.

"Well, that cuts it down to three. Go on, get," said Rifle.

For a moment nobody moved, but then Logan, the dusky barista with the fine behind, stepped out of the line. He made for the door, but Crossbow dropped a hand on his shoulder.

"And you're sure you don't know what he looks like?"

"Maybe we missed him. Maybe this little pissant lied to us," said Rifle.

"I'm... I'm sure! I just heard a few of the workers complain about the speed-up, and joke about pissing in Lee-Smith's coffee," stuttered Logan. "I just wanted to make a fast buck."

"Really? You didn't just screw us?" said Shotgun. He walked over, squatted, and pressed his pistol to Logan's kneecap.

"Oh my God! I saw Joshua make that vegan latte crap! He's here! He's here!" screeched Logan.

"Can't beat the coffee test," said Rifle. "He's here."

"Good work," said Crossbow.

"Go on, get," added Shotgun, prodding Logan's back with his shotgun.

Crossbow let him go, but when Logan got to the window there were a couple of ringing shots from the police outside. Logan put his hands up, and his pants went dark. At first Winnie though he had soiled himself, but then he crumpled, and his front was red with bullet holes.

"Christ, we were releasing a hostage!" screamed Crossbow into the night.

"Sorry!" said somebody on the other side, and there was the sound of a slap.

"Goddamn it!" said Crossbow.

"Watch your tongue. There are ladies present," said Shotgun.

"Hey, you curse around me all the time!" said Rifle. There was an easy camaraderie that was hard to hate, despite the red stains pooling around Logan's body.

While this was happening, Winnie was inching towards the door. Her small frame and dull, professional clothes made it easy to slip under the tables unnoticed, but she still had to be careful to move very slowly, lest the terrorists notice. The blood that was splattered from the window formed trails of droplets across her path, like lava that she carefully avoided. Once she heard Logan talking about her vegan latte, she began to crawl double-quick, trying to make it out before Joshua could point the finger. Seeing the perspiration on his face as he tried not to glance toward her, Winnie wondered if she could have given in to his more pressing needs in that stock room. She hoped it was incentive enough for Joshua not to give her up to the terrorists, but it was a little too late now to go on her knees and open wide.

She was quite close to the door leading back to her office. If she could get to it she could go into the street away from the shattered window. Which way was better? The office would have her vacuum mail to send for help, and a solid steel rail yard door. But her sedan was parked not three spaces down the line, and the attendant would have plugged it into the steam, ready for her regular work hours to end. Across the way, there was another woman who had reached a similar position to the one she had—except she was brushing the table's legs, and the coffee cups on top of it were rattling loudly. Winnie held her finger to her mouth, glaring across the way until the panicked woman stopped moving, her mouth open in terror. Winnie nodded, and made a gesture she hoped translated to the woman as "Wait!"

"All right, Joshua," said Crossbow. Winnie froze. "Your associate just gave away the game. Winnifred Lee-Smith is here now. We want the lying bastard. Which one of these suits is him?!"

Shotgun clocked Joshua across the face with the butt of his gun, for good measure.

"Winnifred? I barely know him," said Joshua when he recovered, rubbing his jaw. He was visibly sweating, but thank the heavens, he had caught on to the terrorists' mistake. "I just make his coffee."

"But you did make it, so he's here now."

"No, I sent it up to his office. He's probably gone now, with all the noise you made and the police here," lied Joshua.

"Liar," said Rifle. She reached over from her reclining position and casually flicked Joshua in his groin, through his apron. The touch was like a firecracker, and the barista jumped a foot in the air. His freeman skin turned the hue of ash over his usual coffee-bean brown. But now Winnie knew they could tell when he was lying, so she pulled her heels up, ready to make a run for the door.

"Christ!" said Joshua. "Okay, okay. Winnifred isn't a man." Damn!

"No? It's a woman?" said Rifle, amazed.

"Yes, yes. It's the woman under the table," he said.

Winnie sighed. That was how much a roll in the hay bought her, she supposed. She couldn't blame Joshua. After all, Winnie would have sold him out in an instant, if the situation were reversed. Winnie had had a dozen like him and one night of jungle fever was no comparison with the rest of her life. Footsteps thundered across the café, shaking the tiles.

But to her surprise, Shotgun did not flip over her table—he grabbed the other one across the way, dragging the woman there to her feet.

"Are you Winnifred Lee-Smith? Did you sign those orders to cancel all our contracts? Think you can just toy with our lives, you spic bitch?" The woman happened to be Latino, probably a Mexican, thought Winnie. She was also shaking all over as the big man lifted her by the front of her one-piece suit dress. When he shook her, spitting in her face, the seams ripped and she crumpled to the ground. That darted hip line might have been armor in the meeting room but it was basically paper now.

"Easy, Shaun," said Rifle, apparently using Shotgun's name.

Meanwhile, Winnie was marveling at what had just happened. Either Joshua was a better man than Winnie gave him credit for, or he hadn't wanted these terrorists to have their way, or Shotgun had simply mistaken which table Joshua had pointed at. In any case, Winnie saw her chance, and she lunged for the door just when the other woman hit the floor and everyone was distracted. She hadn't become senior executive of Human Resources by sitting on her butt and doing nothing.

Winnie made it halfway out the door before she felt her bustle catch, and the back of her skirt threaten to rip. Was somebody hanging on to it? Either way the tug was enough to throw her off balance, and she crumpled against the plate glass of the door, half in and half out. She could see the dead body of the man who had been caught in the first volley, slumped and staining the carpet. When she turned, she saw six inches of wood stuck in the knot of her bustle, pinning her to the wood of the door; a crossbow quarrel, fired with pinpoint accuracy, and it had just missed the skin of her backside by a hair.

"Winnifred Lee-Smith. At last," said Crossbow, grinning.

⋆⋆⋆

They let most of the hostages go one by one, and in that interval the terrorists slipped out the back door and into the offices of Ubique. They brought Winnie with them, hobbled and with her wrists bound in baling wire. The stuff didn't even need to be tied. If Winnie moved her wrists, it bit into her skin and threatened to cut her open.

"Stick to the schedule," said Rifle to the hostages as the three terrorists dragged Winnie out the same corridor she wanted to flee out of. She had clamped a bundle of clockwork and scary glass tubes to the front door; a bomb. "One by one, every ten minutes. The door will ring an alarm, and in that window one person can leave. If you all try to leave, boom. If you miss the window, boom. Ciao!" Then she had locked the back door behind them. They had all seen what happened to Logan.

As they dragged her through the deserted Ubique office, Winnie had time to think that perhaps she deserved everything that was happening. According to Ubique, she had done her job impeccably, and was rewarded. She had consistently sent through every file, managed every contract. She'd found a reliable contractor to handle subcontractors to go into the city and massacre the inhabitants for her client's hopper of corpses. What happened to those people and what happened to their bodies were none of her concern. They were just pieces of paper on her immaculate clipboard to be read by her clockwork sliders and double-checked against different pieces of paper.

Winnie muttered something, a lyric or two she had been listening to that afternoon. Maybe it was her trying to comfort herself, and it wasn't intended for anybody else. But her captor heard it.

"What?" said Shotgun, who was dragging her along. She stumbled, a little, and they paused.

"Bee Oh Eee. B.O.E. The Banality of Evil," said Winnie, shocked into the truth.

"It's music. The name is an acronym," explained Rifle. "It's like fubar."

"What in God's name does that mean?" answered Winnie.

"You don't want to know," said Crossbow.

"Shut your mouth!" said Shotgun. He cuffed Winnie hard enough to draw blood from one lip. Winnie turned back to see Shotgun breathing heavily. The violence was doing something for him. Hitting a small, incapacitated woman was arousing for this enormous man. Winnie swallowed and tried to overcome her horror. Lust was something she knew, and something she could use.

"What are you going to do to me?" asked Winnie. She tried to squeak a little, and she made sure her legs were splayed at an attractive angle. Before Shotgun could react, Crossbow hurried them along.

"Come along now," said Crossbow. "She'll get her just punishment."

To Winnie's surprise they didn't go out to the vehicle steam lot, or the rail yard to escape on a train. Instead they dragged her half-stumbling along the same floor. Winnie recognized Gorvinsky's neat handwriting on the bulletins and doorjambs. They were going on the factory floor, a span of high rafters, large bull-like machinery and vast copper tanks. In the far corner of the room, tracks in the ceiling led out to the hoppers in the train yard. One of the heavy containers stood just under it, parked with its load of fresh material. Beside it were racks of magnets holding up shining cleavers and curved boning knives. Winnie didn't know what half the things here did, but the work floor hadn't scared her as much as the other employees. The stockholders and supervisors never saw it at all.

Industrial chic, they might call it, if they saw.

Winnie hadn't really looked at her captors properly, but now they stopped in the middle of the dark and deserted floor she could see Rifle was carrying her weapon over her shoulder and a large case in her other hand. The case was perhaps half the size of a steamer trunk, lined with durable black panels and shiny chrome corners. Rifle set her gun atop a metallic green pod and set the case on the floor.

"Take off your clothes," said Crossbow.

"Why?!" Winnie's exclamation came unwisely, but nobody rebuked her for it. Shotgun was busy blocking up the exits, with Crossbow covering him. There was nobody to leverage this situation with, no power play she could do.

Meanwhile Rifle had opened up the case, and inside there was a neatly sorted piece of machinery that looked like a figure eight someone had tacked to a miniature calliope. There was a nook in the corner of the case that held a very recognizable steam converter, for tapping the building's pressure. But the machine itself was a mystery until Rifle propped it up out of the case, setting three long legs into the case's corners to stabilize it. She fitted a glass disc to one side, turning it to adjust. Then the purpose of the tangle of machinery became clear; it was a picture machine, a gramophone for the eyes.

They were going to record her humiliations for posterity.

"Take off your clothes, please," said Crossbow.

"He won't say it again, you swine," said Rifle. She gestured at the butchering equipment.

"Come on! You're going to make a pornograph? Here?" said Winnie.

With a twang, a crossbow quarrel stuck fast at her feet, making her jump. Winnie immediately began to undo the clasps at her skirt, hidden under the bustle, crying "All right! All right!"

As she felt Crossbow's indifferent gaze on her, her eyes start to tear, but she fought it down. It was strange, really. Taking off her clothes in a room full of armed terrorists felt exactly like entertaining the succession of fat, wrinkly superiors she had had over the years. And just like that, the clothes came off a little easier.

America hadn't yet come to the progressive fashions of Europe, but thankfully Winnie's outfit was sufficiently Shipster Crap to make it easy to shimmy out of. The air felt frozen as her blouse came off, and then her chest expanded as the modish corset lifted off her small breasts. Her shape immediately lost its hourglass figure. That more than anything made her feel stripped of her armor. Finally she stepped out of her leggings, and stood there shivering, hoping either Shotgun had a fetish for Orientals or Rifle was a student of Lesbos. Maybe if she entertained their sick humiliations she might just get out of this alive, but the air smelled rank and sour, and like rain before a disappointment that smell seemed a terrible portent.

"Now climb those steps," said Crossbow.

Winnie turned to look where he was gesturing at the same time that Rifle found the ceiling arclights switch. White light filled the room, and momentarily the glare blinded her. She stood there, naked, covering herself and squinting. Then the tiles came back into focus around the edges of her eyes and she saw the cast iron steps with their wheels underneath, and where it had been parked as the workmen evacuated the factory floor. Something inside Winnie still derided the slowdown; how would they meet the client's arrival now? Damn terrorists.

The top step of the ladder had been rolled up to the lip of the enormous tub, sat on one wall of the room like a fat, hungry frog. Two round glass portholes showed the clean porcelain interior of the tub, and some sort of dark machinery. Winnie put one foot on the bottom step and jerked back—it was cold! But at the gesturing of the terrorists, she walked all the way to the top. Winnie had no idea what the machine was for, but when she looked down at the slowly rotating chrome of gnashing blades as they spun up with an ominous rumble—she did.

They had put her on the edge of an enormous meat grinder.

"That's good, stop there," said Crossbow. "I apologize, by the way, for the nudity—"

"To this bitch?" cried Rifle.

"—and the picture machine. We were under the impression you were a man... but this does not change our plan, unfortunately. You did a terrible wrong and hopefully we will correct that now."

"Why don't you just kill me, then?" said Winnie. She couldn't stop watching her toes, at how close they were to the shuddering edge of the step.

"Because then you would be a martyr," said Crossbow, as if that was common knowledge. "No, we want you to tell everybody what you've been doing as you look at these horrible instruments in the eye. Then Ubique will know we mean business."

"Yeah. As much as I'd like to give you a good thrashing, Jack says we're not to touch you," complained Shotgun.

"You're going to use me to hit Ubique in the wallet," said Winnie, horrified. "But... but my life might as well be over. They're going to blacklist me from every Ubique office!" Everything she had worked for... everything she had sacrificed for... all those late nights in her superiors' offices... Winnie could feel it all crumbling away from her like wet sand.

"Then find something else to do," said Rifle as she centered the glass eye of the picture machine on the grinder, an air of total indifference about her.

"Ubique is everywhere! You're going to turn me into a Typhoid Mary... I'll never work again!"

"Join the party," said Shotgun, and leered.

"Everyone is going to see what Ubique is up to," finished Crossbow.

Winnie crumpled, hanging on for dear life as the terrorists set up the picture equipment. There was a gramophone attachment to write sound on the thin black tape Rifle wound through the machine, and they spent some time wondering if the grinder was too loud. Crossbow seemed to have a prepared speech he wanted to say, and he kept gesturing with a small notebook as he debated his point. As Rifle tinkered and they bickered slightly, Winnie felt her options dwindling fast. Could she outrun their weapons? No, clearly not. What about suicide? The grinder was still running. But she had a queer idea about what happened to all the product Ubique made for their special client, and she didn't think her suffering would end at death.

All of a sudden the weight of what she had been doing to get ahead, to beat out all the other rats in the race, settled on her shoulders like a sack of bricks. With a start a small epiphany dawned on Winnie, and she clutched her naked shoulders, trying to make herself smaller. She gibbered incoherently. The truth that struck Winnie's tiny frame like one of the freight trains in the quieted yard outside was this: being held at gunpoint and humiliated wasn't any different than sucking off a few powerful people to get ahead. The terrorists had the threat of bullets but the uppity-ups had been blackmailing her life just as much—or rather, her livelihood. Without the title of senior executive of Human Resources, what was she? Just another vagrant, liable to be picked up and brought back to feed this Human Tinning Machine churning under her.

Winnie found herself standing at the edge of the steps, her hands at her sides, when she awoke, as if from a spell. The steel had rumbled beneath her, a mesmerizing rhythm, as if the grinder were an animal that could draw prey into its maw with song. In shock, she stepped back, and realized the terrorists had turned off the grinder, and it was slowing to a stop. The break in the rhythm had interrupted her suicidal walk off the edge. She clutched at the rail, staring down at the floor far below, and the clean blades inside the grinder. Had she really...? Was it so easy to give everything up?

That was how the terrorists decided to show her, with her knees buckled and her private parts exposed. Rifle plugged the steam converter into a port in the floor, and the wheels of the picture machine began to roll. Crossbow began to speak, away from the shot and behind the machine. Winnie didn't catch all of it, but she got the gist of it. Something about the rights of the mercenary, and the skill of the hunter. How theirs was a specialized discipline that went all the way back to the American Revolution and the militia there. How Ubique was destroying their lives by employing heartless machines instead of thinking people. The same kind of would-be revolutionary nonsense Winnie had been getting in her mail tube for weeks, but now it was of paramount importance—or it would be, if she weren't feeling gutted, and miles away.

Winnie was busy gathering the pieces of herself, so when the terrorists asked her if Ubique had hired them to hunt down the blacks and the Hispanics like animals, she said, "Yes."

When they asked her if they were brought to this killing floor, she said, "Yes. Sometimes still twitching. The workmen have to put those down." Rifle panned round to show one of the hoppers in the room. She took the machine off its stand, with its thick black umbilical for the steam, and went to show what was inside.

When they asked her what happened to the bodies, Winnie said, "We put them through this big grinder. Then Gorvinsky and the others give us the full barrels. If they check out on the purity scope a long white train comes to pick them up. It only comes at midnight... it's a scary monster and it goes from station to station when everybody's asleep. They think everything is hunky dory!"

"She's gone mad," said Rifle.

"This is propaganda gold," said Crossbow, who seemed to be less and less an intimidating killer for hire and more like that one fellow from college who joined all the philosophy groups. But as he admired his own handiwork, the picture was interrupted by a twist—the room filling with shrapnel, a din like a million meat grinders and the smell of burning pitch. Then a bright light filled the room from the door to the loading dock, where a dozen sharp metal stakes were ripping their way inside.

Winnie thought the terrorists might have gotten their own deaths on tape. It sounded as if glass spiders were tearing through the place, their fragile skin crackling with gunfire. Huge spiders, spiders from Mars. Hah. That was a good one. Winnie laughed at her funny joke. She supposed she was being a voyeur of utter destruction. Winnie collapsed, tickled half to death by the absurdity of it all, and somehow managed not to see how the work floor became painted with red.

Later, when the rescue team from the local fire brigade found her cantilevered over the carnage by the stepladder, she was still gibbering melodically to herself. The lead rescuer, a handsome fireman, draped his coat over her shoulders and slapped her awake.

She ended up dating him later, during the endless wishful beginnings of looking for a job. The fireman was named Robert Jones Colton, and he had a fine head of punk pink hair. It wasn't long before she found a spot as a barista, and not long after that when she decided to stay at Colton's after theatre and coffee. Not the picture house—she had immediately said no, and Colton had been adorably apologetic. In a post-coitus sharing of thoughts, Winnie discovered the first thing she had said when they finally woke her from her stupor.

"Oh, God, look at the work floor... How will I ever make the morning delivery now?"

7

PLANNING A TRIP IS HARD

As Vanessa Hargreaves clung to a ladder in a burlesque in the seedier part of New York, Arturo C. Adler was negotiating with the remaining members of M.A.D. back across the pond. In a pub perhaps a fifth less shady than Stan Burgess' pleasure palace, Arturo cringed, pulling his scalloped sleeves away from mildew and the pervasive smell of cabbage oozing from the walls. If he left, it would be the first time he quit a lock-in, which was quite unthinkable.

"I know the blasted box is dangerous, Arturo," the old man in the boiler suit before him was saying. "And that's why we're not getting caught up in this."

Arturo supposed Cid Tanner had a sordid history with piracy, but as Arturo was in the confidence of the matriarch of the state, albeit indirectly, he felt entitled to demand a little bending of the law. Not to mention, Arturo hadn't taken rules very seriously since the age of five, when he discovered the rule makers kept treacle tarts in the pantry all to themselves.

"All I want," Arturo appealed once more, putting in every ounce of nonchalance he had in his body, "is for you to help your boss, Inspector Vanessa Hargreaves—"

"—die in a horrible, gruesome way. No, I'm not showing you how to open the damn box."

"*D'accord!* Not opening the damn box!"

"Cezette, stop cursing. You are a civilized lady," Tanner reprimanded.

"But you do, Uncle Cid!" Cezette replied.

"I am an old fart. I am allowed to do things civilized ladies are not. At least curse in French or something; make an effort to humor me."

"I do not know any French curses, Uncle."

Cezette Louissaint calmly sipped her herbal lemonade. A casual observer might think she was completely ignoring the young chavs in the booths, but Arturo knew a fellow *artiste* when he saw one. She had full mastery over them. Even her casual pose was carefully crafted to be heart-stoppingly beautiful, which kept all but the bravest away. Hargreaves had taught her well. Or, she had gone through so much that young men were a piece of cake. Arturo could not help but feel it was the latter, sad though the thought was. She was far too young to start thinking about these things, and thin, from a mishandled childhood. Whatever height she ought have been was indeterminate. Arturo guessed she was somewhere in the midst of her flowering. At fourteen or fifteen, Cezette already possessed the fine sculpted cheekbones to make a great beauty at twenty.

Then there were her legs. The girl's artifice legs were carefully sculpted to match the girl's doe-like countenance, giving her a high-fashion figure. Cid had clearly used the periodicals of the day as a model for the feminine form, resulting in this hyper-Victorian, dress-shop mannequin perfection. A traveling ensemble from Hargreaves' closet hid the legs from view; an espresso-colored pinafore trimmed in ebony, with a dense circle of petticoats beneath to muffle the small mechanical scrapes of cogs. Combined with raven locks and deathly pale coloring from too much time in the M.A.D. tunnels, it made her look like the sequestered daughter of some new steamwork gentry, or some sprung ballerina from a porcelain music box.

Cezette set the glass bottle of lemonade down, and spectral fingers reached out to pick it up, setting it on a passing bar tray. Jean Hallow retracted his fingers and folded over into himself against the sparse crowd, clearly uncomfortable in a social setting. A severely cut suit and his pale complexion made him seem more a comic lithograph than a man, a flat drawing of someone gaunt and pinstriped with hollow eyes. He looked like something native to a cave.

"What good is having a Pandora's box of plagues when there is no way to open it? What if we want to use it as a bargaining chip? What if we want to destroy it?" Arturo proposed.

"Does dear Vicky want it destroyed? Answer me truly," Cid Tanner countered.

"It's an option, I'd say."

"When did you switch from detective to errand boy? Worse yet, a budding war criminal," sniped Tanner.

Arturo sighed. He had expected some resistance, but what he had never counted on was Cid Tanner's immunity to Arturo's charm. The girl Cezette had been quick to marvel at Arturo's impeccable ruby suit, his silk cravat, and the way he handled the pub, firmly, but with a smile as slippery as it was warm. Tanner, on the other hand, was a stone.

"What I want to know," Cezette interjected, "is what you intend to do with the knowledge. The box is no longer in London, *Monsieur* Adler."

"I could wire to our dear inspector," Arturo dodged. He knew it was a futile move; the cat was out of the bag.

"But you have no clue where she might have headed, have you? No reliable telegraph locations, at any rate. It seems to me there is only one course of action, *n'est pas*? You intend to find her."

"Now there is a plan I can nail to a bulkhead," Cid Tanner agreed with a throaty chuckle. He downed the remains of his whiskey.

"None of you are coming," Arturo said, putting his foot down. "No offense, but I work alone. I came to you because you seem likely to keep the secret."

"You're taking the piss," Tanner barked.

"If you are afraid of Maman's reaction, do not be. We will take full responsibility," said Cezette.

"Maman?" Arturo echoed, but Cezette had seen through his bluster at a glance. Yes, he did not want to admit it, but he respected Hargreaves far more than he let on. If she had avoided involving the M.A.D. crew, who was Arturo to thrust them willy-nilly into danger?

"Look at it this way. Alphonse is a precision machine, top-flight and very finicky. He came in sealed boxes straight from the manufactory in Glasgow. Without us, the inspector could easily falter in the middle of an automata brawl. A loose nut or steam leak. With us, there are reinforcements," said Tanner. "You do not have to burden yourself with the knowledge of how to open the hermetically sealed box. Do you really want to be standing there when the seal emits a cloud of Mr. Cook's plague-ridden, vaporized body parts?"

Arturo shuddered with the thought. With the perceptive Cezette's wide eyes on him, the immovable Mr. Tanner, and Hallow perched there like a vulture, he saw no reason to continue pretending. From a dispatch case at his knee, he extracted a folio of documents.

"Now I've been absolved of any responsibility, I've already booked you on the next zeppelin out to New York. You remember Ivanov? He says you are old friend. He helped Hargreaves pull some strings to get there. I've made arrangements for a very private cabin, and the vessel is a fast one."

"You're a right bastard," said Hallow. Arturo started, but was surprised to see the sepulchral figure smiling.

"Not so far as I know. Dastard might be a better description," said Arturo.

"You are a fine, loyal friend," Cezette complimented him. "Maman should be so surprised! *On arrive*, New York City!"

***

London was her usual steamy self. A mile from the city center, an abundance of greenery lessened the signs of Victoria III's steam-driven revolution. In times long ago, this part of London had been used for cemeteries. Later it housed the myriad workforce needed to maintain and drive Britain's budding industry: the Arabs, the blackamoor Africans, and the Indians.

Arturo left the pub with a warm agitation in his chest. He had gambled on much: New York, as the likely place Hargreaves would begin her investigation, that M.A.D. would play into his hands like they did, and that Hargreaves would even continue investigating. But he knew her that much, as well as this neighborhood, in fact.

For whatever reason, a great swath of the place had been saved from the ravages of building to become lush, beautiful parkland. Not even leisure dirigibles chose to land on the green, favoring the flatland of Hyde Park to the bridged hills of Mile End. One wing of a decrepit department store stood like a row of gapped teeth, with one portion missing, bombed out in the last war. The park had been allowed to claim the building, filling the vacant space with grass and benches.

Arturo felt as at home walking these streets as he did in his rooms in fashionable North London. He passed a knot of cockney boys smoking cigarettes outside a pub. The closest, a large bearded fellow, took a long glare at Arturo's shock of bright, spiky hair, until another of them nudged the fellow with an informative jab. Their leader nodded, knowingly. Last year Arturo had posted the leader's bail on a trumped-up charge. Half of these men had been in his pay, at one time or another. Now they were better than hounds when he needed to find someone underground.

By the chip shop on his left, Arturo had found Withers the cat half a dozen times for elderly Mrs. Howell there in the grove of spiny sloe. In the housing complex to his right, he had once saved a young couple's marriage by proving beyond a doubt the tart carrying the husband's child was nothing more than a pretender with a stolen handkerchief. He had people to protect him here, like an armor of whispered tales and rumored deeds. This was his side of the city.

Which made the tail so inexplicable in this part of town. He knew it like the back of his hand. The tail might be hiding his face behind a scarf, but the sharply polished shoes, the immaculate coat, and the way he stepped round the puddles as if they were plague-ridden, all spoke of someone not native to gritty Mile End. Further, as Arturo rounded the corner, the man suddenly picked up his pace.

Arturo gave it some thought. He was surprised it had taken so long for someone to find him. The usual suspects came to mind, of course: British Intelligence? Not Scotland Yard; they were not the cloak and dagger sort. He considered the American thieves, but it was unlikely. Orb Weaver had killed his partners, most likely fled after failing to take the box.

Arturo was so deep in thought that he nearly did not react when the garrote descended past his eyes. But for the glimpse of the first man, he would have been taken off guard. As it was, he was only able to get a finger between the wire and his neck.

"Tell us where the box is," a voice demanded, clearly unaware of how human vocal cords operated. If Arturo could talk he might have remarked his assailant was really quite daft.

Instead, Arturo gasped. The joint at his first knuckle hurt as the wire dug into his glove. A low whirr accompanied the tightening of the wire—a clockworked device. His attacker yanked him backward, into a hedge and against something, maybe a tree. Arturo felt the bite against his neck, a creeping coldness, and disconcerting warmth where the blood was starting to flow.

Even as air became a rare commodity, his brain began to analyze his attacker in the hair's breadths between the seconds. The voice was accented—Liverpool or Ireland, perhaps. Height? The wire was cutting upward, which meant tall, much taller than Arturo. Arturo scouted with his other hand, flailing as if out of control. He felt hard muscle under a woolen jacket, a scruffy beard, and then his strength left the arm as the air began to run out of his lungs. He could track the rate his brain was dying by the white fog creeping into his vision, a London pea-souper in his head.

His attacker loosened the wire. It was just enough for Arturo to grasp a tiny mouthful of air, before tightening again.

"Where is the box?" the attacker asked again.

"You brute, how will the man answer when you've got his neck?"

The tail had arrived, and plunged into the hedge with them. In the dark, it was hard to see, but the man was shorter, and his accent different. Arturo pinned it; Asiatic, likely Nippon. He'd heard one like it not too long ago, at the picture house, some grotesquerie about a lizard monster as tall as Big Ben. An odd match....

Grunting, the tall man released his grip and Arturo fell to the dirt. His hair was likely a horrid mess, he thought. The tall man kicked him onto his back, where he lay unmoving.

"The box is in Whitechapel," Arturo gasped, hacking and wheezing. His attackers leaned in to hear. "Missy Cerise. Red hair, lovely white skin. It's just fifty pee for a look."

Casually, the shorter man took out three inches of steel and sheathed it in Arturo's belly.

At first, there was no pain, just a sudden cold and a shock of seeing the flat, beige handle sticking out of him. When the pain came, the tall man shoved a glove in Arturo's mouth, to silence the screams.

"Basically, we can leave it in there, and you can probably reach a cab or a police box in time," the short man whispered. "Or, I pull it out sideways and let you bleed to death. It won't be pretty, and you'll have a hard time keeping things inside."

The tall man mimed the motion, reeling in the lengths and holding them to his own belly. It was too dark to see their hidden faces, but Arturo felt he must have been laughing quietly.

Arturo was no hero. He told them. He told them everything and more, about his sainted, absent mother, about his arduous youth training in the arts of detecting: acrobatics, chemistry, hours poring over studies of cigar ash in his family library. He told them about the time he got stung in a dozen different places when he bumbled into his father's beehives, and his resulting immunity to bee venom thereafter. He told them everything but what they needed to hear, hidden in the wasteland of his life.

Soon enough, the cockney boys rushed the hedges, drawn by his initial scream, and Arturo gasped a sigh of relief.

"Oh you cunts, you beautiful whoring cunts, yes!" he cried. In the vernacular, of course.

As they chased off the attackers, Arturo held the short man's knife still stuck in him with his left hand. He clung to it desperately, every movement triggering a jarring flower of pain. *It mustn't come out, it mustn't come out*, the thought looped and twisted through his white fingers, locking them like a vise.

In his right, he held onto a sheaf of papers, folded into quarters and hidden under his body. The tall man had probably thought them safe, inside his coat pocket, but discerning and pickpocketing valuables had been the first thing Arturo salvaged from the wasteland of his youth.

*** *

"These blasted scraps of mulch must hold some secret. I've used lemons, I've exposed it to arclight, I've held on to it and spun in a circle. I've even burned a small corner of it. Perhaps it's a spoken command? Come now, reveal your secrets! Abracadabra! Alakazam! Reducto!"

Aboard the zeppelin *Gretchen,* bound for America, Arturo C. Adler was going stir-crazy, shut up in his cabin. Arturo had been confined to quarters after a wide-shouldered German ship's surgeon took one look at his abdomen wound. The M.A.D. members were housed in the same suites, but they had the freedom of the ship.

"Zis is terrible! A velocipede accident, you say?" cried Cezette.

Infuriated, Arturo had devoted his time to two scraps of bloody paper. There were marks on it, in regular lines and dots, but they appeared incomplete, like bits and pieces of Morse telegraph. It was gibberish in Morse, or any of the ciphers Arturo had memorized.

Arturo made all the inductions he could from the paper itself. Repetitive creasing and smoothing had left their marks in nicks and corner folds. There must have been some trick to it, then, some kind of invisible writing. The paper smelled of sweat, and grease from a chip shop, likely from the tall man's pocket. The marks were India black, judging from the distinct smudge pattern. Arturo had turned the paper under natural light, arclight. and gaslight, looking for a telltale shine from invisible inks. It could not be an ink, because the document would then be permanently legible. One corner was discolored, promisingly, but a sniff revealed it to be a spill of common ale, which would have dissolved, not revealed, most inks.

Even in the face of ineffable boredom, Arturo finally ran out of ideas. He leaned back in his bed, his stomach hurting abominably. Though the stitches were good, and the wound relatively harmless despite the small man's threats, the cut still stung. Worse, it itched. His customary laudanum dulled the pain somewhat, but Arturo wanted his mind clear for what lay in store.

Surprisingly, Jean Hallow had been the one most concerned with Arturo's well-being. Cid had seen to it Arturo was alive, inquired of the perpetrators, scowled, and left him to his own devices. Arturo would never subject the girl Cezette to such horrors as his bloodied tum, but she still took time away from the wonders of a passenger airship to read to him in the evenings.

Jean Hallow, in contrast, had immediately asked Arturo to show him the bandaged area. His cadaverous form reminded Arturo of a stiff undertaker, but his fingers were skilled at healing. He'd unwrapped the bandages, checked the stitching done by the London hospital, and applied some top-notch first aid. Then he had arranged for the Gretchen's crew to deliver Arturo's meals to his quarters, all with a businesslike economy of words. His ministrations were efficient, and his bedside manner pitiless, which Arturo appreciated. The only annoyance was Hallow's habit of reading a King James Bible in Arturo's room while Arturo took his supper, but even this was done silently, and was no offense. Occasionally Hallow would chuckle, which sparked Arturo's curiosity.

"Hmm? I'm laughing at the irony. If hubris is a cardinal sin, this God character is the biggest sinner."

"Is it fair to say God is so much like us?" Arturo mused.

"Why do you think it hates the worship of idols? It's trying to eliminate its competition." Well, how could Arturo not enjoy that?

On the third day, Jean arrived with a tray of supper and a blessedly rotund bottle of ruby port.

"Oh, you creepy bugger, that is a Godsend," said Arturo. He pounced on the bottle, swilling the stuff like water.

"You're out of laudanum," Hallow said, gesturing to the empty flask at the bedside. He didn't seem to mind being called creepy.

"Why are you being so attentive? This can't be out of loyalty to Inspector Hargreaves," Arturo said between smaller sips. He passed the bottle to Hallow, who took to it easily enough.

"My father was an army doctor," Hallow said. "We used to care for our neighbors when they got hurt. Hampshire, few doctors and long roads. I'm used to fixing people."

They passed the bottle back and forth. Supper turned out to be a thick bratwurst, mustard, sauerkraut, and new potatoes, enough for one. They picked at it together. It seemed they were birds of a feather, deriving nutrition from a bottle more often than a fork.

"Hargreaves used to favor the aesthetic," Arturo said. He made an odd gesture, indicating Hallow's frayed suit and sunken eye sockets. "Old Gothic, I mean."

"I did not know that. No, I am not a revitalist," Hallow replied.

"It's like pulling teeth with you," Arturo whinged. "Mate, I'm stuck in this room while my belly knits together. The surgeon is afraid I'll spill my guts overboard at the slightest tilt. It would help if you could engage in some conversation."

"If you wished it, I am sure you could sneak out. Inspector Hargreaves often spoke of your resourcefulness."

"You speak with her much?" Arturo felt a sudden pang of jealousy, well buried beneath layers of dense snark. He often wished he could have an honest conversation with the woman behind the detective, but their relationship was built on sniping at each other. It kept them sharp. Still, just once he wished it were otherwise.

"We talk of relevant things," Hallow said. He took out a thick, bound notebook, and began to leaf through, making a mark here and there with a draftsman's pencil. They seemed to be schematics for one of their many automata, though of course they had been unable to bring the other members of M.A.D. along. If Hargreaves was hanged for a traitor, M.A.D. would dissolve.

By and by, Cezette Louissaint and Cid Tanner returned to the room, separately. Cezette had had a grand time in the ship's well-stocked library, a Neo-Victorian affair built to accommodate an onboard horticultural greenhouse. She delighted in sharing it with Arturo. One could select a volume from the secured aeronautical shelves and descend a whirling wrought iron stair to recline beneath the lemon and orange trees. There was even a tea service provided, in a pleasing simulacrum of an English countryside manor. The shelves were taller than the girl, occupying the walls of two decks in the massive, glittering space. Natural light fed herb gardens and flower gardens, as well as some small berry bushes. Cezette, naturally, had chosen to read *The Secret Garden; I, Automaton;* and *Frankenstein.*

Cid Tanner, on the other hand, had discovered the engine room. The instant he entered, the suite was mired in the scent of grease and fume.

"My dear Mr. Tanner, I hardly think you are in appropriate decorum! I am a very sick man!" Arturo mounted a protest, waving one dandy hand before him.

"Injured, not sick," Cid answered gruffly. "Aeon steam is good for healing, didn't you know? 'Course, you'd have to want to be healed first."

"I do not believe in that hocus," Arturo said, sidestepping the sally. He was rather enjoying playing the invalid, what with the gruff Cid to tease and the pretty Cezette fawning over his wounds in the evenings. Besides, he meant it; he did not believe those invaluable aeon stones were good for anything other than moving ships across the sky. The idea of an inanimate object possessing any understanding of a brilliant mind like Arturo's and reacting, indeed drawing power from those thoughts, was ludicrous.

"The hocus is holding you up," Cid remarked. "I took a look at their engine configuration. Eighty-eight aeon bolts inserted into eight reactor chambers; very bold design. It's not as good as pirated lift, but it's close."

Arturo gave him his patented dead-eyed stare, but Hallow seemed to take an interest. Soon the two were deep in conversation.

"It is hard to follow the thinking of experts, *non?*" Cezette remarked. "Look what I found in the library! Shall I read it to you?"

She held a copy of *A Crease In The Firmament*, a fairly recent release. As usual, the first editions had been made available early for dirigible firms. It was bound in sturdy shipboard leather, waterproofed.

"By all means, my dear," Arturo said without a trace of sass.

The light was fading from the porthole outside, so the girl turned up the arc lamp by Arturo's head. Cezette opened the latch of the book and began to read in her lilting, youthful voice. She read in a profoundly French way, lingering on the details and coloring the words somehow with the scent of *framboises* and the sound of the Seine. As she read, her raven locks came loose from her barrette, and she kept tucking them behind her ear or nibbling at them when she fussed over a word. Arturo was more than happy to provide, having a veritable lexicon tucked between his own ears. Cezette made him feel like a tutor, at times, or an older brother, not that he knew what it was like. As she read, Arturo fingered the sheaf of stolen documents, letting his unconscious mind have a go at the problem.

"Tesseract, what is this word?"Cezette finally paused to ask. She had trouble even saying it, the succession of slithering sounds thickening into her nasal vowels.

"If I guess right, the author is about to explain for you. It is by no means a common word in English usage, but one frequented by our academicians and physical scientists."

Cezette continued to read aloud, obediently.

"Ah, I see! It is like when Maman tucks in my skirts." Cezette demonstrated. "I pass the thread through here, and fold the cloth to join the other side. That is how they travel quicker than going on a straight line, by folding space. "

"Has she had to do it for you often?"

"Maman only has her own clothes in the closet, and she is much taller and wider than me. The legs tear when they catch," Cezette said. "But you know how. You have a pattern yourself."

"Pardon?"

"This, this is a pattern for clothes! The lines here, and here."

Cezette snatched up the sheaf of papers and attempted to show Arturo what she meant, lining up the dots and dashes on the paper. After several attempts, she gave up.

"*Quel dommage*," Cezette said, shrugging. She was about to return to the book when Arturo sat up, straight as a rule.

"Louissaint, you are a genius!" Arturo cried. He grasped the sheaf of papers, shuffling them around, then folding them along the creases, first one way, then another. "Why are these creases so worn? Why so much fiddling and tearing, for a simple message?"

Hallow and Cid had ceased their earlier conversation, and were now watching intently. In a moment, Arturo had discovered the pattern, after much folding, cursing, and unfolding. His fingers worked deftly, but carefully, at the delicate paper.

"What is it?" Cezette asked, tilting her head. Her fingers twitched round the thick book, and her legs made agitated clicking noises, as if she was curling her toes. Arturo thought of aeons, and how they were supposed to react to feelings, but it was too distracting at a critical moment.

Arturo produced three different folded sculptures, a monkey, a dog, and a peacock. On each one there was a bit of message, which he laboriously copied out. Soon Arturo had the complete message writ on a piece of the suite's notepaper:

The Detective knows -I

"That's not much to go on," Hallow said, musing on the few words. "Maybe you missed a piece."

"It's an order," Arturo said. "It's short, implying there is a clear objective already in place. The missive is only an update. We know they intend to recover the box. I am more interested in the signature."

"The 'I' could be an initial," Cid Tanner said, joining in.

"Then why one letter? Why not first and last name?" Arturo said.

"More likely an alias, or an organization," Hallow agreed. "I've seen such in the Ministry's secret records. British Intelligence, perhaps?"

"Or...." Arturo mused, but it was too nebulous an idea. What proof was there of that conspiracy's involvement? The men were of various origins, true, and the weapon pulled from his gut was worn from exposure, pitted with salt.

"Spit it out, lad," Cid grunted.

"When I'm sure, perhaps," Arturo said. "For now, let us enjoy the luxuries at hand. I may be able to join you in your library soon, dear girl. Jean Hallow, would you like to come?"

"And what am I, chopped liver?" Cid said.

"You are of course welcome, if you can tear yourself from your nuts and bolts," Arturo added.

"Not going to happen. Mr. Tanner loves them like his own children!" Cezette agreed.

"Harrumph," was Cid's only reply, but he knelt to inspect the girl's legs nonetheless.

INTERLUDE III
A CITY OF TWO WORLDS

The rattle of a chain link fence could be heard winding its way around the alleys for blocks around, though the men guarding it were deafened by their raucous lifestyle and would never hear it.

"Big Brother, did you see? Someone got past the knuckle-draggers."

"Shh. Do you hear it? It could be the police."

"They tore up Tommy Gint pretty bad last week. He was gasping. He couldn't breathe."

"Shhh! I think it's something worse."

The four corners of their alley were bathed in shadow, ominous. After a while a glaring of cats swept through the garbage pails, a sinuous tortoise-and-tabby wave that toppled boxes and tins.

"Just cats," said Little Brother.

"Wait."

And of course, Big Brother was right. A minute or two passed before what spooked the cats emerged from the shadows. The first time the boys had seen one, they were taking a shortcut across a roof, which had likely saved them.

Strangled screams and the shadows playing on the walls were more than enough to keep the brothers from climbing down. They were always too quiet for the police to hear, but Tommy Gint had always said it wasn't that the police couldn't, but that they wouldn't. At best there was a shadow of thinness, nothing substantial, before it retreated into the darkness. The only warning before it got you was a strange clicking, like mandibles coming together.

Big thought they were hole people, vagrants living in the sewers who sometimes emerged to scavenge food or abduct wives. Little, whose hearing hadn't been ruined by begging near the tracks day after day, thought it must be something more. They took men and women both, and had far too many legs. Little knew the amorphous thing in the darkness was what the teachers spoke of when they warned against talking to strangers, a ridiculous notion only the privileged would think was actual advice. Whatever lay in that alley was a living embodiment of Strange. What they knew for sure was this: if it got you, you were never seen again.

After a while the thing left, and took the terrible oppressive atmosphere with it. It was pitch-dark outside the corona cast by the streetlamps. By and by the lions and bears started to return, those regular predators of the night. They used the alley below the brothers like a marketplace, goods and services exchanged in wax paper packets or hushed moans in the night. Some of the people looked rich. Others looked poor, or very sick. Big told Little not to look at them, and Little never questioned his brother until he saw Big down there one night.

Big didn't want Little to know, but Little knew. He saw the tiny glass knobs being passed around, the garnet-red fluid inside turning the bulbs into Christmas ornaments. Sometimes people used right in the alley. It looked like they were having a good time.

Little relaxed, hunched against the wet pasteboard of their house. An accident of architecture had left the brothers this nook, too precarious for an adult but a perfect place to hide two gangly, malnourished boys. They had pushed aside the tin sheeting to find a perfect shelter between two buildings. There was a fire escape ladder on one end and the alley on the other, and they even had a pantry.

Little kept looking at the winking lights through the gap in the tin sheet until Big swatted him. They swam over the spot where the cabaret stood, like fairies over Pleasure Island.

"That place is owned by Stanley Burgess," said Big Brother. He spat the taste of the name from his mouth. "We can't be too careful."

"If you took a job from his men once in a while, we could bribe one of them to let me peek. Or you could let me take one. I'm small enough to run one of their sneak jobs."

"You staying in school is the only way we're ever leaving this place. You're so obsessed with that gingerbread whorehouse! Burgess is a gangster, Little. Everybody he touches ends up dead. Remember Mother?"

"It's cabaret, Big Brother. Not a whorehouse." But Little felt the sting.

"Like you would know what those are," scoffed Big, but it wasn't clear which establishment he meant.

Little didn't like to talk of Mother if he could help it. She'd gone to work in the Cabaret when Little was very young, and never came back out. In his heart of hearts, in a place even Little wouldn't admit to himself existed, he still believed she waited just behind those gilt, blacked-out doors.

When Little went to school Big spent his days begging and running small errands to keep them afloat. It was this or go back to the Gellers, and Big had left Mr. Geller's nose too broken to ever go back.

"I know what whorehouses are. I saw you sneak into the one on Twelfth and Avenue B. What's so good about Beth Brannagan? I bet the cabaret dancers don't wobble when they walk."

It was the wrong thing to say, and Big's calloused hands were hard where they fell. Little clutched at his head, drawing up his knees with their thicker rags to protect himself. Despite that, they were still only a brother's fists, and not the sledgehammers of a day in the yards with a bottle of whiskey behind them.

As he cowered, taking the punishment and feeling his brother's frustration with every blow, Little wondered if Big didn't share some of his sentiments. Big hadn't complained when they found a place with a view of the cabaret. Maybe he missed Mother just as much as Little did. Probably more.

After a while the beating gave way to a bout of sulking, and then

Big pushed over a pastrami sandwich. Lord, it didn't even have trash stains on it.

"Did you…?"

"I did the deli man in the Lower East a favor," said Big quickly. "I didn't steal it."

And night wore on, a thick velum crinkling with trucks going by, the klaxon of squad cars, people fucking. Sounds of commerce.

***

The next time the brothers came across a Stranger, it was on the run from a group of boys in Alphabet City.

Burgess had mysteriously shut the doors to his cabaret. The field had suddenly gone fallow in the Bowery, the fat calves of rich burlesque goers suddenly without a place to indulge their debauchery. Rumor had it he had left the city, having been seen in the airship port at Chelsea. Either way, his thugs scattered and the streets were suddenly full of walkers, backup dancers who hadn't been snapped up by other clubs. The boys had to range farther, aiming to tug at the heartstrings of the families not two streets away, only to find rival whelps vying for the dry teat of the proletariat. They'd run the brothers down with stones and boards and broken shards of glass.

Sprinting full-tilt across sidewalks only to detour into unknown alleys, avoiding the NYPD airships scouring the tall reaches of townhouses, Alphabet City was a maze. Avenue A, Avenue B. The clearly labeled streets should have been easy to run but the letters appeared again and again, like a badly spelled word. Big and Little found themselves beating their shoes ragged. Little's left was already gaping like a broken jaw. Closed shops and boarded-up brownstones flew past them. Avenue A, Avenue B.

In spite of that, Big's pace never faltered, urging them on with curses and wheezing gasps. By the time the brothers lost the gang they had already plunged headlong into the Stranger lurking in the community garden

It was a small space, watered by a tiny clankety-clank boiler in the corner whining away like a tiny copper gargoyle. Walled in between two sheer brick bluffs, the sound very nearly masked the clicking of the Stranger's legs, so soft were they among the only hydrangeas for blocks around. In the darkness, they were a stark picture-house black and white.

Little turned to scale the fence when Big grabbed his shoulder.

"No," mouthed Big, and his eyes were enormous.

Little froze, gathering all his prodigious street urchin senses on the fence, and his heart stopped cold in his chest. The walls all around them had fooled their ears—the Stranger had been behind them all along, hiding in the shadows of a large tree just under the chain links.

The state of the place should have been a warning. By day, it must have been well tended by the local families, a place of rest for perambulatory mothers or weary teachers. Its stone arches were too strong to have been placed. More likely they were remnants of a grand mansion that had once stood in this lot, and some community group or beleaguered urban parent had turned the fallow earth into a paradise. If it were a normal garden the place would have been torn apart by territorial boys long ago, its herbs uprooted, sprouts trodden upon and littered with cigarro butts. The very cleanliness of the walls made it apparent there was something else here, something that kept the evening primroses pristine until morning—like a hunter's trail in the forest.

Past sundown, those same columns and restful lees sprung infested shadows. A stairway to heaven cast a long dagger of night, hanging over the path like a deadfall. The boys had climbed a fence and gone a few steps into the place, but the incessant clicking now barred their way back. Big tentatively inched a step, dislodging a small piece of gravel, and the shadows convulsed in scrabbling silhouettes.

"Big… I'm scared," mouthed Little.

"Me too," mouthed Big. He slowly gestured to the middle of the garden, where a tiny wooden shack had been built. Various tools were piled on a bench in front of it, and there was a large padlock, but the upper level was accessible by a brick stair, probably part of the older building. There was a wooden door at the top, open an inch. It looked thick.

"On three," said Big, without a sound. He put up three fingers, scarcely visible in the shadows of the buildings. "One… two…."

"They have to be here somewhere! Climb the fence and get

them!"

The loud, ragged voice tearing through the neighborhood quiet was jagged, familiar. Big and Little froze, their feet in the air.

"But, boss, that's the Arboretum—"

"I don't give a shit. You get in that tree farm and find them!"

And the chain link fence began to rattle, the clicking grew more intense. Little knew they had maybe one chance to get up the stair. One look at his brother and he knew they had the same idea.

"Go, Little, go!" Big hissed, and bolted.

Little churned his legs, following his brother across the shifting loam, the yelling of the boys behind them surging, playing right into their hands. For a sick moment the gang sounded like they almost upon them, propelled by something not quite right. One of them, the leader, had had his arms pricked by a dozen red marks.

But there were darker things at the bottom of that garden than even the cruelty of boys.

It wasn't long after they reached the top of the building that the gurgled sounds of sharp arms around thin necks chased them into the small room. Big slammed the door against them, sealing them inside. Too late did the brothers look, at the wide benches and large windows, realizing this scenic post overlooking the garden was no protection at all but a breezy deathtrap.

"Little, no!" cried Big, but Little was already leaning out of the window, straining to catch a glimpse of the thing wringing the life from the gang below in bloodcurdling screams. Perhaps it hadn't reckoned on dealing with several at once, but the violence was anything but quiet.

"Get it!"

"Christ, it's as hard as a rock!"

Sounds of clanging and the dull thuds of flesh hitting brick drifted upward, into the room where Big and Little pressed themselves invisible against the door. Strangely, the windows in the cliffs above stayed dark, even though the din could have woken the dead. Little could just see the scene below, as if he himself were safe in a tower. The Stranger with its many arms, strangling with limbs writhing like darkness given flesh. The fence offered no easy way out. Any climber would expose his backside to the shadows, an easy target.

"Oh, God, it's got Takeem!"

"Fucker!"

There was a particularly high scream then, and the moist wind in the room was suddenly brazen with the taste of blood. There was a new sound now, the rushed footsteps and vegetal rustle of fleeing boys, and then the door was rocking on its hinges, somebody banging loudly.

"Let me in! Let me in! I saw you go in there, you little—oh, oh God, no, aughh!"

Big had hardly turned around when the door ruptured, sprouting a protrusion nearly three feet long. The end of it nicked Big in the shoulder, and he screamed. Little nearly retched when he saw the color of it in the moonlight: a bright, fresh crimson, wet like new paint.

"Run, go!" Big howled in pain. "The fire escape!"

Little turned instinctively, lunging out of the window even though he had little idea what Big was talking about. He tumbled through the air, coming up against something hard and crumbly. Big landed on top of him a moment later, pulling him to his feet over the outcropping of bricks that had been left jutting out of the adjacent building. As they ran, they brushed past some of the flowers planted there. The smell of lilacs got muddled with the blood, until Little figured people bled candy violets. They could hear the Stranger behind them, tearing apart the little viewing room over the garden.

At the end of the outcropping, a thick iron ladder hung over the bare brick. With a mighty leap, Big grabbed hold of the bottom rung, jerking his whole weight on his good arm until the ladder came down with a clang. Little found himself bundled up the fire escape, followed by Big with a loose brick. The brick seemed surreal, ill-fit to Little's suddenly one-track world. The night was dark, and though they could see a vague shape following them, there was nothing solid for his eyes to latch on to. That above all was the most disconcerting, as if they were being stalked by a ghost. Big smashed the glass in the closest window with the brick.

"Come on!"

"That's somebody's house!"

But when Little tumbled through the broken window, the apartment was empty and naked. He caught a glimpse of pale white walls, vanilla fixtures like photograms in a brochure, waiting for someone to come nest in it. Splintering the front door on their way out, not a soul emerged to stop them and Little wondered how this beautiful place could stand empty while he and Big huddled for warmth in the alleys below.

The Stranger's crashing could be heard not five paces behind, heavy steps tinkling with glass. They plunged down the deserted hallway, Big dribbling blood on the cream carpet. The hallway was lit, though the gas lamps flickered with the shuddering steps of the Stranger, threatening to gutter out. The floors and walls shook, as if the world was crumpling under heavy fists.

"The light, it won't come near the light," said Little, his voice a strained wheeze.

"Bullshit," said Big, crumpling against the lift's big brassy buttons. Cables run through smooth pulleys whirred thickly, and something moved behind the lift's mesh doors. Cables, pulleys, machinations in the black. Big's shoulder was a red mess, seemingly held together by his tightly clenched hand. His eyes fluttered in a disconcerting staccato.

"Christ, look at you!" said Little. He reached up to help, but the matted gore plastered at the hand shook him, froze him in place.

"Look at yourself," said Big. "Can't even stand up straight. You're shaking like a leaf."

Little hadn't realized just how terrified he was, and now that he had fallen, he found he could not get back up. His legs wobbled, limp noodles.

"Big…." he managed.

"You little shit. Ever since you fell out of Momma I been looking after you," said Big, somewhat bitterly. "Can't you get yourself back on your feet? Useless lump. I oughta trade you to Burgess, see if I can't get her back."

"Big, what? What are you saying?" Little was too scared to feel properly angry, but the fire at his throat loosened up his legs. He felt around for the wall, to haul himself back up, but his hand flailed around in open space. The lift! It was here.

"That's it. That's the stuff. I love you, Little Brother," said Big, and shoved him the rest of the way inside.

"Big! No, Big!"

Little whirled around as he tried to find his balance, and also to strike the round copper button that would hold open the door for his brother. But his fingers fell on no button, only a solid lever that shut the mesh doors on Big's slumped form. That was when the hallway lamps guttered out.

Little threw himself forward then, leaning on the lift's lever, the thing that looked like a steamer's bell command throttle (they'd gone to one, with one of the foster families, hadn't they? And they'd gotten lost, deep in the warrens of the steam boat's innards, hoping to sail away to Neverland or really anywhere else. And they'd found the round throttle lever and tried to make the ship go, only there were no men below decks to answer their call) to go down, down. Bricks fleeing upward, like sea birds.

Little sobbed as he listened to the sound of the lift dropping, a muffled whirring that couldn't shut out the din from above. Doors were no obstacle, it seemed, and the sound of the mesh tearing nearly made Little forget to stop the elevator. The thing jerked, throwing him off balance. Stupid, stupid, he hadn't slowed it down first.

But he got the door open, and was halfway out of it when the ceiling collapsed, in a great roundel of punched-out wood and greasy, dusty machinery. Little felt something long and sharp touch his ankle, feather-light. He tread blood, slick and warm.

An elderly doorman stood in the lobby, and Little reached out to him, watching the man's snowy brow wrinkle at the crying, bloody boy trying to squeeze out from between the lift doors. Then the man was there, grabbing at Little's arms, his pink, papery skin rippling against Little's. The crisp white uniform was rough with starch, probably the cleanest thing Little had touched in weeks. Little's foot came free with a pop, dumping them both on the floor.

"What the...? Damn elevator spewing out negroes now? Boy, are you all right? What in tarnation was that?"

"Mister, you gotta run. Run!"

Adults hardly ever listen to little black boys, but this one did, dragging him to his feet by main force. He pointed towards the front door, the vast, interminable lobby glinting in expensive lamplight. Who was it all for? Nobody *lived* here. The gilt, the live plants drinking up water in their pots. The sofas propped against the walls, untouched and spotless, lonely. There had been nobody in the rooms above to come through this place. Little felt the waste of it keenly, even through sputtering tears. The everlasting lamps in the lobby were sputtering, as if thirsty for gas. Impossible, in all this opulence, how could they?

It took an eternity to cross the lobby, and all the while the mesh of the door was buckling, shearing aside under the force of something dreadful.

There was a telegraph booth near the door, and the doorman ducked inside, waving for Little to go, just go. But the door was heavy, and wouldn't move. Little could see him tapping madly at the graph's points, sending a message for help out over the wire.

He stood there, agape. Where could he go? The door was a thick double panel of gilded sunbursts meant to keep the rabble out of the tower of wealth. There was a window in it, too high to climb, but Little could look out. There was a wide court, a winding drive outside, and blessed be, an actual street. Frosted blocks bricked in the door on either side.

He toyed with the idea of dashing back across the lobby, grabbing one of the heavy cordon pylons and smashing away the blocks, but the thing inside the elevator shaft was shredding away at the wall behind there. It was only a matter of time before it was out, and what if Little was standing close enough for it to grab? The lamps flickered, going out one by one.

Little's fingers scrabbled madly, feeling for a latch, a keyhole, something to force the door open. Big would have known how to pick the lock. The other side of the lobby was wreathed in darkness now, the lamps gone, the only light from the streetlamps outside. Terrible rumbling rippled its way through the room. Realization hit Little like a sack of bricks; the doorman had the key.

Telegraph cables ripped from the wall without a spark, their wires dead, inoperable. The doorman had slammed the telegraph point to the floor. Fear was palpable on the old man's face, but as he stepped forward to open the sunburst door, the last lamp went out.

The Stranger was upon them now, or near as made no difference. Darkness swallowed the booth and the lobby transformed, backlit by the glaring street. Strange shapes lay pregnant in the shadows. The doorman disappeared in a blur, one minute staring wide-eyed into the blackness, the next second taken with a short whoosh of the air being knocked out of his lungs.

Little stood with his back pressed against the glass, feeling desperately for the handle, for a knob, anything to let himself out. He barely registered the clattering of a ring of keys, dropped as the doorman was taken. The darkness was a living thing, shifting with the dust and the rubble that had come from the ruined elevator. He could feel it there, a presence moving just behind the veil of the world. Somehow it made him think of whales, like the ones he'd seen when his class went to the museum. Of sitting at the bottom of the ocean looking at an imperceptible titan, shifting, sending waves of silt and disturbed creatures across the sea floor just by flicking its tail. Something totally indifferent to a small, black boy on the bottom, being tossed about by their currents. Small wonder it hadn't taken him yet. He was a minnow, too small to register on the Stranger's eldritch senses. Were they bulbous eyes perched on stalks? Ears, perhaps, like a cat's? Or the even more terrible, long antennae flicking through the blinds, tasting for his skin?

The darkness shifted.

Quite impossibly, a familiar shape began to form in the darkness, wisps of dust coalescing, like white ink on a black page. A rounded dome of a forehead shone in the street light, a jutting jaw full of defiance.

Little gasped.

He could scarcely forget his brother's face.

Little had seen it every day since Father left. He nearly rushed out to it, to punch Big in the arm for scaring him. It wasn't until he'd taken half a step did he realize Big was far too tall, and his neck far too narrow and stunted.

The Stranger had Big's head held high in one claw.

Little screamed. He screamed so hard, his limbs lost feeling. Then again, it might have been from the desperate strikes against the sunburst door. He punched and kicked at it, blows hard enough to draw blood and dent steel, crack the glass portals that so cruelly looked on freedom. Given time he might even have breached the inch or two of art deco, polished to a high shine that was the difference between vile, murderous darkness and the living realms of the light.

And then it had him, pulling him back through the building, chafing against the rich carpeting. Not up, but down, down, into the basement. The stairs hurt as it dragged him against them. Little caught sight of Big's and the doorman's bodies being carried high up on the creature's back. More pain came, a cruel cleft in the shin from a hard, cold thing covered in a film of filth. He caught a glimpse of brick and grating. Something pierced his eyelid, a loose nail perhaps.

Then there was nothing then but the pain, and the eternal night, the darkness painted on his skin waiting all of Little's short life to eat him alive.

8

THERE AREN'T ANY TURTLES

Vanessa Hargreaves considered the New York Pneumatic Subway System a fair representation of Hell. Still, she was determined to give a good show of following Rosa Marija into the steaming maw of a station not far from the Cabaret.

"I say!" Hargreaves protested as a knot of people peppered her with sharp elbows and hard, unidentifiable baggage.

"Damn tourist," one elderly woman muttered, before muscling her way past Hargreaves and onto the train.

The platform was crowded, and much too hot. Though the subway arrived with a rush of air from the massive fans propelling the cars, the wind was stale and wet, stinking from the rotting seepage at the bottom of the tracks. Rosa Marija had gleefully informed her the men who built the tunnels, and the buildings above, had often been buried in the concrete of the walls. Hargreaves wrinkled her nose at the idea the scent infusing her nostrils was the decades-old rank of death.

"Why exactly are we here, Rosa? Where is Captain Clemens?" Hargreaves asked after the fourth train passed them by.

In London, the underground was no less crowded, but everything was orderly and the people were polite. In New York, everyone seemed to go wherever they pleased, crowding the doors and jostling into one another instead of establishing clear lanes of traffic. Even the trains arrived with the same sort of idle nonchalance, seeming to adhere to no schedule Hargreaves could see. There weren't even clocks hanging from the arched, grubby ceilings, once beautifully appointed with mosaics like stained glass. It seemed to her the entire city needed a lesson in how to queue.

"So eager to see Alby again, Inspector?" Rosa quipped with a smile. She seemed to have a magical knack for being out of the passengers' way. Hargreaves attributed it to the shocking amount of calf Rosa had on display under her black trench. The muscles stood out, raised by a pair of heels with red undersides.

"If you must know, it will be a pleasure," Hargreaves replied. "Did you know the queen wished to knight Clemens?"

"He would rather be hanged," Rosa said, shuddering.

"Do not worry. The captain is a valiant... whatever he is, but I assure you, the impulse was only momentary."

Rosa looked over to Hargreaves and sighed. From somewhere in her voluminous coat, she extracted a pair of boots no less extravagant, but to Hargreaves' experienced eye much less uncomfortable. Rosa tucked away the heels and put on the boots, reaching behind her to tuck in her ankles. It was awkward, like a bird, but there was no façade of drama to it. Hargreaves grinned, feeling at last like she was with the Rosa Marija she had come to know.

"It's about time," Rosa Marija said then, mostly to a large pocket-watch.

The platform was still full of passengers, but the trains were slackening, coming at longer intervals. Rosa turned on her boots and walked straight down the platform, with Hargreaves hot on her heels.

"Won't somebody notice?" Hargreaves asked as Rosa marched off the platform and down some steps, vaulting over a short gate and into the darkness of the tunnel.

"Look around. Does it seem like anybody is paying attention?"

Rosa was right. The New Yorkers around Hargreaves seemed to be absorbed in their own little worlds, bumping past one another with their noses buried in penny dreadfuls. A few more affluent seemed to be engaged in some kind of clockwork diversion, puzzle boxes or games.

Vanessa Hargreaves and Rosa Marija picked their way along a workman's platform running parallel to the tracks. The path was narrow, with nooks in the walls every few feet for a worker to hide when a train passed. Arclights lit the passage dimly. They did not have to walk far. In one of the nooks, Rosa Marija opened a door, and they passed through into an even narrower crawlspace. A ladder led down into the depths below the tracks.

Hargreaves could not fathom why they had waited at all—surely they could have ventured into the tunnel just after a train passed. Rosa Marija climbed out of the crawlspace, and when Vanessa followed, she saw the reason why. The chamber they were in was some sort of drainage or overflow room. Large, toothed gears brooded like sentinels directly in front of Hargreaves, biting into chains as thick as her thighs.

Hargreaves was a Londoner, and so she knew at a glance the vast slabs between each gear were floodgates. More importantly, the high-water mark began somewhere in the middle of the chamber. If they had come a little earlier, the stairs before them would have ended in a flat sheet of water.

Rosa Marija led the way down slippery steel steps. At the bottom of the chamber, two feet of water remained coursing through into storm drains as big as Burgess' amphitheater. A flat little boat sat waiting.

"Most of the city is built on swampland. It's filled in now, but the estuary flows back and forth depending on the tide. These floodgates help move the water from places where it's not supposed to be," Rosa Marija explained.

The two piled into the boat, and Rosa Marija kicked at a contraption at the bottom. With a little hiss, bubbles began to emerge from the back of the boat, and they began to move forward.

"We have to lean. The rudder is broken."

Feeling a little foolish, Hargreaves took Rosa's lead, leaning where the long-legged helmswoman indicated. The little boat tipped alarmingly, but no water seeped over the edge. Instead, they veered marginally, enough to reach the storm drain in the middle. Crisp packets, sweets wrappers and other rubbish floated on the surface of the water. The little boat drifted through a rip in a fine mesh grate leading into a pipe. The pair coursed down the drain, leaning to follow the gentle bend. After about five minutes they emerged into a large chamber dimly lit by a string of arc lights along the walls.

"Here we are," Rosa said.

"Where exactly?" Hargreaves whinged. She was tired of the wet, hot smell of the place, tired of the feeling of damp clinginess.

"Have you forgotten who we are? We are pirates. Air pirates." Hargreaves snorted, but she looked up anyway. Hanging in the air above her was the rounded bulk of the *Huckleberry*, anchored in place to the high ceiling.

***

"What did you expect us to do, tie up on the Wonder Wheel in Coney Island and hang a sign advertising rides in a real-life pirate ship?" Clemens said to Hargreaves later, in the warmth of Auntie's galley. The pirate captain was draped over a paisley armchair Hargreaves didn't remember.

In fact, the entire galley seemed very different. The nailed-down benches had disappeared, replaced by squashy sofas and tea tables. Rosa perched atop the back of the chair, her bare legs dangling into Clemens' lap. The couple was apparently oblivious to how sickeningly domestic they seemed, or simply did not care. Hargreaves could feel the cavities starting to form in her wisdom teeth. But Hargreaves also recognized the nicks in the wood from food fights and Rosa's knives, and the portholes she had looked pensively out of when it seemed the world might end. Being back was a teatime for the soul.

"You had to sneak by the American blockade ships and find a way to come into the city. How did you do it?" Hargreaves, feeling a touch awkward, yielded to the old standby—common ground.

"A magician never reveals—"

"He snuck between two freighter seafarers being tugged into the harbor. We almost didn't find this little bolt hole, but when the tide is right, it's impregnable," Rosa filled in.

"It means you cannot leave, either, when the tide is high," Hargreaves pointed out. "Still, as a hideout, it's not rubbish. Well done."

"Thank you," Clemens said pointedly. Rosa stuck a finger in the corner of his mouth and pulled gently. "Tho what bringth you here, Hargreavthe?"

"It's a long, embarrassing story," Hargreaves began.

"Our favorite," said Auntie, who seemed to appear out of the woodwork. In a corner, Elric Blair waved, to show there was ample company to laugh at Hargreaves. She threw up two fingers in her fellow Englishman's direction. *Jog on!* But it was with a grin.

"Auntie, you know how our inspector takes to teasing," said Rosa. "Vanessa is easy. No point in it."

"That's Inspector—" But Hargreaves trailed off, realizing she was about to prove Rosa right. This sodding crew! She looked to the captain, but Albion was simply waiting patiently. His indifferent presence was familiar and calming.

Something about the room's warmth, being in the *Berry* again, reminded her of the basic nature of these pirates. Sordid thieves, surely, but they had never lacked decency. She told Albion Clemens everything, how she had investigated an automata theft from a moving train, of uncovering the Crown's plot. Her face did not betray her feelings of failure at letting the Orb Weaver kill Feerick, her most important lead, but she allowed her gratitude to show when she spoke of her subsequent escape from London.

Arturo and M.A.D. had been instrumental in securing Cook's hermetically sealed coffin and one Scotland Yard patrol automata, at a cost she still did not fathom. She had not dared to wire to her friends. God, what had become of Cezette Louissaint? What of Cid?

As she spoke, Auntie prepared tea, a perfectly steeped Darjeeling with little thumbprint jam biscuits. It quite took Hargreaves' breath away, and almost made the sewer sojourn worth it.

"In other words, you're a crook, a brigand, on the lam from the law," Clemens summarized. "If caught, you'd be as hanged as the rest of us. Finally decided to join the crew?"

"Captain, I believe you missed the point. Inspector Hargreaves is defying the Pax Britannia to serve the Pax Britannia, isn't that right?" Seated quietly, Elric Blair spoke up from a pub-height table in the corner. As usual, the diminutive man was never without his notebook, but his hair was completely black now, tied back with a thong. His clothes were taut, his pose relaxed, and there seemed to be tight muscle under his one-piece boiler suit. He was wearing a large utility belt jammed with pens, but also strangely, some long wrenches and hammers.

"It's good to see you again, Elric. You're looking... well," Hargreaves replied. Actually, she was having trouble looking into his blue eyes. She'd thought to snap him up herself, in her idle moments. "Yes, you have the right of it. If the British Empire is to use weapons such as this, it will be no victory at all. We will have cut off our nose to spite our face. I must find a way to dispose of this weapon, and to find the perpetrators responsible for attempting to steal it."

"Hum," Albion muttered through a mouthful of biscuit.

For a moment, Hargreaves honestly believed the Manchu Marauder had forgotten their months-long adventure, fighting Mordemere, falling through the sky and looking up at the Laputian Leviathan's blighted promise above them. Of the brief moments of masochistic flirtation, the forbidden fruits, and their deal with each other. Of laughing drunkenly together as the world came apart around them, and their impossible quest to put it right again.

"Oh come off it. You're going to help the girl," Auntie spoke up. As always, she was the voice of reason. "It's just a matter of price."

"You didn't have to be so blunt about it," Albion griped good-naturedly. "I was just wondering how to ask... it seems like she's a little attached to it."

"Attached to what?" said Hargreaves.

"Maybe it will be easier if we show her first," Rosa filled in. She bounced off the armchair and onto the thick pile carpet. "It's always easier to bargain when both sides show their hands."

"Good idea," Albion said, and suddenly Hargreaves found herself being trundled off down the hall, teacup in hand, pinky out.

"Unhand me, you ruffian! Oh, not you too!" Hargreaves wailed. The two air pirates had her elbows in their firm grips, and were bundling her off down the corridor. Elric Blair followed, but Auntie stayed behind. Hargreaves' Darjeeling sloshed pitifully, threatening to spill.

"Hang on to that. You'll need the drink," advised Albion.

It was not long before the inspector remembered the layout of the ship. Not much had changed. Odd trinkets and baubles still hung from pipes overhead, but they seemed more subdued, more feminine somehow. She noted a fluffy unicorn, a dancer with fairy's wings, and a kris dagger in miniature, perhaps one half of a set of earrings. As she passed the crew's quarters, she noticed the captain's door was open, and Albion's chipped cutlass lay over a large chair.

The perilous pair released Hargreaves once they reached the cargo deck, a space she remembered as chaotic. There had been hoards of books and Cid's machinery piled in every corner. Now, the space was clean, the books in shelves, and the tools hung up neatly on one wall. Bright arclights lit a section of workspace.

"I'm not the sort of mechanic who remembers where everything is," Elric Blair said sheepishly as he walked over to a workbench. He placed a hand on it possessively. "I spend a lot of time filing. Still, Cid taught me loads before he buggered off to work for you, and he's been sending us spec telegrams for weeks."

"He's been in contact with you lot? Without my leave?" Hargreaves said shrilly.

"Why would he ask for it?" Albion said. It was true. Hargreaves had, for the most part, left Cid to his own devices. So long as he refrained from his criminal ways, she was content to let the old codger tinker and drink, and play the odd game of bridge with her every so often.

"The frame is actually a kobold. We relieved a crew of Welsh smugglers of it, before they could sell it to a Syrian contact. We have enough trouble with the Ottomans, without the Arabs having these kind of steamcrafts."

"We, Blair? Still loyal to Queen and Country?"

Blair gave her a sheepish grin. "Aye, ma'am," Blair said.

"Either you show me what you brought me here for or I'm going to find another air pirate in these Godforsaken sewers!" Hargreaves complained.

Rosa pulled a lever nearby. A row of arclights sparked into life overhead, revealing a hulk of machinery next to the workbench. Hargreaves' words nearly choked in her throat.

It was undoubtedly an automata, but it was like nothing Hargreaves had ever seen. All trace of kobold was gone from it, and where the scissor claws and bulbous driver's seat had been, there was only a smooth, enameled finish. Hargreaves could not help but draw a comparison. Where Alphonse was all lobstered steel, mail, and pauldrons, this sentinel was made of some light, hard metal, with joints covered in flexible canvas. A long black cloak draped around the shoulders, hiding much of the arms and hips. Grinning inanely, a jolly roger with a dragon skull had been stenciled on the chest plate, and the head had been sculpted to look like a brigandine hat. There was even an eye patch.

"Dragonwell is supposed to be intimidating," Rosa remarked, her brows shot through the roof.

"What's it for?" Hargreaves gaped. "I doubt many freighter captains field these. They would piss off into the ocean the first time a pirate dropped out of the sky in one of these."

"Come up and have a look, Inspector!" Like a child showing off his favorite toy, Albion clambered up a scaffold and into the automata's cockpit. Hargreaves, behaving as if out of professional interest, but really bursting to fiddle with all the toggles in the big machine, followed.

The driver's seat was very different from Hargreaves' own Alphonse, requiring a person not to recline, but lie astride much like on a velocipede. The position seemed unspeakably vulgar to Hargreaves, but then so was Captain Clemens.

"Remember the aeon crystal we destroyed? The one on Mordemere's bridge. A piece of it lodged itself into my shoulder, from the explosion. Cid's always been after an aeon stone pure enough to finish his engine design, but this... We seated the shard in this frame."

"We used it to move my nana's old wardrobe into the ship," Rosa remarked, having appeared on the opposite side of the driver's seat.

"Nana?" Hargreaves asked, but immediately regretted it. Rosa Marija was an orphan, and any nana was likely some unusual, possibly unsavory acquaintance.

Albion was still ranting, interspersed by supportive comments from Blair on the deck below.

"The hardest part was the moisture reclamation, to keep the machine watered. We ended up putting cold condensation on the shoulders. Even the coals only need topping off every so often. Cid mentioned it's an anthro-kinetic phenomenon, of how the aeon particles absorb energy from...."

"The boys will be awhile. Why don't we retire to the galley? You need tea," Rosa said placidly. Hargreaves simply stared. It was hard to reconcile the statement, and the way Rosa looked, with the seductress dancing in Burgess' club earlier that evening. Hargreaves realized she was still holding on to her teacup, and yes, it was ice-cold.

"Yes, yes, I believe we shall. So this is where Burgess' automata parts have gone."

"I did enjoy the work, gorgeous," Rosa reminded her, winking.

*****

"Tell me, what are Queen Victoria III's actual titles?" Albion asked.

Back in the galley, Albion's mechanical fascination finally spent itself, and he had wound down gradually. Hargreaves would have answered facetiously, but it sounded like he was actually about to enlighten her. She felt a bit like she was pulling clues from Arturo C. Adler.

"Alexandrina Victoria Edwardia III, Matriarch of the British Commonwealth, Queen of the Pax Brittania and Ireland, Empress of India, Bastion of the Lands Beyond—"

Albion Clemens seized on the word, never much for Socratic method. He was the most direct person Hargreaves knew, and that more than anything convinced Hargreaves he wanted her support on this, perhaps more than she needed the pirates.

"Bastion. What exactly does that mean?"

"Well, ruler, I suppose...." Hargreaves said.

"Actually, 'bastion' derives from a fortification extruding from a main castle or fort," Elric Blair corrected. "Or a heavily defended area of water."

"A point of no return," Albion said. "The last safe place before the wild."

"The style was invented by Admiral Walter Wilkins of the 587th Dirigible Fleet with the approval of Her Majesty by proxy, on the occasion of establishing Derby Point, the farthest known outpost in the Lands Beyond. Derby was, of course, the hometown of Wilkins. The fortification was later dismantled, but records say a Union Flag still stands somewhere in those coordinates."

"587... that's the fleet sent to explore the Lands Beyond, destroyed under mysterious circumstances," Hargreaves filled in.

"Victoria sacrificed twenty-nine airships to plant the flag there. She had to recognize the feat somehow. There are no queens or emperors in the Lands Beyond. I'll grant her, not a soul has been able to explore deeper. There's the shifting aeon rocks shooting through the air like gigantic bullets, and strange creatures living in the lagoons. Some airmen even swear there be dragons," Clemens said. "But if we could clear the way, with something as adaptable as the Lands themselves...."

"Hence the automata," Hargreaves said, the light dawning. "You want Alphonse. You want the newest M.A.D. automata to go gallivanting into the Beyond!"

"We call them gears, this side of the pond, but yes," Clemens agreed.

"But why?"

"Look around," said Albion, gesturing at the comfort all around him. "Do you think we are suited to a life of piracy any longer?"

"We want to explore," said Rosa. "See the world. Have a rock named after us, or something. Live happily, away from the dirt and chaos of the world."

Hargreaves suddenly felt this was the best possible thing the two could hope for from the future, and something fluttered helplessly in her chest. As usual, her way of coping focused on the logistics.

"Automata will be useless in the Lands," mused Hargreaves. "Every schoolchild has read of the horrors there. It takes a dirigible to fly high enough to even breach the storm walls, and few were ever made to weave through the floating maze. The *Berry* might be able to do it, but when it is too large to fly between the disastrous rocks?

Your anchors are too inaccurate to move them, and automata do not fly," Hargreaves said, and stopped to breathe. "Do they?"

The looks the pirates gave each other, like they had swallowed the canary, said it all. Still, it took the pragmatic Elric Blair to convince her.

"Every British schoolchild knows the dangers, yes. But the tales were spun in part to make Her Majesty's feat seem greater. I have read the accounts. It can be done," Blair insisted.

Hargreaves stared at each of her friends in turn. Whom was she trying to fool? They had saved the world together, had gone through hell together. Hargreaves had even seen each of them naked: Albion, coming out of the bath, Rosa, on purpose and then recently, and Blair, who had torn off all his clothes seconds after they had been rescued from the *Nidhogg*, screaming about dead things seeping into his skin. Hargreaves wanted a vicarious measure of happiness for them, especially since she was hopelessly tethered to this world.

"Show me."

***

Dragonwell took off like an airship, straight up off the deck. Hargreaves expected it to be louder, but the quiet whine of Cid's aeon engine could have been mistaken for a black-breasted tit. It chirped for a few seconds, and then the clunky feet of the automata were suddenly an inch off the cargo hold floor.

"I'll be damned," Hargreaves breathed, before the rush of air nearly knocked her over. Like it was shot out of a cannon, Dragonwell flew across the deck and out through a hatch.

"Go on up to the bridge. We'll show you how we can help," Elric Blair said.

"You're not coming?" Hargreaves asked.

"Don't look so forlorn. I'll be up shortly," Blair said.

"Careful, you're turning into a bit of a rake," Hargreaves cautioned, in jest.

"Not if the missus has anything to say about it," he said, flashing the most surprising thing yet: a ring, an antique of old gold. Hargreaves laughed, embraced him and headed up to the bridge. So he was married, was he? She wondered what his wife was like.

Outside the tall bridge windows, the crew could clearly see Albion Clemens maneuvering Dragonwell through the overflow chamber deep beneath New York City. Lights on either shoulder picked out the silhouette of the automata's billowing cape. The ship was quite high up, but it was clear the lock gates just before them would not admit passage. Huge gears held the gates tightly shut, with perhaps twenty feet between the ceiling and the gate. There were familiar shapes of steam engines at the sides of the locks, for opening and closing, but surely their operation would alert the subterranean masters of New York.

Dragonwell soared up to these slabs of iron, trailing a thin line of steam, and over them.

"And now he's showing off," Rosa murmured inside the bridge.

The lock gears showed the first sign of movement, turning their chains with a groan of stressed metal. Each tooth slid down with a grating like continents, speeding up as they came. Slowly, the iron swung open, releasing a swell of water where the levels were not quite even.

Dragonwell came back into view, at the top of the gate. A dense, bluish steam was vigorously exiting its back, its metal hands braced against one half of the lock gate. It was bodily pushing the gate open.

"How is it possible? There shouldn't be enough room in the automata to hold the fuel and the water…." Hargreaves wondered aloud.

"Now you're interested in the mechanics? Auntie's going to be the only woman aboard who favors a doily to a wrench."

Rosa reached for a throttle control, and the *Berry* slowly drifted forward, through the lock. As they passed between black mechanisms like twin monoliths, Dragonwell released the first lock and flew on ahead, to open the next. When they passed through this one, Hargreaves walked out onto the deck. Far below, she could see the water like a dark mirror before and behind the ship. Powerful lights shone on some blocky, broken shapes in the dark.

"These flood tunnels were built over the first buildings of New York," Rosa told Hargreaves when she came back in. "What you're seeing are the foundations of the prosperity above. These are the homes of immigrants who came to settle in run-down tenements, breaking their backs so their children might find a better life."

"What happened to them?" Hargreaves asked. They were the only ones on the bridge, and the conversation seemed appropriately intimate.

"Progress," Rosa answered. "When space became scarce and the river started to rise, the city's planners simply built over and through them: tunnels to run the trains, sewers to carry the plumbing into the river, and canals to flush the river. There's a skyscraper over this very spot, now, a temple to wealth and power. Art deco, a ziggurat. They even copied the sacrificial altars of old. You can find thousands of these remnants under every large city in the world."

"Britain, as well," Hargreaves said. "I've seen the Yard's old charts and maps. There are nearly two hundred kilometers of abandoned tunnels under London."

"We've flown them," Rosa said.

They navigated the tunnel and through a rusty pair of steel gates to find themselves outside, underneath a wide suspended bridge. The *Berry* flew under a long, raised highway, in the shadow of multitudes of steam lorries and sedan engines packed bumper to bumper, until Hargreaves recognized the raised train tracks of the Bowery.

Dragonwell set foot on the forecastle, its black cape hiding it from prying eyes. At a glance, the sleepless denizens might see a landing jaunt coming to rest on a beat-up old freighter. It extended a hand to Hargreaves, as if picking up a small animal. If Alphonse seemed a comforting old knight to the princess Hargreaves, Dragonwell was more of a veteran lance, battered but no less reliable.

"How about it? We can take you anywhere you want to go. It's only a matter of time before the police discover you're not real British Intelligence," Albion offered. "Having us along will make the investigation go smoother, and we can help you throw Cook into the Atlantic deeps after."

"How gallant to offer. Becoming of you, Captain," Hargreaves said, with only a slight crinkle of schoolmarm about her.

She stood there kitted out in her preferred combat wear, but she felt strangely, comfortably naked. When she was with M.A.D., they were all dependent on her in some way or another, mostly to stop them from tearing Scotland Yard apart. With Arturo, the mask was enjoyable, but not something she could do for long. It was pleasant, not having to hide before people who could speak to her as equals. Throwing away a catastrophic British engine of war was as natural as sipping tea to Clemens. The pirates' very adversity to Hargreaves' proper English way endeared them to her. Odd, that their presence should comfort the turmoil at her breast.

"All right. I will bring Alphonse and the box to your safekeeping, but I will retain mastery over it until such time as your services to me are complete." Besides, Hargreaves would need the big automata to move the enormous box about.

"And no piracy. Don't fret; we're more explorers these days anyhow."

"Seeing as I have no jurisdiction here, and have committed an act of high treason, I may be closer to the gallows than you," said Hargreaves.

The night was cold. If becoming a pirate meant Auntie's warm, comfortable galley, the inspector found she did not mind starting right away.

9

BRITAIN GOES TO WAR.
ARTURO HAS A DRINK.

Though Hargreaves could not know it, her reunion with the *Huckleberry* coincided with the arrival of her old crew. Arturo and the members of M.A.D. disembarked in New York to a hubbub sweeping through the city, though that was not immediately obvious from the famed skyline filling their portholes.

As passengers on a mostly-leisure ship, they docked not at Coney Island, but at one of the ornate towers dotting the West Side. The *Gretchen* slipped up the Hudson, widdershins around Manhattan and sidled up to a forest of towers at Chelsea. They jutted out from the urban cluster at various angles, trees rooted in a mighty cliff of misty copper, steel, and gold. Steam-powered winches raised and lowered the beams to the appropriate height, their spools of cable spanning full city blocks.

Arturo had mostly recovered by the time they arrived, and led the party down the ramp into a hall covered in sunbursts. It was a high-ceilinged place, partitioned into smaller lounges, with a gentle breeze that signaled large ventilation fans somewhere. Arturo guessed the hall ran all the way down the spine of Manhattan, sprouting nerve fibers of shopping arcades and recreation. Plate windows looked on the greenery of residential New Jersey, juxtaposed against the tall ziggurat towers of Uptown on the other side.

The arrivals lounge was more of the same, full of rounded furniture, quadrilateral windows, and liberally gilt borders. A spiral staircase led up to a café area, where a barista was using a tall boiler to make heavenly-smelling drinks with spurts of steam. Underneath, counters with dedicated personnel in sharply tailored uniforms advertised various services. When they arrived, everyone in the lounge was gathered around a news service counter, where an aproned clerk on a stepladder was writing up the news points of the day on a floor-to-ceiling chalkboard.

"Stop writing and read off the details for us!" a sharply suited man in his thirties demanded of the clerk. Beside him, a woman in a shift dress the color of her gray hair shook a manicured finger, one of a dozen accusatory digits.

"What's going on?" Arturo asked of a uniformed constable who had just arrived. The lawman wore blue, but the shield-shaped badge was clear enough to the amateur detective. Arturo checked the collar; he was Officer Paul McGrath.

The police officer looked Arturo up and down, eyes catching on his glaringly magenta frock coat, his perfectly spiked hair, and the way he gingerly favored his stitched abdomen. Thankfully, the rest of M.A.D. were more neutrally attired. Cezette wore tall boots, and a beret poised atop her jet locks. Hallow was his usual pinstriped scarecrow, but Cid had found a bow tie and a frayed brown suit, looking more the aged professor than the plundering engineer. "You sound like you're from merry England," Officer McGrath said in a low voice. "I'm sorry to bear you bad news, but it looks like war has found Britain."

Arturo managed to snag the latest bulletin on the way out, plucking with fast fingers a printed missive from a businessman's dispatch case. It was a telegraphed article, terse and mostly related to which stocks and bonds would be wise to trade for arms companies and logistics firms. Still, the facts were there.

"As of 12:35, May 23rd, Prime Minister Meriweather Falstaff, on behalf of Queen Victoria III, Pax Britannia, and her allies, has declared a State of War with the Ottoman Empire," Arturo read aloud from the missive. They had found a quiet park nearby, a long boulevard of man-made flowerbeds and tall oaks planted on a raised walkway. There were still signs of metal tracks and clinker, from when the platform used to carry trains instead of vegetation. Each of them had a hot drink from a nearby coffee cart, held in a plain pasteboard cup.

"Why in God's name?" Cid gaped.

"According to this, the Ottoman's aerial forces launched a surprise attack on the Falklands, with the aid of allied Argentina, which has long held the islands are a rightful part of their country. Troops were landed with automata units, which quickly occupied several key islands. British patrols nearby were called to respond, ensuing in a prolonged conflict. War Cabinet head Margie Tresser was quick to support the Navy's decision, publicly calling the move 'an informed and apt strike.'"

"That is thousands of miles away from anywhere!" Cezette protested, her accent thick in her aggravation.

"And full of pirates and ne'er-do-wells," Arturo agreed.

"The Pax has declared the Falklands sovereign territory," Hallow explained. "An attack on the islands is an attack on British soil. Argentina has wanted the place back for decades, and for the Ottomans, it's an ideal opening salvo."

"Britain will need to respond with a good portion of our forces, or we will appear weak," Cid said gruffly. "But it will draw our navy away from Europe, where an Ottoman offensive is likely waiting."

Arturo looked about. Under the New York skyline, both Europe and South America seemed far away and irrelevant. These vaulted metropolitan obelisks were likely to be awash in red gold soon enough, but for now they seemed lofty, above it all.

Pressingly, with first blood drawn, the powers that be would undoubtedly expend every effort to track down Vanessa Hargreaves. The Ottomans no doubt had their own agents, but the queen would want to end the conflict quickly, before the declaration escalated into actual war. As of now, it was still possible to reach an agreement with the Ottomans. A devastating retaliation, with a terrifying weapon like the Cook plague, would end the whole thing before anyone got in too deep. Whether the queen only wished to threaten with the weapon, or if she sided with iron hawks like Tresser or Lord Howser in making a demonstration of it, was still up in the air.

"Let's get somewhere more comfortable. I've booked a hotel nearby, and had our bags sent there. We can sort out how to find Hargreaves from the suites," Arturo announced.

"Follow the spiky head," said Cezette, and pranced off between the blooming hydrangeas. They were the last of the autumn foliage, but here in the steel canyons of New York it was still unseasonably hot.

"She's become used to her new legs," Arturo said, watching the girl pirouette and frolic without spilling a drop of coffee.

"Too accustomed," Cid grunted. "She thinks they'll take her anywhere, but one faulty spring and they would tip her off the side of this garden."

"What is the point of new legs if they don't go anywhere?" Arturo asked philosophically. "You have to let go soon, Papa."

"Harrumph."

***

At the hotel Arturo booked, they found their suites as luxurious as the *Gretchen*'s. The lavishly appointed rooms boasted some very modern ingenuities, including a small engine for hot bathwater, a long glass on a tripod for taking in a view of the skyline, and a vacuum delivery tube for the morning post or telegrams. There was also a handsomely folded card on a tray in the master suite. It was refreshingly sepia, with none of the glitz they had seen thus far.

Cezette performed a perfect somersault into the Chesterfield sofa and began undoing the clasps that held her knees to her thighs. The skin was red, but not inflamed.

"Where do you get the money for all of this?" Cid said, looking around.

"I've had some successful cases with successful clients," Arturo remarked. He felt it prudent not to mention exorbitant fees were those clients' guarantees he would keep their secrets. Instead, he picked up the card, expecting some courteous reminder or missive.

You are discovered. Leave immediately -I

Ho-hum, Arturo thought to himself. First a stabbing, then a warning? Perhaps he was being coerced by a group of confused time travelers, who had got things back to front.

"Arturo." Hallow's voice drifted in from the suite's parlor. "There are men in the hallway."

Arturo entered the parlor to find Hallow at the peephole of the door. They were fortunately at the end of the hall, and Hallow had a commanding view of the corridor.

"What do they look like?" said Arturo.

"Prim. Neat. Like crows, with black hats and suits. Their canes are heavily topped," Hallow answered.

Arturo came up beside Hallow, putting his eye to the peephole. For a second he thought he heard the pinstriped scarecrow draw a very uncharacteristic breath. It was not the time to pursue it.

"Those are government agents, or Cid's a delicate Barnsley bird," Arturo confirmed. Particularly the bearded one, he looked straight off an academy rugby team. They were knocking on each suite, behaving as if they were getting the wrong door.

"Our mysterious 'I'?"

"I do not think so," Arturo answered, showing him the card.

He left Hallow at the door and rounded up Cid and Cezette. The old man had the engine going, about to fill a bath. Cezette gave a pout at first, but she enthusiastically clipped her legs back on and drew her stockings over the seam. The limbs were surprisingly natural, their brassy rims and black enamel clicking easily onto the porcelain caps where her knees ought to have been. They bent without a sound to lift the girl on to her feet. Arturo guessed there was some spring mechanism, transferring the nascent energy of Cezette's thigh muscles into the springs in the calves.

Before the men reached the end of the hall, Arturo had the group ready to go. Their luggage would have to be forfeit, but Arturo was able to liberate a few choice items into a traveling satchel. M.A.D. had few belongings to begin with. Cid had a heavy workman's duffel, Hallow an understated messenger bag, and Cezette a utilitarian rucksack.

"Quietly," Arturo said as he slid the window open. They were several stories up, but like every other building in New York, this one was equipped with a fire escape. Metal slats and ladders created an external route to the street below. He had scarcely gotten the others onto the escape when an insistent knocking came at the door.

"Go on, they're not here for you," Arturo said, shutting the window in M.A.D.'s faces. The detective slipped back through the suite of rooms as the knocking came a second time, more insistently.

"Who is it?" Arturo called.

"Hotel management. We'd like a word, sir."

Oh, that was some cheek. They'd even gone to the trouble of accents, an American frontier English the consistency of molasses. The trouble was, they were in fast-paced New York, and stuck out like sore thumbs.

When the two black-suited men kicked down the door, they found Arturo waiting just beside the jamb. The first man fell to a vicious baritsu trip, accompanied by a jab to the throat. While he gasped like a fish on the plush hotel pile, the second man came through, flailing the heavy end of his cane. Arturo danced back, stepping lightly on the first man's cane, which had fallen to the floor. It came willingly, coerced by physics and the fulcrum of the first man's wrist into Arturo's palm.

"Now is the dance of death!" cried Arturo, succumbing to a dapper mood that suddenly overtook him.

Arturo backed off, parrying his opponent's attempts to bash his head in. The second man was a rugby player, all gruff and no finesse, but it was a trained sort of violence nonetheless. Arturo was not fooled, and used the tip of his cane to divert the blows into the hotel's furnishings. He was no fencer, but the cane was weighted well enough, and the suites full of smashing good things to throw a man headlong into. Idly, his detective's instinct for detail uncovered the slight pitch to his attacker's heavy breath, the tint of his skin, the certain hereditary cut to his jaw.

"Come now, you can do better, rarebit!" Arturo taunted the Welshman.

His pinpoint deduction paid off, causing his attacker to lurch out of balance in a lunge. Arturo came down like a sack of bricks, laying his cane headmaster-style into the man's backside. He went down, and the detective pinned the man's fighting hand, while simultaneously producing an item he had liberated from his luggage; a stub-nosed, large-caliber revolver. Unexpectedly, his quarry smirked, before a resounding crash echoed through the suites.

"Eh?" said Arturo. Instead of finding himself laid out on the floor, he spun round to behold the first attacker, his head caved in with a heavy tripod. The suit swanned dramatically into the Chesterfield.

"Thought you might need a hand," Jean Hallow called, still clutching the tripod. "Though it seemed you were having quite the spirited time."

Arturo struck at the rugby man with the point of the cane as he tried to get up, throwing him headfirst into the hot bath engine. A piercing cry came from him as a ruptured steam line seared the flesh from his chiseled jaw. The man fainted dead away.

"If we have a free moment, Mr. Hallow, I will be quite happy to show you a spirited time," Arturo mentioned. He had cheek too, oh yes.

Before either of them had a chance to work out what exactly Arturo implied, the open doorway emitted a babble of concerned voices. It seemed the other inhabitants of the hotel were generally opposed to the sort of ruckus happening in the corner suite.

Arturo and Hallow rushed down the fire escape into a warm New York afternoon. Cid and Cezette were already waiting beside a hired cab, a steaming Fjord Victoria.

"That is the last woman I wanted to see," Arturo said, giving the square grille-and-crown badge of the cab a once-over. They climbed in, urging the driver to go, and never mind the destination.

"Hey, limey fuck, I don't take kindly to no imperialist slurs. You can find your own way. Get out of my cab," the driver chirped at Cid. New York hospitality at its finest.

Just then, a string of sharp reports sounded, accompanied by alarming chunking sounds across the bonnet of the engine. The paint flaked away to reveal strong Fjord iron, punched with regular biscuit-sized holes. Cezette squealed, but she kept her head, taking cover in the bottom of the cab.

"Ah. Apologies, kind sir. And sorry about this," Arturo said. He pistol-whipped the driver in the temple and Cid shoved him out of the engine, taking up the driver's seat himself. The grimy street was probably a safer alternative than Arturo's patronage. They sped sharply away.

"Where are we going? What will we do?" Cezette asked from between the front seats of the cab. She had a big grin plastered across her cheeks. Down Seventh Avenue, the cab made good time for two blocks, but soon ran into traffic. "This engine is bright yellow. Wouldn't that be conspicuous?"

"It's hard to find one particular tree in a forest," Arturo said, indicating the broad sweep of yellow cabs darting in and out before them. They outnumbered the regular sedans, and no horses were in sight, even clockworked ones. "But the bullet holes are a bit jarring. Shall we adjourn to the underground?"

It was easier said than done. Manhattan was a maze of cantilevered valleys, full to bursting with hustle and bustle. There was simply no quiet spot they could leave the engine without attracting undue attention. Surprisingly enough, the bullet holes seemed inconspicuous, unremarkable to the passersby, as far as they could tell. The pedestrians were more engrossed by the rows and rows of adverts overhead, outlined in glowing letters two or three stories high.

"Whatever possessed you to take a hotel suite? You may as well have left our names in these great big arclights," said Cid.

"I did use a false name," replied Arturo, but he felt like a green deckhand being scolded by the experienced captain.

"I would have gone straight to the seediest motel in the city," Cid grunted. "But I suppose they would have found us eventually."

"It was a stroke of luck this cab came along, though," Arturo mused.

"We simply held out a hand, and the cabbie swung round the corner," said Cezette. "I'd read it was impossible to hail cabs in this city. Wonderful book, with sepia photograms. Not very accurate, I think."

"I wonder...." Arturo said. He began to root round the

compartments of the cab, opening wood panels, unlatching patched sheets of upholstery. In a pocket over their heads, he surfaced with another missive, this time written on a crinkled parking ticket.

Five Corners, beneath the bridge. Goldilocks awaits. —I

Arturo flipped the ticket over.

Sorry about the stabbing. —I

"Our benefactor has a funny idea of assistance...." Arturo grumbled. Nevertheless, he showed Cid the message. The old man pulled up to a ramshackle newsstand to ask for directions. His gruff demeanor seemed to work on the ragtag populace hurtling up and down the street, with their multicolored accents and stoic marching rhythm. Arturo sometimes forgot this man had been a pirate with the infamous Manchu Marauder, and Samuel J. Clemens before him. All of this must have seemed all too pedestrian, while Arturo was still wanting for the top hats and discreet parlors of the queen's London. As they drove out of the concrete jungle and into the groves of patchwork buildings, their fronts plastered in every language, Arturo suddenly felt a crushing sensation of impotence. He was starting to feel these were the only four people who made any sense to him, here in the most densely populated city in the world. It was terribly lonely.

***

With Alphonse and the Cook box safely stowed in the *Huckleberry*'s hold, Hargreaves looked toward getting the most she could out of the record book she had liberated from Burgess. It had been a delicate operation. Zampano Ivanov had been sad to see her go, but it was unfeasible to tell him about Albion's presence in the city. For one thing, Ivanov was a legitimate businessman now. Hargreaves did not wish to drag anyone down with her. For another, he might actually be able to help, which would complicate matters. Zampano Ivanov had never been the discrete type.

In the city that never sleeps, the logistics of moving Alphonse turned out to be surprisingly easy to arrange. Ivanov insisted on hiring a moving engine, a flat, stubby wagon with a dozen small wheels beneath. The contraption was slower than paint but it had the torque of a bull elephant. One had to drive it oneself, so after Vera lowered the big bundle of tarpaulin-covered automata with the loading crane, the inspector climbed into the driver's perch. Hargreaves had to wonder if it was the spirit of independence behind the custom, or simple avarice on the part of the owner not to pay a driver's wages.

"You will write, da?" Ivanov said from under the raised driver's perch. From above, the great bear looked more like a sad pup.

"Da, Ivanov. If I can," Hargreaves replied. Ivanov was a wonder. Was he the only sentimental Russian in the world? Certainly the only one plying the cutthroat skies, she thought.

They had chosen mid-morning to drive the engine up from Coney Island. The wide road was packed granules of granite set in asphaltum, making for a smooth ride. There were innumerable Feints and Fjords zipping along on the road, but practically no horse-and-fours or lone riders. In the loose traffic, Hargreaves could see the odd equestrian shy away from the hot, hard road and instead ride along the flat beach and grassy wetland of the shore.

America had long embraced industry, and this country had never had much use for British customs like gentleman's horsemanship. The vehicles passing her now were cheap, efficient transport, working man's steamers. Most of the dock men and subway riders had not spoken much English, and she imagined they did not have much time to learn. Hargreaves recalled the words glimpsed through a pocket-glass as Ivanov's vessel passed into the harbor; "Give me your tired, your poor, your huddled masses." The statue had never promised they would cease to be any of those things.

Hargreaves took the slow lane up the Kings-Queens Carriageway, where she glimpsed domestic airships mooring at the oblique towers of Brooklyn. The shore opposite Manhattan had been transformed into an interminable line of docks and train platforms, inexplicably dotted by residential brownstones. Vast warehouses framed the raised highway, held up by steel girders surely forged in even greater heartland manufactories. The road was pitted and scarred, and there seemed to be an endless battle against entropy waged by orange-suited workers dotted here and there on the dividers. Some were actually laying new tar and spreading bags of gravel. Others looked to be languishing in the gray smoke hanging in a permanent cloud over the road.

The moving engine rolled into Manhattan sometime in the afternoon, taking the Eastside Highway towards the spot where Albion Clemens exited the subterranean tunnels. The pirates were already waiting for her behind a chain-mesh fence. They parked the engine in the mouth of the tunnel, and Hargreaves got into Alphonse to move the hermetically sealed box. Straight and regularly riveted, the box gave her the overwhelming feeling of handling a morgue drawer, even through Alphonse's steel hands. Hargreaves felt a little superstitious paranoia at a job gone too smoothly.

"What about the engine?" Hargreaves inquired of Ivanov's rental.

"Albion's moving it a few blocks over. We'll wire the firm with the location," Rosa explained. "Now, you've had a long, sweaty day. How about a bath? We've installed a real tub, with room for two."

"You've been taking a few too many liberties with this ship, my dear," Hargreaves commented.

"I don't hear a no, gorgeous!" Rosa trilled.

"Ah. Why not? We can tease the captain with its happening later."

10

THE CAPTAIN'S PREROGATIVE

At that moment, Albion was treating himself to a pasteboard container of potsticker dumplings, eaten out of a greasy paper bag. There was a policy he abided by: never waste an opportunity to snack.

Five Corners in New York was exceptionally tempting. The hodgepodge of different cuisines reminded him a bit of Kowloon, like visiting all of China in a ten-block radius. Nestled in the New York tenement apartments were all manner of Chinese immigrants, who had chosen those few gritty buildings to live and work close to one another. Albion went from hole in the wall to hole in the wall, tasting his native Cantonese soup noodles with roast goose, Shanghai drunken chicken, and the infamous Beijing duck, savory and sweet with scallions and brown sauce.

Not to mention, the neighborhood was remarkably convenient. Located off the rows of restaurants on Mott Street were rows of hardware merchants, banks and markets. There was even a telegraph office, selling stationery next to incense and hell money. Clemens sent a message in Vanessa Hargreaves' name to the moving engine company. The Fujian clerk with the distinctive dialect looked at him funny when he handed off the greasy message slip, taking in the burgundy coat with its shiny clasps, the high collar, and the goggles on Clemens' forehead. The clerk decided to conduct the transaction in a broken, lilting English.

Five Corners lay some distance from the mouth of the tunnel where the *Berry* sat hidden, but it took twice as long to walk there, what with all those small mom and pop delicacy shops. Tiny egg cakes cooked on a honeycombed skillet, deep-fried drumsticks—there were even the egg tarts Albion was so fond of having in Kowloon's tea restaurants. It wasn't often he came to Five Corners, and, by helping Hargreaves, he might be leaving New York quite soon. When he finally arrived at the mouth of the access tunnel beneath the bridge, he was loaded down with paper sacks of goodies.

What Albion never saw, as he climbed through the fence and loped toward the gaping opening, was the figure trailing along behind him.

11

GRINDHOUSE DOUBLE FEATURE

"About time you got back. What did you do, take the engine out for a joyride?" Rosa Marija accused Albion as he stepped into the galley.

"The blasted thing can barely hit forty. What about you? You girls look like you've been gallivanting about in your own way." Both Marija and Hargreaves lounged by the steaming row of pipes in the galley. Tall, cold drinks occupied their hands. Auntie was just sitting down to join them. All three had their hair bound up in towels, and their faces were soft and flushed.

"What did you think we did?" Rosa asked pleasantly.

"I say, it has been awhile since I've taken advantage of your hospitality," said Hargreaves.

"I hope you girls know we're helping the inspector commit treason. Those days of going on holiday and just happening to saving the world are over," Clemens said, flopping down on his armchair. When none of the ladies paid him any mind, he went on. "You people act like this mystery is going to solve itself. What, like Dragonwell and Alphonse are going to lumber around and shake things up for—"Albion never got to finish, for as he mouthed the words, everything not nailed down decide to take a step to the left. It would have been hilarious watching the occupants scrabble on the floor, if not for the ominous rumbling. Outside the porthole, the dark tunnel lit up with a bloom of orange fire.

"What the bloody hell was that?" Hargreaves screamed from the floor, where she now sprawled helplessly.

"Never mind that. I've lost my towel. Somebody give me my towel!" ordered Rosa. The three of them sans Auntie bolted for the door at the same time, toppling into each other as the ship righted itself. Rosa's hair swept out in a damp sheet, whipping across Hargreaves' face. It was like being slapped by a fish.

"Nobody's at the helm!" Albion said, dashing toward the bridge.

"What happened to Prissy Jack?" Hargreaves demanded.

"Prissy Jake left to start his flying restaurant business!"

"What?"

Hargreaves took up her underthings, hobbling forward on one leg as she tried to slip them on. Blasted tight stays! Rosa nearly knocked her over in the rush to get to the bridge. By the time Hargreaves made it down the passage, she had her knickers, the ingenious corset, and a pair of striped leggings wrangled. Auntie whistled, and when Hargreaves turned a straight-cut navy jacket with tarnished buttons hit her square in the chest.

"Put it on!" said Auntie. Hargreaves blushed, knowing it was a full-body rouge.

The garment was hellishly tight, but it cinched at her hips, covered everything, and the sleeves were flat to the wrist, surely making for a lovely draw on a weapon. A double-breasted military uniform cut for a woman, with hidden panels so her bust and hips wouldn't catch. There was so much structure to it that she could wear it without underthings. Best of all, there were pockets!

"Where the blazes did you get this?" said Hargreaves.

Auntie gave a thumbs-up and made a shooing motion with her other hand. Hargreaves went.

She reached the bridge to find Elric Blair's voice hollering through the speaking trumpets. The wobbly-headed dolls decorating the consoles wobbled vigorously. A second brilliant light flared up directly in front of them, enough to see a strange shape at the other end of the tunnel. It was approaching quickly, and even more disturbingly, there was more than one shadow. A third blast scraped some splinters of carpentry from the bow of the ship, throwing a wave of water onto the deck.

"Automata!" said Hargreaves. "There's three of them!"

"With six legs? What kind of monster are we talking about here?" Albion said. In the middle of the sentence, his own two legs came out from under him.

Meanwhile, Rosa was unhurriedly flipping toggles and throwing levers, determinedly preventing the *Berry* from suffering further damage. Her hips firmly braced against a support behind the wheel. The contact kept her towel just firmly in place, but that soon became a thing of the past as the ship shuddered, knocking the cloth to the ground. Rosa hurled the wheel to port as the wall there shattered, never minding for a second that she was in her altogether. Eventually Albion reached a locker, holding on for dear life as Rosa pitched the deck this way and that. Her hair swept about her curves, framing muscles in action that looked carved out of tiger's eye stones. Never mind the burlesque, thought Hargreaves. This was her dance. This was where Rosa Marija belonged.

Albion resurfaced with a long shirt that looked like it was the under-suit for some sort of heavier equipment. He swung with his ship, pitching the bundle to drape near Rosa. By then the tunnel outside began to drift past at a steady clip. As a blast detonated somewhere farther astern, Rosa took the opportunity to throw on the undersuit, which was long enough to drape as a white linen dress on her. She began to laboriously lash herself against the padded strut with some built-in straps.

"Alby, there's a set of locks at the far end of this tunnel."

Immediately, the silliness was gone from Albion. Efficiently and fluidly, the captain took off down a different set of stairs. Hargreaves looked on, trying to find a way to be useful, but ultimately settled on strapping herself into a seat and trying to stay out of the way.

"Good idea! Try to use the scopes to find the gears!" said Rosa.

"Err… right! Exactly what I planned!" Hargreaves agreed. She began to manipulate the controls before her. There was a scope at eye level that had a smooth rubber bezel, and she pressed her face to it—only to see a pair of bugged-out eyes staring back at her.

"Christ, what the blazes?" cried Hargreaves. The eyes were gone almost as soon as the words left her lips. There was a jolt rumbling through the ship, and then something landed upon the deck with a loud crunch. A glimpse of fabric whistled over the deck, the only trace of Dragonwell flying overhead. When Hargreaves managed to stand up, she was able to see the wet corpse of something metal and six-legged on the deck. Though each of the still legs was curled against the body, they would be about the length of a man when fully extended.

"Like a cat leaving us a present," said Rosa, and she looked like she wanted to spit. "Can you find him? We saw two more of those things." The ship hovered steadily, and no more explosions shook them. Apparently the *Berry* was tougher than expected, or Albion was putting up a very good fight. Rosa flicked on the ship arclamps, lighting a patch of the cavernous flood drain. Hargreaves puttered about the scopes, and soon had a fine view of Dragonwell.

"There!" said Hargreaves. She indicated the heading. "Don't blind him!"

In response, Rosa shifted the airship until Dragonwell came into view. She kept the lights pointed away, and the tableau before them was a strange stage indeed.

Albion had put the gear high up on one of the floodgates, and it looked like he was fencing with an enormous cutlass. The sewer was dark, but the metal caught the arclight as it danced here and there. Flashes showed fearsome, stabbing legs. Suddenly, bang! Something went off in Dragonwell's hand, and a second later the water below them belched as it swallowed whatever had been shot.

"Gear-sized blunderbuss," Rosa explained briefly. Hargreaves could see the weapon as it was stowed: a brassy trumpet shape that would have been akin to a French horn to a person.

Albion was not done. As soon as the creature toppled off the edge, a second one seemed to appear from the shadows, crawling along the wall. Dragonwell took a step—turned away from the creature.

Albion didn't see!

"Captain!"

"Alby!"

The two women cried out simultaneously, but it was Rosa who seized a length of cable along the bridge ceiling. When she pulled on it the ship's foghorn unleashed the *Berry*'s sizable bellow, cascading into the flood drain like a thunderclap. Dragonwell spun on its heel, and as the spidery metal claw lashed out, so did Albion's enormous blade. A sound like a snapped guitar string rang out, and the claw tumbled end-over-end, severed from the gear.

To everyone's surprise, the gear began to scream, a rasping sound like steel wool over a grate. Then it began to rapidly crawl away, and was soon lost to the darkness beyond their lamps.

"Follow it, Albion!" said Hargreaves. But Dragonwell seemed to settle on its haunches, unwilling to move. When Hargreaves checked the scope, she could see Albion struggling with the controls. Perhaps the gear had been damaged. Rosa steered the *Berry* closer, and by the time they were within a stone's throw, Dragonwell was aloft.

Soon they had their captain back on the deck, and as Albion dropped down from Dragonwell's cockpit, Rosa ran up to give him a kiss. Whatever affection Hargreaves entertained for Albion, she was happy to see the captain reciprocate deeply, his arms around his helmswoman. They clung to each other for a moment while the inspector inspected the one wrecked gear that lay at Dragonwell's feet.

"So what do you make of this?" asked Albion as Rosa finally let go.

"Right," said Hargreaves, not moving from her crouch beside the gear. "This is less of a machine and more of a… creature."

Rosa's brow raised, and Albion gestured at the riveted carapace, the brass cylinders slung under the copious abdomen, and the glass eyes now lifeless and dull. The only sign of anything animal was the copious amounts of gritty, purplish-brown liquid dribbling out of a cutlass-sized hole in the carapace. The wound was full of it. But the stream also bled a collection of broken gears and worm screws broken off inside the spider.

"First of all, can you see a cockpit? It is barely big enough to hold a person," said Hargreaves. "For another thing, this creature looks like a patchwork of scrap."

The inspector kicked the spider over, where a patch of the

carapace didn't look the same as the rest. There was a face of a pig on it, scuffed in long silver lines. It looked like a repair done with a crudely cut piece of white-painted aluminum.

"Wait; I know this pig," said Rosa. "Rosso's. It's a pork and salami distributor in the meatpacking district. A truck comes every week with this pig on it."

"Burgess owns it," said Hargreaves. "In name or just in practice. There's a Rosso's in the log book. It wasn't coded, and the figures look like he was laundering money through it, but not much else."

"Definitely suspicious," said Rosa, but there was a smile on her face. Her captain picked up on it too.

"Let's go pay them a visit then, shall we? The tunnel runs right to the West Side Highway," said Albion. "We'll find out who's caught on to your scent, and why they decided to shoot first, talk later."

"I doubt these things can talk," said Rosa. She toed the spider, which burbled a new slurry of gritty reddish gunk. "There's no room for a person in there. Can we get this off the deck now? It smells like old death."

"Yes, yes. Come on; let's be on our way before that last one gets back," said Albion.

"And here I forgot my calling-on dress," said Hargreaves, grinning. Finally, it felt like they were getting somewhere. It was good to be with her pirates again.

***

Arturo arrived at Five Corners, found the fenced-off tunnel entrance, and came face to face with a clacking horror that emerged bleeding and scrabbling out of a manhole.

"Whoa, bollocks!" he said, but he kept his wits about him.

As soon as the spider emerged, he drew a Webley British Bull Dog revolver and shot the thing in the mouth. The gun had come to him through his mother's inheritance. It had shared the closet with the whips and the masks. It had spent the majority of his crime-solving career in the same box but after being stabbed, the Dog seemed a prudent measure. Arturo hadn't wondered for a second why his mother had it. She was just that type of woman.

The Dog barked harshly, sending an enormous .450 slug through the gear's glass eyeball. It rattled around inside the head like it was a tin can full of jam. Arturo couldn't have said why he felt menaced by the contraption until just then, because the articulated arachnid whirled upon him, its jaws dripping a dark, gritty substance. Arturo fired upon it again.

Sparks ricocheted off the gear's rivets. He could see it had already lost a leg, cleaved by some tremendous force. By chance, his final shot cut through a cable or a linkage. One of the other legs snapped inward as if sprung, clutching to the body as if epileptic. The gear emitted a terrible rasp, as of a thousand cicadas dying.

"Adler! Boy!" Cid's booming voice carried strongly from down the street. The spidery gear stopped, as if it was *thinking*. Surely that was impossible—there was no room for a person in there. Then it scuttled away, leaving a trail of tiny gears and oily wine-red droplets.

"*Sacré bleu! Qu'est ce que ce?!*" Cezette's voice echoed across the street. She had come much closer on her quick ballerina feet. From her vantage point it was possible to see where the spider was going. Hallow stood beside her, seemingly unfazed by the whole situation.

"There's no time to lose! Follow that... that abomination!" called Arturo.

"What? What is going on?" asked Cezette, confused. Her arms flailed prettily as her knees wound to a clockworked halt.

Arturo exhaled, watching his breath mist slightly on the brisk fall air. The Brooklyn Bridge hung sedately over his head, its bricks cast in orange gold by the fading sun. The spider was scuttling northwest, untouched by the shadow of the Bridge. Soon it disappeared, clattering into the alleys of Five Corners. But its trail was distinct against the asphaltum.

"The game is afoot!" cried Arturo, dashing towards their rattle-can cab.

***

Captain Clemens took the ship through the tunnels, and, as promised, they fed out on the West Side under the tail end of the airship moorages. Hargreaves thought it was dangerous until she realized the multitude of passenger ships served to disguise the *Huckleberry*. Their shapes cast huge, bulbous shadows. The *Berry* was a

needle in a haystack so long as Rosa flew the ship like they belonged
there. They took refuge under one of the larger cruise gondolas. With
some convincing, Elric Blair agreed to take charge, flying circles as
lookout.

Application of Dragonwell with its hands cupped and a discrete
landing in a bit of raised parkland allowed Hargreaves, Rosa, and
Albion to alight onto the street. It was difficult to discern the location
of Rosso's until Hargreaves harrumphed, walked into a delicatessen,
and got the address. Apparently neither pirate had the good sense to
simply ask the natives.

"Usually somebody has heard of us," admitted Rosa. "They have
wanted posters up in the bars and rope under the counter."

"Granted, the towns we usually stop in are prone to piracy,"
added Albion. "And our faces are not well known. But America has a
no-tolerance policy for us. It's the gibbet if we're caught."

"More likely shot," said Rosa. "This is America."

She should know. Rosa was American, as far as Hargreaves could
figure. The mocha-dark vixen had the strong brow of the American
Indians, but there was an almost French cast to her nose that made
her striking to look at. Hargreaves knew better than to judge a person
by appearances, especially a friend she had flown with for so long. She
was always cautious of that; the imperial conceit of the English was
strong with Hargreaves. But culture was another matter. Rosa was
certainly boisterous enough to be American, though her passions
would put an Italian to shame.

"Come on. The address is here," said Hargreaves.

Rosso's was a barely marked cinder building with clockworks
sprouting out the back of it. Hargreaves recognized cooling apparatus,
probably for the meat storage inside. The building next door was
much more imposing, a slate-gray block with a coffee shop under it.
One of its large arched windows was blocked off with fresh wood
planks. The pair of buildings backed up to a long pressboard fence
that was starting to rot. Train tracks could be glimpsed through the
holes, and Hargreaves caught the impression of some enormous
locomotive gleaming a brushed silver color. Even passing by in a
fleeting moment, the angled surfaces and spiraling shafts seemed

ominous. She didn't recognize the model of the engine.

Later, resting in her little room, she would bolt upright and realize the train had been the color of meat grinders.

But for now, Hargreaves examined Rosso's in great detail. It was a utilitarian building that showed the marks of constant use. The floor was slick and gross with a layer of fat that could only be spilled viscera. The accumulation of years washed like a tide up to a raised loading dock. One of them was open to the train tracks on the other side of the building. They could see right through to a number of drums on the platform there.

"It looks like they're busy loading the train," said Albion, who had always been the keenest of their eyes. He was right—a number of shadowed figures were loading the drums by the pallet into a box car.

"There doesn't seem to be anything here," said Rosa.

Now Hargreaves knew how Arturo felt when he explained things. Hargreaves could see a thousand clues, the gritty red of something that wasn't offal or animal blood, for example. The scrapes of the building's doorways, signs of sharp metal that had gouged them moving in and out. A patch of softer wood flooring bore the marks of things that had been dragged into the dock scrabbling and fighting. The shapes loading the box car were not human. Their limbs seemed like large, monstrous copies of Cezette's legs. Light winked through gaps in them.

"This way," the inspector said, mostly to avoid sounding trite. Or to avoid throwing up as she passed a fingernail that had been lodged into the flooring.

They rounded Rosso's and Hargreaves found a fresher trail of gritty, oily droplets. They led to a rusty side door. Rosa picked it with a slim pair of stilettos, one flexible, one not. It swung inward to a moist, warm corridor. The lights were off.

"*Allons-y,*" muttered Hargreaves as they stepped into the darkness.

And held her breath as a sneeze threatened to expose their position.

"Ha... ha...." Then, as a strangled sort of squeak, "Chu!"

"Shh!" said Rosa, mostly to take the piss.

Hargreaves held her nose from the dust that had been kicked up by their entry. The corridor was a sort of servant's entrance that ran between the loading dock and the strange, unmarked building that had the boarded-up café in it. On one side, Rosso's was lit by the open train platform, though it was still dark. Apparently the workers, whatever they were, needed no lighting.

The building at the other end of the corridor was lit with Tesla bulbs. A gritty red trail on the floor led through a set of double doors. The whole place had a clinical feel to it, from the green wash of the walls to the tile of the flooring, and it had a feeling of disuse. Like a real spider, their quarry had left no fingerprint when it had come this way, not even disturbing the piles of boxes and canisters piled into the space. Hargreaves, careful inspector she was, had still kicked up clouds of dust. But it had surely come this way. The trail was clear and fresh.

"Let's not go looking for trouble," said Rosa, nodding towards the train loading dock. How perfectly pirate of her, Albion seemed to be interested in the mechanicals, but he wasn't fool enough to provoke the bear. They watched from the safety of the corridor as a pallet of heavy barrels lifted from the floor with little effort.

"I should like to know how they followed me to my ship," said Albion, "and I have a feeling getting thrown around like a rag doll wouldn't be very informative."

"Someone sent the spider automata," said Hargreaves. "Look. There's dust on these shelves. And those loaders are well practiced. And that train! I've never seen its like. Whoever they are, they've been in this city a long time, and they are well established. They were sent not for you, but for me." It was a tenuous connection, but Hargreaves the detective was falling silent to Hargreaves the paranoid. She felt quite sure the latter had her favor.

"How have we never seen hide or hair of them?" said Rosa.

Albion began looking through some of the debris. It was innocuous, and when they opened a box they found more of the canisters, which turned out to be Rosso's Tin Pork. There was a variety of flavors. Hargreaves gestured, and they slowly made their way through the double doors, to find a set of stairs leading up to a sort of storage warehouse hallway. Shuttered spaces lined cinder walls. They followed the trail deeper into the building.

"We're the seedy underbelly of the city," Rosa whispered as they passed the quiet shutters. "How come we've never heard of these spider things before?"

"We have," said Albion now, indicating the plain walls. "What do you notice?"

"What does it matter?" said Rosa, clearly annoyed.

"They're clean," said Hargreaves, who had noticed from the start. She had felt it as keenly as she felt the oppression in the Bowery. "No grafitti. No gang signs, no scratches. There are signs on every other building but nothing on these two."

They continued past two more shutters, each large enough to drive a steamer through. By some arbitrary sign Hargreaves did not see, Albion paused near one of them and bent low. There was a low scratching sound in the deserted hallway. Albion finished picking the lock and raised the shutter quietly on oiled pulleys. It was a room mostly taken up with a large, cold machine and a small pyramid of sealed drums. There was a large canvas hopper suspended over it.

"I've heard stories," said Albion as he held out his hand. Rosa slipped a knife out of her bustier and put it into his hand. "Of people being snatched off the streets, disappearing into the night. Of the Strangers in the Alleyways. Don't go talking to Strangers. They eat the wicked."

Albion drew the blade across the canvas. The steel was sharp, the blade flexible. It opened a slit in the fabric, and what was in the canvas came tumbling out. They came easy, sliding out of the wet inside of the canvas as if the hopper were a stomach that had been cut.

Hargreaves covered her mouth. Rosa looked away.

The floor was covered in grubby, dirty bodies. None of them would have stood taller than Hargreaves' chest. And that was when the clacking sounds in the hallway reached their ears, accompanied by a dreadful moan that spiraled down to the pit of Hargreaves' stomach.

"Lots of urban legends in New York," said Albion as he drew Victoria, his black Colt pistol. "Who knew this one was true?"

***

"*C'est insupportable!*" cried Cezette. She leaned out the cab window and threw a ball of wadded-up papers at Arturo. The ball disintegrated as it flew, swallowing the detective in a cloud of old parking tickets and handwritten receipts. "We are crawling like ants while Maman may be in danger! *Allez! On y va maintenant!*" Cezette's accent grew thicker and higher pitched as she spoke. She found herself constantly flailing her neck about, looking for the garnet drops of the trail Arturo picked out where Cezette saw only a busy metropolis.

"Well, you shall just have to bear it. Detection is as much art as science," said Arturo, sweeping the papers aside with the same hand that held his magnifying monocle out. Scraps caught on the art deco of Manhattan, swirling in the updraft to drape amongst the glitz of the tall buildings. "Besides, this is not Hargreaves' blood. This is not even blood… not just blood, anyway." Arturo paused, then abruptly darted into an alleyway.

"Arturo! *Merde! J'en ai ral le cul! Merde, merde, merde!*"

"Language, Cezzy," said Jean Hallow from the backseat, and Cezette poked her head back in to glare at the pinstriped tutor. How could he be so calm? But Hallow had his eyes closed and his hands folded, proving such an example of calm reserve that Cezette stopped cursing.

Cid, who was driving the borrowed cab, waited until the detective's spiky coif appeared on a fire escape. Other engines honked their displeasure, expelling steam through grubby tubes in the sides of their vehicles. But Cid paid them no mind, and the rest of M.A.D. followed slowly as the figure of Arturo traversed a few blocks of city, before dropping down into the lower neighborhoods in the west. Various signs advertised active butchers and the slick, dark loading docks of meat purveyors. Strangely, those spots were interspersed with the shadowy chic of nightclubs just opening for business. As the cab clacked onto rough cobbles and old wood roads, Jean opened his eyes.

"Ugh," he murmured as a clutch of women trooped past on the cobblestones. "My dear, that is far too much."

Even in the brisk cool of the docks on the west, they were dressed in thigh-length skirts, their petticoats on display. A couple had bodices with a large window cut in the front. All of them had the stork-like gait of high heels on cobbles. Cezette was familiar with the concept of ladies of the evening. But she was perceptive enough to see they paid little mind to the well-dressed men passing them. Those ladies were here to buy, not to sell. Apparently more than one kind of meat was available, here in the meatpacking district.

The cab jerked to a halt and Cezette almost cursed again. Then she saw Arturo standing there in the cobbles, looking down the street to their right. He was motionless, peering, and his monocle dangled to one side. Cezette opened the cab door and rushed towards him. Her heels clicked, but in a couple of steps the fabulous mechanical legs had adjusted to the uneven cobbles. She was about to clobber the silly toff on the head, only to pause herself as a chill swept down her back, shuddering her hips in their lacquered harnesses. Memories she had kept pushed deep down arose unbidden, threatening to upend her. Memories of closed spaces, of stone crumbling to dust in her fingers, of being a terrible titan amongst insects. But her legs were iron, and they held.

A long stretch of railroad yard separated them from the water. Just behind the fence of the yards clustered terrible arachnid shapes backlit by the dying sunset. Each of the clacking eight-legged forms seemed like sewing spindles comes to life, or four of the high-heeled women glued together and submitted to a perverse stretching. There had to be a dozen of them whirring and snapping with the sounds of tensed cables. But what terrified Cezette most of all was the hulking shape they surrounded, which appeared for a second as a rounded hillock, then disappeared into the earth. It appeared once again, and that was when Cezette realized there was a deep *putain* ditch in the freaking ground, and that there was a huge *something* walking around inside it.

"Here we are," said Arturo. "They're going to check their webs, and dear Vanessa Hargreaves is caught on a thread."

"What a lovely *danse macabre*," said Jean Hallow as he strode up. They watched as the long, needle-like shadows touched down, casting a curtain of patterns in the orange-purple of twilight.

"And by the looks of things, the party's going to start any minute," finished Cezette. She took off at a run, her own shapely legs joining the regular ballet of shapes blocking the sun.

***

The moans reached their ears almost as soon as Albion's words dropped into the quiet room, and the lights went out at the same instant. Hargreaves heard the clickety-clack of spidery metal limbs striking tile. Shuffling ghouls these were not. Neither were the sounds a pure twang and whirr of steam-powered automata. What monstrous creatures had caught their scent? Then came the scrape of sharp things against metal shutters. They were right outside the room!

"Quickly!" hissed Rosa, and ducked behind the pile of canisters.

Albion slipped behind a tall cabinet, which seemed to be a tool locker of some kind. Hargreaves slid behind the huge machine in the center of the room, and almost retched. From this angle it was very clearly a steam-powered grinder. Chrome gleamed on its surface, and the worm screw looked freshly cleaned, but the smell so close to the hopper was still overpowering. It was also cold enough to make her gasp as her side pressed into the bare metal of the hopper's frame. She covered her mouth.

"Shh!" said Albion.

Hargreaves shot him a dark look. Why, oh, why hadn't she insisted on Dragonwell's presence?

There was a moment of quiet in the room as the sounds of movement ceased, be it from the hunters or the hunted. Moonlight slanted in as a white knife from the eastern window, cutting the room in half. Hargreaves could see motes of dust in it. She held her breath, expecting the tiny dust particles to swarm and betray her. The smell was unbearable. The moment lingered longer than it was welcome. Shadows crept across the room. Hargreaves could see the thing come closer, a daddy-long-legs shadow that was far too thin to be human. She tightened her grip on her .22 Tranter, its tiny rimfire cartridges not as comforting as she'd hoped. Something dribbled upon the floor with wet splashes, and the umber shape took another step into the room.

That was when Captain Albion Clemens made his move. In two long strides he emerged from behind the tool locker and fired two bursts into the shadow's back.

"HUWARRRRR!" roared whatever it was. It wasn't simply a feral cry of pain but something mechanical also, rasping deep within an infernal organ. Hargreaves was ready, and she had taken a step out and fired before she registered the nightmare in the middle of the room. It was eight-limbed, like the gear that had attacked them before, but the thing in the middle of those machined the meat grinder to shame. An empty soul peered from lidless eyes trapped within a tangle of hoses and finely wrought steel. Limbless porcelain stumps glimmered from the gleaming embroidery, and teeth grinned from behind snapping pincers.

There was a child strapped into the gear's frame.

"No... no!" screamed Hargreaves, emptying her gun into the abomination's center. Great gobs of sloppy viscera fell from the holes, drifting through the moonlight to land with a splat upon the killing floor. Somehow she thought of Cezette Louissaint. And of 'Rose Cottage,' the nickname Nessie Drake had once called Rosa Marija. Why did she think of that? Even as the screaming, whirring monstrosity fell to the ground, Hargreaves could not help but wonder. Was this the true form of the thing in the Cook box? Was it somehow the malevolent will of those who had crafted this poor creature that had created the plague strapped to Hargreaves' back?

"Come on!" said Albion, stepping over the twitching legs and wresting Hargreaves' arm forward.

Hargreaves discovered she was not in fact held down by a great metal coffin, and she could move after all. Rosa's skirts swirled in her periphery, following Albion to the hall. Just outside the shutters, there was a crash as another sharp armature crashed down, aiming to gouge out Albion's innards. At the last second he rolled out of the way, and the arm struck bright sparks as it punctured one of the great drums. Even as a sickening slop rolled out of the drum, the flash illuminated a multitude of bright lacework steel and the quiet grin of teeth that had lips no longer.

"This way!" said Albion, and they lunged down the corridor, away from the clacking of claws and the teeth in the darkness.

"Oh, God!" came a cry, and the two of them turned to behold Rosa Marija frozen in the hallway—with one of the monstrosities descending upon her, its limbs upraised to plunge through her breast and into her heart.

"Rosa!" screamed Albion, and through his hoarse voice Victoria barked two sharp reports. The limb shattered in a rain of bright sparks, lighting up the lions and tigers and bears hiding in the nightmare of night. Albion ran back, sliding to catch Rosa as she crumpled to the ground.

"The church! The children! Oh, I'm so sorry!" Rosa sputtered uncontrollably.

"Rosa! Rosa! It's all right! It wasn't your fault!" cried Albion.

He lifted a hand, whether to caress or to strike, Hargreaves did not know. But whatever it was, it changed into a plunge for the inside of his coat as Albion drew his pirate's cutlass, lashing out against the sharp limb descending upon the two of them. Even as Albion's cutlass bit into the monstrous creature, Rosa's grief and madness had already begun to change.

"I'm sorry," she said. With that Rosa leapt upon the nearest of the monstrosities, her cream skirt whirling into a cloud of death. Her hands disappeared into the depths of the cloth, and when they reappeared they were already driving a knife in each hand deep within the guts of the... creature? Machine? It screamed, anyway, and the same sickening liquid gushed from its innards. Hargreaves glimpsed Rosa as she pitched with the monstrosity, and saw a different gleam come upon her brow. Her eyes were lost deep within a furrow of fury.

"Go!" cried Albion. He dashed the creature aside, then drove his blade deep into a different part of its anatomy. "While we have these things distracted! Find what truth is here, or all this will have been a waste. I'll get Rosa out!"

"You melodramatic knob!" cried Hargreaves.

Albion was hardly paying any attention. There were at least three of the sickening spidery creatures, and now Hargreaves could see them in the flashes of light, they made her still sicker. One of them was bending low, and she thought she saw it reaching to lap up the spilled contents of the ruptured drum in the grinder room.

Hargreaves nodded towards Albion, turned, and fled down the hallway. As she did she glimpsed boxes behind the opened shutters. Boxes made of riveted metal, with a heavy smoke pouring from them. Boxes that were at once terribly familiar and chilling to the bone. They looked, each of them, exactly like the Cook box in Alphonse's care.

As she ran, Hargreaves reloaded her Tranter with shaking hands. The bullets clattered to the ground as they missed the chamber, but she had two loaded when another of the monstrosities ripped its way out of a shuttered room just before her. Hargreaves steeled herself. She looked directly into its bright teeth and shot them out in tight formation. The wall was plastered with its thoughts, whatever thoughts it might have had.

But a second one was just behind it, so Hargreaves tore the pin off the last potato masher she had brought all the way from merry England, hi-ho jolly pip, here's a gift from old John Bull, may you use it in ill health. It lobbed through the air like a ridiculous jester's baton, end-over-end, and stuck in the monstrosity's elaborate rib cage like a flower in a button hole. The mandibles clicked twice. The child inside turned to look at the sudden appearance, an expression coming over the ruined cheeks as if it hadn't seen a toy in years. Then there was a click.

When it exploded, the bloody thing nearly took Hargreaves' head off.

"Damn! Bloody Nora!" shouted Hargreaves as loud as she could, because she couldn't rightly hear and she was afraid she'd lost it for good in her right ear.

She had thrown herself behind the first spider thing and the shrapnel had largely missed her. The shock seemed much larger though, as if the monstrosities were packed full of black powder. It had thrown her completely off her feet and into a cart full of dirty rags.

But she could still walk. So she picked her way through the wreckage, trying only to step on the dry bits and avoiding the wet ones gleaming in the traces of moonlight. She coughed. Then she retched, as she tasted the rubbish that had gone down her throat. It was a dry heave that tasted of bile. Hargreaves spat it out and kept going. She felt her breath returning in a reeking rush.

But at the very least, as Hargreaves stumbled through the rooms, she had figured out two things. Firstly, whatever these abominations were, they were under orders not to harm her. She had gotten close

enough and hesitated long enough to be killed outright. So they were
after her, or the box, or both. Secondly, whatever they had been doing
to the people in this building, it was done. Finished. The rest of the
rooms were cleared out, and the pallets stood lonely. Empty. There
was another exit on the other side of the corridor, and Hargreaves
plunged through those double doors to find herself on another train
platform,

"What? Bugger," said Hargreaves, casting her eyes around.

For a moment, she was completely confused. When she had first
come in, she had glimpsed the train's engine on the other side of the
building. But now, she stood on an emptied cargo platform, looking at
an identical engine steaming up the place with huge clouds of steam.
Close up, the engine was enormous--clods of chromed muscle,
cowcatchers that could make mince of whole herds, and smokestacks
that breathed fire, like dragons out of myth. The bloody wheels were
the height of Hargreaves herself. There was a mirrored window just
ahead, in what looked to be a station master's office. In the reflection,
she thought she saw the head of the train as an incredibly angry skull.

Before Hargreaves could make heads or tails of it, there was an
equally enormous clunk and a blast of steam vented out of the
engine's flanks, knocking the inspector over once again. Having just
had a go at this merry-go-round and not liked it one bit, Hargreaves
took the tumble badly. She did, however, survive, rolling over her
shoulder and avoiding the sharp stays of her corsetry.

The opposite edge of the platform arrived with alarming swiftness.
Hargreaves tried desperately to stay away from it, fighting the
numerous cuts and bruises that now covered her body. But that body
was sliding towards the gap with the force of the steam. Mind the gap!
Some insane twaddle forced itself through her mind, looking for its
partner in sense.

Hargreaves felt her hand clasp for a moment upon the leg of a
bench. Fighting every burning fiber of muscle in her arms, she locked
her fingers around it, praying her bones would hold. The heels of her
pretty boots dangled over the precipice, and that was when
Hargreaves realized she was high up over tracks suspended on a trellis
over the street. Only a bit of wood and empty space stood between

her and a five-story fall to the hard cobble. Unlike with a passenger platform, a fall off this station would surely kill her.

"Mind the sodding gap indeed!" cried Hargreaves. That profanity helped force her painful arms back to the task of pulling herself back to her feet.

By the time she did, the train had itself a head of steam, and was rolling its way out of the station. Desperately, Hargreaves aimed her Tranter and pulled the trigger, only to hear the hammer clacking furiously against six empty chambers.

"Arghh!" screamed Hargreaves.

The inspector took off at a run after the implacable wall of boxcars. Her breath came like fire. Tracking the adamant nut to America, for nothing. Infiltrating a notorious gunrunner's lair in a foxy dress, for nothing. Enduring an assault by abominations in stinking sewer and reeking cannery. For nothing? The thought was frankly odious to stomach.

"Hey! Hargreaves! Inspector!"

"Hargreaves! Vanessa!"

The sharp pain of Rosa's palm across her cheeks woke Hargreaves from her raging stupor. When she came to, Hargreaves realized she had reached the end of the platform. She was standing there screaming at the passing boxcars.

"We have to go!" said Rosa.

Albion's gun let off a trio of loud reports. Hargreaves turned to see two of the spidery automata leaping off the passing train, landing on the platform with the tinny clanks of their sharp feet. Victoria's bullets clattered off of their carapaces; these weren't half-made things like the children in the cannery.

"It's time to exercise the better part of valor," said Albion. He made to run off the edge of the platform, only to be stopped by Hargreaves as he almost pitched leg-first over the edge.

"What are you doing?" she admonished.

"There's a bloody ladder there!" said Albion. And there was, a long maintenance access that ran to the ground. But it was exposed to the elements, nothing more than a series of bars set in the trellis iron.

"You think those things can't climb?" cried Rosa. A flurry of strange hisses, pops, and sizzles accompanied her voice: her plethora of trick knives doing their best to distract their pursuers. "We'll be sitting ducks!"

"The train!" said Hargreaves desperately. "We board the train!" The line of cars was surely almost at an end, and with its passing went the truth. Why were they hunting and processing people wholesale? For these sinew and spring monsters? Did the Cook plague make them? For Queen and Country, she had to know!

But the moment passed, and the grinning skull of the train's second engine passed her by. Hargreaves straightened up from the cliff face of the platform. Something in the shadows snarled, producing an ominous hiss and a smell of burnt wire. The darkness was slowly encroaching, but it wasn't just the coming of night. Something enormous was slowly making its way towards them. The ground shook in a strange, eight-beat rumble. This one left footprints.

Vanessa Hargreaves took one look down the length of the tracks, slowly reloading her .22 with steady hands. She took one step forward, planting her shapely thigh firmly in a Yard shooting stance.

There were monsters here before her. And now her way to the truth was through them.

12

ARACHNOPHOBIA

"Well. I suppose the inspector has found some help," said Arturo.

He couldn't help but follow the path of the *Huckleberry* as it swooped down, pausing in the midst of the ruckus, and flew up again.

"Look at the engineering," said Hallow.

"There's my girl," said Cid. An enormous shape blotted out the starlight of New Jersey across the river as something the size of a house lashed out at the airship. The *Berry*'s lights wobbled like an ornament batted by a cat. Then it righted itself, doused its lamps, and disappeared towards the west.

"*Merde,*" said Cezette simply. Then, "Maman! Maman!" But the efforts were for naught.

A moment later, the shadow presumably followed as it disappeared as well. Then the earth shook momentarily, and from that Arturo deduced the chase had gone underground. If he was feeling optimistic, he might have admitted to seeing the distinctively well-turned outline of Vanessa Hargreaves' shapely form and her leonine mane clinging to the rails of the *Huckleberry*.

"The girl always loved her dusters," Arturo attempted to convince himself.

After Arturo and the rest of M.A.D. saw the shadows of spiders in the tracks, they had walked through the meatpacking district, trying to discern the spiders' destination. It was getting a little later, and more of the well-dressed people were showing up in the area. The butchers were closing and the other sort of flesh sale was happening on street corners. Cid, the protective uncle, tossed Cezette his coat to cover up. Cezette's long raven hair, form-fitting black pinafore and dense petticoats hid her age from the casual eye. But it was hard to know what Cid was protecting more, Cezette's honor or the perfectly formed clockwork legs under her, slotted into black leggings.

It wasn't always possible to separate the predators and the prey, but Arturo's eye for detail caught the subtly expensive shoes and the more conservative cut of the gold diggers' bodice. Possibly to sort out the chaff, the nondescript doors of secret clubs deployed large burly men in waistcoats and rolled-up shirtsleeves. Hallow whistled as they passed one.

"Lay off," said Arturo, but he didn't like the look he got back. "We haven't time for treats. There's the inspector's life at stake."

"You think so?" replied Hallow, at the same time as Cid's empathic harrumph.

"Absolutely," Arturo said. "Our mystery benefactor, 'I,' wanted us to follow. They clearly thought these arachnid villains up to no good. I would bet you thirty pounds Vanessa Hargreaves and the Cook box were hiding in Five Corners."

Arturo's hunch had borne out rightly, for as they came upon Rosso's and the adjacent building, all the lights suddenly went dark in them.

"Oh, no!" Arturo had cried, and they ran towards it even as shots rang out and flashes of light escaped its windows. With his eye for detail, Arturo had noted the subtle mismatch in elevation, and that the building concealed the deep pit of the rail yard behind it. He couldn't shake the image of the enormous shadow M.A.D. had glimpsed just before.

That was when the *Huckleberry* had come into view, its lights setting the club goers in the district to whooping and hollering. It had rescued Vanessa Hargreaves, or so Arturo dearly hoped. He looked down a long avenue as the rumbling passed them by, traveling along unseen channels in the bowels of the city.

"I suppose New York's subway system could use the odd cleaning," said Hallow.

A manhole popped a long ways away, and a couple of cars sank into the street.

On the streets of Manhattan, Grant Sullivan was walking widdershins around First Avenue when the ground dropped out from under his feet.

He wasn't drunk in the middle of the afternoon, nor had he been to an opium den. He was loaded down with shopping bags, mulling over how to inform his girlfriend Maddie he had no way of paying for these things on his overdrawn line of credit. The transactions went through the telegraph, of course, but the charges wouldn't add up until the next business day. One day was not enough for a man of Sullivan's means to escape the collection agents.

He would have been glad to know the fall wouldn't kill him, but it would be enough to mount a lawsuit on the City of New York and throw off the loan agents in the interim. The resulting settlement would be enough to pay off his debt several times over. It was just as well. There was no way Maddie would continue to see a man with one leg, anyhow. She liked a man who could stand up for her in a pinch.

***

In a teashop on a corner of Alphabet City, Thompson Wong had just sat down for a rare treat. He hadn't expected to find such a rare tea in a western teashop, let alone in a tiny basement shop like this one. The aroma of cliff-grown oolong wafted into his nostrils, filling the newly arrived immigrant with reminiscence and nostalgia.

It was a shame about the clientele, though. The woman at the counter was raising hell, and all about nothing. One look told Thompson everything he needed to know: the expensive clothes, the thick mask of makeup, the reek of perfume barely covering an unwashed, rude smell. Thompson knew entitlement when he saw it.

"What do you mean I can't use your bathroom? Where am I supposed to go?"

Thompson was considering telling her to find a jar, when the bottom of the shop fell out and took the screeching banshee with it. It was a strange thing, to see the clean tiles of the place suddenly give way to a neat, square pit. The smell of tea was suddenly replaced by the rank odor of sewage. The shopkeeper looked on in horror, until her fine aquiline face scrunched up with the smell of it.

"Ah. Well, I guess she can go down there," Thompson remarked blithely in Mandarin, and took his teapot out into the shop's garden.

***

Two blocks over, a Jewish family of four had just sat down in their sunny front parlor for a simple lunch of lox and bagels. Little Nathan Wiseman had just put his fork to the plate when the plate, knife, and table simply vanished down a hole in the middle of the parlor. The last things he saw were the tips of the unlit candles as they sank into the hole.

"Daddy, where did my lunch go?" Nathan asked.

Geoffrey Wiseman looked at his son quizzically. It would never do for the boy to doubt his father, or have any inkling adults in general lacked the faculty of omniscience. Wiseman was a teacher at the local elementary school. The latest studies said a child who doubted his parents was likely to grow up a rebel, a criminal, or worse yet, an atheist.

"Son, God works in mysterious ways. Now let's step round the hole, and see if your Mother has some more of that salmon in the pantry."

***

Down in the tunnels, Hargreaves could tell Rosa was having trouble keeping ahead of their pursuer. Past the first couple of locks at the west end of the labyrinth, they found themselves flying through a wriggling section of tunnels. Though Rosa didn't have to wait for the blue streak of Dragonwell to open the locks here; the turns were too tight to push the *Berry* through at full steam. As they fled, they cast their arclights back, to show their pursuer in all its ghastly detail.

Furtive glances were all Hargreaves could afford to keep abreast of Rosa's piloting. Hargreaves' eyes were glued to her scope once again, which was only marginally effective as a means of targeting. Mostly, it gave just enough of a view to terrify the wee out of Hargreaves.

The machine following them was having no trouble at all within the tunnel. Its six limbs punched deep into the stone. It moved like a tarantula, thick mechanical limbs scrabbling for purchase on all sides of the passageway, dragging along a vast cylindrical abdomen studded with rivets. Puffs of steam marked its passage, and the twang of steel cable echoed all down the tunnel. Terribly, as Hargreaves looked at it, it was looking back, with eight swiveling glass eyes rimmed in copper.

Hargreaves fired a salvo of anchors, unhitched from their chains to make sharp, heavy cannonballs. The steam filled the tunnel, making it difficult to see, but she was a good enough shot to guess from a glimpse. She was also livid, and though the anchors did little, they served to bleed off some of her rage. Sparks flared off the sides of the tarantula, but the anchors did little to slow the machine. Its sides seemed impervious, gleaming a pale white like some cave-dwelling horror.

Hargreaves considered tactics. Perhaps the six-legged machine might simply not have the angle to fire in the twisting tunnel. She remembered the explosives the smaller automata had fired upon the *Berry* earlier. As they shot into one of the large overflow chambers, the explosions did not resume. Instead, Hargreaves looked into a viewing scope to see two smaller limbs unfold from the machine's belly. Those long metal tubes, the belts feeding into the body....

"Gatlings!" Hargreaves cried. "Large caliber!" She had barely done so, before a ghastly thunder echoed from beyond the *Berry*'s flanks. The walls outside the ship began to powder in long lines of wet brick dust.

"Albion! We can't stay ahead of it!" Rosa's voice came rolling from the horn on the forecastle. The motor guns wrung splinters of wood from the *Berry*'s flanks, as if great dogs were worrying at her sides.

There was no way for Albion to respond, except to pilot Dragonwell in an acknowledging arc. He had jumped into the gear almost as soon as the trio scrabbled aboard the rescuing airship. Now the red streak of Dragonwell screamed over the bridge of the ship, towards the rumbling, stalking enemy. With a start, Hargreaves realized there was a six-foot long cutlass clutched in its metal hand.

"He's going to fight that thing? Up close?" Hargreaves protested. "It's a Goliath to his David!"

"Be quiet and help!" answered Rosa. Her brow was furrowed, her grip on the throttle lever white-knuckled. Pretty brown limbs braced desperately against the wood of the bridge.

Hargreaves dearly wanted to comply, but the daring Clemens was flying in erratic arcs, staying just ahead of a line of bullets. She could not risk hitting him. Dragonwell would try a pass with the cutlass, or deliver a fast kick, knocking the pursuer for a loop. The Goliath tarantula leveled its globular eyes at the spot and lashed out with its heavy, squat legs. Ammunition glinted whenever it passed through the arclights, as if a mirage. Shots pummeled the walls to rubble, sending up great sprays of water and punching craters in the solid iron gates.

"There's a lock!" Hargreaves cried, pointing.

"I see it; I see it," Rosa answered. "The water is too high!"

She was right. Tides were still draining from the other side of the chamber. If they opened the lock, the chamber would fill with brackish water.

Rosa threw the ship round in a wide arc. The tarantula machine was focused entirely on Dragonwell now, which gave the ladies a second to recover. Hargreaves, out of anchors to fire, darted out of the seat and joined Rosa at the helm.

From their vantage point the mirrors showed a cavern of horrors. Dragonwell was having difficulty keeping up with the tarantula, occasionally taking a blow from a lashing leg despite Clemens' spirited piloting. Its cape was ragged with bullet holes. If they did nothing, eventually he would be shot.

"We ram it," Hargreaves suggested.

"Don't be stupid. This is not a Balaenopteron-class. We don't even have a figurehead, let alone the alloy ram chassis," berated Rosa. "What we do have...."

Rosa ran a merry frolic up and down a panel of instruments at her elbows, releasing a furious whine from deep inside the *Berry*. Two leather greaves popped out of the panels, each digit wired within an inch of its life.

"What are you up to, Rosa?" Elric Blair's tinny voice sprung out of a speaking horn.

"Elric! Move all the surplus pressure into the arms!"

Hargreaves knew what would come next; the *Huckleberry*'s ace in the hole, the hidden manipulators tucked away inside her flanks. Each arm was two-thirds the length of the ship, fully articulated, and ran on smooth, agile rails. Its machinery took up a whole deck by themselves. Rounded alloy discs topped the knuckles, perfect for punching the lights out of an enemy dirigible. Now, it seemed, those hands would be made to squash an insect.

Rosa grabbed for the tube connected to the external horn.

"Albion! Get out of the way!"

With a turbulent groan, the *Berry* surged forward, its right manipulator thrust out like an iron tree trunk. A red streak flashed through their forward arclights—Albion, dodging within a foot of the limb. Thunderous crashes announced their connection with the pale white tarantula. Hargreaves fell out of her post, and when she looked up there were eight glassy eyes spinning wildly outside the portholes. Then it was gone, punched away and out of a tunnel mouth they had just reached. The Goliath spun wildly and skidded into the water, throwing up a tidal wave. With shock, Hargreaves made out chunks of buildings and old foundations–the lock had been built over a flooded neighborhood of the old city.

The *Berry* roared, surging forward, with Rosa lashing furiously at her controls. Instead of a punch, Rosa threw an open-handed blow, sinking the *Berry*'s fingers deep. They pinned the Goliath down, smashing it in a long, dragging ditch into the wall. Ominous rumblings and wildly flying debris went everywhere. Rosa threw the other arm in, pinning two of the tarantula's thick legs.

Before the enemy could swivel to bear on the ship, Rosa threw the first arm into the fray, forcing the main body of the tarantula away from them. Hellish rattling came from its cacophonous guns, but they did little but splinter the *Berry*'s carpentry some more. Her screw whined fearsomely, throwing a streak of white steam into the chamber, but she held.

"Rosa? Oh, I see. You were trapped," Albion's voice drifted in from outside, tinny with machinery. He floated just over the deck.

"What are you waiting for? Finish it!" Rosa screamed back.

"Can't. The steam cutlass just slides off. Some kind of reinforced ceramic," said Albion. "Look, we can't let it get a hold of the Cook box. I'll distract it as long as I can. You open the locks and we'll drown it!"

"What about you?" Hargreaves yelled, snatching the tube from Rosa. The helmswoman gave a shrill noise of alarm, but was too busy holding down the tarantula to take it back. "You'll be caught in the deluge!"

"There's no time! It's getting free!"

Albion was right. At the expense of its trapped limbs, the horrific machine was tearing out of the *Berry*'s grip. Spurts of steam seared the walls clean. With a snap, one of the cables cut free and lashed a deep gouge in the *Berry*'s hull. One of the tarantula's free limbs crashed down on the pinning arm, denting it deep enough to produce a worrying plume of steam. Gauges all over Rosa's panel suddenly began to spin like whirligigs.

"Don't worry! This tunnel goes all the way to the Bronx. Dragonwell is tough. We'll find you later!" said Albion.

"Alby, no!" protested Rosa.

He didn't wait for a reply. Leveling the point of the cutlass like a knight's lance, Dragonwell pointed it at an exposed chink in the tarantula's armor. With a burst of bluish steam, the Gear leaped forward, sinking in deep and releasing a torrent of smoking machine oil. Where it touched Dragonwell's chest, the enamel tarnished black.

"Arghhh!" Albion screamed. One of the Gatling arms stopped moving, hanging limp.

Albion thrust Dragonwell's free arm into the thing's glass eye. A vast column of thrust erupted from the back of Dragonwell, momentarily lighting the dank waterway blue. And impossibly, tremendously, the huge Goliath began to move. The metal beast scraped slowly along the wall, marking deep gouges before crashing into a corner of the chamber. Then faster, and faster, driven away from the *Berry*. Crushing limbs came down on Dragonwell's shoulders. Regular flashes lit from where the tiny automata fought on, with Albion firing some kind of weapon from Dragonwell's chest section, in bright blue arcs. With another boom, one of the tarantula's limbs fell, sinking into the water in a dark plume.

"Rosa!" Hargreaves shouted, stunning Rosa Marija out of her blank stare. Rosa looked round, dazed, then threw the wheel before her into a free spin. The chamber whirled about them. The screw at the stern of the ship gave a quick burst, and then Rosa was digging the *Berry*'s fingers into the space between the lock gates.

"Open, you mother!" Rosa groaned, her arms wrenching at the control gloves. Gauges squealed and waved everywhere, and Elric Blair's voice was barking reports from seemingly all over the ship.

With the left manipulator arm still leaking from its wound, it seemed like the locks would never open. Hargreaves cinched it by rushing over to a bank of controls, throwing levers, and turning wheels according to Rosa's orders. With a sudden groan, the arm surged with power, damaged lines circumvented by their combined efforts. The vast slabs began to grind agonizingly open.

All at once, the lock gates burst apart, nearly overwhelming the *Berry* with a wall of surging, dark water. The torrent was high, but as the mass of water came, it left a space at the top. Rosa hurled the ship forward, instead of back, and they shot into the tiny corridor between stone and surge.

"Albion! Albion! Albion!" Rosa cried, even as she put more and more distance between the ship and her captain. Hargreaves caught sight of the tarantula behind them striking out at the valiant Dragonwell, before the water overwhelmed them both.

13

STILL SHARP

Arturo could not believe he was standing over yet another crater, peering into the steaming darkness for a clue to help Inspector Vanessa Hargreaves. A column of dust and soot filled the concrete canyons, driving people to seek the shelter of cafés, stations, and public buildings. When the cry came up and down the block of sinkholes opening up in the street, Arturo had decided the only civilized thing to do was to carry on looking for a decent cup of tea. After all, he had just tracked his erstwhile crime-solving partner to an abattoir of horrific implications, only to have her chased into a sewer by a gigantic metal spider. Tea was, as in most circumstances, the correct answer.

The police of New York, seemingly slothful, verbally abusive and dull-witted, took to a crisis like ducks to water. Barriers of wood and authority were erected. Curious tourists and journalists with photogrammers were efficiently herded away. Enormous Tesla lamps had been exhumed from enormous warehouses somewhere and brought to light the scene of the disaster. Arturo could see the glow of other spotlamps in the distance, other places where that enormous shadow had ripped through to the surface.

At the lip of the hole, several plainclothes detectives consulted with each other and some men in hard hats, who were commanding a platoon of workers in sealing off the more dangerous apertures. A civic dirigible had been pressed into service to cast an arc lamp on the scene, and another flew ready to haul up the worst of the debris. It was a remarkable exercise in damage control, but it limited Arturo's detective work considerably. All the more frustrating, as the sinkholes had crushed any hope of tracking Hargreaves and the *Huckleberry* in the first place.

"Hand me another of those." Arturo gestured, his eyes never leaving the pocket-glass. The soft fingers of Cezette Louissaint obligingly placed a ring-shaped pastry into his saucer. Arturo nibbled at it (amazingly, creamy and crumbly at the same time) following with a sip of black coffee, before scribbling something in a pad at his elbows.

"This is a mockery of a failed croissant," said Cezette, taking a luxurious bite of a pastry herself. "But not bad."

The four of them had finally parked the cab—no easy task even in the best of times—and climbed a set of narrow, advert-plastered stairs to find a trendy little coffee bar carved out of a pair of three-story brownstone suites. Naked bricks and wrought iron held a raftered ceiling over squashy armchairs and tasteful oil paintings, each one with a discrete price tag. Most importantly, an espresso machine sprawled in metallic tentacled glory over the back of the counter, like an old god risen from the caffeinated depths.

From a teat so numinous must come a milk to end all coffee, Arturo thought.

It was loads better than simply standing about eating the ubiquitous hot dogs from carts everywhere, although the cafés were not completely free of questionable meats. Arturo might be used to spotted dick from a can, but he wasn't quite ready for the pink pudding that passed for tinned meat on this side of the pond.

"If it weren't for the businessmen, these artisanal coffee houses would never survive. Look at all the customers using it for a personal office," Hallow remarked.

The coffee and cloistered interior seemed to loosen his normally absent voice. It helped that the cafe was buzzing with a susurrus of voices; the businessmen's ether boxes were chattering quietly on their tables. Their smooth black surfaces rippled. Words streamed across as intricate pins pushed up through the material, so it thinned out and was legible. If you skinned those tablets you would find a watchman's nightmare combined with a toymaker's wet dream: rows and rows of pin drums, delicate springs, ether crystals a hair's breadth wide, captured in tiny bottles.

"I don't like it," Cid grumbled. He had a badly brewed cup of English Breakfast in his paw. "They cheapen the whole experience somehow."

"It does not matter whether we like it," Cezette reminded them. "We can see the whole scene, and it is only a matter of time before we find Maman."

"The girl is right," Arturo said, putting down the glass. "There's a line of destruction straight across Manhattan that can only be from the enormous spider we saw moving violently through the sewers. It was after our own dear Vanessa Hargreaves."

"We may simply be looking at the fruits of a city growing too quickly," Hallow said. "Surely Alphonse would not be able to do this."

"How do you know it's her?" said Cid. "How do we know she's even alive?"

"Look around," said Arturo. "Do you see any heavy machines bigger than a steam shovel? That pattern is no explosion, or normal collapse. I've only seen such a wanton use of automata once before, at the stable in Mile End." He shuddered to think of it, what little they had seen. But the ship had taken off, and he had seen Hargreaves at the rail. He had to believe she was alive. "Pursuit means the quarry is running. The inspector is alive. And besides, our sometime malefactor 'I' must have led us here for a reason."

"*Mais oui!* Of course Maman is alive. The people after the Cook box want to know where the box is hidden," Cezette said. Arturo felt a warm something welling up in his chest. The girl hadn't doubted Hargreaves' survival for a moment.

"You are shaping up to be a fine little detective," Arturo praised, and the teenage French girl purred. Really, they were getting on thick as thieves. "Indeed. The situation is more dire than I had supposed. Apparently we have stumbled into the enemy's back garden, and they are comfortable enough to commit wholesale destruction in so fantastic a manner. There's something afoot that doesn't mind anyone knowing it is here."

"A deduction fraught with flaws," Hallow said, in a way that was more constructive than not.

"Induction, sir, is my method," answered Arturo, but he was stung.

"What's your plan, lad?" Cid asked bluntly. He tried a scone, and spat.

"It is not my plan, but Inspector Hargreaves', we ought to fathom. I presume some as-yet-unknown pursuer is hot on the trail of our inspector," said Arturo.

"This 'I' personage who has hounded our steps?"

"No. I get the singular impression our mysterious malefactor has changed tack, and intends on guiding us onto the inspector's trail. We must assume they do not intend to harm the inspector, which leaves another party that does," Arturo finished. "The Ottomans?"

"More likely the person who murdered the circus man, Feerick," Hallow said with unerring attention to detail.

"It is unimportant. If Hargreaves is running from machines, where would she go?" Arturo said. "What is it all steamcraft have in common?"

The group was baffled, and in the space of the moment Arturo languidly sipped at his coffee. The early morning sun speared through a skylight, illuminating an imitation Dutch landscape of some New England hills. He did enjoy his drama.

Cid was the one to break the silence.

"Us," he grunted calmly.

"Precisely. Automata are fairly new. They require precision tuning, customized parts, and skilled technicians. All of it can be improvised in a city, but the rural states of America offer no such things. Once out of the city, the inspector's pursuers will be limited as to how they may deploy their dastardly machines."

"But so will the inspector. Alphonse will likely be needing maintenance soon enough," Hallow interjected.

"Ah, but if we are to reach the inspector first? Then she will have the home advantage, so to speak," said Arturo.

Cid rummaged about in his satchel, coming up with a map run off a public library's photogram press. The ink was still grainy from the impression.

"What?" Cid protested. "I ran to the library while you lot jawed with the shop girl over the espresso machine." He spread the rolled sheet onto the table. Everyone weighted the paper with their coffee cups, holding the world in place with copious amounts of caffeine.

"Here, the South has little in the way of steamcrafts. They were far too dependent on their slave economy, and still have not recovered from the Civil War to produce an industrial revival," Hallow pointed.

"The rail lines run thick," Arturo said. "The South is still one of the breadbaskets of America. It would be easy to run men or automata in to overwhelm our dear inspector."

"New England is much too industrial, too many ports," Cid said. "Clemens and I often stopped to raid them of lobster and wenches." When he noticed everyone leaning away from him, he amended, "The elder Clemens, I mean," which helped not a jot.

"She cannot possibly stay. Every steam-monger and alchemist has offices in New York. We must assume some of them are in the power of our enemies," Hallow said.

"There, the Niagara Falls! I have heard they are beautiful!" Cezette crooned.

"Your Maman is no simpering, romantic buffoon," Cid chastised.

"It is a way to dispose of the Cook box," Arturo mused. "Buried beneath tons and tons of surging water. Even the most powerful automata would be torn limb from limb beneath it...."

"The box would be impossible to retrieve," Hallow said. His brow creased, deep in thought.

"But the falls are treacherous. Hargreaves is unfamiliar with the lay of the land. The inspector will not follow so obvious a route as the Hudson," Cid pointed out. "And what if the seams were to burst?"

For a while longer, M.A.D. sat grimly contemplating, none of them ready to admit not a single clue looked promising. Cid got up to try the coffee, muttering about the machine he had built when he was fifteen and comparing notes with the barista behind the counter. By all accounts, the review was favorable.

Cezette struck up a conversation with a group of nearby youths. While they were shockingly dressed, adorned with polka dots, corsets worn on the outside, piercings and death's head motifs, they were amiable, and soon a twitter of fashionable gossip drifted through the café. They seemed to be enamored with the stylings of a musical group named Heinous Anus.

Hallow picked up a paper left on a nearby table. It was a late edition, already reporting on the wave of collapses throughout the city. One enterprising journalist had climbed a tall building, taking a far-seeing shot of the line of collapses. The article suggested a sewer line collapse all along one stretch of the city, already being leveraged politically against an infrastructure that had already been operating on shoe strings. There was also a piece on the continuing mine fire, out on the west coast, which had already consumed most of a town with flaming sinkholes.

Suddenly, Arturo felt the tips of his sparkly up-do tingle with the beginnings of an idea. Or, rather, a non-idea, so daft it couldn't possibly fail. He didn't know what to call the opposite of an idea, even with his prodigious intellect, but it was rather a lot like trying to find one's way in Whitechapel. It was pointless to look at the house numbers or the streets, plastered over with a dozen languages. Fighting the *eau de toilet* for your senses. Rather, you simply had to plunge in, sample the whore-boys, and drink the little bottles, trusting your hedonism to see you through and coming out the other end where you wanted to be in the first place.

"What are you thinking?" Hallow laid down the paper, engrossed.

"I'm saying we stop thinking, I say, the hole goes in one direction, why don't we go that way?"

"That seems absurdly simple and suspiciously like instinct," said Hallow.

"Why not? Municipal sewers follow very basic patterns. They're shit pipes; they go where you don't want to. It can't be hard to figure out where their exits are, what's big enough for an automata to get out. If we don't find anything, we simply turn around and check the other end. But it gives us a *direction*."

"Why that's so daft it might just work," said Hallow, his nose crinkled in disgust.

"Sometimes it is better to just start walking. We shall *rendezvous* with our dear Vanessa *tout suite*!" But of course the inspector wasn't there to be annoyed by his French.

The French did draw Cezette, who returned in a pinafore covered in printed cherries. She'd traded clothes with a native. Strangely, it made her blend in, with her cheekily cocked beret just another young metropolitan girl with a flair for the retro. At the same time, the espresso machine gave a gurgle and a bang, issuing a fantastic cloud of steam.

"And that, my boy, is how you extract Blue Mountain. If you'll excuse me...."

"That would be our cue to exit," said Hallow. Arturo thought he imagined it, but Hallow was looking up at him strangely.

Having a plan was all well and good, but to get there was another issue. Once they returned to the cab, they discovered a cold puddle beneath the engine and a dry tank. Their cab had developed a leak, gored through and through in a vital pipe, and once the engine was cold there was no stopping the liquid water from escaping. "It's an all-nighter," Cid said, "I'll have to scrounge the parts from shops, but the fastest we can do it is morning."

"But Maman is already on her way!" Cezette cried.

Who knew what was following? Arturo thought.

"Can we get a different vehicle?" Arturo proposed aloud, but he knew it was hopeless. A leased vehicle would leave a paper trail, as good as breadcrumbs for whoever wanted the Cook box. He was loathe to steal another engine, and draw the attention of local law enforcement. The sun was sinking fast between the tall skyscrapers, its golden glint coppery on the edges of airships drifting past overhead. Buying one outright was outrageously flashy, but if only they weren't being pursued, would definitely have some appeal.

"Alphonse needs fuel and water. Hargreaves is human, no matter what she may think," Cid said. "Relax, lad. Have some fun. When do you get a chance to visit New York? We'll rumble on out of here as soon as I get this patched."

"And I will help," Cezette said, eager for engine work. "You get some rest."

The urgency was as palpable as the mysterious stinks on the streets, but Arturo saw the sense in their words. Cezette had fast fingers, and even as Arturo turned to look, Cid had half the pistons in pieces on the sidewalk. The old codger thrust a scrap of paper into Hallow's hand as the lanky figure loped past.

"We will need food, and sundry. This may be a long trip, and—" Hallow looked at Cid's list "—there are some basics for Alphonse."

"I can get them," Arturo said. "It is a good chance to put my ear to the ground."

"I will come with you. You will need help carrying it all, with your healing stomach," said Hallow.

"We will have need of expenses here," Cid reminded the two of them. "Food, incidental parts, more coffee."

"Aye. Damn pirate," agreed Arturo. He handed over a sheaf of dollar notes. "If you need rest, there should be enough to get a room nearby."

Arturo and Jean Hallow left Cid and Cezette to their tinkering, and headed towards a nearby market. Sundry was simple enough to procure, but for Alphonse's specific items, New York was a walking city.

"We will need to take the subway," Jean Hallow said matter-of-factly, after Arturo had finished at a local telegraph office. There was a directory, and a map, and even a rudimentary calculating engine for finding one's way in the labyrinth of the city.

They descended into New York's train system, only a short walk around the block. Arturo, with his keenly honed senses, could not help but admire the efficiency of the transit system. In a city of millions, there was an easily accessible, constantly running way of getting from place to place. Oddly, though the passengers closed in to Arturo's sides, there were absolutely no destitute or beggarly people on the platforms or the cars. He would have been glad of it, if those same platforms weren't devoid of the street performers, vendors, and musicians he had read so much about. Hallow stalked the platforms like a thing native to the dark, and the passengers seemed to part and flow around him.

Once in the proper part of the city, finding a Ubique mercantile was no issue. Even at night, surrounded by New York's glittering finery, the mechanical giant operated a storefront like a glowing beacon in a barren waste. The arclights in the forward display alone could have brought Rohan to Gondor's aid.

Inside, gleaming spanners lay in neat rows, bins were stuffed full of pressure pylons and folded piles of airship envelopes stacked by color. One could build an entire conveyance from the showroom floor of an Ubique. The parts Hallow needed off Cid's list seemed common, stocked in large cubbyholes behind the counter.

"Those look like parts we could have scavenged from the cab," Arturo remarked of a knot of twisting pipes.

"Essentially. Mordemere had to build his inventions so they could be easily repaired. He was an alchemic genius, but also a businessman," replied Hallow. "To hear Cid tell of it, the vital parts of Alphonse are sealed in black boxes. We do the maintenance, but the instructions come from Leyland directly, and Glasgow, where he was assembled."

Arturo hadn't expected Hallow to be so forthcoming. The scarecrow-like man examined the part with interest, manipulating the moving components and testing the metal by tapping it with a coin. He seemed unusually adept at it, for Hargreaves' archivist. Then again, the man could operate automata with ease. He must have picked up a taste for motor oil from Cid.

The Ubique mercantile was situated across from a grubby-looking eatery. Both Hallow and Arturo were worn out from jostling through the train crowds, and the smoky aroma wafting out the doors was an easy choice compared with the all-too-human smell of the train platform. Shopping was hungry work; the pair were famished.

They clambered through with their paper bags and boxes in string to find themselves in a well-lit, relatively clean place. Arturo noted the sawdust on the floor, the skulls of livestock nailed to columns, and the butcher paper spread for tablecloths. He realized the dirt was simply an aesthetic reminiscent of the frontier west, a land tamed only on some politician's map. Out there, the points of civilization were so far apart, even the long arm of the law could not string them together. Somehow it felt both comforting and terrifying, all at once.

Arturo was pleased at finding a variety of barbecue options, named for different places of the country. New York City was a sort of nexus for everything American, and they had stumbled across a node of southern hospitality. Arturo was glad to find a wide selection of whiskey, while Hallow stuck to sweet tea. Neither was what they expected, but both were excellent. They ordered, but to Arturo's horror, the waiter returned almost immediately with huge, sloppy plates piled high with dripping meats. Arturo rolled up his tightly clothed sleeves, looked around, and shrugged. He was simply too tired and hungry, and besides, he was in America. There was nobody to judge his attire here.

With the first mouthful, Arturo was hooked.

"Civilized!" Arturo proclaimed between bites of robust, smoky sausage. He had gone for the items most familiar to him: bangers and mash. The side of garlic potatoes was lackluster, but the meat was engulfed in a cloud of hickory smoke. He dipped into a sauce that made him feel like he just kissed the inscription on the gates of hell. All hope indeed abandoned—the stuff was addictive!

At a more measured pace, the quiet Hallow sat eating a pulled pork sandwich with a knife and fork. He seemed well practiced at it, placing a small portion of bone-white coleslaw onto the cut section of sandwich, tucking in all the strands of meat before tapping at his puddle of sauce. Even though others around him were slathered in reddish goo, he went on calmly chewing at his meal, working through the mess methodically. He seemed unaffected by his surroundings.

"That's right; you've lived in this country before," Arturo mentioned, as he mopped up the last of his sauce with a piece of cornbread. "You told me as much on the airship from England."

"Yes, I did," Hallow answered. He hadn't spilled a drop of sauce, and his plate was clean as a whistle. The napkin at Arturo's neck was drenched, even though he was used to eating in frilly sleeves. "Though it was not in New York. I traveled quite a bit. My father paid to have me attend the finest schools in the country, after secondary school."

When Hallow fell silent, Arturo put his highball down and ordered another round.

"Not all of them, I presume?" asked Arturo, when Hallow had his first sip.

"No, no," said Hallow. His scarecrow limbs hovered, flying clear of the tabletop. "But I had to change quite often. I am afraid not many of them were tolerant of my... behavior. It was hell on my poor mother."

"Come now," began Arturo, but Hallow interrupted him by grabbing Arturo's bourbon and downing it, two fingers, all in a shot.

"That was precisely the problem," said Hallow at last. He went on in a rush, a hurried whisper full of strain. "I do not mean to be indelicate, but surely a person's preference in mates is his own business!"

There was an uncomfortable silence. At first, Arturo meant to say something with a little more cheek, but he had realized, for quite a while now, what Hallow meant by 'mates.'

"They were... intolerant of you," said Arturo delicately. "I am sorry. Did coming back here remind you of things that were buried?"

"There are some things that ought not to be exhumed."

Arturo was intrigued. He had entertained the notion of seducing Jean Hallow ever since he caught a glimpse of the man, in Hargreaves' office during a social call. The introverted, shy clerk had captured Arturo's attention, not simply because of his slim, boyish figure or the grim cut of his jaw. Arturo had had plenty of that in Whitechapel, or more discreetly, in the parlors of London society.

No, what caught his eye about Jean Hallow was the ineffable quality surrounding the man—a *je ne sais quoi*, as Cezettte Louissaint might have put it. Hallow was hiding a secret, some darkness in his past that clouded his every movement, made his step cautious and careful. It knit his brows and drew the corners of his mouth down, qualities only a practiced observer of Arturo's caliber might have remarked as unusual. Yet, they told him nothing, which was the quintessential draw. Hallow was a puzzle Arturo might never solve, and it drove the spiky-haired detective crazy.

Hallow was speaking once again. Arturo ordered more drinks.

"We are born into this world expecting to have choices. The idea that we don't is put into our heads, you know, by our betters. To be respectable in society. To succeed. Why do we tell our children to be lawyers, men of influence, or men of science? Or doctors."

"Your father was a medic," Arturo recalled. "An army doctor."

"Yes, I have said. A country doctor, later in life, but a great name in the Pax Britannia as I was being shunted from place to place in America. His name was influential enough for him to indulge in some... unorthodox practices."

"Wait... you don't mean Jacques Johannes Hallow? The Snipper?" said Arturo. He hadn't meant it, but the moniker had just slipped out. Doctor Hallow had occupied the spotlight during the War as a proponent of the most drastic kind of eugenics. Even his peers in America had thought his methods extreme. Thankfully, he did not find favor for long, and was denounced as a hack once the current Queen Victoria donned the crown and men who favored evidence over ideology were put into public service.

"The Snipper. Yes, that was the name the British public gave to him. He hated my kind, yet he never knew... or perhaps he did. Ironic, isn't it? Someone of my persuasion is guaranteed not to have children of my own, yet his method was uniquely targeted for the termination of progeny."

Arturo could imagine the young Jean Hallow, alone in a strange country, swooning over some dashing American boy. Finding out his father's legacy through the teasing of other students and the disdain of the teachers.

"Then again, he was convinced the passing of unfit hereditary traits had to be stomped out, by the knife and in polite society."

"The exchange of mnemonic propagations. Memes. Yes, I've read of this, the idea that ideas can reproduce of their own accord, very like natural life. It has been a popular topic these past months, with telegraphy so popular and ether wave devices becoming affordable. Albeit in a very different context. Those ether tablets are mostly used for pornography and photograms of cats."

"Like the ancient Egyptians before us, the worship of cats is once again in vogue. But, the exchange of pleasure is the very core of the mnemonic propagation. My father sought to terminate his 'aberrations' at their source—oh yes, they were his as well. I saw the way he touched his subjects, peeking through the doors of his laboratory when he thought nobody was looking. His tastes ran young, very young." Hallow spat. "I have never wondered why my mother left us."

"If fate had been kinder, perhaps he might not have been so twisted," Arturo remarked. "Today, he might have the acceptance to love openly."

"If he had loved them, he would not have put this through their skulls," Hallow said. He drew from somewhere in his tight suit a piece of wrapped velvet, which, when unfurled, revealed a foot of thin surgical chrome. The padded hammer was peeling from age, but the tapering tip was still horribly recognizable: a lobotomy needle.

"You carry this around with you?" Arturo said, his eyes wide.

"When he succumbed to the pox, his fortune passed to me. I sold everything he owned, the townhouse, the medical journals, down to the buttons in his wardrobe. Except this."

They fell into an uneasy silence. Arturo mulled over his drink, and eventually Hallow put away the terrifying spike. When they left the restaurant, Hallow turned to travel back to Cid and Cezette, but Arturo took him by the arm, gesturing instead towards one of the many hotel towers lit up by Tesla lighting. Arturo wasn't sure what he intended. To comfort? To distract? Was it a selfish obsession of his own? Probably. That felt preferable.

Later, in the room they took for the evening, Arturo awoke to the sound of tinkering in the bathroom. He groped around in the dark, found his pocket watch, and threw it away without looking. He groped about some more, and discovered a finger of bourbon still in his glass. The bottle was missing. He downed the finger and gagged on the taste of tobacco ashes.

The silken sheets were too freeing on his bare skin, and he had trouble sitting up. When he finally got the hotel's plush robe on and padded into the bathroom, he found Jean Hallow standing before the mirror.

Hallow had the lobotomy needle up to his face, his fingertips gently touching the steel, and was staring down over the point. The tip brushed one of his eyelashes. It fell like a leaf in autumn, drifting to settle on the pure white countertop.

"Still sharp," Hallow said, and set the needle down to take a drink from the bottle.

14

INSIDE THE ROSE COTTAGE

While Arturo and Hallow made ready to rejoin Cezette and Cid in the morning, a bulbous airship hull bobbed up and down over the brilliant orange foliage of the Hudson banks. Her port manipulator dangled, scraping the treetops, like a gimp's crippled arm. Her screws churned a broken staccato. The deck tipped starboard, spilling a brackish drip. It threatened to dip below the Hudson's calm surface, there to fill with water and drag the ship to its depths.

Inside the *Berry*, the situation was no less dire. Rosa Marija was strapped behind the helm, her adept hands busy in the quagmire of controls. Half of them were useless, shifting loosely in their mountings, some twitching dementedly from the *Berry's* mangled steam lines. Rosa's mascara had run, in black streaks down her cheeks. She had to keep this ship, Alby's ship, in the air, for as long as she could. Every so often, the helmswoman found fresh salty droplets on the panels, but her sleeve soon put it right.

Hargreaves would have offered some kind of commiseration, but Rosa was a cruel taskmaster as she doled out the things that needed done. Where to patch the boilers, which valves to shut and which to open. If the veins of the ship stopped circulating the vital aeon steam the ship would fall, and fall fast.

In the corridors of the *Berry*, Inspector Vanessa Hargreaves' long legs took her through in bounds and strides. The ship opened up to her, guiding her along unlocked portals and around buckled bulkheads. Occasionally the corridors would become crumbling deathtraps, but the *Berry* was careful, even so badly wounded. Hargreaves skid to a halt as a panel before her slammed nearly on her toes, the space beyond filling up with boiling steam.

"Thanks, old girl," Hargreaves said, giving a nearby bulkhead a good thump. She darted into a side corridor, ripping a grate aside to thrust a long pair of clamps onto a quivering nut. Four deft turns closed the line, but whistling tore through the corridors, signaling another leak. Thick work gloves shielded Hargreaves from the worst of the hot metal, but shiny burns still spotted her arms pink. It was far too hot for the jacket at her waist, and she ran about in a linen chemise, her corset ribs popping up through the damp material.

"Rosa! Trees!" Hargreaves hollered into a speaking tube between sealing breaches. The pointed treetops she glimpsed through the misted portholes were alarmingly intimate.

In the echoes from the bridge, the harsh bark of Cockney Alex and the wheeze of a running Blair could be heard, interspersed by Auntie's calm, matter-of-fact damage control. As usual, the massive, burly Londoner had been impossible to find until the ship needed him. Hargreaves began to wonder if he was tied to it somehow, as if it birthed him from her bulkheads when needed like some attendant drone. All of them were, now, scrambling through the *Berry*, desperately healing her hurts.

"Forty yards and I can set her down," Rosa hollered through the brass of the ship. Her voice was terse, tinny, like they had been dropped into a void.

Rosa was good as her word. Before the *Berry* burst apart at her seams, Rosa landed her in a jarring skid through a gauntlet of creaking, breaking pines. Their flexible limbs held the *Berry*'s bulk. A last jerking halt nearly threw the inspector from where she clung, tangled in a nest of cold pipes. Her joints threatened to tear from her sockets, but after a nerve-wracking thirty seconds, the ship settled to a halt.

Hargreaves bolted up to the bridge, where the cracked, bullet-pocked windows showed a dense sea of leafy branches. If she looked behind them, the sky was a riot of color from the rooster tail of pine needles and fall leaves thrown up by their passing. Rosa was still busily throwing switches, one of which released a cloud of dense steam into the forest. The plume seared the branches naked, making the treetops sway and roil like a real ocean. At the edges of the venting, the white waves were freezing boughs solid. Cid had once explained it was an effect of the steam rapidly cooling to liquid water.

"Rosa," Hargreaves said, slowing to a stop. Her sweat dripped on the wood floor.

Rosa was restless, moving from still gauge to still gauge. None of the needles showed any sign of quivering, but the helmswoman still plunged through the grove of instruments, tinkering.

"Rosa!" Hargreaves repeated, but the helmswoman would not stop.

The inspector stepped up and put her hands round Rosa's middle, halting her clicking boots mid-step. It was a smart decision. Had she struck her, or simply stepped in her way Rosa might have become violent. There was no Captain Clemens to arrest her excesses this time, Hargreaves knew. After a while, the helmswoman's tears began to cool through Hargreaves' damp shirt, and she knew it was all right to let go.

"He's all right," said Hargreaves.

All the steel had gone from the normally adamantine Rosa Marija. The inspector stood stunned, holding her limp, sobbing form. Then a warm wetness began to dribble down her cheeks, empathy blowing the dam of pragmatism in a torrent of quiet tears. It wasn't just empathy. In small moments in her bed in Kensington, Hargreaves had entertained guilty thoughts of Albion as her own white knight. Between her disparaging quips she'd grown used to the idea of the Manchu Marauder in the world, drinking hard, cracking heads, and righting wrongs where the law wouldn't reach. Most of all, he said the things Hargreaves never could, purged the ghosts from her conscience. The *Berry* put to her bed with the forest in early winter all around them, the two women began to weep, and it seemed the ship wept tears of aeon water with them.

They found tea in abundance in the galley, and blankets. The fireplace was undamaged, and soon they had a roaring fire going. Hargreaves balanced the teapot on a poker, holding it over the flames. The others had gone to replenish the ship's water stores, wisely leaving them alone.

"I had nowhere to go," Rosa said after a while. Hargreaves finished setting out the chipped cups and plates, being mother.

"Nowhere to go. Nessie Drake had gone, setting up her empire. I'd cheated half the airmen in the sky, scorned the other half. And then there was my moniker…."

"Rose Cottage," Hargreaves said. "I remember Drake mentioning it. I don't know what it means," she added hastily.

"You would be the only one who doesn't," Rosa said. "Most of the underground knows the name, even if they don't know my face. It was before I met Albion, when I was running with Drake and a couple other like-minded individuals. Grifters, to put it bluntly."

"There was Eyre Cantilly, you might know her as the Francisco Fraulein, with a dozen formerly rich, formerly alive divorcés to her name up and down the West Coast. Johnny Bracken, oh, he was a card, with his fake Aussie accent and the way he used to smirk when you caught him looking at your bottom. And then there was Sister Anna Marie Clementine, the one who got us all together…." Rosa drifted off.

"What happened to them?"

"Eyre Cantilly got stabbed through the liver two years ago. She picked the wrong gentleman millionaire, either that or her legendary physique could no longer keep up. Nessie, we know is still out there, curse her undead Lolita heart. It's no surprise Johnny Bracken got caught in Mexico City, in a shitty brothel with a teenage *señorita*. Her father was the leader of El Gancho, the local Mexican gang. El Gancho means 'hook,' in Spanish. You can imagine what happened. As for the Sister…." Rosa paused, realized she had got ahead of herself. "We were sixteen? Seventeen at the time. Long story short, we put together a heist."

And so Rosa told the tale.

***

"It was supposed to be an honest job, but the Sister was a bird of another feather. She showed up in a dive, at the dirigible port in Baltimore, walked straight through those jeering aeronauts, and posted a job with Blue Crab, in the back. Crab, now, he wasn't particularly bright, but he had been around the block, and he had this low sort of cunning that made you comfortable knowing exactly how you couldn't trust him. He wasn't ever quite liberal with the details of the job, information being his trade, but you could count on him not to screw you if you'd ever bought him a drink.

"There were plenty of suspicious characters in the bar that day, men bitter with the weight of the world. Maybe it wasn't the smartest thing the Sister ought to have done. Crab, well, he knew a determined face when he saw one, and he took her money, which for me was a sign of earnest employment. Good as gold.

"Nobody else seemed to see it, but I could tell right away, the old codger had his claw clamped tight around this one. It was just as well; most of the numbskulls there thought the Sister too green to work with and too poor to con.

"So, I say to him, 'Cough it up, Crabs, she's on to something big, isn't she?'

Well, that crusty crustacean put his big wooden leg up on the bar and dug a little deeper into his bottle of rum, flicking soft-shells out of his teeth. Crabs are cannibals, you know.'

"He works the bolt in his leg, because we didn't have those fancy jobs you said Cid was building for Cezette Louissaint. Blue Crab had a piece of an airship's mizzenmast, the bit with the big coil in it, attached to the stump of his right hip. Every time the spring caught he had to work the bolt, so he wouldn't be walking round sideways. If the cannon had taken him any higher, he used to say, he'd be standing on a very different sort of wood.

"'Rosie,' he says to me, 'you stay 'way from Sister Anna. The woman done showed me what it meant to be a man.'

"'I don't know what that means. Don't even think about telling me,' I answer him.

"''Aight, I won't tellsya,' Crab says, and leans back, dead to the world, his leg going creak-creak as he works the bolt.

"Well, I didn't have any choice, now, did I? I laid on some

persuasion, not too heavy. With my knuckles skinning his fresh-shaved head, he gives in.

"'Give! Give! Uncle!' he cries, and I let him up. 'Not doinya any favors, ya hear? The Sister is lookin' to pull a job. A thievery, a rustlin', a good old-fashioned burglary.'

"'What sort of a job?' says Nessie, who just rolled in, lolly in hand. I could pass for a twenty-something back then with the right heels and eyeliner, but Nessie didn't even try. She was wearing an upended crucifix, the same color as her carbuncle eyes. She had an affectation for the upsetting that drew more trouble than Nessie was worth. It did no good to nettle her about it. Even in those days, before the Lovelace business, all her black lace and white trim made her stand out, let alone the gothic paraphernalia.

"Oddly, Crab looks her up and down, nodding. 'Aye, ya'll do fine! The sister might not have requested y'all specifically, but in the absence of an altar boy....'"

"'A priest? We're robbing a priest?'

"'An orphanage, to be precise,' Crab says, looking up from Nessie's flat, beribboned bosom. He showed no guilt about it. I knew for a fact what Crab's type was, and I propped one leg up on a chair, an incentive on two fronts.

"Crab noticed. I also had enough of a reputation, and he valued his remaining limbs.

"'The job needs Nessie, but it don't need you, Rosa. Ye're too much of a loose cannon,' Crab says.

"'There are others,' I deduce.

"'Aye. She's got a tank already, and a fingerman. She don't need a pepperpot spicing things up. What she does need–' Crab leers at Nessie again '–is a trapper.'

"'I can handle it,' Nessie says nonchalantly. 'But Rosie's my partner. She goes, or I don't.'

"'Too smart for yer own good, ye are,' groans Crab. 'Most girls yer age are playing dolly, or worryin' about yer pretty ball gowns, not coverin' each others' fannies. Here be the meeting place. Make sure ye get there on time.'

"I snatch the slip of paper from him, a slip he evidently kept to hand for the minute I showed up. Blue Crab was an old, cynical pervert, but underneath, he had a weary, beaten heart of gold. I suspect he thought we could stop the Sister from what she wanted to do, but even he didn't know the extent of her plan. We turned to leave, flicking him the requisite fee. Honor amongst thieves, and all that.

"'Oh, and girls?'

"We turn at the door.

"'Be careful with this one. Jesus might have saved a spot in heaven for a thief, but his followers? They're like to send you straight to hell,' he says, counting his money and downing the rest of his pint.

"We rendezvoused with the Sister at a library near Baltimore's historic district in broad daylight. It made us uncomfortable. There were lots of straight-laced suits around, and plenty of police. A raised thoroughfare blocked the front of the library's beautiful clock tower, progress slowly eating the city's beauty from the inside out.

"'I did not sign on to babysit children!'

"Eyre Chantilly was the first to notice, and it was only by the virtue of the private reading room's thick walls she did not topple the whole building on top of us. She was in her prime then, a regal figure exaggerated to epic proportions by medieval corsetry.

"'And we are not in the profession of caring for the elderly,' Nessie Drake shot back, her voice sharper than cheddar bay biscuits. I giggled. We had had this conversation before, and I loved to sit back and watch.

"'Ladies.' The Sister's voice was firm, stern, betraying none of the madness we would know all the more keenly later. She was young, in her early twenties, but her gaze was stern. 'I am sure they are simply lost, from a school group. Kindly move on; I have reserved this room for private business.'

"'We are your private business,' I answered her, and it was just as well I had come along with Nessie Drake. Simply by flashing the wristlet I palmed from Chantilly, I was able to convince the Sister of our unique talents. She seemed to disapprove of Nessie, who wore a backless dress that day, with an exaggerated bustle that showed off her concave spine.

"'Let's not waste time bickering,' Chantilly said. She displayed one elegantly manicured hand, with three of my own throwing knives pinched between her fingers.

"'The fingerman,' Nessie said.

"'And the tank,' said a man who had, by a remarkable feat of stealth, managed to hide amongst the stacks. When he moved, he shed a brown cloak to reveal about a mile of stubble. Bracken crossed the room, and in an instant, had my chin in his right hand. I felt the left start to slide up my thigh. 'Why don't you show me what those fingers can do?'

"'You mean these fingers?' I asked, but I didn't really expect a reply. I had a cold stiletto between his thigh and scrotum. Johnny Bracken's ice-chip eyes were full of low cunning, like an animal calculating whether he could snare the bait before the trap fell on him.

"'Hmph,' Bracken answered, and backed off.

"The Sister, on the other hand, was looking at us with naked fear.

"'No. Never,' she said. 'You must leave right away. I cannot use you for this.'

"'You posted the bill,' I pointed out.

"'Never played this game before, have you?' Nessie said, hopping into a chair. She could have been a student, out for the day on a research trip. 'If Crab gives us the job, it's ours.'

"'It is not a game for children!' the Sister insisted, but when she looked into the eyes of the adult shysters in the room, she found there was nobody in her camp. Protection of children only existed within the bounds of schools and nurseries. Hell, in Bracken's eyes, we were old enough to breed. They all knew the rules, and were indifferent.

"The Sister sighed, and began to unfurl a map she carried in a dispatch case. We crossed to inspect it, but were careful not to gather too close. There was nothing in the Sister's clothes to show who or what she was. Plain, conservative clothes, yes, but no habit, no cross, just a straightness to her back. A whip-smart quality to her wrists that made you want to move all the rulers away from her.

"What she unfurled, at first glance, were plans to a heavily fortified gaol. The thick walls, barred windows, and the lack of emergency exits were clear. There were larger rooms, with observation levels built in, looking eerily to be surgical theaters. Then the clues began to click: the long wings, tacked onto the short central hall, the dots showing reinforcing supports all along the walls, and the tall tower in the middle of the building, with an empty space within. Nessie was the first to catch on.

"'This is a church,' she said.

"'No—this is something else,' Chantilly corrected. She pointed to the rooms along the flying buttresses, each one reinforced with steel bones and concrete.

"'It may once have been a church. Now it is an abomination,' the Sister said, bitterly. 'There is something of great value in this room here. I need you to steal it.'

"Though the Sister would not give us any more information than we needed, she had planned the heist to meticulous detail. Nessie and Chantilly were to infiltrate the building, posing as mother and daughter, and charm the authority there to a private interview. Apparently a lecher and predator of children, he would no doubt want to get Nessie alone, giving Chantilly the time to scour his rooms for a most essential key.

"Johnny Bracken, Sister Anna Marie, and I would storm the inner sanctum through an external storm drain. There would likely be guards, which we would readily dispatch. The meeting point was in one of the cellars. Nessie would hand off the key. Then the three of us would enter the hall of reinforced rooms, entering a certain one and liberating a certain item.

"The Sister was awfully insistent about telling us nothing.

"We did not question the Sister overmuch. For one thing, she had a third of the payment ready to hand in Spanish galleons. Full faith and credit, hah. For another, the job seemed easy. All of us knew the building in question. The church of St. Francis was an imposing building but full of pleasantly bleating sheep. I can assure you, we were all thinking the same thing—that Sister Anna was full of it, and we could make off with the loot all for our own. We separated jauntily, the best of friends, our money rattling in our pockets.

"Perhaps because of some religious piety on the part of Bracken or some feminine feeling from the rest of us, we all showed up at the rendezvous with time to spare. In a job like this one, you would expect one or two hitches, maybe one of the players not showing up, but from the beginning it went smoother than silk.

"Bracken, the Sister, and I headed toward a tidal access, under the disused seafaring port. The official tunnels dead-ended a mile in, but a deep fissure in the wall led us into a maze of catacombs. There were signs of regular activity, stone surfaces scrubbed clean of dust and scored in regular lines. Despite the guide, I spied Bracken marking off the path with tiny arrows. He didn't trust anybody, not even someone devoted to God. It was smart.

"I kept a steady hand on my torch, and another on my stiletto, and so when we ran into the guard it was a simple matter of holding the mouth firmly while running the blade, covered in sleeping tincture, across the thigh. He was a slight man, short enough for me to grab. The panicked throbbing of his heart pushed the sleeping draught through, downing the man in an instant. It was dark, and I didn't think too much of it.

"'I would have just killed him. Kinder,' Bracken said, flipping his Bowie knife through the torchlight. I felt his gaze crawl along my shadowed backside. Disgusting, yet he had a point. These tunnels were dark, branching left and right. The guard would wake, befuddled and full of visions from the drug. If he had friends down here, they'd be chasing us in a labyrinth we could not know. The walls we passed were damp stone, from the tide. We would drown if we dwelt too long.

"Sister Anna seemed anxious to go on. We left the guard and continued, soon reaching a wall of brick, not stone. Turn-offs split every which way. If she hadn't known the way so well, we might still be wandering down there.

"A wood pallet leaned against the stone, but once removed, proved to be hiding an open doorway. It had been the wall to a cellar stuffed full of bottles and wheels of cheese aging on boards. A cunning secret door. Sister Anna took out a pocket watch, and counted down the minutes. Ten minutes past time, the door to the cellar creaked open, and the gaslight came on. A disheveled Chantilly and pristine Nessie Drake appeared on the stair.

"'The vicar was on sabbatical. This one likes them on the altar,' Chantilly said, still adjusting her bustle. 'Quite vigorous, for a man with a cane.'

"'I lifted the key,' Nessie said, her face screwed up in disgust. She held up a strong iron key the length of her arm.

"Sister Anna breathed a sigh of relief through tight lips, a sign Nessie and I caught even if nobody else did. This was a fortunate turn of events? If Nessie had wanted, she would have just knocked the vicar out.

"We entered the fortified corridors we had seen on the map, just off the cellar. The walls were old, made of mortared stone, and there was a burnt powder smell in the air from some building engine grinding stone to dust. We passed closed door after closed door, heavy old bronze with frames dug into the rock. There was a guard in a nook just inside a turning passageway. Bracken kicked him in the sternum and stove his face in. He hadn't even the chance to come into the light.

"We stopped before one of the doors, a bronze sheet like any other, tarnished a layered gray. There was a meal slot in the bottom, and an elaborate keyhole. The long iron key slipped in up to the ring, and turned with considerable effort. Things clicked inside, like a thousand scurrying beetles, and the door opened like a jaw, two halves sliding away from a middle seam, gaping up and down.

"'Is this a safe?' Chantilly asked, tucking the last strands of her hair in place. 'Whatever's inside must be valuable.'

"'Hamish!' Sister Anna cried, and rushed into the room. Inside, there was a washbasin, a drain, and not much else, save a small boy in brown rags that the Sister clutched to her breast. His ribs stuck out from his chest, and when we tried to stand him up, he crumpled like a paper doll.

"I'm sure you've guessed by now what we were really there to steal, though it didn't matter much to those of us gathered—so long as we were paid. We did feel right pleased with ourselves watching the Sister cradle the slip of a boy in her arms, though. As we wound our way back to the cellar, the Sister admitted to us her dreadful sin: that of having copulated with one of the priests, a Father Michael with kind eyes. She had been fifteen.

"'He took him. My child. Claimed he was the fruit of the devil, an unholy union, and he kept him from me for five long years. I stayed in the church long enough to find out where he was being kept,' the Sister said. 'At the same time I discovered these plans in Father Michael's offices, I found a hoard of Spanish galleons in the foundations of the wedding chapel. All of this used to be a pirate bay, you know. They ran the gold in crab barrels.'

"'You are one brave sister,' Chantilly said.

"'All mothers are,' Bracken said.

"'Get us away from this place, and the galleons are all yours,' the Sister said.

"The child, Hamish, lay an unmoving bundle in her arms, though he occasionally blinked at us.

"'But why all of this?' Nessie Drake wondered, turning so the corridor spun like a carousel. 'Are there children in all these rooms?'

"She spun, fitting the key into the nearest door.

"'No!' the Sister cried, plucking the key from her fingers. She did not offer any explanation, nor did she look capable. All of a sudden she looked no more than a child herself.

"'Something fishy is going on here,' Nessie said. That was when everything went to hell."

***

Rosa took a deep breath. Hargreaves refilled the tea, and stoked the fire silently. They moved the chairs closer to the fire, their armrests touching.

Eventually, Rosa spoke again.

***

"The halls filled with the worst sound a brigand could hear: the piercing drone of alarum. It nearly drowned out the chittering of all the doors unlocking, each one getting ready to open.

"'Are they going to go so far to protect one child?' Chantilly screamed over the din. 'I'm getting out of here!'

"We took off with Chantilly in the lead, dashing down corridors filled with the groan of opening doors, clashing with the shrill throb of the alarum. We could see the shapes of children, none older than ten or so, stumbling out of the openings, groggy or disoriented. Chantilly nearly ran headlong into a figure in priests' clothes, a greybeard full in the paunch but fierce, with a gray carven face.

"The father's eyes were anything but kind. He had a look to him, a terrible look… of sadness, and betrayal, but also a sort of furious madness. We paid him little mind. He was old, old enough to be Sister Anna's grandfather, not enough of a threat to bother with. That alone ought to have tipped us off. Sister Anna called to him, by name, but we just pulled her along, shoving him aside as we bolted for the exit.

"He said nothing. He lifted a sort of whistle, a plain whistle like any schoolchild might have. He blew on it, two blasts, and all the children screamed, holding their heads in pain.

"I never found out why they were all down there. None of us did. We just knew when Father Michael stopped blowing, they weren't children any more. They were beasts, animals. Their eyes practically glowed with malice, their mouths drooled, and there was a bitter smell as if their soft skin dripped with hate. They surrounded us.

"The closest of them lunged for Johnny Bracken and gave him his scar, the ragged one across his collarbone. The silly man was reluctant even to punch the child gnawing on his shoulder. It was strange seeing the coarse thug suddenly hesitant, even kind. Then we saw bone and Bracken tossed the little body aside like a sack of potatoes, child or no.

"Chantilly tore her bustle, using it to blindside their heads before they could bite into her thighs. Nessie was about their height, but she was smart, she turned and pretended to attack me, all the while shoving us down the hallway instead. When I turned to take Sister Anna with us…She tried to bite my face off.

"She was one of them. Father Michael must have done whatever he'd done to the children to her when she was in his care. The horrors in that rotten place ran deeper than any of us could guess.

"Sister Anna dragged us back into the throng. That was when I stopped seeing them as children, but as simply things that had come out of the darkness, scenting for prey. There was nothing we could do but fight back, and we weren't so grown up to feel for them like they were our own progeny. To us, they were simply attackers, not cute, not helpless. We lashed out with Nessie's sharp fingertip claws and my knives, taking an emaciated limb here, a grubby hand there. There wasn't a lot of blood in them, but soon the floor was slick with it, the air copper with the steam. It was a wonder we got out at all.

"I reached out through the slaughter, snagging Father Michael's collar. Something came away in my hands, and I realized I was holding his whistle, the whistle that started all this madness. Without thinking about it I blew, hard, the slimy texture of fresh gore staining my lips. Immediately the children, and Anna, and even Hamish the wretched child, scrabbling for murder with stubby fingers, they let loose a bloodcurdling howl. When I stopped, their murderous eyes fixated on us once again, so I did not stop. I drew one enormous, deep breath and I blew, hard.

"We backed up, four cutthroat robbers bleeding at a dozen places. We scurried back, back into the tunnels. I blew until my breath gave out. When they started emerging from the black tunnel mouths I took another, and blew again, and again, until the children's eyes bugged out, their faces ran red, and the nearest one turned and began to bang his head against the wall. Even then, there could be no stopping. We kept retreating, my heaving chest putting forth blast after blast of the diabolic whistle. Somebody, I think Chantilly, wet themselves, and that byzantine hell stank more than a charnel house.

"In the end they tore themselves to pieces trying to get at the sound in their heads, until there was no need to run any longer. Then we followed Bracken's chalk traces to get out of the tunnels.

***

Rosa stopped, tears beginning to slowly well in the corners of her eyes. She sat silently for a moment, allowing them to fall.

"Nessie, of course, delighted in the macabre of what we did. It bought into her counterculture, her stupid anti-establishment rhetoric, making it seem like we eviscerated the rotting heart out of the pristine body of God. Some shit like that. She started telling people, exaggerating the horrible bits, like I was the one who had no compassion at all. Of course we sold it as if the Sister had set a trap, which we cleverly clawed our way out of. They ate it up, helped build our reputation… but only as nasty and not to be fucked with. It was useful, until we split up. Then I found no captain would take me by my lonesome, no matter how much leg I showed."

"But why? That sounds to me like a reputation any pirate would be eager to have."

"Eager? Certainly. Proud? No. Not for a woman. The men of the world might look gruff and autocratic, but their protectiveness for children often runs deeper than ours. With Nessie around they thought I was not a threat, but without her, they compared me to Gryla. To Pierre Fouettard. To the Countess Bathory. The child-eaters out of myth."

"Instinct. The drive to protect one's legacy," said Hargreaves.

"A Rose Cottage is a morgue for children, did you know? I was a child killer anywhere there were men, you see. 'Nervous' is a kind way of putting it. They despised me. Only Albion looked past that. He took the time to listen. He convinced me I had no other choice down under the church. Those poor babes... some no more than toddlers, really, unable to do anything but shriek and run headlong into our shins. Unbelievably, he said he had seen worse. He offered me a place on his ship. From then on I was his, and his alone."

Rosa stopped, and the silence was filled with the dying embers of the hearth fire. She tore a piece of broken bulkhead from the *Berry* and threw it on the flame, smoothing the spot with her sleeve.

15

HARGREAVES RIDES
INTO THE SUNSET

"He's alive," the inspector insisted after a bit.

"Of course he's alive," Rosa said, as if the inspector had pointed out the sky was blue. She stepped back, straightening her skirts. "The question is where we should rendezvous."

"I have Alphonse. We should make good time, if you still keep a sedan engine in the hold," Hargreaves began.

"We're not leaving the *Huckleberry* here," Rosa said curtly.

Hargreaves whirled around, shocked. "Rosa, she's shot through in a million places," Hargreaves said. "You can't expect her to carry us, not without water, and lift. More of those things may come upon us at any moment."

"Lift we have, backed up in the reserves," Rosa said. She was tapping at a row of glass tubes in a panel, half of them bubbling with some glowing blue liquid. The others were shattered or empty. "We can seal the breaches, and we've got a hold full of gear parts. One anchor launcher is functional. There's a pond not far back, and we can filter the water."

"How long? With what crew? You've got Auntie and Elric and Alex, and us," Hargreaves said. "Unless you're hiding a merry band in those skirts, it's going to take you a week! What about the manipulator arm?"

"So it will take us a week," Rosa insisted. Her fingers busily opened panels and unrolled foolscap schematics from the copious recesses in the bridge's walls. "This ship is Albion's home. We'll drag her fat backside to water and then she's going to look for him."

"There are men with automata after us, Rosa! Albion stayed behind so we could do this!" Hargreaves shrieked, her voice higher than she intended. "You knew! You knew even when he stayed to confront Captain Clemens. For all his talk of profiting off this, he's always had an eye on the greater good."

"What greater good?" Rosa said, her voice deadly calm.

"Stopping this Cook plague from being used in war," replied Hargreaves, but her voice was shaky, unsure. Just before the spidery automata attack, Albion had brought back news of an Ottoman incursion at the Falklands. Hargreaves was no longer sure keeping the Cook box from the queen was a choice she ought to make now, nor whether she had the right to make it. How many lives would she save, by giving up the weapon and ending the war early?

"To think of the greater good, a girl has to have a future. Without Albion, I have no future," Rosa said.

So there it is, Hargreaves thought. They had gone beyond games, little rivalries. Rosa was in love, and she was determined to rescue the captain, despite his noble intentions.

"All right. I'll take Alphonse and go it alone. The least it will do is draw our pursuers off of you," said Hargreaves. "Mind, the captain may very well be coming after me himself. He's as reckless as you are."

"Then I will be there for you, Vanessa. You know that."

"Humph."

Hargreaves strode off the bridge in a huff, half expecting a sassy quip. When she looked back, Rosa was buried in her schematics, conversing hurriedly with Blair through a speaking tube.

Hargreaves set out on Alphonse, but she wasn't alone in her endeavor. Inside the warm, thrumming belly of Alphonse's cockpit was a satchel of parting gifts from the crew: comestibles from Auntie's larder, and a stock of ammunition in a cookie tin from Alex. Blair had kept Alphonse in pristine condition, his handwritten notations pasted everywhere with spirit gum.

Hargreaves had labored over what she would do, where she would go. In the captain's quarters, she pored over his charts, devising a sensible route towards the Niagara River, where she would dispose of the Cook plague forever. Or could she? What if the queen had lied? What if there were more bodies?

There was a series of arc power manufactories on the river, with large filtering sluices and deep tunnels for running the arc cables. The power of the falls had long been in use for mills and nearby townships, and in the early 1800s the first arc generators were constructed. Unfortunately, the churning power of the falls proved too readily accessible; the company maintaining the manufactories found they could only sell the energy at dirt-cheap prices, and soon defaulted on their debts.

Today, only the smallest manufactory at Lewiston still operated, and the hulks of its larger, more powerful cousins stood sentinels all along the Niagara River. Hargreaves' plan was to make for the trinity of falls at the town of the same name. There, she would use Alphonse to throw the Cook box into the Bridle Falls, where a current capable of grinding boulders to flour would keep enterprising evildoers from it. The sealed plague box would sink to the bottom, the terrible load lost under a frothing maelstrom forever. Rather than conspicuously tossing it into the Atlantic and having a spy aboard Ivanov's ship relay it back to her pursuers, she would choose a spot where she felt confident nobody would find it.

She had other ideas: burying the box somewhere, or hiding it in a cave. Throwing the box down a shaft, in a town she had read about, perched out in the frontier and built over a mine that had caught aflame. The unsure ground would periodically open up the gates to hell, and swallow an innocent person. An inferno to burn out the sickness. If all else failed, she could go out as far as the Pacific, out west towards the gray veil of the Lands Beyond and dump the box into the eternal divide there. But the falls seemed... practical. She wanted closure.

It was only halfway out of the forest when Hargreaves discovered the folded clothes slipped behind the seat of the rumbling Alphonse. By then it was too late to return. She stopped by a stream to clean and change, throwing on the sensible traveling ensemble and pinning her hair so she wouldn't appear to have just survived a dirigible crash. There wasn't much flair to it, only a thin line of lace at the hem, drifting over her ankles, but such was the point. The skirt was librarian green, just sufficient to set off her eyes but not flashy enough to draw unwanted attentions. She tucked one of the eight throwing knives into her hair, where it lay hidden with an anodized dullness, and slipped the rest into the heavy carpet bag full of firearms.

From over a sun-dappled ridge, Hargreaves looked back down on the *Berry*, her flanks speared and torn, ground beneath her soaked into a sucking mud. Hargreaves could just make out the sparks of a torch, the faint snoring of a saw at work on the forecastle.

"Thank you," she said.

She steered Alphonse gently away to pick her way into the wilds of America.

Interlude Exeunt
Parting Shots

The customer had been going on about the third piston coil on his velocipede for ten minutes when the rattling taxi pulled into my lot. It was strange to see bright yellow so far North of its hunting grounds. Maybe it was a really fat fare.

Already I could tell from the sound it was going to be an easy fix, a loose belt or a leaky nut along the steam line. Those old Fjord cabs, if you gave them a good oiling every once in a while, they might just run forever. This one was not well maintained, likely a victim of round-the-clock business from drivers preoccupied with green mattress stuffing. Truth be told, I was just glad for the excuse to be rid of my first customer, even if the excuse chose to disgorge a load of tourists. My final exams were coming up, and I didn't need the stress.

"Sir, for the last time, I can't fix a third coil that doesn't exist. Yours is a two-piston model—excuse me; it seems these folks need some assistance."

Turning on my heel, I crossed the ten steps from the office to the lot like a man summoned by the President himself. I was glad. Any more of the customer and I might have taken a pair of valve calipers to his face.

"You folks all right?" I spoke to the nearest of them, a young slicker type in a bright frock. It was the graybeard coming around the front who began to give commands.

"Lad, we need a top-up and a new four-eighths belt, pronto. Hurry, now! time is short!"

Despite the state of the machine, the limey graybeard seemed to know what he was doing, so I jabbed the hot water hose into the port and went into the garage to get the part.

When I came back, a big circle of taffeta was buried in the hood of the cab. As I approached, the circle straightened up, and suddenly a girl stood there with killer legs and a smudge of grease at her brow.

"*Bonjour*. Is that a timing belt I see? Just the thing," she said, and I was floored.

Those eyes captured me from the first. I'd only seen the like in the picture house, those dusky butterfly flutters in the first act. The girl had an air, like she would make it worthwhile to do anything for her. Her hair looked impossibly long, and deep, like it would suck up my hands if I stroked it. She'd clipped it in a barrette, and it flowed down one side of her like an ebony river.

The graybeard was deep in the other side of the cab, and his hands flew around inside it like nothing I'd ever seen before. I was so amazed by his expert dismantling, buffing, and spitting, I barely noticed those were my spanners and screwdrivers he was working his magic with. Even more amazingly, those tools he was pulling off the messy cart were being mystically sorted by size and type, as he enlisted one after another to work in the steaming hot engine. I saw the pointed tips of the fop's hair in the garage shop.

"Blasted American standard!" the graybeard said. "Thank you, Cezette."

"Don't you Brits use the same measurements?" I said, idly watching the girl handing him a set of points. Cezette. Her name was Cezette. And she was just as familiar with my tools as he was, all the while doing it in a pair of wedge heels.

The graybeard looked up to reach for the tools, found them ready to hand, and gave me a searching kind of look. The tips of his beard quivered in the steam.

"Aye, more or less. I'm a convert to metric; the increments are smaller," he replied. He tossed a rotted, melted canvas belt over his shoulder and I handed him the new one, which he fit to the timing gears with a few precise movements. I crouched in closer under the hood; the customer from earlier was loitering, poking his nose around like a pup, curious.

"Look, I'm glad you're doing the work for me, but we still have to charge you for labor," I said lamely. Undeterred by my assertion, the graybeard silently tested the new belt's alignment. Unsure what else to say, I continued to hand him screwdrivers and bolts as he needed them, trying to keep my hands from touching the girl's. With a final flutter of the pressure throttle, he slammed the hood down again. The taxi was still rickety, but at least the engine hummed a little smoother, spinning idly in an empty gear. The whole thing had taken maybe ten, fifteen minutes at best.

"Look, you seem a bright lad. You think a wise old mechanic like me would put up with a piece of rubbish like this?" the graybeard said, jerking his thumb toward the rumbling taxi. The clunker in question sputtered ominously. "Frankly, my boy, we are not the type to be taking the piss with."

"We have a solution for that." I jerked a thumb towards the hulking owner in the back of the garage, and mimed the cocking of a scatter-gun. There wasn't actually a gun. Mr. Elmer just looked the part, but he was a gentle giant who paid all right. The best I might do was run someone over with my velocipede, parked next to the pickup.

"What's your name, lad?" the graybeard asked.

"Frances Dolores Derry, on account of my birthplace and my dear aunt Dory," I said, proudly. "Friends call me Derring-Do," I made up on the spot. The girl Cezette must have been fourteen, fifteen. My age.

"Well, Derring-Dolt, why don't you take a look here through this pocket-glass, and tell me what you see?"

Like any strapping American lad, I was possessed of a certain invincibility complex and what my poppa liked to call 'damn fool antics.' Yet, I had to be smart to keep all my fingers around fast-moving machines. Steam could be erratic, moving in sudden bursts, and a certain degree of long-nurtured caution seeped into my head at this point. When I put the long tube to my face, would I then find one of my own spanners headed for a collision course with the back of my head? The graybeard looked on, tapping his foot, as I backed up from him enough to watch him and the glass at the same time. Then I put the tube to my face.

Then I put the tube to my face again, one eye squeezed shut.

And a third time, just to be certain, turning the focus this way and that.

"But... but... but...."

"Yes, yes, it has a great big metal butt. I'm sure the bollocks are also quite impressive. The point is the thing is headed this way."

It was something straight out of the *Popular Steamcraft* magazines in my room, in an article about today's American arsenal. In the article, the government claimed to have an army of these things, all commissioned at great cost and able to defend our borders. In fact, the article claimed they were doing exactly this, in Ottoman-allied Argentina, which begged the question of what they were doing so far from our borders. They could be seen only on the elaborate propaganda picture-house reels.

The thing I had seen through the pocket-glass differed from the magazine articles in two major respects.

Firstly: The gear was four stories tall, quite a few heads over the ones I had seen in the periodical.Secondly: It had a rather prodigious amount of legs, some of which appeared to be damaged. Despite this, it seemed quite capable of crushing buildings and engines underfoot.

The one thing that appeared unchanged was the presence of two underslung, many-barreled guns. Unfortunately, as they were approaching with now-tangible shakings of the ground and the distant snaps and thundering of explosions, these were little comfort.

At this point the fop returned to the taxi, accompanied by what appeared to be an undertaker. He tipped his hat to the graybeard, who grunted and returned to work. I could only assume the copious amounts of snacks and sundry in the fop's arms were offerings for the great metal god descending upon us.

"My word, everything they have is bacon flavored," the fop said. He extended a paper bag of potato chips. He offered one to the girl, who took a nibble.

"My tongue is digging a grave through my jaw, and I have the

French affair with lardons," my beautiful angel said. I could feel a breeze on my teeth as a smile took over my face. The girl was a swan in black lace.

"Do not fret. Here is a boiled sweet," the undertaker said. He spat. "I retract my statement. Fret, this candy tastes like bad laudanum."

"Give it here!" the fop answered.

The undertaker delivered his judgment with what seemed like fondness, if one could call a minuscule crease in the pallor of a corpse 'fond.' Both he and the fop looked too old for my angel, a fact emitted from me as a dreamy sigh. They looked back and forth between the graybeard and me expectantly.

"All done," the graybeard said calmly. Somewhere in the distance, a giant's leg came down with a boom. My velocipede customer fell on his bottom, breaking something in the office with a tinkling crash.

"What are you, crazy? There's a runaway gear over there!" I hollered. "Run! I mean, drive!"

"Run away? I think not," the undertaker said. "At least not right away."

"Yes… it might be looking for something," the fop said.

"Maman?" my angel asked. Her whole face lit up as she said it.

"Possibly. Shall we investigate?"

Somewhere in the backwater of the country, there were some dedicated skywatchers who consorted with metallurgists to build some truly monstrous vehicles, which they then drove into the hearts of storms and twisters. I looked at the rickety taxi, sitting there without a single panel of armor, occasionally flatulent with a misfiring pressure piston.

"You people are insane," I declared to empty air. The four of them piled into their cab, and the graybeard got the boiler started with a characteristic hiss. "And you haven't paid for the timing belt!" I added, as they began to pull away.

I do not know what came over me, perhaps some ragged scrap of responsibility for settling the account. More likely it was the gleam from my angel's eye as she passed within arm's reach. Seizing the moment, I made a mad dash toward the garage, where my velocipede was parked, waiting. The starter churned the smoldering embers into a roaring flame, a flush of steam from the garage's hose burbled through her streamlined chassis, and then I was off, the pressure churning her pistons from a ragged chortle into a roar. She shot out of the garage just in time for me to see the back of the taxi disappear round a corner.

Was I love-struck, as mad as the New England writer with the morbid fear of seafood? Very likely. The severe cut of her jaw, those graceful limbs, the color of her hair like some indescribably deep abyss, had in a short moment engraved in my mind like a pressure hammer on some warped velocipede frame. The cautious part of me was a reluctant passenger, watching on as the driver took our body closer and closer to some stomping, crushing doom. I think at one point I thought myself a hero, going to save her. So yes, I was an idiot, as all teen boys are.

When we reached the beginning of the destruction, the sane part of me began to regain control. By that time, it was far too late. As I whizzed over a covered bridge, the crushed bedrock under it gave way and the whole bridge collapsed in a spectacular spray of water and rocks. My rear wheel barely made it across.

The road was pocked with craters, new round, shallow manholes the footprints of the gear's passing. The overcast sky and dust raised by the destruction occluded the monstrosity. From a distance it looked like an elder god, descended from the Tartarus of space to kill us all.

What the fuck was I doing?

My velocipede could weave between each crater, her enameled fairing reflecting the light of burning homes and carriages in streaks of writhing, glowing serpents. Soon the taxi in front of me slowed to a careful crawl. I pulled up beside them as they stopped before a downed tree.

"Hey!" I hollered.

"My, you are persistent," the fop said, leaning out of the window. He began to leaf through a sheaf of notes, not all of them green.

"No, you have to get out of here! Before we all die! I know the way!" I said. There was a way, at an intersection just past the tree. If we turned left, we joined the larger road away from town. If we turned right....

"Listen, you seem a decent sort," the fop continued, "there's no reason you should endanger yourself on our account. Here's some money. Run along and get somewhere safe."

I took the wad he held out to me, and stood there with one foot on the ground as the little taxi started to bumble away.

"Aw, shucks," I said, and pulled my velocipede's big front wheel round to meet them on the other side. She was a direct descendant of the first two-wheeled vehicles to touch this side of the Atlantic, a finely tuned, 800 psi Jack Winner custom I'd refurbished myself. When the branches of the tree tore strips of paint from her sides, it was like tearing the skin from my flanks.

Fuck it. I'd already come this far.

"*Allors!* The knight returns!" cried the girl, as I pulled up beside them. They'd stopped at a shoulder, peering at the distant destruction, the ominous shadow of the colossus stomping through the dust of my home. That fact had barely even registered, but now it hit like a sack of bricks.

"Look! If you're going to do this, let me come with you. I know all the shortcuts and roads around here," I implored, one last time. I managed to push down the dread, the sinking feeling. The pretty girl at my elbow helped. "The least I can do is guide you out when you finally realize it's a suicide mission."

The four of them looked to one another, shrugging in turn. The girl turned to me and smiled. We reached the intersection, and turned right, not left. The ground rumbled beneath us. As we came on the town church, the bell tower veered past and the bulk of the gear swung grandly into view. Up close, the machine defied comprehension, even for me. There were materials and parts that were utterly alien, like growths, or cancers. And the way it moved, the scale of it! Not a machine but a tornado of howling, scraping steel slabs, bleeding miasma where it was torn.

"Whoa!" I cried, wheeling my velocipede around. We were close enough to hear some kind of staccato popping. It didn't take long to see the flash of gunpowder, and the little trails of brick dust spurting out in a long line on the ground.

"Look at the bore of those guns!" my angel said, awed.

"And the perfect gear ratio." The graybeard's voice drifted over the rushing air.

I marveled at the seeming obliviousness of these people. Instead of running for their lives they were marveling at its construction like art fiends. I had to admit, however, the gear was magnificent, at the same time a feat of steam age engineering and some kind of childhood nightmare brought screaming to life. The only noticeable flaw was a deep gash along the ventral side, and a stubby limb that looked like it had been lopped off, but that didn't stop it from continuing to smash my hometown with apparent glee.

One of the tree-trunk feet came down on a truck full of baking goods, momentarily blanketing the street with a cloud of flour. The limbs rose and fell, appearing and disappearing, as if we had entered some strange new planet, whose gargantuan inhabitants dwelt in a perpetual fog. It was a bad picture-house feature, an exploitation flick about something ludicrously impossible. As if self-reflective, one of the legs descended upon the town's tiny one-screen palace, crushing a million little bulbs of arclight as if stepping into a bucket of popcorn. I'd kissed Janet Winter there, two summers ago. That had been my first.

One of the bulbs must have ignited the cloud of flour, because there was a clap of thunder and a powerful wind rolled over us, stopping us screeching in our tracks.

"We're in the thick of it!" I yelled. I pulled a rag from my pocket, tying it around my face so I wouldn't breathe in the dust. My riding goggles came out of my saddlebag. "Can we leave yet?"

"No! Bring us somewhere we can get a good look at it!" the fop answered.

I nodded, the debris getting to be too much for my makeshift mask. We wheeled right, climbing a wooded path between the library and the Millers' general store. There was a little promontory where the students would go for those fumbling nights of initiation.

From this vantage point, it was easy to see the trail of destruction. The beast had come from the South, stomping flat *Delilah's*, my favorite roadside diner. A little caravan fled before it. I recognized the

Finns' little red wagon, Principal Meyers' brand-new Paddy, and Sheriff Patterson parked by the tough old townhouse, taking potshots at the gear with her buck rifle. Occasionally it would sweep the Sheriff with its guns, riddling the brick hall and deflating the tires on every engine parked there.

"Ho-hum. It appears our dear inspector is not in the crosshairs," the graybeard said. He had come out of the cab to get a better look.

"We had better get clear of this mess," the undertaker said, behind him.

"Agreed. Derry, can you get us out?" said the fop.

"What? How can you say that? Those are people I know down there!" I protested. A sudden wave of indignation washed over me, taking me by surprise. Here I was, risking my ride and my life to help them, and they were so damnably calm. "You were all gung-ho to get close, but now your own people are safe, you're going to flee? I know you know something about this. Help us!"

It was ridiculous, I know. But the anger I felt then overrode my initial fear, and even my crush over the girl. My cheeks bloomed, and I felt ashamed, embarrassed, demanding something of these strangers. But hell, whatever led me here, even some teenage folly, I was here, and I was the only one who could ask.

"Why ought we?" the fop asked. He leaned on the warm cab, his feet up on its grille. His flinty up-do was even more obnoxious seen in the light of the burning town. "We have our own problems. This knackered taxi is about to fall apart. Even if we knew something about this, how could we possibly help?" He gestured towards the destruction, as if to say, '*Derry, you're fucked.*'

Instead of staying annoyingly condescending, the fop suddenly fell over into the dirt. To my enduring surprise, there was my angel, her hands still palm-open, stretched out in front of her from pushing the fop over.

"Arturo! That is not how Maman would have it!" she screeched. "You may not be able to help, but we are M.A.D.! We can take this monster apart and build a *crêperie* with the parts!"

"She is right about that," the undertaker agreed lazily, not caring about the fop's predicament. "The creature... contraption appears to be already damaged, and lashed together with cable. I would have chosen a pneumatic propulsion, sort of like a true spider...."

"We can take it in the legs," the graybeard grumbled, a bit sheepishly. "I have a bolt cutter in my toolkit. Get close enough and I can tell you which lines to cut."

No matter how angry or insane these people were, suddenly it felt like I had an army at my back. I looked towards my angel, blinded by a brilliant smile.

"I'm Frances. Frances Dolores Derry," I said.

"Cezette Louissaint. *C'est la destin*, Frances. It is my beloved France you are named for," she answered. The others must have grunted names, but I barely registered them.

The hill road let out again farther along, leading to the main road by the townhouse. I guided my velocipede away from the cab, as a decoy, and emerged close to the gear just in time to see Sheriff Patterson leap aside from being crushed by a heavy footfall. The blow flattened her cruiser, steam hissing in angry clouds through the crumpled seams.

"Derry! Get out of here before I put you in the tank again!" she cried from the shattered front steps of the town hall. Even tussled and knocked down, she still reloaded her rifle with thick, callused fingers. "You ain't a minor for long; it'll be jail this time!"

"Just get on, Sheriff! We have a plan, just get on and don't stop firing!"

I whipped the velocipede around and began to weave, threading between the gear's legs. Behind me, Sheriff Patterson kept up an ear-splitting caterwaul, but to her credit, she continued to fire. The bullets tinkled along the gear's belly, even as it lurched doggedly forward. The gun wasn't doing much to hurt it, but I could see the head section twist around to follow the gunfire, away from the Finns' fleeing wagon.

"What's it up to?" the Sheriff hollered into my ear. I shook my head to clear the ringing, shedding droplets. All the steam in the air was soaking into my clothes and hair.

"I don't know, but the plan is working. It's following us," I answered. Even as we lured it aside, the Sheriff's question nagged at something. This big metal monster was pockmarked all over and leaking fluids. What could it want with a small town like ours? There were no military bases, no foundries or even a modest logistics depot. The closest thing to a store of parts was the garage I worked in.

"We're losing it, Derry!" the Sheriff said. The metal spider, deciding a buck rifle that could demolish a deer's skull was merely a peashooter against its dense hide, turned its many glittering eyes back towards the closest target: Principal Meyers' Paddy, tail-up in a ditch, unable to run from the horror at his heels.

"That's okay! My friends are over there!" The graybeard brought the taxi around, looking for a way to sidle up to a leg planted in the flower garden outside the school.

I watched the arachnid gear slowly lean forward, its pincers looking to close on the principal's struggling Paddy. Principal Meyers, normally so calm and disciplined, desperately spun his wheels, unaware they were getting no traction. The rattling taxi pulled up to the leg, and the fop climbed out of it, agonizingly slow to my eyes. He clutched a long, strangely top-heavy tool: the cable cutters. The graybeard pointed toward a spot in the gear's leg, behind a joint. The thrumming between my legs seemed to slow, each piston fire in my velocipede coming with a few extra beats between.

Beat. The monstrous mouth descended creaking upon the Paddy, ripping open the door.

Beat. The fop dropped the cable cutters, fumbling in the petunias.

Beat. The mandibles reached in, deep, groping like a real spider's nightmarish mouthparts. It gripped with ambulatory bits, like fingers. The principal must have retreated to the far side of the engine, but the door on that side was jammed against the ditch.

Then everything happened all at once. I saw Cezette running forward with the cutters, the graybeard gesticulating madly. The mandibles closed with a sort of finality around something in the Paddy. Cezette closed the cutters on something in the gear's leg and leaned all her weight on the severing handles. As the mouthparts emerged, clutching the screaming principal between them, Cezette fell over, her black hair landing in the grass. The leg suddenly crumpled, all the strength going out of it, and the gear lurched sideways.

"Everybody get down! Find cover!" I found myself suddenly screaming.

What a buck rifle could not do, the gear's own weight and the sharp, sturdy clock tower of the brick townhouse could. With a rending, screeching noise, the gear lost its balance and impaled itself upon the tapered weather vane, issuing a final gasp of raging steam from its terrible wound. Clouds of hot vapor bleached stone and wilted plants.

When I jogged the few yards over, I saw a shadowed enclave, all that remained where the bulbous eyes had flipped up on a hinge. The pilot of the gear had opened the driver's perch and fled. The fop and the undertaker were heaving at their cab. I breathed a sigh of relief when I saw Cezette, whole and graceful, attending to the graybeard. The steam parted to reveal Principal Meyers, still clutched between the mandibles two stories above ground, his pants stained dark. What the gear wanted with humiliating Meyers, nobody could say.

"Is the old fella okay?" I asked as I approached.

"Cid? He will outlive us all," the fop breathed through heaving efforts. The graybeard sat on some rubble in front of Cezette, but as he straightened up, he seemed hale enough.

"Good. You are alive," my angel replied. She looked me up and down, satisfied I was in one piece. I felt a blush under the layer of soot and grime, all down the front of my chest.

"And he was supposed to get the dangerous part of the job," the graybeard grumbled.

The undertaker looked about to snap like a twig from effort. I walked over, and between the three of us, we rocked the taxi back on its wheels. A look under the hood confirmed the health of the machine: rickety, but it would run still. Old Fjords, they'll show you every time.

"I hope you have some explanation for this," Sheriff Patterson said as she arrived, limping slightly. She gestured toward the smoking ruin, and the faint sound of klaxons arriving from fire engines nearby, but doubtfully, like she would rather be home soaking her feet. "But if not, then I don't have a reason to detain you."

"It might be better that way," said the fop flatly, but pointedly.

"We still have to catch up to the inspector."

"Maman," said Cezette. Oh, tragedy; my angel was getting aboard the taxi again.

"But you've only just arrived!" I gaped stupidly.

"What a gentleman," Cezette said. "I would love to see the sights with you, but it looks like the sights are all gone. Perhaps next time, Frances." She leaned down, and scrubbing a patch clean with one ebon-black sleeve, planted a kiss right on my cheek. "*Au revoir, mon chevalier. Nous vous reverrons, mon cher ami!*"

Stunned, my face tingling with her touch, I barely registered the old Fjord wheezing into life, bent wheels climbing doggedly over the rubble and onto what remained of the road.

"She called you a knight," the sheriff said suddenly.

"What?" I gaped.

"You just asked me what she said."

I had no memory of saying so.

"Chevalier means knight, and she also said she would see you again," the sheriff explained.

"A knight." I found myself echoing the word. "Tell me the whole thing."

"She said," the sheriff began.

A warm flush was filling my body, my eyes tracing and retracing the contours of the beautiful Cezette. Never in all my life had I met someone more exotic, more beautiful, or so elegant. A knight!

"She said, 'Goodbye, my knight, and we will meet again, my sweet friend!'"

My pleasure swept over me for a good four seconds.

"Wait... friend?!"

THE END

Thank you for reading! Find book one, FUTURE THAT NEVER WAS, of the *Lands Beyond* series available now. Find Kin S. Law across social media.

Facebook: https://www.facebook.com/kinslawauthor

Twitter: https://twitter.com/VoxVorago

Website: https://voxvorago.tumblr.com/

Please sign up for the City Owl Press newsletter for chances to win special subscriber-only contests and giveaways as well as receiving information on upcoming releases and special excerpts.

All reviews are welcome and appreciated. Please consider leaving one on your favorite social media and book buying sites.

For books in the world of romance and speculative fiction that embody Innovation, Creativity, and Affordability, check out City Owl Press at www.cityowlpress.com.

ACKNOWLEDGEMENTS

This book would not have been possible without my beta readers, the encouragement of my family, and the City Owl team.

ABOUT THE PUBLISHER

CITY OWL PRESS is a cutting edge indie publishing company, bringing the world of romance and speculative fiction to discerning readers.

www.cityowlpress.com

ABOUT THE AUTHOR

KIN S. LAW is a Chinese-American author who looks to include diversity, representation, and truth in his steampunk. Instead of a historical fiction where one event has changed things, his worlds represent what could have been, what should be, and what always was. He draws from a life lived in multiple cultures, but always with a love for everything weird and geeky.

Facebook: https://www.facebook.com/kinslawauthor

Twitter: https://twitter.com/VoxVorago

Website: https://voxvorago.tumblr.com/

www.ingramcontent.com/pod-product-compliance
Lightning Source LLC
Chambersburg PA
CBHW020821260626
47169CB00003B/766